NEW STORIES
FROM THE SOUTH
The Year's Best, 2003

The editor wishes to thank Kathy Pories, Dana Stamey, and Anne Winslow, colleagues whose talent, skill, patience, and tact are essential to this anthology.

She is also most grateful to the many journals and magazines that, year after year, provide the anthology with complimentary subscriptions.

PUBLISHER'S NOTE
The stories reprinted in *New Stories from the South: The Year's Best, 2003* were selected from American short stories published in magazines issued between January and December 2002. Shannon Ravenel annually consults a list of about one hundred nationally distributed American periodicals and makes her choices for this anthology based on criteria that include original publication first-serially in magazine form and publication as short stories. Direct submissions are not considered.

Edited by
Shannon Ravenel

with a preface by Roy Blount Jr.

NEW STORIES
FROM THE SOUTH

The Year's Best, 2003

Algonquin Books of Chapel Hill

Published by
ALGONQUIN BOOKS OF CHAPEL HILL
Post Office Box 2225
Chapel Hill, North Carolina 27515-2225

a division of
WORKMAN PUBLISHING
708 Broadway
New York, New York 10003

ISSN 0897-9073
ISBN 1-56512-395-6

CONTENTS

Roy Blount Jr.

PREFACE:
FIRST TELL ME WHAT KIND
OF READER YOU ARE

What do you do?" people ask.

I say, "I'm a writer."

And outside the South, people don't respond the way you'd think people would. They don't say, "I knew a writer once. He could never sit still in a boat," or, "Yeah, that's about all you *look* like being, too. What do you do, make it all up, or do the medias tell you what to say?" or, "Uh-huh, well I breed ostriches." I could roll with any one of those responses. One reason there are so many Southern writers is that people of the South either tell a writer things he can use, or they disapprove of him enough to keep his loins girded, or they just nod and shake their heads and leave him to it. But people outside the South act like being a writer is *normal*.

"Oh," they say with a certain gracious almost twinkle in their eye, "what kind?"

What am I supposed to say to that? "Living"? "Recovering"? They'll just respond, "Oh, should I have heard of some of your books?" I don't know how to answer that question. And I'm damned if I'm going to stand there and start naming off the titles. That's *personal!* Can you imagine Flannery O'Connor standing there munching brie on a rye crisp and saying, "Well, there's *The Violent Bear It Away* . . ."

What I want to do, when somebody asks me what kind of writer I am, is sull up for several long seconds until I am blue in the face and then, from somewhere way further back and deeper down than the bottom of my throat, I want to vouchsafe this person an utterance such that the closest thing you could compare it to would be the screech of a freshly damned soul shot through with cricket-song and, intermittently, all but drowned out by the crashing of surf. But I was brought up to be polite.

I was also brought up Methodist and went to graduate school, so I can't honestly say what I want to say: "Self-taught annunciatory. I received a vision out of this corner, of this eye, about 7:45 P.M. on January 11, 1949, and since that moment in earthly time I have been an inspired revelational writer from the crown of my hat to the soles of my shoes. And do you want to know the nature of that vision?

"The nature of that vision was a footprint in the side of an edifice, and the heel of it was cloven and the toes of it was twelve. And how could a footprint be in the side of an edifice, you wonder? Especially since I stood alone at the time, stark naked and daubed with orange clay, in a stand of tulip poplar trees some eleven miles outside of Half Dog, Alabama, way off a great ways the closest man-made structure in any literal subannunciatory sense. That footprint could be in the side of an edifice for one reason and one reason only: because —"

But then they'd just say, "Oh, a *Southern* writer. What *are* grits?"

I don't live in the South anymore. I maintain you can't live in the South and be a deep-dyed Southern writer. If you live in the South you are just writing about folks, so far as you can tell, and it just comes out Southern. For all we know, if you moved West, you'd be a Western writer. Whereas, if you live outside the South, you are being a Southern writer either (a) on purpose or (b) because you can't help it. Which comes to the same thing in the end: You are deep-dyed.

Whether or not anybody in the South thinks you are a Southern writer is not a problem. Englishmen think of Alistair Cooke as an American. Americans think of him as English. So he's in good shape, as I see it: Nobody keeps track of whether he goes to church.

One thing to be said for being outside the South, and you being Southern, is that it provokes you to keep an edge on your Southern-ness. Sometimes I'll bring up obscure examples of anti-Southern prejudice —"You ever think about the fact that in the book, the good witch is the Witch of the South, but when they made the movie they changed her to the Witch of the North?"

Also I make a point of taking no interest whatsoever in what passes in the North for college sports. When I was a boy in Georgia, college sports was Bobby Dodd versus Bear Bryant immemorial. Compared with that the Harvard-Yale game is a panel discussion. When all the college sports you can follow in the local media are Nehi or Lehigh, or whatever, against Hofstra or Colgate, or some-body, why bother? You know what they call the teams at Williams College? The Ephs. Let me repeat that: The Ephs. Pronounced *eefs*. Do you think that anybody who is willing to be called an Eef is capable of playing any sport at a level anywhere near root-hog-or-die? Caring about college sports in the Northeast is like caring about French food in South Carolina.

A good thing about being Southern is that it often involves get-ting to a point where you don't know what to think. People of the rest of the U.S. act like they have never been to that point before. Certainly they know what to think about Southern things. When-ever such people try to prove they are down with Southern culture by professing love for, say, Garth Brooks, I look at them with a cer-tain expression on my face and ask whether they haven't heard of the real cutting-edge genre, Faded Country—songs like "I Guess Fishin' Is Sufficient, But I'd Like a Little Love" and "I'm So Lone-some I Could Go Out and Ride Around on I-285." Or if people start telling me how deeply they respond to B. B. King, I'll say, "Y'all know they've isolated the blues gene?"

I freely say *y'all*. The language needs a second-person plural, and *y'all* is manifestly more precise, more mannerly, and friend-lier than *you people* or *y'uns*. When Northerners tell me they have heard Southerners use *y'all* in the singular, I tell them *they* lack structural linguistic understanding. And when they ask me to explain grits, I look at them like an Irishman who's been asked to explain potatoes.

All too often outside the South, *writers themselves* seem to regard being a writer as normal. When people ask a Northeastern writer what kind he or she is, instead of expostulating, "What do you mean what *kind?* Getting-by-the-best-I-can kind! Trying-to-make-some-kind-of-semi-intelligible-sense-out-of-the-god-damn-cosmos kind! If you're interested, see if you can't find a way to read something I wrote! If I knew it by heart I would recite the scene in *Marry and Burn* where the fire ants drive the one-legged boy insane (which I'll admit I think almost comes up to what it might have been, but it's not *simple* enough, there are too many *of's* in it, I couldn't get enough *of's* out of it to save my life!); but I don't carry it around in my head—I was trying to get it out of my head; and even if I did, reciting it wouldn't do it justice! You have to read it"—a Northeastern writer will natter away about being post-structuralist or something. And everybody's happy. Writers fitting into the social scheme of things—it don't seem right to me.

Grits is normal.

NEW STORIES
FROM THE SOUTH

The Year's Best, 2003

Brock Clarke

FOR THOSE OF US WHO NEED SUCH THINGS

(from *The Georgia Review*)

I was driving through Savannah, Georgia, and discovered that the city was deserted, agreeably so, and so I made some inquiries and one thing led to another and I ended up buying the whole city, cheap. Of course, the city fathers had to sign off on the deal first. They were suspicious of my motives, and asked: "Are you one of those fellows who buys up abandoned cities, remakes them into sanitized versions of their former, authentic selves, and then sells them off at a huge profit?"

"Oh, no, not me," I said, because I had heard of these men, had read about them in all the major magazines, and it gave me a little bit of revulsion, what they did to perfectly good, deserted cities like Santa Fe, New Mexico, and Monterey, California, and Charleston, South Carolina, the way they hired people from the suburbs and had them move to the city and pretend to be genuine adobe-dwelling Pueblo Indians or authentic downtrodden cannery workers or fourth-generation Gullah basketweavers. "Not my style at all," I said to the city fathers.

"So why in the world would you want to own a whole city?" they asked.

"It's complicated," I said.

"Try us," they said. It was clear that the city fathers weren't going to finalize the sale of the city until I told them the whole story. So I sighed and told them the whole story: of how my wife had just left me and moved back to upstate New York, where her parents lived, because of certain personality conflicts which had caused us to grow apart after three years of marriage. And one of those personality conflicts that had caused us to grow apart was that I had cheated on her, once, with her best friend, and then lied about it, and my wife happened to be the kind of upstanding person who needed to be able to trust her best friend and her husband, and she was also the kind of upstanding person who hated cheaters and liars. Even so, it was an amicable breakup, so amicable that it became clear that I was losing a wonderful, singular woman who had such extremely high moral standards that, if you were a cheater and a liar, she wouldn't give you one more chance even if you begged her. It pained me to know that I would never find another woman like my wife again, and it also pained me to sit around our house in Jacksonville, Florida, which was so cramped with regret and despair that I couldn't think straight. So I decided to find a bigger place, a place like Savannah, where I could be by myself with my few worldly possessions and contemplate how I had ruined my marriage and how I might someday set things right again.

The city fathers sat there quietly and listened to my story. When I was done, they asked: "You mean you've got yourself a broken heart, don't you?"

"Yes, I suppose so."

"Well god*dam,* why didn't you just come out and *say* so," they said, because the city fathers were highly sympathetic toward broken hearts, themselves having been divorced by wonderful women for cheating and lying. We all got teary and agreed how difficult it was to live in the cruel, cruel world, and then we talked about the weather for a few minutes, and then the city fathers stood up, smoothed out their khaki pants, hitched up their belts, signed over the city to me, got into their Lincoln Town Cars, and drove back to their duplex condominiums and their youngish second wives on Tybee Island, just outside the city.

So that was that. I moved my stuff and myself into an enormous pink brick house off Bull Street. For a long time, I simply walked around Savannah and surveyed my new property. Even though it was run-down and mostly abandoned, it was still a very pretty city, with all its lush parks and waving palm trees and sagging wrought-iron balconies and that good, rotten salt smell blowing in off the water and all that spooky, dying sunlight filtering through the Spanish moss. Yes, it was a fine Southern city I'd purchased, an excellent place to be by yourself and contemplate your broken heart and store your few worldly possessions.

But then I got lonely, as will happen to owners and sole inhabitants of decent-sized American cities, so lonely that I called my wife at her parents' house in upstate New York. I told her how I'd been living in monastic solitude in my new city, how I'd been thinking hard about what I'd done to her and how I'd broken her heart and mine, and how the solitude had been good for me. Except that now I was lonely.

My wife, if she were a certain kind of person, might have said how lonely it made her to see me and her best friend, drunk and pawing each other at our annual Labor Day barbecue, and how lonely it had also made her feel when her best friend and I had feebly denied that anything "funny" had gone on between us, even though we were standing there with out clothes half off. But instead she said: "If you're so lonely, you should join a club." This was constructive advice, and not at all mean-spirited. So I said to myself: "What kind of club would be appropriate for my fine, Southern city?" Because I didn't want to go off half-cocked and form just any club to ease my loneliness: sure, I wanted a group of people with whom I could share my city, but I also wanted the right kind of people, the kind of people who wouldn't be too out of place and ruin all the good salt smell and wrought iron. So after some careful consideration, I went out to the western suburbs, hired twenty overeducated old ladies, set them up in the abandoned movie house, and asked them to start a literary society. In doing this, I was not at all like that man who bought Omaha, Nebraska, and ordered that the paved roads be made into dirt roads and ordered that all men wear denim overalls and that all women wear calico dresses and that livestock be herded through the dirt streets twenty-four seven, and that Omaha be referred to on all promotional materials as the Original Cowtown, USA. No, I hired the old ladies because I'd never been to a Southern city that didn't have a literary society run by overeducated old ladies, and because it seemed appropriate for me, as the owner of the city, to be concerned about the city's cultural life. Besides, my wife had always been something of a patron of the arts and for many years had been a season-ticket holder for the Jacksonville Philharmonic. I wanted her to approve of my choice in clubs and see that I was someone who deserved a second chance, because it occurred to me now that my city wasn't just a place to contemplate my sins, but also to atone for those sins by making the city into something better than it was and thus make me look better in the bargain.

Anyway, the whole thing was slow going at first, because it took the ladies some time to apply for the appropriate federal grants and write their manifesto and to organize their first symposium on the future of Southern literature. But I was careful to stay out of the ladies' way and not to meddle too much or micromanage in any way. Soon enough the grant money started rolling in and the symposium definitively answered all the relevant questions. It was a great comfort, believe me, to smell the cigarette smoke wafting up from the street to my bedroom window after the symposium concluded, and to hear all the voices agreeing with each other as the symposium contributors walked away into the inky night.

But the old ladies didn't stop there. Encouraged by the success of the symposium, they began to hold regular Monday night poetry readings. They were nice enough to ask me to attend the inaugural reading as their guest of honor. It was the first poetry reading I'd ever attended. I can't describe the feeling of walking out of the dank, salty air and hearing a professor from the local college reading a poem about that dank, salty air, and then walking back out into that very same air after the reading; well, it's enough to make you feel real again. And when people from the audience came up to me after the reading and said: "This is a nice little city you've got here," I agreed with them and felt very lucky indeed. This was what I told my wife on the phone afterward: how lucky I felt to own such a nice city with such a fine literary society, and yet how strange it was to feel so blessed and to miss her so much at the same time and to have such mixed feelings about things. My wife, if she were a certain kind of person, might have mentioned the mixed feelings she had when her best friend and I tried to excuse our cheating and lying by saying: "We were drunk," and "It didn't mean anything." Instead, my wife said kindly, patiently: "You just went to a poetry reading, so why don't you write a poem about all your mixed feelings?"

And I would have written a poem, I really would have, but right after I talked to my wife Thanksgiving hit, and the literary ladies got hungry, and we had a problem, because I wasn't much of a cook.

"What is it you want to eat?" I asked them.

They said, "We wouldn't mind a mess of collard greens and some sweet potatoes and maybe a nice deep-fried turkey since it's Thanksgiving and everything."

"OK," I said. My first thought was to hire a caterer, but there's something very distasteful about caterers, something temporary and mercenary and nomadic about them, and I didn't want something like that polluting my nice little city. So I went out to the northern suburbs, met with several black women who jointly owned a chain of soul food restaurants, and explained my situation to them.

"What do you want us to do about it?" they asked.

"I'd like you to open up one of your restaurants in my city."

"So those white ladies have something to eat," they said, deadpan-like.

I said, "I know, I know." I told them I appreciated the long, troubled history of such a relationship and insisted that I wasn't insensitive to how offensive my proposal might seem to them and made it clear that I was all too aware of the intersections between race and commerce and the imbalance of political power in our supposed democracy and stated and restated my sympathies until they said: "We'll do it if you shut up. Plus, we want to bring our husbands."

So we had a deal. The women opened a restaurant on Abercorn Street and brought their husbands with them. I was nervous at first, not just for the obvious reasons of race relations, but because I was concerned with my nice, empty city becoming too crowded for a man to think about his broken heart and do penance for his sins and maybe even win back the affections of his estranged wife. Then there were the husbands, who couldn't cook and had nothing at all to do with the restaurant. I frankly wondered how they were going to occupy themselves.

But I needn't have worried, because it turns out that the husbands were good men, very engaged men, who as it happens, were involved in neighborhood politics and who were also involved in community theater. These were not men to sit idly for too long, and one day, soon after their wives opened the restaurant, the husbands came to me with a proposal. They reasoned that if their wives were there to make the old literary society ladies feel comfortable, then it was only fair that the husbands be allowed to make the old literary society ladies feel uncomfortable.

"What do you have in mind?" I asked.

They said: "We want to sit on the park benches right outside the restaurants and wear heavy, tattered clothes, even in the hottest weather, and drink forty-ouncers out of paper bags."

"Paper bags," I repeated, thinking about it, letting the idea soak in.

"Except they won't really be forty-ouncers," the men explained, "they'll be forty-ounce cans filled with water, but they'll be in paper bags, and when the old white ladies walk by, we'll feign inebriation and harass them."

"Will you cackle at them incomprehensibly?" I asked, because

I'm not afraid of a little innovation now and then, and because these men were very good at setting the scene. I could envision the whole thing already.

"We might," the men said. "But wouldn't it be better if we hurled fake voodoo curses at them?"

I agreed that it would be better, and so they made it happen, and it ended up being a wonderful piece of guerrilla theater. The white women complained about the black men to the black women and the black women, who knew all about their husbands' plans, complained theatrically about the men to the white women and went outside and said "Shoo" to the men, who stayed put. Then the black women went back inside the restaurant and everybody ate their turkey and their collard greens and complained a little more. One of the black women was so wise and artful in her complaining that the white women suggested that she write some of her thoughts and ideas down in a book. The black woman said, "Already did that," and then handed the literary ladies a manuscript, which was a collection of the woman's life lessons and recipes entitled "In the Kitchen." The manuscript was a complete surprise to all of us. Before anyone could catch their breath the literary society named the woman its first writer-in-residence, and there were hugs all around. The husbands even came in the restaurant to hug their wives and managed to do so without breaking character and soon the emotions were running so high that everyone got completely exhausted and had to call it a day. Somehow all of it was both genuine and ironic, which, as I told my wife on the phone that night, is all you can ask for in a modern city, which is something those hucksters who buy abandoned cities, etc., never seem to be able to understand: that you can't just hire fifty Salvadoran migrant workers and set them up in state-of-the-art Ogunquit roundhouses off the pedestrian mall in downtown Portland, Maine, and have the concessions people sell Coca-Cola out of calcified squash gourds and try to pass the whole thing off as the real deal without the least bit of self-consciousness and then expect the Salvadoran Ogunquits and the paying customers and everyone else not to feel horribly empty after a while.

"You've got to be honest, even when you're dishonest," I told my wife, not even trying to hide my double meaning; which is to say, not trying to hide the fact that when I spoke of the Ogunquit roundhouses I was really talking about the way my lying and cheating had derailed our marriage and how I'd never, ever do anything like that again. Because this is not the same world it once was, and if you hurt your wife you can't just go out and buy her flowers and expect her to forgive you, you've got to do something dramatic, like buy a city and do something real with it and distinguish yourself from those other men who buy up abandoned cities for the wrong reasons, and once you've done all this, you have to apologize for breaking your wife's heart and you have to do so both directly and through analogy. "You've got to be honest, even when you're dishonest," I repeated.

"That's true," my wife said in a wistful faraway voice that seemed plenty promising to me.

"I've got something really special going here," I told her. "You'd be proud of me and my city."

"I think I would," my wife said, and she didn't even tell me to write a poem about how proud I thought she'd be of me and my city before she hung up.

Well, it was quite a beginning for me, the owner of Savannah, and I had high hopes that my wife would continue to see what a sea change I'd undergone vis-à-vis my city and soon she'd move to Savannah and we'd reconcile and run the city as equal partners. This was exactly what I was thinking when the former city fathers came in to Savannah one day, saw what I had done with the city, and wanted to be involved in the city's "renaissance," which is what they called it. I understood what they were saying, completely. Who could blame them for wanting to live in a real place again after dying a slow death in the gated condos and planned communities out on Tybee Island? And I would have been happy to include them, honestly, except that they had gone out and done some reading and all they would talk about was rebuilding the city's infrastructure and how we needed to improve the city's bond rating and so on. Understandably, I didn't want this kind of boring, officious stuff coming out of the mouths of my city's fathers, because it's very difficult to ease your wife's broken heart and your own when people are spouting figures and acting fiscally responsible. So I told the former city fathers "No thanks," and sent them back to Tybee Island.

I should have left it at that; I know this now. But I was still thinking about how my running of the city seemed to have changed my wife's mind about me, somewhat, and I was also thinking about the black men and their fake forty-ouncers and fake voodoo curses, how cutting edge their work was and how their guerrilla theater had made the city innovative and authentic at the same time. I was inspired, maybe too much so. In any case, instead of leaving well enough alone I went out to some of the suburban golf courses and found eight colorfully dressed, overweight sixty-year-old men who would only talk in sports metaphors and didn't give one shit about going through the proper channels or due process, and who were not averse to making wild, sometimes nonsensical, sometimes offensive public proclamations, and I hired them on the spot to be my new city fathers.

Once their salaries were agreed upon, I gave the new city fathers offices in city hall and I also gave them an endless supply of Early Times bourbon and a team of press agents who taught them to always speak in the infamous misdirectional Southern doublespeak we see so often on television, which, at the time, seemed like a nice little flourish on my part. Sure, my city was a bit more cluttered than I would have liked it, but the city fathers and their oversized personalities made the place more true to life, it was undeniable. And if the new city fathers said a couple of things that set some of the black women into fits of quiet rage and the black men into heavier fake drinking and the overeducated white ladies into making fierce *tsking* sounds while they read their poems during open mic night, well that was true to life, too. Besides, I made sure everyone was well compensated for their work.

"Don't worry about a thing," I told my wife on the phone. "It's all under control."

"Are you sure you aren't overdoing it a little bit?" she asked.

"You sound like you're worried about me," I said hopefully.

"I *am* worried about you," she said. "Maybe you should stop and take a deep breath or something."

"OK," I said, and told my wife how touched I was that she was thinking of me. I swore to her that I'd stop and take a deep breath or something.

But then the old men came back to town, the old widowed white men who had moved out to the lower-middle-class suburbs in the 1970s, and I didn't have time to take a deep breath. The old men, whose wives had all recently died, took note of the white literary ladies and the black women and men and the outrageous, corrupt city fathers, and they got sentimental over how the city used to be, before they abandoned it for their brick ranches and fenced-in back lots. These old men began to trickle back to the city—first as visitors, then buying the assisted-living condos I'd built in the old warehouses on River Street. This was nice, and I welcomed it at first. For one, it's expensive to own and run your own city, and I was happy to get some cash flowing in via the condo sales. For another, it was certainly nice to see the emaciated old widowed men sitting on the benches on the public squares with their legs crossed and dangling at the knee, chain-smoking Winstons as they no doubt used to do back in the days of old.

But the thing is, old people, as a rule, are on tight budgets and thus prefer to sit on a free public bench and *look* at things and not buy anything, not even Styrofoam cups of sweet tea to go. This freeloading upset the black women, who were not making any money from the old men; and it upset the black men, who had grown used to having the benches as their own private stage; and it upset me because the old men looked so lonely and sad and so *near death* that they made me think of my wife, so far away in upstate New York, and how sad and lonely I really was in my heart of hearts and how I was afraid I'd never win her back and what it would be like to die all alone some day. My mood was grim is what I'm saying, so very grim that one day, just before Christmas, I asked one of the old men if he could at least pick up a banjo and play it while he was sitting there, just to add something to the ambiance of my nice little city. I said: "Maybe you could play something high and lonesome and transcendent, a tune by Ralph Stanley or Bill Monroe or the yodeling Jimmie Rodgers, that kind of thing."

Well, when I suggested this the old man stared at me for about a half-hour before going back to crossing his legs and not getting his banjo and not playing a Jimmie Rodgers song and not buying anything, either.

It was at this point, three months after I purchased Savannah, that I learned a valuable lesson: you cannot feel good about your city if you have too many old people living in it. So first, I instructed the city fathers to put a cap on the number of retirees allowed to live in the city at one time. This caused some grumbling from the condo dwellers and bench sitters, and it also caused some grumbling from the city fathers, who accused me of being Machiavellian and exactly like those men who we all read about, those men who buy up abandoned cities and sanitize them to hell and then sell them off at a huge profit. This was a sore spot with me, for obvious reasons, and the accusation almost made me rescind my cap on the elderly population. But in the end I didn't and in the end the city fathers did what I told them to, because, as I pointed out to them, it was my city and I could do whatever the hell I wanted with it.

"You actually said that?" my wife asked when I told her about the old men and my showdown with the city fathers.

"I sure did."

"You're sounding a little weird," she said. "A little out of control. You don't sound like yourself at all." And if I had listened carefully, I would have heard what my wife was really saying, which was simply this: "Remember that deep breath I told you to take? Will you please just stop what you're doing and take a deep breath?" But instead, I heard what I wanted to hear, which is: "I'm proud of you, the way you're working so hard, keep working hard, the more the city changes the more you change, so keep proving yourself to be a different man, almost all is forgiven."

"No time to talk," I said, because I was inspired by what I thought I had heard, and because I was late for an emergency meeting with the old literary ladies and the black women and black men. I had called the meeting so I could ask them what we could do to make the city a little less depressing, a little more lively. To a person, they said we needed more young adults.

"Are you sure?" I asked them.

"Adults ages twenty-one to thirty have more disposable income and dine out ten times as often as people in the next highest age bracket," the black women said, reading directly from a government study.

"They don't sit on benches, either," the black men said. "Those benches are our stage. Without a stage, we've got no theater."

"Yes," the old ladies said, and they also said how young they felt at heart and how just the sight of the old bench-sitting men was bringing them down in a big way.

"OK," I said. That very afternoon I got in my car, drove to Atlanta, assembled a focus group of men and women ages twenty-one to thirty, and asked them what it would take for them to move to a nice, little Southern city like the one I owned.

"We'd like to see Irish pubs and deep-dish pizza joints," the focus group told me, in unison.

I thought perhaps I'd been misunderstood. So I repeated the question.

The focus group said, "We'd like to see authentic Irish pubs with trivia games on Wednesday night and folk singers on Thursday and pizza joints specializing in deep-dish pizza."

This presented something of a problem, understandably, because it was my city and I had gotten plenty attached to it and so

I didn't want to ruin it with any kind of quick fix. Besides, I wasn't sure that Irish pubs or deep-dish pizza places were the kind of thing the old literary ladies or the black women or their husbands had in mind, and they had all helped so much in easing my broken heart that I didn't want to betray their trust. And then, in the back of my mind, I thought of those men we all have heard about and loathe, the men who buy up the abandoned cities and turn them into theme parks and manipulate tourists and residents alike with their bogus notions of authenticity, and then resell the cities at a huge profit. I didn't want to be like them, it was true: but were Irish pubs and deep-dish pizza joints something these developers would be interested in or not? On one hand, the developers might not think Irish pubs and pizza joints were authentic-looking enough, which would be reason enough alone not to allow them in my city. But on the other hand, were these developers so concerned with the bottom line that they would do anything to make a profit? It was confusing in the extreme, and I called my wife to get her opinion on the matter, but she was out, running errands. Without my wife's guidance I had to rely on my own instincts, and my instincts looked around and saw the old skinflints loitering themselves into slow, certain death on the benches and bringing the whole city down with them and depressing the hell out of me, the guy who owned the city *and* its benches, and my instincts said: "All right, let's do it."

So I did it: I made the necessary contacts and hired the appropriate restaurateurs and beer distributors and converted some of the assisted living condos on River Street to singles pads and in general made way for this infusion of youth that my fine little city so badly needed. And it worked, in a sense: before I knew it my city was invaded by armies of young men dressed in Duckhead khakis and young women dressed in tight pastel T-shirts, all of them chewing gum and drinking beer at the pubs, eating pizza after the pubs closed and then on the way home singing out the fight songs from whatever universities they'd just graduated from with degrees in accounting and industrial management. And while

I didn't exactly appreciate the young men and women puking in the public squares after the bars closed; and while I quickly got sick and tired of the Irish folk singers belting out "Margaritaville" in the pubs five times a night; and while I loathed the way my new young citizens referred to me as the "mayor guy"; and while I became near homicidal every time the kids insisted I yell "I *own* that shit" whenever they would name a building or statue or anything else that fell within the city limits of Savannah, it was true the city was full of something—*life* maybe—that it wasn't so full of before, and it was also true, in terms of population growth and cash flow, that my Irish pub and deep-dish pizza experiment worked out extremely well.

In another sense, though, it turned out disastrously, as I found one morning when I woke up and found that my house was being picketed—the old literary ladies, the black men and women, the college professors who read their poetry at the literary society, the old bench sitters, all of them holding signs and walking in circles in front of my pink house, all of them irate over my Irish pubs and deep-dish pizza joints. The black women were seething over the pizza joints, which were taking away some of their business; the black men were upset that there were too many kids walking around with plastic cups full of beer from the pubs, which lessened the shock effect of their forty-ouncers; the literary ladies and professors insisted that it was impossible to write poems about the dark, forbidding night and the whispering palm trees and the haunted hallowed ground with all this pizza and beer and youthful exuberance to contend with; and the old bench sitters pointed out that many of the kids who washed dishes and glasses at the pubs and pizza joints were also skateboarders who used the benches for ramps and whatnot and made freeloading almost impossible and potentially life threatening. Then, once everyone had had their say, a memo was read from the city fathers, saying that their mood was black and that I'd hired them to be city fathers of a Southern city and that if Irish pubs and pizza places were Southern then they didn't know *what* and that as history and football showed you could knock a man into the dirt and you could make him eat the dirt but you couldn't make him like it.

"Listen," I said from my front stoop. "This was your idea. I did this because of you."

"We hate you," they said.

"Go to hell," I said, because I'd absolutely *had* it by this point. After all here I had been, interviewing people in Atlanta and hiring contractors and worrying about the literary ladies and the black men and women and *busting my ass* all over the place, and yet I wasn't enjoying myself or my city one bit. "Go to hell," I said again.

"We thought you'd say something like that," one of the literary ladies said. With that, the picketers all turned heel and marched toward the city hall. If I'd been thinking clearly, I would have been concerned about this march in the extreme. But I wasn't thinking clearly: I was too busy thinking how hard I'd worked and how unappreciated I was and how I deserved the chance to let my hair down a little for once. So I went back inside, let my hair down a little for once, which is to say I drank Early Times bourbon straight out of the bottle until I passed out, and I didn't wake up until the next morning.

When I woke up the next morning the damage had been done and I'd more or less lost my city, but I didn't know it yet. In fact, I felt good, real good, because the sun was bouncing off the wrought iron just so and the thick sea air was seeping in through the window and Bull Street was absolutely quiet. The city felt properly spooky and real again, like it was when I bought it, and I was once more proud to be its owner. I was feeling so generous I even allowed myself to regret some of the things I'd said to the picketers the day before.

With this regret in mind, I went straight to the city hall and my city fathers, thinking that I would have to make up with them before I got the rest of my city in order.

The city fathers were all sitting in the conference room when I arrived.

"We've got to talk," I told them.

"You *know* we do, boy," they said.

I didn't like this "boy" stuff, and I also didn't like the way they were looking at me, angry-like and eyes squinty.

"What's going on here?" I asked.

"You've made a mess of this place," the city fathers said. "So we got ourselves some outside help."

I didn't like the sound of this, either, but before I could say anything else, a man in the corner of the room, a man I hadn't noticed when I first walked in, stood up and walked to the podium at the head of the conference room. The man was young—in his early thirties maybe—with expensive casual khaki trousers and a white knit polo shirt. He was so handsome he made your teeth hurt.

"Don't even tell me," I said, because I knew exactly who this man was: he was the most famous man among those men we've all heard about, the man who had bought up Times Square and kicked out the real prostitutes and drug dealers and hired all of Epcot Center's most experienced employees to be fake prostitutes and drug dealers and instructed them to offer the tourists blow jobs and rock cocaine but to do so in such a way that tourists wouldn't be uncomfortable and to also do so in such a way that parents could turn the whole thing into a cautionary learning experience for their children, if they so desired.

"Listen," I told the man right off. "I'm not sure if you know this, but this is my city, I own it, and it's not for sale. Besides, you're not exactly welcome here."

"That's not what *these* crackers told me," he said, hooking a thumb in the direction of my city fathers. The city fathers seemed taken aback by his remark, and I was encouraged for a moment, because I had grown up in Florida and so I myself had a healthy amount of regional resentment. I thought, perhaps, the man's comments would turn the city fathers against him. But it was strange: the more the man insulted the city fathers, the more he put them on the defensive and thus the more at ease they seemed to be. Before I knew it, the city fathers were making a number of familiar, sly jokes about the man being a carpetbagger and this being the second wave of construction; and then the man made some familiar, aggressive jokes about the city fathers' social backwardness and the ruinously high fat content of their food. Soon they were getting along like fraternity brothers.

"Hold on a minute," I said. "I still own this city."

"Shouldn't we let the people decide who owns the city?" the man asked. "Isn't this a democracy?" It was a clever question, I'll give him that, because I couldn't very well come out and say, "No, it's not a democracy," and still be perceived as the kind of city owner I wanted to be. So I reluctantly agreed to call a town meeting to let the people decide who they wanted to own their city.

The town meeting was held that very afternoon. The man spoke first. He argued that he sympathized with the citizens, that he had worked with many, many cities and so he knew what it was like for a city and its people to go through this kind of identity crisis. He added that if he were allowed the privilege of buying up the city, it would still be, in a very real sense, *their* city, and he knew they wanted their city to be an authentic, Southern city, didn't they? They did, obviously, because there was much clapping and whistling.

"Super," the man said, and then explained that he'd done some research and found out some interesting things. Did the citizens know, for instance, that the Irish had been among the first residents of Savannah, and so the Irish pubs—*my* Irish pubs—were boh genuinely Irish and genuinely Southern and didn't that make the citizens feel better? It did, obviously, and so did the man's plans to hold an annual St. Patrick's Day parade, during which the pubs would serve free green beer courtesy of Budweiser, with whom he had some sort of connection. More clapping, more whistling, a smattering of encouraging hoots.

"But what about those damn pizza joints?" someone in the crowd asked.

"Not to worry," the man said, and he explained that as part of his research he learned that as long as the pizza joints were operated and staffed by citizens of Georgia, then they could be considered authentic, too. "I looked it up," he said.

A huge wave of relief passed over the audience. The more the man spoke the happier my citizens got, and the more discouraged I became—not because my citizens hated me, but because they had forgotten me so quickly and so completely. I overheard some of the college professors telling the literary ladies that perhaps they had underestimated the tragic, lyrical qualities of youthful exuberance. The old literary ladies said that they would organize a symposium on that very subject, pronto. Everyone seemed to have a renewed sense of purpose. I even saw the old widowers smile grimly and clap their hands a little. Indeed, it seemed that the black women and men were the only people who weren't appeased by the man who had bought Times Square and who was about to buy my city, too.

"What about our restaurant?" the black women asked.

"What about our benches?" the black men asked.

The man simply shrugged his shoulders and held out his hands, as if to say: "What can you do?" And when the black women and men stormed out, vowing never to return, the man bugged his eyes out in mock horror and everyone laughed. It was all disheartening, so very disheartening that I forfeited my turn at the microphone. And so the meeting broke up and everyone went home satisfied, until it was just me and the man. He had all the proper documents in his briefcase and he took them out, laid them on the table, and handed me a pen.

"Well," he said.

"Is it usually this easy?" I asked.

"Yes," he said, not gloating, just telling the truth. And so, without saying another word, I sold him Savannah, and I was so saddened by the whole thing, I sold him the city for less money than I paid for it in the first place.

After I was done selling the city, I went back to my house, called my wife, and told her everything that had happened. Because I had it in my mind that we were still in love, despite everything, and so I had high hopes that even though I'd failed to save my city from the kind of man who we all hate, I thought that maybe I'd done enough to ease my wife's broken heart and win back her trust.

So I told her the whole story, how I'd lost the city, etc. When I was done, she said: "I'm so sorry, I really am, I know how much this meant to you."

"It doesn't matter. You mean more to me than this city ever did," I said, really pouring it on and desperate.

"Oh," she said.

"Will you take me back?" I said, and I got down on my knees, even though we were on the phone and she couldn't see me.

"I'm sorry," my wife said. She really was sorry: I knew this because she started crying. But before I could say anything else she hung up, leaving me all alone, on my knees in a house that I didn't own anymore, in a city in which nothing was mine except for the broken heart and the few worldly possessions I'd come there with in the first place.

I assumed that would be the last time I would ever hear from my wife, and so, in the absolute pit of despair, I went about packing up my house, getting ready to move to someplace, I hadn't yet figured out where.

Then, a few days after our last phone call, my wife called.

"Listen," she said. "What are you going to do now?"

I told her I didn't know. "Why?"

"Because," she said, and then explained that two paper mills just closed down in her hometown, Little Falls, way up there in upstate New York.

"Yes?" I said, hopeful, and yet afraid to be too much so.

"The workers don't know what to do with themselves: they're walking around town like zombies, giving the people who still have jobs the creeps."

"Yes?" I said.

She said, "So the city is looking for a consultant. Someone who can show the guys what it is they're supposed to do: someone to help them buy flannel shirts and grow out their beards and develop a taste for Utica Club beer and drink all day in bars that don't make money and should close but never will and generally stay out of people's way. That kind of thing. I thought of you, obviously."

"Do you want me to take it?" I asked.

"I do."

"Does this mean you still love me after all?"

"I don't love you," she said, and then sighed. "I could never love you again after what you did to me."

"Well, Jesus," I said, getting less hopeful and more angry. "Then why do you want me to come up there?"

"We won't be in love," she said. "But at least we could pretend."

"*Pretend?*" I said.

"It's better than nothing," she said. "Is it not?"

"I'll get back to you," I said, and then hung up. My first thought was to say: No way, because there was something extremely demeaning about my wife's proposal; because it seemed to me that it was, in fact, worse to pretend to be in love than not to be in love at all. It was the principle of the thing. This was exactly what I was going to tell my wife when I called her back: I was going to say: "No way," and then, when she asked why, I was going to say: "It's the principle of the thing."

So why then did I call her back and say, "OK, I'll do it"? Why did I leave Savannah—which I hear is now full of tourist trolleys and guided voodoo tours and stores on the Riverwalk that only sell products featuring peaches and pecans—why did I leave Savannah with a light heart and no ill will? Why do my wife and I say, "I love you," each night before we go to bed even though we know better? And why don't we feel so horribly bad for doing so?

Because the world has changed, I've said it before, and you can't just buy a two-hundred-and-seventy-year-old city and expect it to be real, anymore than you can cheat on your wife and expect her to truly love you again. And if you can't have real cities and true love, then you settle for the next best thing. This is why I moved to upstate New York and this is why I'm happy enough to live out my life and pretend to be in love, and this is why I sit down on a daily basis with the laid-off millworkers and help them buy the proper clothes and drink the proper beer and feel the right kind of desperation and act the way they're expected to act, and this is why I will continue to work hard to create a world that looks true and real for those of us who need such things.

Brock Clark is from upstate New York, and now lives in Cincinnati, Ohio, where he teaches fiction writing at the University of Cincinnati. He is the author of a novel, *The Ordinary White Boy*, and a short-story collection, *What We Won't Do*, the latter of which won the Mary McCarthy Prize for Short Fiction. His stories have appeared in or are forthcoming from *Georgia Review, New England Review, Southern Review, Five Points*, and *Mississippi Review*, and in 2002 he was a fellow at the Sewanee, Breadloaf, and Wesleyan writers' conferences. He's currently finishing a novel—*An Arsonist's Guide to Writers' Homes in New England*—and short-story collection, *Carrying the Torch*.

LANE W. CLARKE

A few years back I moved from Rochester, N.Y., to Clemson, South Carolina, and while plenty of things changed with the move, one of the things that remained the same was that I liked to read those free weekly newspapers you get in the mail—you know the kind, dominated by modular-home advertisements and outraged letters from senior citizens. Anyway, one day, I received one of these newspapers and on the cover was the header: "New York Man Buys Savannah." I had a decent idea why a New York man might want to buy a medium-sized Georgian city, and so I wrote this story.

By the by, it turns out that the Savannah of the article, the one that the New York man purchased, was not the city in Georgia, but rather a prized pig with some high local celebrity.

Patricia Lear

NIRVANA

(from *StoryQuarterly*)

W ho knows what it was that happened between him and his business partners that made him move us out of Memphis, move us all the way to Uncle Winn's moldy old farm in that furnace blast of a summer, where, granted, we were to live only until our new house was finished being built, but still, we were Country Club kids, my brother and I, happy as clams back in Memphis, and us living on that piece of corn-growing grasshopper-infested family dirt was as bad as anything I ever knew, just so bad that I hated every choking minute of it.

And even though we were out of Memphis and he didn't ever again for any reason have to lay eyes on his bad business partners, he was always in a bad mood. He got exasperated if gas station attendants mumbled when asking if he wanted his oil checked, or if waitresses mumbled while taking his order. He would go, *"bluh, bluh, bluh,"* right in the waitress's face, and say, "What did she say?" to my mom, with the waitress standing right there like she was an idiot.

Uncle Winn was old—he had Parkinson's and elephantitus of the balls. I once overheard someone say that this was why he had never married but when I asked more about *that,* everyone acted like I was rude. They walked off in disgust, left me for dead—but his pants were lumpy with balls and he was always sitting next to me in the backseat when we went to the drive-in movies.

In the mornings he would be sitting up in his hospital bed in the parlor window, set up there by my dad so he could see outside the fields and the blacktop highway and the barn where my brother had raised, on that first day of our arrival here in the North, like a fist, the good old Confederate flag. Before he went off to work, my dad would help Winn get ready for the day. He would help him onto the porta-potty, help him with the seventy-five or eighty pill bottles that sat on the TV tray next to the bed, and then help him with some simple breakfast, something my dad would toast in the toaster. Then together my dad and Winn would sit quietly, murmuring in deep men tones, while my dad would slowly turn the pages of the business section of the newspaper.

About my dad and his Uncle Winn—I thought this then and I thought it many other times too—that Uncle Winn was his beloved but my mom said no, that what my dad felt for Winn was respect for things I knew nothing about, and that maybe someday I would feel some of that too.

During the day, other than staring at Uncle Winn in his hospital bed or looking out the window at my brother bagging up grass clippings, there was nothing to do. Sometimes I would lie on one of the old iron beds and put my mom's face cream between my toes. I would eat ice-cream bars and then go out the back kitchen door and throw up in the black-eyed Susans, then sit on the stoop and watch as a cat would come out of the bushes and eat it. Sometimes when it would build up in me, about what things were lost from my life (riding polo ponies with Kathy Klyce out in Germantown, drinking iced tea in the hammock in my Aunt Peggy Gotten's ivy-and-squirrel-filled garden), I would go outside, right into the blaring breath of that molten dusty grasshopper-plagued summer, go right past my mom who had the absolute certainty of the completely choiceless, and I would go out in the yard and fall down in the grass—grasshoppers hitting my body like missiles— and I would yell and scream and tear the hem of my shirt with my teeth, and pull my hair and shudder, and yell to the heavens and have heaving gut-wrenching sobs until finally my brother—who had the dignity of someone who mowed the grass—would leave his rusty push-lawnmower and walk up the yard and punch me in the stomach.

When I would lift my head and look around, always there would be Uncle Winn looking out the window at me from his hospital bed, and there would maybe be people looking at me from cars out on the road, and this one time there was also my mom watching me from where she had come outside on the porch, and the first thing I thought was, *good,* now I can launch myself at her about how rotten her life is, because usually it was about this time that I would implore her with, "You know you miss playing bridge in the card room at the Country Club with the *laa*-dies," (all drawn out and obnoxious) and "You miss going to the Pauline Trigère trunk shows at the Helen Shop. You didn't want to leave! Why don't you just admit the truth for once in your (pathetic) life?" And some-times I would get to her and sometimes I wouldn't because my mom was someone who could just take it and take it and take it, and from everywhere did she take it, and me, I would go just short of death with her and it didn't much matter. She had the kind of power only true, determined victims have, but even so, that day it never even got so far as me starting in on her because when I looked up at her, something about her was clearly different, a sub-tle change to be sure, but it was discernible, or I was seeing it for the first time since we were forced upon each other all that sum-mer, but what I saw that day was something in her eyes, a flatness to her look, and I felt it and knew it, like you know with some spe-cial sense in ways not direct—a fine mist going over the back of your legs, or you sense a slight darkening to a bright, torn blue sky. What I saw in her eyes for the first time that day was that *I* was the place where *she* drew the line in the sand, that whatever else she had no choice about, and there was plenty, that *I* was the one place *she* never had to give in, and that *she* was as clear about me as she was about herself, and what I saw of myself in her gaze that day was something that literally made me fall back in the grass and lie there, practically shuddering, until finally, after a time, I just got up and went on back into the house.

Looking like a pork sausage in the flight suit from when he bombed all the Germans in the war, my dad would come home from working all day at his new ice-cream plant, and after sitting with Winn and talking to him about business, he would come in the kitchen, take one look at us, and become poor old oppressed him. He would look off in the distance as if none of us was worth looking at, and start heaving sighs like the old ladies in church did. He would key open a can of Metrecal and tilt back his head and drink it all down. This one night he said, "Let's just go to the drive-in movie," which meant there was a war movie playing.

With me packed in the backseat between my brother and Uncle Winn, off we went, deeper than we already were, into the inky-black countryside. My angry brother, who could make the sounds of bombs dropping and machine guns firing, was singing the Fire-stone Hour Song, which went (opera-like) "Eff I cud tell you, of my deeevotion . . ."

Uncle Winn gazed out the window at a herd of Black Angus, his thick ironed khakis lumpy with balls. I scrunched up my face in disgust. I stuck out my tongue. I leaned my face over and gagged.

I still hear the crunch of the gravel under our car wheels as we, all those times we went to the movies, would slowly make our way around the Stardust parking lot, trying to find ourselves a good place to watch the movie from. We would pull up on the little mound there always was in each parking slot, and reach way out for the speaker. Half the time the speaker wouldn't work so we would have to move our whole show to a different speaker. I can still feel the heft of that speaker in my hand, the coolness of the pockmarked metal, remember the way there was a hook on the back, remember how after the movie, we always forgot about the speaker and left, tearing it right off its stand.

This one night though, my mom said something none of us

quite heard and my dad said to her, "You said *'bleh, bleh, blah, blah'* bunny rabbit?"

"No," she said, "I just said, 'Don't any of you all forget, tomorrow we are going to Aunt Roney's for Fourth of July.'"

"Aunt Roney is a slovenly bitch-on-wheels," said my brother.

Big heaving sigh from my dad, then really twisting his mouth around and letting his lips go extra loose so they would really blubber, he said to my mom, "Well, then, why do you mumble so nobody can understand you? You sound like *bluh, bluh, bluh, blah* to everybody."

There were a couple of beats while we all just sat there, my mom looking like a little idiotic furry forest creature sitting up in the front seat, her brow furrowed up, thinking way beyond her capacity. I wanted to hit her on the head or pull her big ear. I wanted to go *bluh, bluh, bluh* right up against the back of her head.

"You talk like a little baby," my dad said, then he sighed real loud. "It's exasperating."

Pretty soon after we were all settled in with our candy from the snack bar, and during the fighter plane dogfights, my dad turned into Mr. Charming Dad. Smelling up the whole car with his Good & Plentys, he was banging his fists on the steering wheel and grinning his big white choppers around at the rest of us. When our eyes would meet though, my dad's and mine, I made my eyes go as cold and flat as I could make them. I tried to make him feel as *alone* as possible. I tried to scrunch away from Uncle Winn and his lumpy balls, and I tried to fart in the direction of my brother and blame it on Uncle Winn, and then finally I stuck my filthy feet, with the ground-in summer dirt, up between the front seats on the armrest under my mom's arm where she was by now searching her hands around to lace fingers with my dad.

Then it started happening what usually happened in movies. The candy, the drifting, the thinking, the humming the Firestone Hour song, the just listening to the crickets and smelling the fields and the cut grass that edged the drive-in, the dozing, the watching the blinking lights from a far-off radio station tower, the fireflies, and then seeing the moon through sheer summery cottony clouds and also twinkling stars, and as I did all of this, I thought about Memphis and all my friends there, and the people that I was related to there, and this made me think about what people I might be related to *here*, and how I didn't really even know any of them, or really *want* to know any of them either—such as my Aunt Roney, my mom's sister, who often dropped by to sit and have a Coke with us whenever her kids were taking their various lessons—clarinet, ballet, tap, acrobatics, baton twirling, trumpet, 4-H Club, Charm School, football practice, swim club, and Youth Group at the Methodist Church. Just to see her lugging her big Jello-ass up our yard was embarrassing, and there always seemed to be boxes of Modess Sanitary Napkins piled up on top of her grocery bags in the back of her Oldsmobile stationwagon.

Her one boy, my cousin Ox, was a football star at the High School, and he played the trumpet like my brother. They even had a pony named Scout. I was thinking about how last time Aunt Roney came by one side of her Olds was bashed in like a stepped-on empty can of Tab, from Big J.B. ramming her with his car.

I drifted and thought some more.

Out of my mouth came, "I want to go to charm school!" and my mom looked over the back seat at Winn and winked and said, "We can't afford it," and then said to me, "I know you, you'd want to quit," and it is true, I did quit everything—I quit making up my bed, I quit brushing my teeth, I quit ironing my blouses, I tried to quit going to church, so I guess I did quit everything.

My brother said, "It wouldn't do her any good anyway."

"How do you know?" I said.

"Because you are rude, crude and you stink."

Because I was rude, crude and I stunk, I didn't know who to hate the most, I was completely cornered by hate, and all I could think of was my mom saying to me what she always said, *If you are a happy person, you can be happy anywhere,* and that made me madder than hell, and then I thought of the song lyrics, *If I could tell you of my devotion, If I could pledge all my love so true,* and then, out of nowhere, I suddenly saw the movie up on that big drive-in movie screen, and then next, I may as well have been *in* the movie with the way that I was caught *up* in the movie. That night, suddenly up on that screen in that war movie I saw things and people with such spirits and human character, like elevated-beings I saw these people-to-be—people who shared and cared, who said what they meant and what they meant was something worth meaning and I began wondering what in the world I was doing with the way I was acting, with my attitudes towards life? What difference did it really make where we lived, Memphis or this (crummy old) farm? In that movie, at that time, I was made to see that there was a whole world out there, other ways to be—none of them any way I had been—and I saw the values of family and country and doing good and doing the hard thing and facing down fear and evil, and I *vowed* to be different. This movie was just what I needed to feel love for my family, and it was so powerful a love that I thought they must be feeling it too. They weren't blind or anything. Hell, no, they were my family!

All of living started to make sense, and I realized that our childhoods were over, my brother's and mine, and also that that was fine and good. I realized that my mom and dad did the things they did for a reason, reasons I could not even yet imagine, but good and right reasons all the same, all so I could have a wonderful life, all for my benefit, and if they weren't there to teach me, and my brother too, I would not do anything, not one thing. Look at the slovenly waitresses in the restaurants, at the lazy gas station attendants.

Kindness, innocence, bravery and patience and Christianity came into my heart. My hatred softened, yet I retained a spark of my old spunkiness too. I desired to radiate inner as well as outer beauty. I wanted to do good and help people. I saw my dad as the war hero he was, not the fat, cranky guy he had become. I admired him for following his dreams. I thought about how sometimes I would catch sight of my mom from where I would be lying by the pool with my friends back in Memphis, see her walking across the

Country Club terrace in her Mr. Galanos dresses and her black high-heeled shoes, and just thinking about her like that made me almost weak in the knees with love.

And Uncle Winn didn't have such a good deal any more, him living out his days in the hospital bed and carting those balls around with him his whole life. I felt instant compassion. I looked over at him and told him I liked his nice ironed khakis.

Then this one scene in the movie started up that had all our eyes like saucers. Nobody even ate so much as a Good & Plenty while this scene was unfolding up on the movie screen. If this scene had never come, I know now, I would have been infinitely better off. If that movie had just been left where it was—expanding and inspiring me and changing my view of life—my life would have had a chance of succeeding, of embracing the hard things, and I may have actually made something of myself. But this scene derailed me—just as some such scene in a movie, a book, a magazine article, a story, a dream—had derailed my mom years before me. Scenes such as these were how she could look at me with such chilling certainty as to me having the same measly-eyed future as her.

What happened was this Air Force guy, when he came back from flying his forty-eighth mission in his fighter plane, and once he had climbed down onto the tarmac and unstrapped his leather cap, he went looking for this Italian girl (who might have been Jane Russell) who had spit curls and a silky ribbon-tied blouse, and he had been thinking about her the whole time that he was having his dogfight in the sky—she had inspired him to keep going when it got rough—and it *did* get rough—and when he found her in this bar, he grabbed her and dragged her out and she screamed that she hated him, and he called her his little spitfire, his wildcat, and he drank in her mouth deeply (my brother said *bluh, be-luh, blaaaah*) while her legs were kicking and her black hair was thrashing back and forth and her blouse was coming loose and dipping lower and lower over her heavy breasts that rolled loose over her ribcage, (plus there was her little waist, and her kicking thighs) and the next thing you knew, she was going *mmmm, mmmmm, mmmm* and grabbing him around the neck and he was saying, that's right, kid, don't fight it, and our whole family, we all sat there with eyes like saucers, silent, all of us each acting like nothing at all was happening, but what was happening was what the weeds were doing that were growing up out there in the gravel in the parking lot, and what the birds were doing up in the trees and the bees were doing in their beehive, and what my mom was doing lacing her fingers in between those of my dad—it was the force that spun the world, what was happening.

Then while the dancing cartoon soda cups and smiling candy bars were doing the Charleston up on the screen, my mom and I felt around with our feet down on the floor for our sandals and we unlocked the car doors and walked through the gravel to the ladies room together and by then nothing was the same. Nothing. I walked taller and up on the balls of my feet, and I balanced my head like a flower on the stalk of my neck, and my face felt to me utterly and forevermore awash in moonlight—moist, dewy, glowy. As we were washing our hands side by side at the sinks, I was thinking I would cut spit-curls in my hair, and suddenly my mom started telling me one of the same old things she always told me, which was that college was the best time of her life. Ordinarily the things she told me I always felt were some new trap, but this time I heard what she had to say in a new way, and I heard that now, for once, because of this movie, this was the honest truth coming from my mother, like she was my friend and wanted me to know things. She said what she said like we were two girls together and she was speaking to me with such heart I almost reached out my hands to hers there in the middle of the washroom as she started saying that in college I would date. She said, oracle-like, that I would really miss something if I didn't go to college. She said that I would meet someone my sophomore year, get pinned my junior year, and get engaged my senior year, and then get married. She had married my dad before she had graduated but I would probably want to wait until graduation, although if I was in love, maybe not. I *would* fall in love. She was excited for me but dead serious about what I needed to know. She was all but holding onto me and telling me this secret—this thing I just had to know—with an honesty that was chilling.

Actually she had been saying this to me since I was a little kid when the afternoons were long, after my nap was over. She said to me before bed that I would have to brush my teeth or no one would want to marry me. Everything I had to do or no one would want to marry me.

The telephone lines scalloped black pencilings against the Fourth of July sky. We were packed into the car with a bunch of red, white, and blue Bomb Pops packed on dry ice in a Styrofoam container on the floor in the backseat under my feet. My brother had brought along his trumpet in its case.

In the trunk we had the firecrackers. We had snakes for us girls, and sparklers of course, and bottle rockets, pinwheels, buzz-bombs, ground spinners, helicopters, Roman candles, fountains, cherry bombs, M-80s, aerial bombs, airplanes.

Hanging onto my spit-curls, which were getting blown to smithereens, I started thinking about my boy cousin Ox and wondering if you could marry your cousin. Pretty soon, as we came up over a final hill, we could see Fourth of July smoke signals in the sky from all of the black smoke rising from everybody's Fourth of July grills. After a couple of turns, we pulled into Aunt Roney's and Big J B.'s driveway, and parked behind Aunt Roney's bashed-in, red Oldsmobile station wagon. A tan Cadillac was marriage-bedded right up next to it, with sets of glittering cats' eyes skulking around underneath.

Somebody had written *I love Ox* in the cement walk going to the front door. Brainless grasshoppers jumped up with every step we took. My brother stomped on as many as he could as he walked up the walk.

"For pity's sake!" said my dad about all he had to endure. He was trying to pull the Bomb Pops out of the backseat and the Styrofoam box was wedged in tight. We were standing at the door reading a note that said, "Come on through! We're out back!" The house was like walking into a dark movie theatre but we found our way around the furniture and out the rattly metal back door.

Big J.B. was grinning and struggling to get out of a mesh lawn-chair, revving up to be hosty and social. He was hanging onto an aluminum hi-ball glass that was beaded with sweat. His forehead made me think of a boiled potato or a hardboiled egg. Aunt Roney was steaming around the side of the house in a twirly Mexican skirt, hair flying loose—a kind of a jumbo version of the spitfire from the movie last night. She said, "Get up, J.B., for Christ's sakes, they're here," and put a wooden tray with chips and onion dip, oily smoked oysters on toothpicks and Ritz crackers, down on a round redwood picnic table. Off to the side, there was a half-flat, blow-up kiddy pool, and further out back, in the *back* backyard, there was Scout standing in his little pasture.

We all had our stiff zombie-hugs all around.

Ox wore a football jersey, scissored off just above his waist, with the number 17 on it. He stood strong on solid, touchdown-running legs. His shoulders were big even without shoulder pads. Across the yard, he and my brother went towards each other like magnets because they were boys together, my brother saying, "Hey, how's it going?" *(ha, ha, ha)* "Well okay, how's it going with you?" *(ha, ha, ha, ha)* "Yeah, I remember that time you all came to see us!" and Ox said, "Yeah, and we went to the Pig 'n Whistle for bar-b-que? You had three malts!" and "What do you think about all these stupid grasshoppers?" *(ha, ha, ha)* and "Remember when we taxidermed that old squirrel?" and "How soon is it going to be dark enough for the fireworks, *bwammo! Kaboom!*" and "Daddy and I went out and we got enough we can blow this whole town up if we want to." *(heh, heh, heh)* Like that they went on up to Ox's room and pretty soon we could hear them up there talking, then they got quiet and pretty soon a couple of cherry-bombs flew out the window over our heads, making us all scream, and Aunt Roney put a stop to that, and then one of them started playing the trumpet to a Stan Kenton record, *"doo be, doo be, doooooo, Candy, they call her Candy—"*

Then Big J.B., with his mouth half open, suddenly got real serious and said, "What can I get you all?" He looked steadily at us, from one to the other, and kind of jiggled his glass a little, like, hey, how about one of these? "There's pop for you kids in that tub over there. See all that, with the ice over there?" I looked and saw a big galvanized tub sitting on a corner of the cement slab patio.

I grabbed a couple of those smoked oysters on toothpicks and went over to dig around for a cream soda.

Aunt Roney said, "What do you think about all these grasshoppers?"

"I can't *stand* them!" said my mom.

"They're just a bunch of boogers," said Uncle Winn, his balls hanging down one leg of his khakis.

"Isn't it just the dickens? When are they going to do something?" said my mom.

My dad said, *"Bluh, bluh, blah, blah,* bunny rabbit. That's how she talks. Nobody can understand a word."

Then Aunt Roney said to me, "Taylor, did you see Larissa inside? No? She is in there making us a Fourth of July cake! If she was a snake she would have bitten you!"

I thought about this girl Candy and wanted someone to write a song like that about me some day. I wolfed down my smoked oysters. Finally I walked inside to see that cake Larissa was making. Two cats ran out the door as I opened it and three fought their way in with me. My Keds looked white and cartoonish before my eyes could adjust to being inside, and they seemed to be all I could see.

"I learned how to do this in cake-making class. I want it to look like a bakery cake," said Larissa. A couple of cats jumped up on the counter. She was paving the frosting on a crumbly cake trying to get it to look smooth. She had her daddy's boiled-potato forehead and was wearing a ruffly midriff top that showed a wadded and twisted belly button thumbed into her belly.

"How do you make the frosting?" I said.

"Why do you want to know? That's my secret I learned in cake-making class, you silly," she said, giving an orange cat's butt a boot off the counter. "Oh well, so you'll know, I scooped it out of that can over there in the garbage," she grinned, looking like her dad. "Don't tell anybody." She picked up a toothpaste tube of frosting and started writing a big 4 on the cake. It took a while, and I just sat watching on a kitchen stool. The orange cat came around my feet, and jumped back up on the counter. When I petted him, he stuck his rear end up in the air. Next she was sprinkling pink sugar onto the cake from a little shaker to make the tops of sparklers. She had lots of different stuff to decorate the cake with. I said, "Can I do some?"

"You don't know how."

"Let's go and ride on Scout," I said.

"Nobody ever rides Scout. He bucked all of us off. You want him? We are going to give him away."

"Give him away!" I screeched.

"You would give him away too if he bit you with those great big teeth and then bucked you off. Don't you know anything?"

"Let's go and put our feet in your kiddy pool."

She started laughing hysterically. "You silly billy, it's full of grasshoppers, or haven't you noticed? Where have you been, on the moon? I am going to be a doctor, what are you going to be?"

I went outside to get a better look at Scout. Grasshoppers boinked my legs with each step I took. He was just standing out in the middle of his pasture with his head hanging down. He looked like a little Indian pony. Scout was a pretty good name for him. It was hotter than Hades. Why couldn't these cousins understand how wonderful it was to have their own pony? I would be whooping around on him right now if he were my pony. After I finished baking the Fourth of July cake, I would go out and whoop around on Scout, then lie in the kiddy pool and have cake and ice cream to refresh myself.

My cousin Frances cart-wheeled down the yard to the fence to

be by me. She was a little younger than me and pretty, in a ballerina way, with the kind of creamy skin that has black moles. I was
leaned up against the fence like I was an old cowhand, and together
we surveyed Scout. On closer inspection he had a hairnet of flies
all around him and he looked dirt-caked in the sun. Grasshoppers
jumped up with every move he made. I knew if I petted him, dust
would poof up off his hide. Suddenly he lay down and rolled
around on his back like a dog, twisting this way and that, his hooves
flying up in the air. His fly-hairnet got a lot wider. The grasshoppers went crazy. Frances was saying he was pretty much wild by
now, that her daddy had won him in a poker game and that he was
trying to lose him in another poker game but nobody wanted him,
and that she didn't care if they ever had any pets again, that they
were overrun with pets. It's true, they had a lot of pets. Easily seven
or eight cats were swarming around our legs.

Over under the tree, Uncle Winn and my dad and Big J.B. were
sitting together—my dad cradling a can of Metrecal in his lap,
sticking to his diet. I thought of this picture of him on his bureau,
him all slim and young, leaning up against his airplane, cap pushed
back on his head, grinning—and the plane had a hula-girl, I swear,
painted on its side. Big J.B. was talking and my dad's eyes were all
lit-up, charming as all get-out, and he was murmuring interested-
sounding things, such as, "Well, for heaven's sakes," and "I never
heard of such a thing." Then my dad was telling the story of the
fighting part of the movie last night, and they started talking about
somebody killed in the war, Skillet or somebody. They got all quiet
and my dad turned his can of Metrecal around and around in his
hands.

Aunt Roney and my mom were going in and out of the house,
bringing out platters of hot dogs and ground meat made into hamburgers, all covered with waxed paper. Mustard and pickles and
ketchup were already on the picnic table. Big J.B. would struggle
up from his lawn chair from time to time and squirt more lighter
fluid on the grill. Aunt Roney: from the back, her hips lifted up

one side of her skirt and then the other side, as she walked. Looking at my mom and Aunt Roney, it was hard to believe they were sisters.

The hamburgers tasted like lighter fluid and were not cooked all the way through, and they were delicious. To try to keep the cats away while we ate our hamburgers, we sat with our Keds off and our feet in the wading pool. We kept a hose running to squirt the cats away from time to time, but still every cat from twenty miles around was crawling over us, practically standing in our plates. Dead grasshopper bodies were floating like water-soaked cigars around our feet. The dying ones were paddling their dumb legs.

Since the adults were still sitting around yakking and making no moves towards firecracker lighting, we dumped our paper plates in the garbage barrel and went upstairs to Frances's room to see her new bedroom set. Her white canopy bed and chest were painted with delicate gold curlicues. There was a wooden box with a kitten painted on top on her dresser, and when I opened it, I saw that it was filled with Modess Young Miss sanitary napkins with a little belt curled up, ready and waiting in the corner. Larissa came in with her doctor's kit and we started giving her Vogue Dolls shots, telling the dolls, "This will kill." We gave each other shots by using the plastic shot needle and pinching hard with our fingers so it felt real.

Pretty soon my top came off and I lay face down and Frances and Larissa were trailing their fingernails across my back. I thought of this thing my dad would do when I was little. He would hold me in his lap and run his fingers in little circles on my knees saying, *If you are a lady, as I think you be, you will neither laugh nor giggle, as I tickle your knee.*

Out the window, Aunt Roney said, "Goddamn it, J.B."

"Oh shut your blowhole," said Big J.B. back, but I was happy and content because them out there meant there were parents, and somehow that meant that no matter whatever else, if anything really awful happened, they would fight it before we had to.

The next thing I heard was *Candy, they call her Candy* booming from Ox's room next door, and pretty soon, outside, I heard trumpets playing along with the music, and I leaned myself up on my elbow, the girl cousins now sitting on me, and I looked out the window where I saw my brother and Ox, with their trumpets sparkling in the sun, playing along with Stan Kenton, the parents all quiet, respectful, legs crossed, listening, seeing how the boys were coming along with their trumpets—boys having the dignity of ones that could play the trumpet.

Pretty soon they called us for dessert and I rolled Frances and Larissa off of me. Larissa got her cake and we got the Bomb Pops out of the freezer. The cake was funny looking, did not look anything like bakery-bought. Big J.B., when he saw it, said, "Well, I'm not eating that thing! She always has these kids taking all these crazy lessons. Roney, how much money did this dumb-looking cake cost me anyway?" But my dad said he wanted some of that $100 cake, what the heck, it was a holiday, he could go back on the Metrecal tomorrow—but did they have any vanilla ice cream to have with it? And he said he wanted a mixing bowl to put his in, not one of those silly tiny dessert dishes Aunt Roney was bringing out on a tray. My mom got up out of her lawn chair and went inside and brought out a mixing bowl. I was squatted down, lighting a snake and watching it pump up—like a Dairy Queen—from out of the little aspirin tablet those things come in, and Aunt Roney was holding blubbery, red faced Larissa in her lap and saying to Big J.B., "Now why do you have to do that with her? You are always making her cry."

Then Ox, with the dignity of someone who is a football star, went over and jabbed Larissa in the arm with his knuckle and said, "She is such a little crybaby. You are just a whiney little girl!"

"From their mothers, that's how girls are supposed to learn how to make cakes," said Big J.B. "That thing isn't even what I would call a cake."

"She probably got the frosting out of a can," said Ox.

"I did not," screamed Larissa from Aunt Roney's arms, snot spewing.

"You are such a liar," said Ox and started coming over towards her with his knuckles again.

"She did get it out of a can, a Betty Crocker can," I said and ran inside to get the can to show them all.

"I'll have some of that cake," said my dad, "but I need ice cream with it."

Ox said, "What a pile of crap! I have to get the hell out of here."

Lordy, but didn't I do a U-turn and follow him out of the yard, trotting along like that pony Scout would have if he ever moved. I had scared myself, because I had said Larissa had gotten her frosting out of a can, and that seemed to be an especially low yet powerful thing for me to do.

Aunt Roney said, "Don't you kids want any dessert? What about your dessert?" Larissa was looking at me out of eyes I knew well, out of black eyes full of rageful hatred.

"You girls don't touch a single one of those fireworks until I get back," said Ox to Frances and Larissa. My brother was already upstairs with Stan Kenton on his trumpet.

I petted Scout on his forehead as I went by—but I was careful in case he went for my hand—then Ox and I went on down the crumbling sidewalk past the older houses with open screen doors, front porches and American flags, and wheelbarrows full of pansies sitting out in their front yards. We went on to the corner, turned right and went up the hill past the high school where Ox was a football star. Near there was where the Dairy Queen was. I liked the way the gravel felt under my rubber soles, I liked the sweet ice-cream smell of the Dairy Queen mix, liked seeing the people sitting around spooning up Peanut Busters at the picnic tables, their skin slick summer skin. I was wondering if the girl who had written *I love Ox* in Aunt Roney's cement walk would now see us and think we were having a date.

We got chocolate dip cones but didn't talk or anything—he was mad about something that I knew nothing about—Larissa's cake or something—and I couldn't think of anything to say so I said, "Do you all have a country club around here?" Suddenly, he started trotting down the street, breathing heavy and blowing out air in swooshes. I stood there a minute, then kicked into gear and began running along with him, holding my dip cone out in front of me.

"Bet your house isn't like this one. God, I hate her," he said.

"What?" I said.

"Frances."

"Frances?" I said.

"She is a moron. I hate those girls. Larissa is okay, but Frances, I hate her."

"What did Frances do?"

"Girls are morons."

All I could think of to say was, "You silly billy." Ox then threw himself down in the tall grass right there by the main drag. Where he was sitting looked to be full of grasshoppers and other stuff like old cigarette wrappers.

"Are you in a bad mood?" I said as he sat there, licking at the melting drips of his dip cone. A grasshopper jumped on my leg and spit tobacco juice on me. I just looked at it and didn't know what to do so I said, "You silly billy," again. Cars and a tractor went by. Pretty soon a Cadillac honked at us, *beep, beep,* and it was Big J.B. and my dad with him going someplace, looking at us out the windows with big grins on their faces.

"Now, where are our dads off to?" I said. My dip cone dripped all over my hand and I sopped up what I could with the one toilet-papery napkin I had. Finally I threw the whole thing away in the drainage ditch, and my mouth was a mess and I had no napkin.

"I hate those grasshoppers. I'm going to get some M-80s down here and blow their dumb heads off," said Ox.

I just looked at the grasshoppers. "Where are our dads going?" I said.

Ox shrugged. "Well, here, they have some really big choices. They could be going down to the airfield or to get more beer. People around here think it is a really big deal to go down to the airfield and watch planes come in." I thought about the movie from last night, then what I thought of was my dad in that picture on his bureau, him with his fighter plane, and skinny as me in his flight suit. Ox said, "Then this rinky-dink fair comes here and people think that is a really big deal. We're just a bunch of hicks. Oh, yeah, we have some really big deals here. Now, here, *you* would be everything. You would be Homecoming Queen, you would be the biggest deal. You would have any guy you wanted. You would have them eating out of your hand, now—you, here, you would really be something in this po-dunk town."

I was flabbergasted, absolutely flabbergasted. All I could think of to say was, "Oh, stop being such a silly billy." I also remembered the Italian girl from last night in the movie. I knew there was something I'd forgotten.

"I am getting sick of you saying silly billy about everything," said Ox.

This shut me up.

"I think you are beginning to get boobies. Let me see. I have sisters, you know, and I see them all the time."

We sat out there like that for a long time and were quiet, him saying *come on, come on,* every once in a while, and pulling me back where the weeds were deeper, and I could hardly breathe and I knew one thing for sure, that this, now *this,* was thrilling. *Thrilling.* I would do anything for more of this, I already knew. It was almost as if every part of my life leaped into focus with the idea of showing him what I had under my top, and I wanted to, but didn't know how—just pull up my top? Like a total idiot? But, it was that he wanted me to, so much, and it was that *wanting* I was so broadsided by. *Pop, pop, pop, pop, baaaaa-wham!* We could hear firecrackers in the distance, and Ox finally said, well he's bored, sitting out here in the weeds fighting off grasshoppers, if nothing is going to happen with me, and we should get home because it is almost time for the fireworks. *Oh no, oh no, oh no,* I thought, and I yanked up my top and he stopped his getting up and dropped back down in the weeds, and he ran one callused football-throwing finger, his trumpet-playing finger, over my little bumps, like the girls' fingers were trailing softly on my back earlier, and I really liked it. He rubbed his finger back and forth and with his big flat hand pushed me down in the grass, a bit back from the side of the road. I lay there and looked up at the gauzy charcoaled burnt-wiener sky, his fingers and whole hands going back and forth on one and then the other of me. He brought my hand down to his pants and I touched his thing.

"You are giving me a hard-on and you aren't even all that big yet. Boy, you are going to be something." He rubbed my hand on his thing, I didn't have to do a thing, I was a wanted girl. Never in my life again would I have to do one thing. He said to me, "I am going to go off like one of those molatov fountains, or whatever they are called," *heh, heh, heh.* I wondered, if I acted like the little spitfire I saw in the movie last night, would he tame me, and maybe next I would even buck around like Scout. I wanted to get married and have him put babies in me, I wanted, I wanted, I wanted. I wanted, I wanted, I wanted. Grasshoppers jumped all over me. I was floating on one of the clouds up in the sky. He finally stopped but I never wanted to stop. "Let's go back and shoot off those fireworks," he said, standing up, adjusting himself in his pants. He swiped his hand through his buzz-cut, and then stuck it out for me to pull up on. "Come on, I am supposed to be shooting off firecrackers with your brother now."

The Cadillac rumbled down the road and crunched over on the gravel as Ox pulled me along behind him—me, sex drunk, my arm pulled out straight and long. If he would have said, *lie down,* I would have lain down again right then. He was telling me about myself, "You want what all girls want, you are going to have a time of it, I know about these things, you are going to have to beat them off with a stick."

My dad leaned his face out the passenger side, all happy as can be, and said, "Would M'lady like a ride back to set off some black snakes? Wave some sparklers in the night sky? Eat some of that fine cake cousin Larissa has made for us? What can I do for you, Sweetheart?"

"Crap, they've been downtown," said Ox.

Big J.B. was red-faced and *hardy-har-har*ing and tipped his head back for a pull of whatever he was drinking.

"Hop in, Ox," my dad said, leaning forward so his seat could tip forward.

Ox was too big for that so my dad opened the door and stepped out so Ox could fit in the back, and I sat on my dad's lap, with my dad holding his drink out so I didn't bump it, and also holding me so my butt didn't slip off his lap, and like that we went the four blocks back to the house. "You sure have pointy hipbones," said my dad, and Ox said, "Awww, she's just a runt," and messed up my hair with his big football-throwing hand, then secretly kept his hand on my neck and squeezed and let go and squeezed and let go.

You want to know about happiness? I put my feet with the ground-in summer dirt up on the dashboard and Big J.B. gunned that Cadillac home, dust and gravel probably making a whirling Burt Reynolds tornado out the back, and with me all gooey and girlie—now *that* is happiness.

Back at the house, my brother was sitting in a rocking chair eating a whole cherry pie. He had a half gallon of vanilla ice cream down in the grass beside him and was adding scoops to the top of his pie as the ice cream would soften up enough so he could dig more out.

"Where'd you get that?" I said.

"It's mine," he said.

Ox was pulling out the snakes and cherry bombs and bottle rockets from paper sacks like a kid tearing through Christmas presents. Us girls mowed through the sparklers and snakes in about ten minutes, and we laid ourselves (me squirmy and breasty) out on the stomped-down eaten-up grass with the grasshoppers and Scout to watch the show. Cats darted around, ricocheting from bush to bush, scared of the firecrackers. Scout ran around kicking up his back heels in his pasture. He had forgotten that this same thing happened last year and that he survived to tell the tale. Ox had forgotten all about me but I did not know this yet. Pretty soon my dad came over to where us girls were lying in the grass and he picked me up and sat me in a lawn chair with him. His Metrecal was long gone, nowhere in sight. He said to me—as we were watching a giant firework arcing in the sky and then sending out spinning stars that go off and keep going off, the boys saying, *oh man, look at that, oh man, that is so great*—my dad said to me, as he folded me into him like the little baby girl I used to be, he said what he used to say, he said, "If you are a lady, as I think you be, you will neither laugh nor giggle, as I tickle your knee." Then he said, his hand on Winn's shoulder, Uncle Winn sitting next to us in a *chaise longue*, he said, "I am going to say something to you that Winn here said to me when I was about your age and I will never, ever forget it, and I want the same for you, all playing aside. I want you to remember this night. I want you to remember how it smells and how it looks up in the sky, all what you can see up there. Now, you look around and remember all of this—who was here, all these people that are your family, and how it smells out here with the firecrackers, how it feels, how it feels to be you right now, and to be with me right now, because this time will never be again. I want for you to remember every bit of it." And I looked around at all of it—at Aunt Roney in her twirly Mexican skirt, at my mom sitting with her legs crossed and watching me with suspicious eyes, at the boys squatting down, heads close together, putting a match to a firework, at Uncle Winn next to me with his balls in his lap, at the girls lying together in the kiddy pool, their heads resting on the soft smushy side, and at Scout running around and bucking in his pasture, Scout mostly dark and unseeable but with the white spots positively incandescent in that most indelible of nights.

Patricia Lear was born in Memphis, Tennessee, and lives in Evanston, Illinois. Her story collection, *Stardust, 7-Eleven, Route 57, A&W and So Forth,* was included in the 1992 *New York Times* Summer Reading List, the Editors' Choice, and was also named one of their Notable Books of the Year. Her stories have appeared in *Triquarterly, The Quarterly, The O'Henry Awards, Best of the South: From Ten Years of New Stories from the South,* and *Best of the Decade: The Antioch Review.*

The skeleton of "Nirvana" was drawn from my early life. Yes, when we left Memphis we lived on a farm for a while, yes, there were cousins in a nearby town, yes, there were drive-in movies that we indeed went to. But the anger and rage of my brother and I was never so deep, my dad never so mean, my mom never so distant, and most of the scenes and especially the big sex scene never happened. (Note to Mom: it never happened.)

The story was the usual struggle, but I have to tell you that the ending was one of those rare gifts that occasionally happens in fiction writing. It just came to me in a rush as I was looking around for a kick-ass ending. And such a moment between my dad and me did happen—just not in the context of the events of "Nirvana." I am happy that I got that moment down on paper, the emotion of it and the sweetness of it, before it disappeared—like everything else has from back then. That last paragraph's for you, Jim Merritt.

COOL WEDDING

(from *Shenandoah*)

D ear Lakshmi:

In the summer, this place is like India: Bombay, Madras, only fancy name Houston-Pouston, America. My skin feels like bubble gum even after fresh-oil bath. I am wearing eggplant-color handloom sari, oiling and plaiting hair, putting *kumkum tikka* on forehead and going to *puja* room in closet. I am placing banana bunch and broken coconut on stainless steel *thali* before Ganesh, lighting four sandalwood incense sticks. Please God, remover of obstacles, I am saying, wake up my *shakti* part. You have placed me here in America. Help me influence husband Cheenu, children, Sudhir, Sushila, and Siddharth. I am doing *namaskaram* prostration then crossing my hands, touching opposite earlobe, and squatting and standing, squatting and standing, physical penance before Ganesha. He is kindly forgiving all wrong tendencies on my part. This also helping my fitness program.

You know I always say we Indians not believing in psychologist, therapist, why talk to strangers when you can talk to close sister, after all, nothing like family, though spoiled children and husband make me question that wisdom sometimes. Did I know married life in America would turn out this way, that day when Cheenu came to our flat in Matunga, and I was only nineteen, rosebud-faced in emerald Binny silk sari? Even after marriage, and Sudhir and Sushila coming along in New Jersey, then Siddharth belated surprise in Texas, I did not have any inkling of my present life.

Anyway, you asked about my job, my trip to Louisiana—our nephew Vikram's wedding; yes, cousin Leela was there with Dhakshisriramabadran, and I saw the Patels, Ila and Arun. I will try to tell you, bring you up-to-date on all those things including the difficulties in my family life.

Since I returned from the wedding, too many things to attend to: children's academics, health problem, matching client difficulties. I tell you, often I wonder, what is the meaning of this modern life?

Last Wednesday evening, I went to Sudhir's school meeting. You know hubby Cheenu is not going, always watching sports on TV. Coming home from work, then sitting with potato chips in front of TV. He is paying for ESPN, golf channel, God knows what else. You know I am not having time for TV, all rubbish they are showing anyhow. I am only watching news and i channel. International channel is showing nice Indian movies; you know I still like to watch Hindi movies, I don't like to forget language I learned in Bombay since childhood, this America and all, it is not reaching my blood.

You know Sudhir is in expensive private Episcopal school, very fancy that one. All mothers wearing such strong perfume, so crowded in chapel where we are meeting with college counselor, it is too much, I am sneezing too many times. You know Sudhir has to take SAT in a few months. I hope and pray he will do well. Lakshmi, you will not believe the competition in America. What with all the smart Chinese children. Thank God for the Americans. Without them, how will our children shine in America? I, personally, am very glad about the policy of one child only per couple in China. Wish the Chinese in America would also take it up.

Anyway, so I come home from the meeting and put on fan in the family room.

"Bring me some water," I am telling Sudhir, that boy. "All that perfume your school mothers are wearing, I am getting headache, bring also that Tylenol."

"I need the car, ma," he is saying, "I have to visit Karen, group project for math. Everybody's meeting with their groups. Promise, I'll be careful with the car."

"Don't talk to me about car, buster. Those two traffic tickets, who is going to pay for that?"

"No more tickets, I promise, please mom, please."

I am telling that boy, "You better shape up after all this sleeping and sleeping in the summer. Your father and I are working like crazy, you better work like anything. Just wanting to do medicine is not enough. Nothing we want is going to fall from the sky." That cheeky fellow, your darling nephew as you call him, you know what he says?

"Who told you I want to do medicine, I'm thinking maybe law, history, dentistry. Am still undecided, ma."

"This undecided not deciding and all is fancy American talk, you will make me old talking like that," I tell him.

Tell me Lakshmi, you think that Vimala Vaidyanathan's children, son-in-laws and daughter-in-law talked like him? She is displaying blown-up family photograph in her oversized den always saying pathologist, cardiologist, oncologist, neo-natologist, urologist, neurologist. Already there is one black sheep in our family, my daughter, your niece, Sushila, doing math. Don't get me started, I tell you. All that praise from her teachers, "Your girl's so bright, Mrs. Srinivasan." What is the use of that?

"Pure math is what I want to do, ma," Sushila said, and I replied, "What are you, famous mathematician Ramanujam?"

Too much of this confidence-ponfidence, that is your niece's problem, Lakshmi, I am telling you.

"He's so cute," she is saying this summer talking to her friend on the phone about some idiot classmate in UT Austin, thinking I am deaf in the next room. "So sue me, ma" Sushila says, in that stylish way of hers, "I like him, so what?" I am thinking, am I a fool?

Why should I sue her when I can pinch her if I want? I am telling you, Lakshmi, mothering in America is so stressful. When I start to think of all that freedom in college, I cannot sleep sometimes. What is this cute-shoot rubbish showing off her figure wearing tight T-shirts all the time? It's not nice for a grown-up girl advertising everything like that. Really this Cheenu, your brother-in-law, should also be doing father's job. What is the use of only mother scolding children all the time? The way some of the other Indian parents are suffering, I am telling you, it is very worrying sometimes. Daughters and sons jumping over fence after lights are out, American dates waiting in Cherokee Jeep cars, so many children lying, parents not knowing, no communication, very sad, this America, too much pressure to conform.

"What is the point?" I am asking Cheenu. "Talking about others, what are you doing to help me in this house mister, never scolding children, making me the heavy (American talk), always working and watching sports, is that job of good father?" Again he is smiling and pushing up his specs, I am getting mad and walking out. Anyway, sometimes I am getting so fed up feel like being American myself saying none of my business, let them all fly a kite.

Yes, yes, don't worry, I'm getting to the wedding in Louisiana.

I know it is more than three weeks since your letter came and I am writing back late, one section yesterday, another today. What with one thing and another thing. I am only wanting peace and quiet to be good matchmaker, sensitive mother and wife, you know I don't like to complain, that's not part of my style. But for peace and quiet, you need cooperation from family, husband, and children, none is forthcoming from either direction, I can tell you that. Sometimes this matchmaking job I tell you, it is too much. But thank God. Since Cheenu helped me with my web page on the internet, my phone bills are not so fat. That is something at least. Tell me what you think of my new web site. Copied it down for you to read next. After all, if you cannot depend on close sister for advice, criticism, who can you turn to?

www. *ShubhMangalam.SiteofAuspiciousMarriage.com*
Say yes the Hindu Way: First comes marriage, then comes
love:
Earthly bliss and Heavenly joy.
Celebrating Whole Decade of Fruitful Matchmaking.
When it comes to the needs of your family and friends,
Shoba Srinivasan is capable of attachment and detachment.
I take care to meet your subjective mate requirements on this
end while performing all potential spouse search tasks with
objective outlook on other end.
All cases accepted:
Caste/Nationality No Bar.
Single-Time Sincere Divorcees Okay.
We are not discriminating on basis of color, religion or mixed-
marriage results.
This is the **Shubh Mangalam** way, where list of potential
spouse is always qualitative and quantitative, in short—*fantastic.*
We cater to astrology/horoscope believers and
modern nonbelievers.
ShubhMangalam.Site ofAuspiciousMarriage
Say yes the Hindu Way.
Sugar Land, Houston, Texas, USA.
Cash (only) transactions arranged after first meeting.

Anyway, next month, matchmaking results will be good. Pros-
pects are promising, let me leave it at that. With Syrian Christian
Malayali family in Chicago, I will hopefully be making four thousand after taxes, not bad. Psychiatrist boy wanting demure wife,
not job-taking type. "Enough stress in my job for both of us," he
said. "What to do," I thought, "difficult to find modern girls to
agree to such demands." Luckily for me, I met grandmother visiting from Trivandrum at Onam festival lunch in big Woodlands
house. Very grand affair with real rose *kolam* design at the entrance,
so many fancy cars: Mercedes, Acura, BMW and all, they are asking us Toyotas to park very far from the house. "Patience," I am

telling Cheenu also, *"arre,* you know my matchmaking job, I need these people, what to do, such is life."

"C'est la vie," as our sister is saying in Louisiana during the wedding, I am coming to that, wait.

Really Lakshmi, why all this materialism? Very sickening, this attitude. Woodlands house for Onam lunch has big swimming pool like lima bean. Everybody standing around, no place to move, so I am bumping into elbow of Trivandrum grandmother with demure granddaughter, loving States, watching *Dallas* on TV, crazy about Texas, only twenty, finishing senior year at Loretto House in Calcutta, very easygoing, fair, slim, smiling type. Now only remaining problem is matching horoscopes and you know that is not in our hands, God will do the rest. I am going regularly to the temple you know we have Meenakshi temple in Houston, very beautiful and nice.

This squeezing in motherhood, wifehood into my demanding job, it's very obstructive sometimes. And on top of that, like a fool, I tried to make the children and Cheenu *puri, korma,* fresh rice for yogurt rice, and condensed milk *payasam* for dessert because it was Friday. You know I make a point of the family observing some prayer time and proper South Indian meal at least one auspicious evening a week. Keeping in touch with our culture is so important I tell you, I am seeing so many who are lost.

I am hurrying up, finished grinding the coffee beans for *dikak-shun* extract, Saturday night before going to bed. Sudhir and Sushila being teenagers do not get up till ten o'clock on Sunday morning. If we slept late when we were growing up in Bombay, Amma scolded and Appa turned off the Bajaj fan and dragged the pillow from under our heads. India built character muscle. Not that we need to brag. A little discipline, some suffering, it's good for the soul, no? Otherwise, how do these children grow depth? Too much cushioning and softness, all this choice in America, it's not very good. Anyway, what is done is done, I married Cheenu and now we are here not there. Not that I'm complaining. Still.

Your dear brother-in-law Cheenu can enforce some discipline, give them deadline for waking up, not encouraging bad behavior, you know this is how problems start. "Who knows where it will lead?" I tell him, giving him coffee in nice stainless-steel tumbler. He is nodding as if serious and pushing his specs back to the top of his nose, whistling all the way to the den. By the time I finish my bowl of Golden Grahams (you know my weakness, I am loving American sweet cereals), I hear him laughing and watching *Simpsons* with Sudhir, Sushila, and Siddharth.

At last children are in their rooms—Sudhir on the phone telling me homework, Sushila washing hair using enough water for whole family in India, Siddharth, my innocent baby, really doing homework, having slight problem with fractions, never mind.

Anyway, Cheenu and I are both relaxing for few minutes. I am telling him also, "What are you doing? What is the meaning of working all week and watching news and sports on TV every weekend? Same same all the time. Do something new with your time. Always the same business, it's not nice."

On Friday afternoons, he is going with friends for golf, talking about playing sports, sitting and driving around course in cart, then nicely lying to me, saying, "Working out. . . ." On top of that, he is drinking beer with friends, saying, "Why not enjoy only?" when he comes home and I ask. Then he is thinking he can make up by trying to kiss me. But you know how your brother-in-law is. He thinks he knows everything, only office business and golf; tennis scores swimming in his head all the time. Life is also about other things, no? I am telling him, *"Arre baba,* do some sit-ups, some exercise, this golf-polf once a week, it is not enough."

"I know about you," I tell him. "Your type-A personality, look at your Ganesh tummy like big coconut, work, work, all the time, lifting your company on your head, Fluor Daniel this and Fluor Daniel that. I am not Mrs. Daniel, remember that. There are three children to be educated in this family, buster, I can't do it alone. I want you healthy so you can live a long time. What is the point of being married becoming widow stuck with children all the time?"

Only yesterday, before my bath, I am looking at myself in the full-length mirror and thinking, not bad, talking to myself. Forty-two years old and still curvy-purvy, like slightly plump Janaki from Chingelpet. "Now you better get serious," I am thinking, "in this family, if you don't get serious, then who will?" Then your brother-in-law Cheenu is coming in, whistling at me like I am some blonde on TV ad. *"Arre,"* I am saying, "what is all this middle-aged lust? I am not your Monica-Ponica sitting in some White House. This is Shoba Srinivasan from Matunga, remember that."

Yes, about the wedding in Louisiana, I am coming to that soon.

I am going to the kitchen, cutting *brinjal* and onion for *sambhar,* finished frying mustard, then comes Siddharth, saying, "Call me Sid."

"Arre," I am saying, "why I am bothering suffering with you big, American, super-size son, cesarean section, labor for hours and hours, coming out saying, "'Don't call me Siddharth, ma, my name is Sid.' What is this dirty habit, nice Indian name Siddharth—this Sid-Pid—chopping your name so rudely like that?"

He is saying, "What's this brown stuff, ma? *Sambhar?* Not *again.* I like fried chicken, Kentucky, man."

"I don't do this chicken business," I tell him, "eating birds and such. You want smart brains, eat fried *bhindi,* okra, we ate that for good grades in math. You become back-talking like your big brother and sister, I will pinch your buttocks, buster junior, remember that."

In the middle of all this commotion, you know I have to help prepare for the wedding in Baton Rouge. That dear sister of ours, Padma, very stylish and sophisticated, I don't want to gossip and complain all the time, you know I don't like to do that, but she is calling me ten times a day, saying, "What do I do about this and what do I do about that?" *Arre,* what is the use of post-graduate degree in psychology and women's studies, cannot help organize son's wedding? Why all this botheration when Cajun bride's Robichaud family in Denham Springs, Louisiana, offering house, having only pool wedding, fifty people, saying they don't believe in anything grand?

Anyway, so I am calling bride's mother for names of Cajun dishes, then phoning catering people, ordering: *palak paneer, pulao, dhal,* chicken curry, gumbo, jambalaya, crawfish étouffée, this strange combination Padma wants, and I am telling her, "You better set up separate vegetarian and nonvegetarian tables, why did you invite cousin Leela and family from Calgary, Alberta, they are coming with purist Hindu food notions and all?"

Then she is saying, "Never mind about that, I am worried about Cajun granny from Gulf Coast, she wants rehearsal dinner, supposed to be given by groom's family. Did Esther's mother talk to you about that?"

"No," I am saying, now worrying along with Padma. I am telling you Lakshmi, Cajun granny is behaving like Pope's right foot. What is the use of Catholic-matholic tradition? Granddaughter not even wearing white dress, choosing pistachio gown from Dillard's. Bride Esther and groom Vikram Bakram having it off months before the wedding living in same apartment. These children today, no respect for marriage, holy institution should be approached with respect. Even those of us approaching with respect getting problems back. Those two should be ashamed, none of my business, I tell you, you know I don't like to interfere, let them do what they like.

So I drive down for a week to Baton Rouge leaving Cheenu, children, and clients, since Padma calling and pleading too many times. She does not know what to serve for rehearsal dinner, menu planning and cooking, she cannot do that. Anyway, so I go into her kitchen and think, good that I'm adjustable, eating eggs and cheese and baked goods because her fridge is full of brown, organic, oval eggs laid by chicken that run wild not caged in pens.

"Padma," I am saying to our dear sister, "this eating scrambled eggs, toast, salad, soup, all the time—no wonder you cannot think, nervous about small thing like cooking. Get some *dhal, chapati,* rice in your life." But she is not listening to my sensible words, inviting me to join her awareness workshop in massage therapist's office same evening.

Anyway, so two days before rehearsal dinner I go with our sister to awareness workshop in borrowed massage therapist's office. Very crowded with office furniture, tables in the middle, chairs pushed against the wall. All the women wearing black leotards. Me in my purple sari with yellow border, you know I still wear only Indian clothes, this is best in humid climate, airy feeling, breeze flowing in and out. Padma's assistant friend is putting on new-age music, strange hollow-tube noises, everybody starting out, inviting wild Kali woman inside to come out. Wriggling like caterpillar black bodies on the floor, then rising, opening pieces of netted fabric from Michael's (famous American craft shop), cloth wings stretching into butterflies. Women dancing all over the place, around massage therapist's table, I get knee cramps pretending like the rest. For the remainder of hollow-tube song, I am standing near filing cabinet in the kitchen, which is so narrow my throbbing knee is jutting out.

"This goddess-poddess game, wild woman thing, is not for somebody like me," I am telling everybody.

They are saying, "Let it out, push the anger out." What is the use of so many angry women in black leotards playing caterpillar-butterfly? Metamorphosis should be happening in your head, not happening from dancing around office furniture. I, too, am angry but smart enough to know that. Anyway, none of my business I tell you, this awareness-shewareness, strange modern invention, did Cajun granny become demanding granny doing butterfly dance?

I am calling Cheenu daily, telling that Sudhir to work hard, that Sushila she is by nature hardworking, only has this eye for the boys. I am telling her also, "focus on studies, that is your job." And my baby Siddharth, you know he is the innocent type, only interested in food, chicken, chicken, nothing else.

On day of rehearsal dinner, Cheenu is calling me from cell phone, Sushila late coming from Austin, they are leaving soon, on their way in no time. Next phone call is collect from Leela they are also arriving soon, plane late leaving from Calgary, you know that Canada, all that Quebeçoise French-Canadian nonsense, efficiency going down toilet, what to do, such is life. Anyway, four hours later, cousin Leela and husband are walking into the house. She has not changed a bit, I tell you, wearing heavy jewelry like Christmas tree, so much ornamentation is not nice.

At rehearsal dinner, you know I made my specialties: *pulao, korma, kofta* curry, *puris, idli,* chutney. Everything came out very nice. Leela is talking loudly like always. Joking and laughing with Cajun granny, who does not seem so tough, liking my cooking, after all. Our dear co-brother-in-law, Leela's husband Dakshisri-ramabadran, wearing pretty red-velvet bowtie, sitting quiet like meditating mouse, while our dear cousin talking and laughing with everybody, again and again, all that jewelry shaking, no moderation, decorum, always bumptious, that one.

The Cajuns cannot pronounce our beautiful Indian names. Americans cannot say "Dhakshisriramabadran Velayathur Venkatraman" or any long name like that. Same problem all Indians are having, talking on the phone, giving our name for reservation or anything like that. If American at other end, typing name on keyboard, South Indian speaking, spelling out the letters, saying, "D as in Donkey, A as in America" and so on till the end of the name and American on other end saying computer screen space not enough, name too difficult, long, which country is that from? Anyway, so poor co-brother-in-law Dhakshisriramabadran, trying to be adjustable, telling bride's father, "Mr. Robichaud, call me Dhakshi." But all Robichauds and Boudreaux men already giddy from Budweiser beer, saying together,

"Say what, bubba, Ducksheet?"

And all children and teenagers within hearing distance laughing, including my own Sudhir, Sushila, Siddharth. I tell you, these children today, no respect for adults.

Anyway, rehearsal dinner is big success. We are finishing off with *laddus, pedas,* and *gulab jamuns* from Bombay Sweets in Houston. "Sweets and all," I told our dear sister, "better order only, I cannot do that." Thank God, after rehearsal dinner, Cheenu and I are getting one day rest. Everybody else going to Nottoway plantation and Padma's organic picnic lunch. Only hubby and I are not going.

We are getting invitation from Cheenu's old office friend, Patel— you know Ila and Arun from when you lived in Toronto. He used to be with Fluor, now with Exxon. They live here in Baton Rouge, owning chain of motels on Florida Boulevard. That Ila and Arun, too forward I tell you, having love marriage twenty-seven years ago, now throwing big party for anniversary. You remember from before, they have one show-offy son, always wearing cellular phone, beeper, whole Radio Shack store on his belt. Twenty-four years old, already earning six-figure salary in motel business. What is the meaning of money? No value these days, I can tell you that. Anyway, so Cheenu is showing me invitation from Patels, big pink-carnation flower on left side, glitter powder stuck on the petals, dewdrops on the leaves and Hinglish words on the right. You know these Gujeratis, thinking in Hindi-Gujerati, writing in English, always mixing Indian English and American English, they cannot talk good English like us South Indians to save their life. Anyway, I copied the words for you. I know you like to hear everything, leave nothing out, you always say, I am giving details like you want.

ANNIVERSARY PARTY INVITATION
Before our happy, auspicious marriage,
people said we were an
UNLIKELY AND UNMATCHED PAIR
Some said PERSONALITY-wise difference,
Others said NATURE-wise difference
Elders said HOROSCOPE-wise incompatibility,
Neighbors and friends said OTHER-wise unseen difficulty
**HEY, Y'ALL: WE ARE STILL JOYOUSLY MARRIED
TO THE SAME PERSON EACH OF US!!!**
Merry times await you at

Plantation Banquet Hall
Quality Inn, February 8, 7:00 PM
No gifts please. Your presence will be our present.
Ila and Mukesh Patel
4656 Inverness Drive,
CCLA: Country Club of Louisiana (housing golf course designed by many times winner of emerald jacket Golden Bear Jack Nicklaus)
Baton Rouge, LA 70808

At the party, Ila is the same like always, talking with lipstick on her teeth. "You know my *beta,* son Suresh (whole Radio Shack store on his belt, I am adding) went to Bombay to brush up Gujerati, seek prospective bride. So far, nothing worked out," she said, licking her teeth, swallowing her lipstick, and holding my hand. "Poor fellow," she said, "landing in Bombay during monsoon rains so much water, car stalling, people pushing taxi, shouting *dhakka marro,* water over knee caps, nothing changes back home, only girls becoming too westernized, they used to be so reserved and homely types."

Then Arun, her husband, joining us and boasting to me, "The men in this family, we are always very peripatetic. Only Ila, she is homely type, does not like to deal with jet lag. Everybody in Indian community saying to her, you have everything, only waiting for daughter-in-law. So, Mrs. Shoba, I am requesting you to look for suitable girl. Keep an eye out. No rush. After all, my *beta,* you know he is only twenty-four. We want girl with topnotch character. Only thing, you know our lifestyle, girl must be sociable, know how to talk with people, smile and be without stress. You know we men already have too much of that. We want women with calming effect. Must be cultured. You know Ila is culture-vulture type."

Outside I am saying, "All right, we will see what we can do." But inside I am thinking, "Why they want to take some too-young girl, mold her into this foolish wife?" Before finding answer for my own question, I see Radio-Shack boy coming near me, wearing big smile. He is having good manners, politeness I see, bringing me juice and saying *namaste*. He is asking, "How are you auntie?" and offering plate of *masala* cashew nuts. Ila and Arun are leaving to greet new arriving guests. Radio-Shack boy turns off on buttons of communication gadgets hanging from his belt and pocket: click, click, click and red-glowing buttons turning black. He is bending his head low American-style and talking to me softly.

"I hear that your business is doing well, auntie; all my friends are saying so. You are listening closely to the parents but not too much. They are saying you understand very well young people's views. That is very modern and good, auntie, I like that." Then he is smiling and winking at me, that foolish, charming boy. "You know I like mature and bold professional type," he is whispering. "Not this teeny-bopper business *desi* Indian style."

On the day of our dear nephew Vikram's wedding, bride is appearing in pistachio-color gown, looking very nice. Good girl, that one, only has to learn our Indian ways. Not looking decent, sitting on Vikram's lap at breakfast time. Why these children today, wanting to do everything in front of everybody? All this flaunting is not nice. Anyway, that civil judge-priest, in black suit, very punctual, coming on dot of eleven, and all of us standing around pool, bride and groom exchanging vows, reading poetry, both looking into each other's eyes. Robichaud women crying, bringing Kleenexes out, and me praying, our dear nephew and his wife, dear Brahma, Siva, Narayana, let them stay together always, no divorce American-style, that is all we simple people want.

After the wedding, reception is in backyard. Behind the big azalea bushes Robichaud and Boudreaux men arranging barrels of beer with tube spout coming out. I am standing near cake table, so many fern leafs stapled to lace cloth, flowers here and there, champagne glasses wearing ribbons, very beautiful and nice. Then I see Sushila with bride's brother Claude, English major at L.S.U. Cajun granny said he is writing love poetry Esther and Vikrain exchanged to each other. You know English-major type, long hair, black clothes even in Louisiana heat, smoking cigarette, dirty habit. I am watching very carefully, walking from cake table. Claude is pushing away strands of Sushila's hair, they are pretending to be Sonny and Cher, I can see that. I am staring at her very hard shaking my head no, all this is not nice. Then that Claude has seen me, too, I can tell Sushila is mad by the way she is walking off. She will be complaining about me to him, but that is okay, I say quite all right. I am only doing mother's job.

That husband Cheenu is nowhere to be found.

I find out Sudhir is in front of Acadian porch of Robichaud house, parking cars with other boys. Padma is calling me, something about Siddharth. I want to tell Sudhir, "No, not good idea. I don't know what kind of insurance policy those people have." You know he brought home two traffic tickets since summer. That brother-in-law of yours, Cheenu, he should be talking to Sudhir, doing father's job.

My baby Siddharth is in the kitchen complaining of tummy ache. He has eaten shrimp, he is saying. "How much?" I am asking.

"I don't know—maybe forty—something like that," he is saying.

"All that oily dip. Why this behavior, am I not feeding you?" I ask. I am taking him upstairs, saying, "Lie down. Maybe go to bathroom. Where is your father?" That Cheenu, you know he is always carrying Rolaids to neutralize Fluor job? Really, these children, troubling like babies in middle of family occasion. I am giving Siddharth Maalox from Robichaud medicine cabinet, taking him to spare bedroom saying, "Lie down."

When I am opening the door, I hear the TV and who is there but your dear brother-in-law, Cheenu, no wonder I could not find him anywhere downstairs. He is watching TV, golf, I can see, smiling foolish smile. "Shoba, baby, it's PGA Finals. Don't be that way." I see reason for baby, foolish smile. Empty beer can near the chair, he is holding second can. I am always worrying about children, what is next problem, what are they going to do now? And he is drinking beer, enjoying life.

After lunch, catering big success, Sudhir and Sushila, all teenagers and American adults, dancing to music inside the house. Then Leela going in and joining. That silly Padma encouraging her. You know those two women in our family, never knowing limits, always getting carried away. Again poor Dhakshisriramabadran, standing and smiling and watching cousin Leela, teenagers, many adults doing macarena. You know this is a fad now, latest American dance. Cajun granny also joining in. Everybody shaking bottom and slapping thighs, and sweating, really, this Leela must be knowing middle-aged Indian women do not have hips and figure to dance macarena in public. Leela is looking like *chapati* dough shaking in earthquake. "Chee! chee!" like we used to say in India as children, "shame, shame, poppy shame." Dhakshisriramabadran now sitting in corner again like meditating mouse.

Anyway, between you and me, hubby Cheenu is not totally zero father, he is telling Sudhir that boy in car driving back to Houston, "Be practical, career choice and all is okay but remember you have to look after yourself." Hubby also telling Sushila that girl, "Everybody having lust like Jimmy Carter. That is quite all right. Only hide this from public view, you know our Hindu community, pretending sex is okay on rocks, temple sculpture and all but not for people made of flesh and blood." And to baby Siddharth he is saying, "It does not matter if you are not clever at math. What is the use of being engineer working your balls off?" You know ditchwater language is very cool in America, what to do Lakshmi, cool becoming worldwide disease nobody wants inoculation for that one. Even I am doing fusion Bharath Natyam dirty dancing in shower. Those three children listening or not listening to hubby Cheenu, I don't know, only God knows. Anyway, for one minute, I am thinking, "Not bad, I married smart man."

"Too bad you missed Vikram Krishnamoorthy and Esther Robichaud's cool wedding," Sudhir says to tell you. He says you would have loved that. I am not saying anything. You decide for yourself. You know my nature. I am not gossiping like the rest. We are family, after all, if you let down own family what is left in this modern life?

Anyway, after cool wedding, we are coming home exhausted and I have frozen *dhal* thawing in microwave, fresh rice from pressure cooker and *papad*. We are all happy to be home, even the children, though they don't admit anything. Going out and all is nice, but nothing like coming to our own place, I tell you, I need same pillow, bed, even different bathroom is giving me problems, that Padma's organic sandwich, stomach making noise all the time. Good to eat rice, have oil bath, and rest my head on my own pillow, nothing like that I tell you. But when I am lying down after dinner, my mind still vibrating like *pambaram,* wooden top, must be all the excitement from cool wedding, I cannot fall asleep, my eyes are open like bird wings in the sky. So pretty soon I am counting baby elephants, praying and talking to Ganesha about job and family.

Anyway, between you and me, hubby Cheenu always laughing and understanding all my jokes. What is more important than that? Good sense of humor, that smart man. You know America, very optimistic country, people are always saying, "Shoba, you are only forty-something years young," so I am also thinking for some things, when in America do as the Americans do, keep trying to change hubby, never give up, men are like bread, be patient, give them time to rise.

So in the dark, I am turning to Cheenu, and saying, "What is all this, mister? Sleeping sleeping night after night always the same thing, it's not nice. What is all this Hingis-Pingis only watching tennis and golf why not care a little about wife, family? Only sports, office, sports, office, so American, that is not our style. Let us do something different. Why not imagine oval office, round office, I am getting feeling like playing White House."

Yours in affection and devotion,
Shoba

Latha Viswanathan has published stories in
Shenandoah, Other Voices, Fiction International,
Weber Review, Rattapallax, and *StoryQuarterly,*
among others. She attended the Sewanee Writers
Conference in 1997, as Tennessee Williams
Scholar, and in 2000, as Borchardt Scholar. Her
stories have won awards and also nominations
for the Pushcart Prize. In 2001 she received a
grant from the Austin Writers' League. She lives
in Houston, Texas, and is currently working on a
novel.

Years back, I hosted a rehearsal dinner for a young Indian student and
his bride-to-be, a girl from Louisiana. I watched bits and pieces of the
story unfold—the comparison and contrast of the two groups in all their
complexity and richness, the hilarious and touching moments. The rest of it,
I made up.

Donald Hays

DYING LIGHT

(from *The Southern Review*)

It's a Sunday afternoon in early May. Bud McMahon, who's
eighty-one and dying of esophageal cancer, has been to church
with his wife, Annie. Friday they went to the clinic, where they
were given the diagnosis. Tomorrow they have an appointment
with a surgeon, but they've been warned there is probably nothing
the surgeon can do. Now McMahon's sitting in the living room
with his son, Web. Annie's in the bedroom resting. But McMahon
knows it's not just that. She wants McMahon and Web to talk, just
the two of them. She hopes that now, at last, they'll learn to get
along.

McMahon has always had problems with Web. He's never been
the strong, stoic son McMahon wanted. He's smart; he teaches
painting and art history at the university. When he was young, he
wanted to be a real painter. And maybe he could've been, maybe
he had the talent. McMahon doesn't know about that. He just
knows that Web's cynical about it now. About what little painting
he still does, about the students he teaches. And he's been married
for nearly twenty years to a successful woman, Ellen, who despises
McMahon. They've chosen—Web and Ellen—not to have children. They had their careers; Ellen's a psychologist, some kind of
therapist or counselor, and neither of them wanted to sacrifice that

for children. *Careers*. They didn't talk about their *work*. They talked about their *careers*.

McMahon knows that Web's here now because he wants to get things said before it's too late. Web's had a breakdown. He had an affair with a student. (One of many, probably, McMahon thinks: Web's always been attractive to women young enough and dumb enough to mistake his weakness for wisdom—or at least sophistication.) Ellen, who had probably been looking for an excuse for some time, ordered him out of the house. Web then drank and drifted his way into a depression that ended up with him playing Russian roulette by himself in the middle of the night. (Or so Web had said. McMahon doubted there'd been bullets in the gun. The empty-gun suicide attempt, that would be Web. All self-pity, no risk.) He took sick leave from the university. He was just out now, after spending a month in a high-dollar moon ward called Harbor View. McMahon knows what kind of advice he would've gotten there: Go to the root of the problem, talk things through with your father. Using the kinds of words McMahon had heard Ellen use. *Closure*, that was the one he hated most. Well, if that's what he wanted now, all he had to do was wait a few months and McMahon would be dead. Real fucking closure. But Web's not the kind to let it go at that. He'll have to pick at the sores. And on account of Annie, McMahon will have to let him do it. It irritates McMahon. His son, he thinks, was lost to him a long time ago. Why should they kid themselves about that now, either of them, just because McMahon is dying?

Just now, Web looks like he might get up out of his easy chair and leave. He doesn't know what to say, how to start. McMahon can see that. He gives Web a little more time, then says, "The Braves are on the TV, I think. You want to watch?"

Web perks up, as if that were the cue he's been waiting for. "I'm thinking about making it up with Ellen," he says. "I think she'll take me back."

Well, Christ, of course. It's the way of the weak, always going back to the suffering they're used to. "You want that?"

"I think so."

What can McMahon say to that? It was a terrible marriage, Web's and Ellen's. For the last seven or eight years, Ellen has been sick with something or other all the time. She'd get so bad she couldn't breathe. But the doctors never could find out what it was. They said it was psychosomatic. McMahon thought she was allergic to Web. She'd be better off without Web. If she stayed away from him, she'd probably never cough again. And, God knows, Web would be better off without her. Even Annie agreed with that—and she thought divorce was a sin.

"I don't know," McMahon says. "Are you telling me that's what you want to do? Or are you wanting my advice?"

"Your advice, I guess. You and Mother, you're as different from each other as Ellen and I are."

McMahon can hear Annie moving around in the kitchen. "That's right. Your mother and me," he says, "we were as different as daylight and dark. I drank and cussed and roared around. I wasn't happy when I got out of the navy. I thought I would be, but I wasn't. I was hard to be around. You know that. But your mother, she waited it out. She stuck by me. It was part duty that kept her by me. Religion. Fear of God. But I don't think even that would've been enough. So it was love too. She's always loved me. I don't know why. I didn't deserve it. But that's what it was."

Web looks at him. He seems a little confused. "What are you saying then? You think we should stick it out too? Ellen and me? That it's our duty?"

"I don't know, son. I never liked Ellen. You know that. Just then, I was trying to tell you to go back to her. But that's just because I thought that's what you wanted me to tell you. But I couldn't do it. Truth is, you were bad for each other, you and her."

"I could change. That could change."

There it is, a thing that has always bothered McMahon about his son. The way he has of seeing weakness as duty. He says, "You asked me, I'll tell you. Sometimes a man's better off with a stump-broke goat than he is with a woman."

. . .

By the time Annie wakes up and finds her way into the TV room, Web's gone and McMahon is watching the Braves. Annie stands in the doorway and leans over her walker. She's looking around the room as if Web might be hiding somewhere. "What happened?" she says.

"He's thinking about going back to Ellen." McMahon speaks loudly, slowly, and clearly. Even with her hearing aids, she's almost deaf. "He's gone."

"What did you tell him?"

"I told him not to. I told him they were killing each other."

She stands there for a long moment and stares at him. She's trying not to say what she wants to say. McMahon can see that. She's always blamed him for the troubles they've had with Web. And she wants to blame him now, for this. But she doesn't. She won't. It's one of the things about dying; people stop telling you what they think. They start trying to protect you from life.

"He just wants to know you love him," she says. "That's all."

"I've loved him since the day he was born. I love him now. I'll love him till I die. If he doesn't understand that, fuck him." McMahon believes that's true: He loves his son, he just doesn't like him. Can hardly tolerate him.

"May God forgive you."

She steps back out of the doorway, pulls her walker to her, scoots it around so it's at her side, turns into it, and lurches, precariously, angrily, away from him.

McMahon turns his attention back to the TV. Maddux is pitching against the Mets. This is what McMahon wants to do now, watch someone do a hard thing as well as it can be done. Someone who has to work with a very small margin of error doing something that, in any real sense, makes no difference whatsoever.

He tries to concentrate on the game, tries as if he were the catcher, Bako, to call the pitches and the location before they're thrown. He's good at this. He knows the game. But today his mind won't be diverted. It returns to Web. He'll be back, sooner or later, McMahon tells himself. His father is dying. Guilt will drive him back.

Guilt. You get down to it, he thinks, maybe that's all that holds us together, all that makes us a family. Maybe guilt's all that can come to you when you see that your love hasn't been strong or pure enough.

"There's nothing I can do," the surgeon says. He's a man in his fifties with a strong round face. His hair is gray, and he has a thick mustache that still has some red in it. His eyes are a clear blue, and McMahon likes the honest way they hold his gaze. This is not one of those doctors who looks down at his charts when he has something hard to say. This surgeon is a man he can trust.

"I want you to cut it out," McMahon says. "Or try to, anyway. If it don't work, I'll die on the table. Clean."

"Mr. McMahon . . ."

"Only problem I got now is I can't eat. Food won't go down, just lumps up and comes back. All I expect you to do is go in there and clear a path. That's all. I like to eat." He glances at Annie, who was in her youth the most beautiful woman he'd ever seen. Now she's old and confused. He's sure she hasn't heard anything that's been said. "It's the only pleasure I got left."

The surgeon, still looking straight at him, opens his hands, a gesture of helplessness. "Mr. McMahon," he says. "I'm a surgeon. It's my nature to be direct. You understand that?"

"It's why I'm talking to you."

"Yes sir. I see that. So what I'm telling you is that with this kind of cancer—esophageal cancer—by the time we find it, most of the time it's too late to operate. I'd go in. I'd find that it's spread. I'd close it up. And you'd be way worse off than you were when I started. You'd suffer more and die sooner."

McMahon nods once, then looks at his Annie again. "What did he say?" she asks.

"Says he can't do anything."

She looks at the surgeon, who has swiveled on his stool so that he faces her now. "That's right, Mrs. McMahon," he says in a loud, clear voice. "Nothing I can do."

It seems to McMahon that Annie's eyes, made bright by a film of tears, look almost young again. Jesus, he thinks, what will happen to her? That sweet woman.

He gets up and walks over to her. He stoops and places his hand over her elbow. "Well, Annie," he says, "I reckon we best be headed home, let these folks get back to business."

"What?" she says.

"Home," he tells her.

"There are things we can do," the surgeon says. "Sometimes radiation helps."

McMahon doesn't respond until Annie is on her feet and balanced, her little claw-footed metal walker in one hand, his elbow in the other. Then he looks at the surgeon and says, "Cure me, will it?"

"It might give you more time. It might let you eat a little."

"What's the odds?"

"I'll make you an appointment with Dr. Johns. He's the specialist."

McMahon gives him a half-grin. "First one you dodged," he says.

The surgeon smiles, shrugs. "Odds are good it'll give you a couple more months. Might let you eat a little. Eggs maybe. Even that's a long shot."

"Eggs." He laughs outright. "Well, fuck it then."

"Donald!" Annie's the only person on earth who calls him Donald. "You have to do what he says."

He looks at her, surprised that she's heard.

"I mean it," she says. "You have to."

He turns back to the surgeon. "My Annie," he says. "You make the appointment. I'll think about showing up. We'll split it up that way. All right with you?"

"The girl at the desk, she'll give you a time."

• • •

He pulls in at the White Spot on the way home. "What are you doing?" Annie asks.

"We're going to go in here, and you're going to order yourself one of their burgers with the fried onions on it, and I'm going to get me two of them, like I always have, and we're going to eat." He says this at such volume that the man getting out of the truck next to them turns and looks.

"You can't eat," Annie says.

"I can die trying," he says.

He helps her out of the car and lends her his supporting arm, and they make their way slowly inside the diner. He orders and then tells the waitress they'll need a pitcher of water. "And bring it now, you don't mind. Got to get the skids greased."

He and Annie don't talk while they're waiting for the food. He'd have to talk so loud that it would be like making a public speech. McMahon would like to say something, tell her maybe that he doesn't want to go back to the clinic, doesn't want to let strangers decide how he will spend the little time he has left. Or maybe he would just talk about how much he's always liked these little burgers, the thin patties, the fried onions. He can remember when the place opened, back in the '50s. The first time he ate here, he was home on leave from Korea. The hamburgers were twelve for a dollar. The man who ran it then was the father of the one who runs it now—that man there, flipping the patties and wearing the white T-shirt that has JOHN 3:16 printed across the back. And, hell, this man, the one here now, he must be sixty. Christ, it comes and it goes. They give you a little time in the sun, and then they drag the darkness down.

He reaches across the table and lays his right hand atop Annie's left. She stares at their hands for long moment, and he knows she's trying hard not to cry. Then she looks up at his face. She leans forward, touches his cheek with her free hand, and tells him she loves him. He nods and says he loves her too. She can't hear him. He knows that. And maybe he should say it again, loudly enough so that she—and everyone else in the diner—can hear. But he doesn't.

Instead, when she takes her hand away from his face, he takes that hand too. And he holds it. And as he looks at her then, he thinks how old she is, how frail, how weak.

When the food comes, they move so the waitress can set the plates down. Annie folds her hands in her lap and lowers her head. He watches her. Grace. She's never doubted that.

Of course, he can't eat. Nothing gets down. He goes to the toilet and gags up the bite he tried to swallow. He returns to the table and watches Annie eat her burger. She does it without appetite. A duty.

McMahon believes in nothing outside of this life. Not really. There may be some kind of God, but He doesn't pay much mind to any of us. World War II taught McMahon that. He'd been on two ships that had been torpedoed and sunk off the coast of North Africa. He had floated in an ocean full of dead men. Who lived and who died—it had all been shit luck, cold chance. But he's glad now that he went to church with Annie almost every Sunday of the forty years since he retired from the navy. Maybe that will let her see him as one of the redeemed. Maybe that will be enough to get her through.

He tells himself that next time he'll try to do better with Web. He owes it to Annie. Pretty soon, Web will be all she has.

It's a twenty-mile drive from the White Spot to their old white hillfarm house. McMahon drives and wonders how long he'll be able to do that. When they pass the county hospital, he says, "That's where Josie was born. She was the only one of us born in a hospital." Josie was the youngest of his nine brothers and sisters. They're all dead now. He thinks about how they died, each of them—and where. All but two of them died in a hospital.

It's a bright afternoon. The middle of May. The trees are lush. There are flowers everywhere, bursts of color in every yard. As they pass the veterans' cemetery, he's tempted to stop and sit for a while on one of the benches near the ground he'll be buried under. But he decides that would worry Annie, and he drives on.

When they get home, he gets out of the car and helps Annie. As they're walking, he looks over her head at his garden. The tomato plants are already thigh-high. "Well," he says. "I reckon a man's still got to tie up his tomatoes."

McMahon is right. Web does come back. He's with them now in an examining room at the clinic, and they're listening to the radiological oncologist. He's a small, neat, soft man who speaks in a low, smooth voice. McMahon decides there's no point listening to this man, much less talking to him. Here he is, this doctor, surrounded daily by the dying, and he doesn't know anything but to lie.

"It's terminal, you're saying, this cancer?" Web asks the doctor.

The radiologist offers Web a solemn nod. "Here at the Hooper-Krock Clinic," he says, "we don't believe in terminal illness." He smiles.

Web rocks back a notch. "What?"

"We have to remain positive," the doctor says. "Attitude is everything in a case like this."

"In a case like what?"

"Like this," the doctor says. "Life-threatening."

"But not terminal? He won't die."

"We can't say that. But we can't give up."

Web looks at McMahon, who shrugs. He's a little tickled by this, McMahon is. After all, it was Web who persuaded him to show up for the appointment, Web who told him over and over again that he couldn't just think about himself, that he had a family, that he owed it to all of them to let the doctors do what they could. That he owed it to all of them not to give up.

"No point in this," McMahon tells Web. "You looking for straight answers, and this man, he's a fucking radiation salesman."

Web laughs, a big, loud, good laugh. McMahon likes that. It's one of the things he's always liked about his son. He says, "Let's take your momma home."

But then the doctor changes. He gives them a brisk, blunt assessment of what the radiation might do. It can't hurt anything, and there's a fair chance it could help. It's a statistical certainty that it won't save McMahon's life. An extra two or three months, that's what they're talking about. A little time. "It won't make you sick, not the way it used to. We've gotten much better with that. You might lose some hair. You might feel a little weaker during that time. But you'll just have to come over here once a week for a month. Then it'll be over, and you'll feel better for a while. I can't say how long."

"What did he say?" Annie asks.

"Two or three months," Web says. Then he raises his voice. "He says the radiation might give Dad two or three more months."

She turns to McMahon. "I want those months," she says.

McMahon nods. "My Annie," he says.

A week later, Web's back. The three of them are in the living room in the old farmhouse. McMahon is sitting in his recliner. He's not wearing a shirt. He took it off to show Web the blue cross at the top of his chest, just below the neck. It's the target for the radiation machine. Just yesterday, McMahon had his first treatment. Web sits at the end of the couch nearest McMahon. Annie's on the couch too, at the other end. Of course, she can't hear anything that's being said. She just looks at one or the other of them every so often and smiles. As long as Web and McMahon are talking without raising their voices, Annie can hope they're making up. McMahon knows that. And he's decided to try. He'll talk to Web. He'll listen. He'll do his best to understand. He won't say anything hard, even when he thinks it's the hard thing that needs to be said.

They have finished talking about the radiation for now, and Web is telling McMahon that he and Ellen have talked. They've decided to take some time and think things through. She wants to be sure. She wants Web to be sure. She doesn't want them to make the same mistake again. They need to wait.

What they're waiting for is for me to die, McMahon thinks. But he doesn't say anything. And, Christ, who knows? Maybe his death is what they need to make their marriage work.

Web's waiting for him to say something, so he does. He says, "That makes sense to me. There's a lot of pain there. You want to go easy."

"Too much, maybe," Web says. "Too much. I don't know." He leans forward on the couch. He looks down.

McMahon wants to tell him, *Buck up, be a man, cut her loose.* But he doesn't. He doesn't say anything.

Web looks up, sits up, shakes his head. "I'm sorry," he says. Here you are with cancer, and I'm complaining about my problems."

"Hell, death's easy," McMahon says. "Nothing you can do about it. But you now, you got choices to make, one way or the other."

McMahon watches Web think about this. "There've been times," Web says, "when the thought of death has been a solace to me."

It sounds like a line he's rehearsed. This isn't the turn McMahon wanted the talk to take. "Ought not be," he says. "You're way too young and smart to be looking for solace. There's too many other things to try."

Web nods. "Painting," he says. He looks toward the front window as if there might be something out there he could paint. Then he looks down at his lap. Then he looks up at McMahon. "When I understood how good you had to be at it to make it matter, I quit trying. I got scared. I played games with paint, but I never painted." He nods again. "That's what I've decided to do now. I'm going to paint."

McMahon wonders whether that's something Ellen told him, or maybe the moon-ward doctors. But "Sounds good to me," he says. "It's what you've always wanted to do."

"Yes. Yes, it is." He hesitates, and McMahon can feel an edge in the air. "Look," Web says. "I haven't talked to Mother about this. I know what she'll say. She'll say yes to anything I ask. And then you'll say yes. For her. I don't want it to happen that way." He stops again.

"Want what to happen? Say yes to what?"

"I want to paint you. I want to move in here—for a while, anyway, the rest of the summer, maybe. And I want to paint you."

Now it's McMahon who doesn't know what to say.

"You must think I'm some kind of vulture, asking this. And maybe that's right. I don't know. I just know I want to do it."

"And if I say no?"

"I won't mention it to Mother. We'll go on the way we are."

"You think you can stand living here?"

"If I'm painting, I can. This matters to me. You, me, the painting. Even if I can't do it, I'll know it mattered. I won't be able to kid myself anymore."

"Well, all of us, you know, we're good at finding ways of kidding ourselves. No matter what."

"Not about this," Web says. "I know the difference between a real painting and a fake one. For a lot of my life, I've wished I didn't." He gives a half-nod to help make the point. "Look," he says. "If I fail, it'll be an honest failure. I promise you that."

"Well, then," McMahon says. "I can't say no to that."

Web moves in two days later. He sleeps in his childhood bedroom. It's still got the old twin bed in it. The same pine desk he used in high school is there too. There's an end table and a lamp on one side of the bed, a window on the other, a cheap chest of drawers against one wall. Otherwise empty. It looks like what it has been—a room no one uses.

Other than his painting, drawing, and writing materials, Web doesn't bring much. A few changes of clothes, the necessary toiletries, a couple dozen books. He says he'll do the cooking and cleaning, drive Annie to the grocery store or Wal-Mart or wherever she needs to go, and do whatever McMahon wants him to do in the garden. He wants to help, he says. He doesn't want to be any burden.

He offers to drive McMahon to the clinic for his radiation treatment, but McMahon says there's no need for that. Not yet. He'll drive himself—and Annie, if she wants to go—as long as he can. Helplessness will be on him soon enough, he says.

And so they settle in.

The radiation doesn't cause McMahon any real problems. He doesn't even lose any hair. And he enjoys the weekly drives to the clinic with Annie. He keeps the window down, the air conditioner off. He likes the sun, the movement, the way memory seems to enter the car with the warm wind.

They don't talk much during the drives. He's fine talking to Web or most anyone else. He still tells stories to whoever comes by the house for a visit, anyone who can hear. But if he says more than a sentence or two so that Annie can hear them, he can feel a strain in his upper chest, can feel what he calls the termites in his throat. Sometime before he dies, he'll probably lose his voice. The termites will take it. He knows that. If you look at it one way, it's funny. An old man who can't talk, an old woman who can't hear. A marriage.

Six weeks go by, and McMahon loses thirty more pounds. He's down to 160 now, 50 pounds less than what he calls his living weight. He's getting by on juice and broth and Ensure. Once in a while he manages to choke down a little yogurt, but it's not worth the trouble. "Hell," he tells Annie, "you go to all that trouble, it's still yogurt." He still hasn't lost any hair—or not enough to be noticed, anyway. The radiation therapist tells him he's lucky, almost everyone loses some hair, and a lot of people lose it all. "Hell, me," McMahon says, "I got hair with a positive attitude. It'll keep growing after I'm dead."

McMahon is so weak he lets Web drive him and Annie to the clinic every Tuesday. A couple times a week Web also drives Annie to the Superstore, pushes her up and down the aisles in a Wal-Mart wheelchair and helps her pick out groceries and toiletries. Nights, Web sits with McMahon in front of the TV and watches the Braves. Sometimes, Annie sits with them. Now and again McMahon catches her looking uncertainly, hopefully at him or Web. Usually, though, she falls asleep after an inning or two.

One night McMahon's in bed asleep, and then, just like that, for no good reason, he's awake. He feels an absence beside him. Annie's not there. He raises his head a little and sees her kneeling against her side of the bed. He looks at the nightstand clock. Nearly three o'clock. He lies there on his back, watching her, tears in his eyes. He knows what she's praying for. She's been praying for it since Web was a teenager. She's praying that her husband and her son, the two people on earth she loves, will learn to love each other.

McMahon's on morphine now, and he spends most mornings sitting calmly in the sun. He takes his paper and his coffee on the back porch, sits in the old high-backed, split-cane rocker, and stays there until nearly noon. Most mornings, Web is out there with him for the first couple hours. He begins by taking photographs of McMahon from different angles and distances. He uses two cameras, one for color, one for black-and-white. When he has taken his photographs, he sets up his easel, places his sketchpad on it, and begins to draw. All this photography and drawing—and, even worse, the apologies Web keeps offering—bothers McMahon. He doesn't want Web out there—doesn't want anyone there, not even Annie most of the time. He just wants to sit on his own in the silence and the sun. And this . . . well, this seems so, what? Scientific, or something. Some kind of experiment Web's doing. It would be just like him to think that if you did everything just so, followed the right set of rules, gauged the light and the shadow perfectly, you could figure death out.

The first few drawings each morning are quick, rough sketches. Web finishes one—or gives up on it, maybe—tears it from the pad, lays it facedown on the floor, and starts the next. As the morning goes by, Web devotes more and more time to each sketch. He'll sometimes spend an hour on the last one. When he finishes, he puts all the morning's drawings in a folder, carries the folder to the porch swing, and sits there for a while. He and McMahon talk a little then, or try to. Neither of them knows what to say. It's very awkward. Web makes the silence that surrounds them seem unnatural.

At the end of the first morning, McMahon asks to see the last drawing. But the request makes Web dodgy. It takes him several nervous minutes to explain that the drawings aren't ready to be seen yet—he's still getting his eye, his touch. It has been so long, he says, and it will be a while longer yet. This seems so painful to Web that McMahon lets it go, and nearly three weeks go by before Web carries a morning's final drawing to McMahon and holds it up before him. McMahon is surprised by how much he likes it. You can see death in every line of the face, but a dignity—or maybe just the memory of a dignity—remains in the eyes and the mouth. McMahon looks at Web. He understands that his son has made him an offering, an offering he has worked hard to make right. "I forgot how talented you are," McMahon says. "An awful thing for a father to have to say. But it's true. It's something you have that has nothing to do with me. So I forgot about it. I'm sorry."

There are tears in Web's eyes. McMahon watches him control himself. He appreciates the effort. He thinks it would be wrong for either of them to let the moment go soft on them. They'd lose its truth that way. So he gestures toward the drawing. "A man like that at a time like this," he says, "you know what he wants?" He looks up at Web. "A cigarette." He cocks his head, nods once, smiles. "You do that for me, son? Go get me a pack of smokes?"

There's a confusion on Web's face, but then he lets out a little laugh. "You serious?" he asks.

"Camel straights, son," McMahon says. "God's own."

Web is back in fifteen minutes with the Camels and a black Bic lighter. "Been fifteen years," McMahon says. "Got to where I had bronchitis about two-thirds of the time." He taps the pack sharply against the arm of his rocker. Then he opens it and takes out a cigarette. He looks at Web and offers him one. Web takes it without hesitation, clearly pleased to have been asked. With the Bic, McMahon lights first Web's cigarette, then his own.

He coughs once, then again. He's dizzy for a moment and a little queasy. He lets his head and stomach settle before taking a second drag. Much better. And the next drag is better still. He holds the cigarette out and studies the burning tip. "By God," he says, "I've loved these sons of bitches."

Web laughs, that good deep laugh.

And then they begin to talk, light talk but real, about smoking and quitting smoking.

In the days that follow, Web continues to start their morning by taking photographs, but now he's painting after that instead of drawing. Some days he works five or six hours without a break. McMahon is content to sit that long and longer. Sometimes he thinks he could just sit there day and night until he dies. Often now Annie comes out on the porch and sits with him. They rarely say anything. She watches Web paint, and McMahon can see pleasure on her face. He knows she thinks her prayers have been answered. It's funny, McMahon thinks: All they needed to become a family, the three of them, was a killing cancer, a steady supply of morphine, and, on Web's part, about thirty years of failure.

One evening McMahon and Annie are sitting at the kitchen table. Annie is eating a bowl of chicken noodle soup and a pimento-cheese sandwich she bought that afternoon when Web took her to the Superstore. McMahon's having his Ensure, which Annie has poured into a fluted glass. The stuff looks like Pepto-Bismol. McMahon wishes it tasted as good. He'd rather be in the den watching the game, but he does this for Annie. He has gagged about half the Ensure down when the front door opens. McMahon hears Web walking through the living room and dining room, talking to someone. McMahon can't make out the words, but he knows who the other person has to be. And he's right. When he turns, he sees her just behind Web, in the doorway. Ellen.

They're dressed up. Web's wearing a wheat-colored jacket, a tie. Ellen's in a nice blue dress. Good-looking people, for their age. They should've had kids.

McMahon looks back at Annie. She's intent on the soup. She still hasn't heard anything. He says, almost yelling, "Annie. The kids are back."

She looks up at him, then turns and raises her gaze to take in Web and Ellen. "You all sit down," she says. Her chair jerks backward. I'll get you some . . . some supper?"

McMahon holds up his glass of Ensure. "Got plenty of this. Buy it by the goddam case."

Web goes to Annie, puts a hand on the back of her chair, bends down and kisses her on the forehead. "We're fine, Momma. We've already eaten."

"Oh."

McMahon looks up at Ellen. "Come on in," he says. "Sit down." She does. Web sits across the table from her. There is a silence.

McMahon doesn't know what to say. This is the woman Web has loved and hated and can't get over, the one who has marked him for life. Maybe he ought to just live with her, do the suffering face-to-face. McMahon takes a sip of Ensure, sets the glass down, shakes his head. "Cure you of wanting to live, this stuff. You get done, you got to lick a dog's ass to get the taste out of your mouth."

Web laughs, but Ellen merely smiles politely, tolerantly. "It's our anniversary," Web says. "We went to Bella Italia over in Ft. Smith."

"You bring me a sausage?" McMahon says.

Web smiles, says nothing.

"How long's it been?" McMahon asks. He looks at Ellen, then back at Web. "Which anniversary, I mean?"

"Thirty years," Web says. "1971."

McMahon nods. He lets them watch him think about the thirty years. "You're back together then?"

"We don't know," Web says. "We're talking."

McMahon looks at Ellen.

"We want to be sure," she says. "Sometimes I think we were always wrong for each other."

McMahon shakes his head. "No such thing as being sure," he says.

"You and Mrs. McMahon," Ellen says. "You're sure. Anyone can see that."

McMahon cocks his head as if in surprise. "Me? Annie? Oh, no." He gives a short nod and a half-smile. "I been married fifty-eight years." He lets the smile broaden. "To the wrong woman."

She laughs. It's a nervous laugh, unsure of itself. But she laughs.
"Piece of wisdom," McMahon says. "Only one I got to pass on
to you. You fall in love, and then sooner or later you going to find
out it's to the wrong woman—or man, your case. Question is,
what do you do then?"

"What's he saying?" Annie asks Web.

"He's telling Ellen about marriage." Web enunciates the words
loudly, slowly. "About you and him."

"Lord have mercy," she says. And then she laughs.

Two weeks later, on a Wednesday, McMahon loses his voice. The
cancer is in his larynx. He can make himself understood if the lis-
tener sits close and leans forward. But it's all breath, little rushes of
air. And he's in his wheelchair almost all the time now. He can walk
no more than a step or two. He has to have help in the toilet, in the
bathtub. He needs more and more of the morphine.

Web is still taking pictures every morning and still painting too.
He's finished three portraits, but hasn't been satisfied with them.
McMahon doesn't think any of them is as good as the drawing. But
he's in a morphine haze, and, like everything else, his eyes are
going. So he doesn't know.

Ellen hasn't been back. Web says they're still talking, still thinking. They've hurt each other a lot. They still don't know what
they'll do. McMahon suspects that whatever they do they'll be
sorry. Sometimes that's the way it is.

In the evening Web wheels him out on the porch. Annie joins
them. Web begins saying the things he needs to say—that he loves
McMahon, that he's sorry he hated him so long, that he's going to
keep painting, that he'll paint as well as he can, do honest work,
that he'll take care of Annie, that he'll always do that. McMahon
listens and nods. He reaches over and touches Web's arm. Web
takes the hand and holds it. He quits talking. McMahon is staring at the sunset. "Annie," he says. But there is only the forcing of
breath, no sound she could possibly hear.

Still, the sky—an old glory of dying light. It is beautiful. It is almost enough.

He knows he will not see another.

Donald Hays is the author of two novels, *The Dixie Association* and *The Hangman's Children*. Recent stories of his have appeared in *The Missouri Review*, *The Malahat Review*, and *The Southern Review*. He is working on a novel and a collection of stories. He teaches in the Programs in Creative Writing at the University of Arkansas.

My father died of esophageal cancer. He had been a big man, but the cancer ravaged him, taking him from about 215 pounds to about 140. About a week before he died, my mother and I took him to the clinic. The cancer had spread to his larynx and taken his voice. He could speak, but only in a whisper, willed rushes of air. When the doctor entered the examining room, my father motioned him close and then said, "How long, you reckon?" The doctor, the kind of inane Christian who always had a yellow happy-face decal pinned to his breast pocket, started to answer then stopped himself. I could almost see him rummaging through his stock of equivocations and euphemisms. "You'd think," my father said, "you sons-of-bitches'd be used to death."

This story grew out of that memory.

Chris Offutt

INSIDE OUT

(from *Tin House*)

Today's deceased required little preparation on my part. A young man is simpler than an old lady who needs extensive makeup and hairstyling. Her breasts have to be taped so they'll stick up when she's lying on her back. Deceased lungs are empty, and the bosom falls into the armpits. The bereaved don't like the looks of that. Thank god for duct tape. It's the little things that get repeat business. As Great Uncle said, you've got to cater the dead to the living.

My official title is Director of Grief Proceedings, which has a more savory connotation than Mortician or Undertaker. What I really am is a businessman, the only one who gets everyone's business, regardless of station in life. Many people believe that I understand death, but I don't; I understand the bereaved. The fancier death is made to appear, the more the mourning seems to matter. We crave an afterlife because otherwise our dead grandfather is the same as a possum hit by a car and swelling in the ditch. My job is to dress up death and transform Grandpa from outdoor roadkill to an indoor centerpiece surrounded by flowers.

I shooed the bereaved away on schedule and sat in my office completing the bill. Someone knocked on the door. The bereaved often think my occupation can offer insight into sorrow, which is like assuming the worker at the Salvation Army knows why someone donated a toaster. I am not a therapist. I am a professional of the mortuary arts with fifteen years' experience in Lexington, Kentucky. My livelihood is based on the perpetual public expression of sympathy when, quite frankly, I don't care. I keep this to myself. I keep a great deal to myself.

A woman entered my office. Her open shirt revealed the intricacies of her collarbones like a topographical map of an exotic country. I arranged a sincere expression on my face and used my most dolorous voice.

"I'm afraid that the viewing hours have ended, but I can allow a final good-bye to your loved one."

"No thank you," she said. "I've said all the good-byes I've got. Don't you ever get tired of saying them? I bet that's all you do— good-bye, good-bye, good-bye."

"Won't you please have a seat?"

She entered my office as if stepping into a throne room that was rightfully hers. I thought of lost royalty, an illegitimate child waiting to discover her birthright. Her neck was lovely and strong.

"My name is Lucy Moore," she said.

"Please tell me how I can serve you, Ms. Moore."

"Thank you," she said. "But I have to say, when someone says that to me, I get suspicious. Men especially. A man's idea of serving me is mostly a long ways from mine."

"I'm afraid I don't quite understand."

"I'm afraid you do."

Of course I knew what she was talking about. Death produces an irrational need for tidiness and a surprising amount of spontaneous sex. I've found people in the coatroom, the foyer, the restroom, even the chapel. Great Uncle warned me of this. In adamant terms he said I should deflect a woman's attempt to seek temporary solace in my arms. It would be short-lived and bad for business.

"Ms. Moore, it is my duty to serve the family. I retrieve the deceased from the hospital, prepare them for viewing, and arrange for cemetery proceedings. If you are here to discuss such provisions, I suggest we make an appointment."

"I was a friend of the man in the other room—Billy Chandler."

Great Uncle taught me that calling the deceased by name would hinder my ability to perform the necessary tasks. It was similar to naming livestock intended for slaughter. She passed me a manila envelope containing the last will and testament of William Chandler. It was signed by the deceased and countersigned by his attorney. He bestowed his liquid assets to alternative energy research, his books to a community library, and his household belongings to a homeless shelter. His collection of animal skulls was bequeathed to the Portland Museum of Natural History. Lucy Moore was the sole individual recipient of goods. In explicit terms, it was made very clear that she was to receive the personal and actual skull of the deceased.

I inhaled and pressed each of my fingertips against its mate on the opposite hand. I exhaled while slowly relaxing the pressure. Great Uncle taught me to do this when facing a bereaved upset over the cost of arrangements.

"Are you with a TV show?" I said. "Is this some kind of promotion?"

"No, it's real."

"Are you protesting the amount of real estate given over to cemeteries? Because I'm with you on that. I can be of service."

"No," she said.

"Animal rights. You throw animal blood on people wearing furs."

"Of course not. That's disgusting."

"So is taking a human skull."

"Are you saying you can't do it?"

"Oh, it's my department, all right. In the trade we call it a skull extraction or a cranial harvest."

She didn't smile and I called my attorney, who requested an immediate fax of all documents. People are eager to provide me with assistance. They believe that if they are prompt and competent with death, death will do the same for them. What they secretly want is a financial break on an eventual coffin, a deal I always offer, since I can eat 10 percent without batting an eye.

We had half an hour to wait for the legal response to her request, which was not only a first for me, but quite possibly for the entire industry. Lucy Moore exuded a remarkable repose. People who aren't afraid of life have no fear of death, and I was surprised to find myself admiring her resolve.

"Was Mr. Chandler a special friend?" I said.

"My whole life there's always a man telling me what to say and what to wear and how to act. But not Billy."

"A close friend."

"Are you married?" she said.

"Divorced. No kids. And you?"

"Never married."

"Most people," I said, "meet their spouse at work, but I work alone, and I never get involved with a client. That makes it difficult because in the long run everyone becomes a client."

"You made a joke."

"Yes."

"I hate when people laugh at their own jokes," she said. "It's worse when nobody thinks it's funny. Then the person usually laughs harder. Know what I mean?"

I nodded.

"But a smile is ok," she said. "You're allowed to smile."

"Great Uncle taught me never to smile because a smiling undertaker is a fearsome sight."

"That is the saddest thing I've ever heard."

"Great Uncle passed on, and I am proud to continue."

"So you inherited a funeral home," she said. "How about a tour?"

"It is against policy to conduct tours."

"I might be some sicko, right? Or maybe I'm just curious. And don't go giving me that curiosity killed the cat stuff, I've heard it all my life and it makes no sense. Besides, I'd be in the right place. Can you imagine being an undertaker for cats? All those lives. No business."

She laughed then, a low tone.

"See," she said. "You smiled. Glory be, what would Great Uncle say? Come on, let's have a look. I won't touch a thing."

She rose from her chair with surprising grace, considering the swiftness of motion. Her jeans were old, frayed at the cuffs. She was one of those spectacular women who actually looked better when she dressed down. She was as beguiling as a card trick. I wanted to touch her, which was startling because I had recently lost my curiosity for bare skin in general. People are reluctant to shake hands with me. Lurking in the back of everyone's mind lies the omnipresent possibility that an undertaker is somehow inexplicably drawn to unnatural relations with the dead. This is tantamount to thinking that a plumber might eventually begin eating from the toilet.

I led Lucy Moore into a private chamber, where a portrait of Great Uncle hung on the wall.

"This was my former office," I said. "After Great Uncle passed, I made this room a history of the business. The artist is local and enjoys a strong reputation. He recently painted the wife of the lieutenant governor."

"Nice frame," she said.

"Yes, quite tasteful. I chose that. It is burnished dark cherry, also available in a casket. The color is musteline."

"You don't have to sell me. I'm not in the market."

"Yes, of course. I apologize."

"I never heard of the color musteline."

"Me neither. Great Uncle called it Monkey Brown."

She laughed again, a sound I wanted to hear forever.

"Tell me about him," she said. "Uncle Monkey Brown."

Hair wisped into her eyes. Mine was trimmed weekly by a barber whose brother had died intestate and destitute in Cincinnati and for whom I had arranged an elaborate funeral without charge. It was a justifiable expense, I felt. The barber's family was very large and all would eventually die.

"Great Uncle learned embalming during World War II when he was stationed in Alaska. He came home at the same time that funeral homes were opening, which was also the golden era of home building in Lexington. In those days, most people died in their own bed instead of a hospital and the family prepared the body and held final viewings at home. Each house had a special room called the funeral parlor. With the emergence of professional undertakers, every home gained an extra room that Great Uncle began to call 'the living room.' The term swept the country like influenza, which frankly never hurt our business."

"Ah," she said, "another joke."

"One of Great Uncle's, I'm afraid."

The fluorescent tubes swathed us with a garish flickering that made my eyes hurt. I wanted to be in the same room with her forever.

"When I was a boy Great Uncle used to give me a ride in the city ambulance. He let me turn on the siren and the red light, and we'd fly down Savoy Road. It's my fondest memory from childhood."

"That is the second saddest thing I've heard."

"What is your fondest memory of home?"

"Leaving."

A part of me envied not only her honesty, but the fact that she had left. I have lived all my life in my hometown and never regretted it. Sometimes though, usually at night, a sense of dissatisfaction crept through me like a shadow. I thought of running away and starting again in a place where people didn't avoid me on the street. I wished I could be a supper guest, a block parent, a board member of an arts organization. I craved a different wardrobe and a flashy car. I wanted to be liked by people who knew nothing about me.

"Do you ever wish you could go somewhere new?" I said.

"I change jobs a lot," she said. "Waitress, copy shop, temp sec. I tend to burn my bridges."

"That sounds sad to me."

"I don't have an occupation or an inheritance. I'm always new, a constant visitor."

"I am never a visitor. No one invites me anywhere. When I run into people at stores, they hurry away. The worst part is that no child ever comes to my house on Halloween. I leave the porch light on. I carve happy pumpkins. Nothing works. Every year the children skip my house."

"Kids do things they're afraid of all the time. It's the parents who won't let them come to your door."

The planes of her face worked together as if made smooth by a craftsman's touch. Her jaw ran taut to her chin, yet there was a softness present that I wanted to trace with the back of my finger. She turned away abruptly and moved along the wall of various framed photographs and awards. She didn't notice my official commission as a Kentucky Colonel.

"What's this picture?" she said.

"That's Man o' War. It's from the *New York Times,* 1947. Great Uncle embalmed him. He invented a special sling to hoist him into an oak casket. It was six feet by ten feet and weighed half a ton. That horse took twenty-three bottles of embalming fluid. Afterward Great Uncle 'retired' the tools. They now reside on permanent exhibit in the Texas Museum of the Mortuary Arts. I would prefer to have them remain in Kentucky, but the Texans quite generously provided a substantial fee that was tax-deductible. I take a cavalier approach to taxes since morticians are rarely audited. When it comes to death, even the IRS would rather not know."

"How'd Man o'War die?"

"Heart attack."

"Is this what I think it is?"

She was pointing a delicate finger toward Man o' War's loins. He lay on his side in the immense casket, his penis proudly exposed rather than tucked demurely from sight. The photograph had been cropped to hint at what lay beyond the edge of the frame, as if the horse had been circumcised.

"Yes, it is," I said. "Man o' War sired three hundred eighty-six foals."

"Believe me, that sort of thing means a lot more to a man than to a woman."

The room suddenly seemed like a pathetic attempt to chronicle a record that no one particularly cared about—including me. I am no fan of horse racing. Anyone can become a Kentucky Colonel, and no one really cares about mortuary awards. I was looking at a picture of a dead man and a dead horse and feeling proud. It occurred to me that my photo was next to join them.

We walked to the foyer, and I felt thunderstruck by her very presence. To prevent staring at the contours of her posture, I admired my parking lot through the windows. I keep it freshly blacktopped and clearly marked with bright yellow lines. The machinations of death are clean, well lit, and orderly. More automobile burglaries occur at funeral homes than anywhere else because people commonly leave their cars unlocked. I am proud of my lot, which is the most secure in town.

"It's peaceful here," she said. "I'll give you that. I like the quiet."

"It's my world."

"And the dead. Don't forget your bread and butter."

I guided her through the visitation rooms, well appointed in dark paneling with potted plants and alcove lights. Pastel sofas were placed against the walls. Many years ago I converted a room previously used for private moments into a smoking area. The smell of cigarettes served as an excellent antidote to the pervasive reek of perfume. Before attending services, most women feel compelled to douse themselves as if applying bug spray. Lucy wore no scent that I could detect.

We entered the coffin showroom. They were arranged hierarchically by cost, with the most expensive occupying the best light. Over the years I have noticed that a poor family wants a fancy funeral, and the wealthy want to get out cheap. The absolute top of the line—mahogany rails, brass finishings on all the joints, silk interior—is invariably chosen by adult children who had seldom visited the deceased. As Great Uncle used to say—guilt translates to gilt.

"So," Lucy said, "how much do these boxes run?"

"Between two and ten thousand."

"That's a lot of money."

"All the general public sees is the price tag."

"It's like eye doctors who sell glasses. How can you trust what they say? They run a test, tell you how bad your eyes are, and sell you a pair of glasses on the spot. The exam is cheap, but the glasses cost a fortune."

"You have no idea of my expenses."

"I bet you're tight as the end of a woodpile."

"Naturally we have slumps when no one dies, but we can never complain."

"Then you get a rush. Like lunch hour."

"Cremation is on the rise," I said. "It's faster and cheaper. It is also a scam, since no bereaved actually receives the ashes of the deceased. You get a smorgasbord of that week's incineration. Consider for a moment—when you vacuum your house, do you change the bag after each room? Of course not. And no funeral home cleans the ash hopper between procedures. My competitors think it's a betrayal for me to expose this practice, but I believe the public has the right to know. Especially since I can charge a higher rate to guarantee the ashes are those of the deceased."

Gleaming empty boxes surrounded us, the lids open like mouths. The only sound was Lucy's breathing and the white noise of my own blood rushing through my veins. I wondered vaguely how fast blood moves and if the velocity differs with each person. The flow of blood slows as it gets farther from the heart.

"Do you do autopsies?" Lucy asked.

"No, that procedure is performed at a morgue by a medical examiner."

"Then what do you do?"

"Drain the body of fluid. Extract air from the organs. Introduce an embalming agent."

"That's it?"

"That's a lot. It's not fast, and once you start you have to finish. Sometimes there are difficulties, depending on cause of death."

"What do you mean?"

"If the family wants an open casket and death was due to head trauma, my task can be quite challenging."

"How about a quick peek?"

I shrugged and led her to the lab, where an alarm system accepted my digital code. We passed through a small corridor, and I unlocked the heavy lab door.

"What's that smell?" she said.

"Embalming fluid. Some people consider it the scent of death, but I find it soothing. I associate death with the bouquets that fill the visitation rooms. Flowers die here, not people."

I turned on the powerful overhead lights to a stainless steel table, storage cabinets, and shelves. My instruments were carefully stored. Everything was orderly. I felt pleased and relaxed, as anyone does upon entering the place of work. Aside from medical personnel and the occasional anatomy student, no one visited my lab.

"Embalming," I said, "is not as necessary as people believe. Our food is so full of preservatives that the deceased take twenty years longer to decompose. That doesn't mean we'll live longer."

"Another joke," she said. "What's the point of embalming anyhow?"

"If you get the deceased in the ground quickly enough, it's not necessary. The only reason we embalm is for viewing. At death, the skin draws away from the fingernails, giving the illusion that they continue to grow. The face stretches so tight it can pull wrinkles away, making the person seem still alive. The organs swell until they burst and blood is forced out of the mouth. This is what gave rise to the vampire myth—a deceased feeding on blood and remaining young with fingernails that grow."

"So you embalm a body because people are scared of vampires."

She released a stream of laughter that echoed from the tile floor to the high ceilings. I remembered Great Uncle's delight in my attention twenty years ago. His weak jokes were attempts to amuse me in the same manner that I was now trying with Lucy. She turned to the door. I wanted to prolong her presence but wasn't sure how.

"Kentucky doesn't have a female funeral director," I said. "You are patient, smart, and steady. You could be a pioneer in the field."

"No way, Jose. I like the living."

"An effective system of mourning is one that blurs the line between the living and the dead. When the baby boomers die, we'll need you."

"When the boomers die, we'll need ground space."

We returned to my office and faced each other across my walnut desk, bequeathed by Great Uncle when he entered his early retirement. The phone rang. My lawyer had communicated with the deceased's attorney, who was dismayed that the beneficiary was actually seeking her inheritance. My options were limited—give her the skull, buy her off, fight in court.

I thanked him and replaced the telephone on the receiver. This funeral home was built on the basis of a horse and I was not going to lose it over a skull.

"My attorney believes you to be a valid heir."

"No surprise there."

"Have you thought this through?"

"I believe that's your job."

"Should I ship you the skull after removal and cleaning? Or maybe you want me to just cut off his head and give it to you in a duffel bag right now?"

"Shipping is fine."

"First of all, it's illegal to mutilate human remains. To honor the will, we have to inform the family and delay the funeral. Then we'll go to court. That means newspapers. The media will undoubtedly portray you as a contemporary ghoul."

"It doesn't matter to me.

"It does to me. I can't have citizens think I'm over here giving away body parts. We need to work out a compromise."

"All my life men have told me that. I'm sick to death of it, Mister Undertaker Man. Why is it that men always want women to bend but don't want to give an inch?"

"I can't answer for other men."

"That's what they all say."

"You can do whatever you want with your body. You can pierce it or tattoo it or give it to science. Donating body parts to private parties is ahead of the curve. I respect the foresight of your friend. It might be the wave of the future. But it's just not feasible to hand over his skull."

"Feasible doesn't have a hand in it. Neither does compromise. Or your business."

"That's selfish."

"I'm not here for myself. I'm here for him."

"Maybe you need to meet a different man."

"I finally did," she said. "He went and died on me. There were times when just knowing he was out there kept me going. We never even kissed, but he was my backup man. Now I don't have anyone—in back, in front, or on the side."

"I can provide you with a fully articulated skeleton discarded by a medical library or an art school. The skulls are intact except for the cranial cavity, which is always open for removal of the brain. It latches together like a screen door. You can have an Asian peasant or an American who died in prison. Perfectly legal. Delivered to your door free of charge."

"I want Billy's."

"Why?"

I enjoyed the prolonged silence that ensued. The room faded as if she were able to dispel time and space by speaking. Her voice was tinged by a mountain lilt that became more pronounced the longer she spoke.

"I'm not the collector type. Billy got me started on bones. He liked to walk in the woods without a plan or a map. He found skulls hand over fist. It was like they found him. He thought he kept part of the animal alive by saving the bones. Life was what he liked, not death.

"Bones are hard to find because they get scattered. Billy showed me where to look—along rivers, and on cliffs. Animals die at the high and low spots of the world. Other animals gnaw their bones for calcium and they go for the skull first because it's thin. Finding one is rare. Billy said a skull was the last footprint you left. He had gobs of them. He set them on shelves. We always talked how a human skull would be the prize for a collection, but they're hard to find. If you do, you're supposed to call the police. One place to look is Civil War battle sites. We didn't want that because it felt like prospecting or something. They got a place in New York called Manfred's Mandibles where you can order all the bones you want, but we never thought that way.

"Billy knew a lot of people from traveling and they sent him things in the mail—bones, shells, feathers. A neighbor sent him a camel skull years after he moved away. I think people gave him so much because he never wanted anything. Nothing. He never asked anyone for a thing. He wanted nothing. He wanted to find bones without meaning to. The whole thing was to come across a skull by accident.

I started living that way in general. Thinking inside out, I called it. If I wanted to escape from my life, that really meant there was something inside of me that wanted out. If something was eating at me, I was hungry for something else. If I felt sorrow, it meant joy was trying to find me. Thinking inside out changed my life. For the first time I was a little bit happy. I quit wanting. All my life I'd wanted more but I turned that inside out. The less I wanted, the more I got.

"Then Billy moved to Portland for a job. My thinking went back the way it was before. At Christmas I mailed him a skull. For his birthday I sent a letter saying he could have my skull if something happened to me. He sent me the will. It was supposed to be fun. Then he died."

She stopped talking as if all the air had leaked from her head. Her face held a forlorn quality, buttressed by a scaffold of strength, like an old building that was half-renovated. After a lifetime of professional compassion, I was shocked to feel genuine sympathy for her. For years I'd handled the dead, massaging their muscles to help the embalming fluid enter the veins. Like anyone wanted to be more than a statistic at the courthouse, more than a name engraved on a rock in a grassy field, more than a thirty-line obituary in the Sunday paper. I wanted to live on, but would never leave an heir. Four million years of genetic memory ended with my death—I was history turned inside out.

"Lucy, you should consider your trip here as a hike in the woods. Amid the concrete flora and fauna of the city, you stumble across something by accident—a human skull. It's not the skull of a friend, or a prisoner, or a forgotten soldier. It's my skull you found. Mine. An average skull of an average man."

I turned my head side to side for her scrutiny. She gazed at me as if I were a deceased twitching on the embalming table. Her eyes were heavy-lidded and lovely of lash. She never blinked.

"Through my industry contacts I can guarantee a swift and simple process of acquisition. No fuss. No courts. No media."

"You don't know me," she said.

"It's not about you. I'm trying to think inside out. Undertakers are never remembered after their death. I have directed over three thousand funerals and have nothing to show for the work. Nothing. All of my achievement is slowly rotting under the earth. Great Uncle was remembered for a horse, but I have done nothing. When I die, my business rivals will prepare my body. No one will attend my funeral. Who mourns the mortician? Not a soul."

She reached across the desk and placed her hand on mine. Her skin was soft and very warm. The feeling I'd previously had drained away as if pumped from my body, replaced by something new and fresh with a completely different purpose. She slowly moved her hand beneath mine, turning her palm until the inside of our hands touched each other.

"You are a good man," she said. "I don't meet many."

"With your help," I said, "I can live forever."

"If you think inside out," she said, "death means permanent life."

"Will you take my skull?"

"Yes."

I stepped around the desk and traced her jaw with the back of my fingers. Her eyes never left mine. She tipped her head to my caress, her breath warm on my hand.

"You understand," she said.

"What?"

"I want to turn my loneliness inside out."

"Forever?"

"For now."

I pressed my forehead against hers. The sudden warmth of her skin flowed through my body. I felt as if I knew her a thousand years ago and a thousand years from now.

Slowly I rolled my head against hers. Our breath mingled. The lashes of our eyes brushed each other as if straining to entwine. I moved my cheekbone along hers, first one side, then the other. My lips touched hers. Our mouths turned inside out.

———

Chris Offutt is the author of *No Heroes, Kentucky Straight, Out of the Woods, The Same River Twice,* and *The Good Brother.* All have been translated into several languages. His work is widely anthologized and has received many honors both in the United States and abroad.

SANDY DYAS

Shortly after getting married, my father broke contact with his family and encouraged my mother to stop seeing hers. To facilitate matters, my parents moved their four kids deep into the hills of Kentucky. I grew up without benefit of cousins, uncles, aunts, or grandparents, all of whom lived a few hours away. There was never any explanation for this. My mother spoke quite fondly of her family, but they didn't call or visit, and neither did we. As a kid, I thought that meant our relatives hated us.

Fourteen years ago my mother sent me an obituary for her uncle, William P. McCarney. The list of pallbearers and survivors did not include anyone I knew. I suddenly realized that I had never attended the funeral or wedding of a family member. This saddened me greatly. My sorrow was offset by the astounding information that Great Uncle Billy had embalmed the racehorse Man o' War in 1947. I wrote a very bad essay about Great Uncle Billy, revising it three times before putting it aside. Nine years later I returned to the material as fiction.

Today it occurred to me that much of my writing has been an effort to populate my life with absent family.

John Dufresne

JOHNNY TOO BAD

(from *TriQuarterly*)

"You're going to run to the rock for rescue.
There will be no rock."
—The Slickers

Barbie

I'm not proud of this, but I'll tell you anyway. My dog Spot has a
Barbie doll that he carries with him everywhere he goes. She used
to be Malibu Barbie, but then Spot ate her splashy little lounging
outfit, and now she's generic, brunette Barbie, or as my girlfriend
Annick says, she's Housing Project Barbie. Spot stole the doll from
Layla Fernandez-Villas who is five and lives two doors down.
Layla's mom Gloria (Call me Glow!) hammered on my door, told
me what had happened, said her daughter, her baby, was in her
bedroom right now weeping hysterically. I told Glow to take a
deep breath, offered her some iced tea. Sweet or un? She said
something to me in Spanish, something about my *cabeza*. I stayed
calm. I explained that while Spot was admittedly rambunctious
(how could I deny the *chorizo frito* episode?), and while, yes, he was
decidedly mischievous, though I preferred the word *frolicsome,* and
certainly he could be naughty on occasion, and granted, he is im-
pervious to discipline, I'll give you that, Glow, still he's an honor-
able dog, and he would never—

I heard the clicking of Spot's toenails on the terrazzo and turned to see Barbie dangling by her legs from Spot's jaws. She was naked to the waist, her buttery body slimed with drool, her belly punctured, her arms flung above her head. Her hair was perfect. I ordered Spot to come. He backed away, wagged his tail. I snapped my fingers. I said, Drop the doll! He shook her. Glow said she didn't want the goddam doll anymore—what good is it? I said, Please, let's not make this any harder than it already is. Spot dropped Barbie on her head, dared me to reach for her. He snorted. I said, My goodness, Glow, is that the Greenberg's cat on our couch? Spot looked at me, at recumbent Barbie, back at me. He growled. When I reached for Barbie, Spot snatched her up and bounded toward the kitchen. He stopped when I refused to chase him. He woofed. Had I forgotten the rules to Keep Away? Spot hunkered down on his forelegs, Barbie between his paws, his butt in the air. He lifted his brow. Glow told me her husband Omar would not be happy about this. Omar sells discount cosmetics and knock-off perfumes out of his silver Ford Aerostar. He claims to be the man responsible for this new look where women paint their lips a conventional red and then outline them with a violet or brown. So we know he's a dangerous man. Naturally, I bought Layla a new doll—Los Alamos Barbie. She wears a spiffy, starched—and discreetly revealing—lab coat, high-heeled hiking boots, and she glows in the dark.

Bigfoot Jr.

Yesterday afternoon, Spot and I walked to Publix, our supermarket. Usually, I'll buy Spot a scoop of butter pecan at Ice Cream Cohen's next door, but today he wouldn't release his beloved Barbie, so I tied his leash to the bike rack and went inside. The place was mobbed. I stood in the express checkout lane with a twenty-pound sack of dog food. There was some confusion at the register. The customer, a great-bellied fellow in a white T-shirt and black Speedo, spoke only French, the cashier only Spanish. Apparently the trilingual manager was being summoned. I put down the sack

and plucked a copy of the *Weekly World News* off the rack. A woman
with a hirsute toddler on her lap posed for a rather artless photo.
The headline over the picture read I HAD BIGFOOT'S SON! I wasn't
sure we needed the exclamation point. Krystal Drinkwater had
confessed to the astonishing copulation, but did not reveal the how
or the why, did not mention where Dad was at these days, whether
they kept in touch, shared custody and support. I wondered, too,
if Krystal had simply used Bigfoot for reproductive purposes or
had she been in love with the big palooka all along. And what do
her neighbors think? (I imagined a trailer court at the edge of the
woods, gravel yards littered with rusted hibachis, baby strollers,
automobile tires, and Big Wheels. In the window of a yellow and
white Skyline, an aluminum Christmas tree.) And is the child, Kirk,
being ridiculed by his playmates at preschool, pitied by the teachers? Is breeding outside the species something that Bigfeet regularly engage in or was Krystal's inamorato a sexual pioneer? I wanted
to learn about the ecstasy, the trepidation, the dream. I wanted to
be in that delivery room. And, of course, I wondered what had made
Krystal so — desperate, was it? — so reckless that she would make
this preposterous claim to her family, her friends, the world. Because, really, there is no Bigfoot, is there?

And then I heard folks behind me in line talking about the approaching hurricane and how Publix was already out of bottled
water. I turned. Hurricane? I said. *Fritzy,* the Asian woman told
me. I saw my incredulous face in her sunglasses. Hurricane Fritzy?
I said. Was she joking? She wore a coral-colored, low-cut T-shirt
with *Hottie* in blue letters embroidered across her breasts. She
wasn't joking. How had I been so preoccupied that I'd missed the
news of an approaching hurricane? I excused myself and went in
search of batteries. Once again, I'd waited too long to order storm
shutters.

Victim Soul

I made grits and cornbread, sat in front of the TV. The folks at the
Weather Channel said it was still too early to determine the storm's

landfall, but we should all stay alert and tuned in. You could see how sober and calm the meteorologists were trying to be, and how really jaunty, cheery, and hopeful they felt. No doubt, Jim Cantori was home packing his Gore-Tex windbreaker and his personal anemometer. I knew that Channel 7 (*I, Witless News,* Annick calls it) wouldn't think it too early to call for a direct hit on South Florida. I knew they'd already be reveling in the potential devastation. I switched channels, but the local news was over. The *Jeopardy* theme music played, and Spot came zooming into the room, dropped perforated Barbie, and howled. I put the TV on mute. Spot looked at me and whined. How many times does he have to tell me he hates that song? He collapsed on the floor, his muzzle against Barbie's back. I apologized. When I saw Alex Trebeck, I put the sound on. Defending champion Betsy wanted *Geography* for $200, Alex. Alex said, It's the largest freshwater lake in the world. Betsy buzzed in. She said, What is Lake Superior? And Alex said she was correct, but she was not. Am I going to have to dash off another letter to these people? The truth is (or the fact is) that Lake Baikal in Siberia contains 20 percent of the world's fresh water, more than all of the supposedly Great Lakes combined. I hate misinformation.

I surfed through the channels and found an *Unsolved Mysteries* segment about a miraculous girl from Worcester, Mass., and naturally I watched because Worcester's where I grew up (in a manner of speaking). Turns out that the girl, Little Rose, drowned in her family pool ten years ago, but did not die. Not quite. She's in what the doctors call a state of akinetic mutism. She seems to be awake—her eyes are opened and mobile, but she is fixed and unresponsive. People call her a victim soul, say that she's crucified on her bed, that she takes on the suffering of others. She's developed the stigmata. Oil drips from the walls of her room, oozes from the holy pictures at her bedside. A statue of the Virgin on Rose's dresser weeps. The oil and the tears are collected on cotton balls, packed in Ziploc bags, and given to visitors who use them to swab their tumors, their ulcerated skin, their arthritic joints, and so on.

Little Rose's mom says that her daughter was visited by a woman with ovarian cancer, and the woman was healed. When Rose manifested symptoms of the cancer, X rays of her ovaries were taken and showed not a tumor at all, but an angel.

During the commercial, Spot the Vigilant heard me shift in my chair, or he sensed my larcenous intentions, and he bolted awake, took Barbie to his sheepskin-lined bed across the room—a very expensive bed that he's never used except for storage—and dropped Barbie inside next to his squeaky tarantula, his plush duck, his soccer ball, and his wooden shoe. Then he lay in front of the bed and stared at me. I said, She's not good enough for you, Spot. He blinked and yawned.

The Little Rose story resumed with a shot of a football stadium where a Mass was to be celebrated in her honor on this the anniversary of her drowning. Paramedics wheeled her into the end zone on a gurney. She wore a white gown and a gold tiara. Her abundant black hair tumbled off the mattress and trailed to the ground. I was afraid it would tangle in the spokes. People in the stands wept and prayed. They raised their arms to the Lord, shut their eyes, swayed their bodies.

When I was a boy I worked at this very stadium selling soda at Holy Cross games (only we called soda *tonic,* so I sold tonic, and we called a water fountain a *bubbler,* and pronounced it *bubba-la;* we called lunch *dinner;* dinner *supper;* sprinkles *jimmies;* a submarine sandwich a *grinder;* a hard roll a *bulkie;* a porch a *piazza;* a cellar a *basement;* a rubber band an *elastic;* and a milkshake a *frappe.* We called a luncheonette a *spa).* And then I saw myself at ten, no gloves, maroon woolen jacket, holes in my P. F. Flyers, torn dungarees, nose dripping, Navy watch cap pulled to my eyes and over my ears, lugging a tray of drinks up the stairs in Section 14 where I knew my old man and his buddies would need cups of ginger ale for their flasks of Canadian Mist. I could smell November in the air, and I knew when the game ended I'd have two dollars, and I could stop on the way home at Tony's Spa for an English muffin and a hot chocolate, and if the schoolyard lights were still on,

Bobby Farrell and I would shoot some hoops. I heard a cheer, and I looked up to see if Tommy Hennessey had scored a touchdown, and I saw Little Rose being carried to the altar at the fifty yardline. I wanted to be cured of my aging. I said, Little Rose, take away my years. I waited. I switched off the TV. This was one miracle she could not perform. And apparently there was another: she could not heal herself. Which made me think. What would all of these people do if she were no longer the victim soul, just another fifteen-year-old girl in love with pop singers and sassing her mother? And what about Mom? Does she want her little girl back or does she want her little saint?

What I know and what most viewers of *Unsolved Mysteries* do not, is that Worcester is mad for the miraculous. When I was at St. Stephen's grammar school, Dicky Murray's sister Mary and her friend Patty Shea were praying at the side altar in our empty church when they saw the statue of the Blessed Mother move. Patty hyperventilated and passed out. Mary Murray wept and pledged her life then and there to Jesus. She would become a nun. When word of the miracle got out, the church was mobbed every day with pilgrims come to give praise, come to witness the dynamic evidence of God's love and compassion. And many were not disappointed. The plaster Virgin might wiggle a finger one day, cast a glance the next, flare a nostril, flex a toe. Her movement was subtle, not grandiose, that being her way.

Dicky told me that at night when he was in bed he could hear his sister through the walls speaking with Jesus. She wrote down their conversations in her diary. Dicky knew where she hid the key. Mary claimed that she could taste the love of the Sacred Heart, could smell sin on people's clothing. Jesus called her His Maple Sugar Valentine. Mary told the nuns at school that Jesus had asked her to suffer for their sins. This did not go over well. Eventually, Mary was pressured by the Monsignor to recant, to admit that fasting for communion had left her and Patty dizzy and befuddled, that perhaps the flickering lights of votive candles on the altar, the dancing shadows, had tricked them into thinking the statue had moved.

Not long after the Ecstasy of Mary Murray, a father Leo D'Onofrio was assigned to St. John's parish down the hill, and he set about healing the infirm. His hands, it seemed, made whole. Busloads of crippled and otherwise ailing supplicants arrived from around the country on the first Sunday of every month. Father D'Onofrio made the lame to walk, the deaf to hear, the dumb to speak, the blind to see. He shrunk tumors, cleared arteries, purified blood. People abandoned crutches, prostheses, and wheelchairs in the aisles of the church. We took my uncle Armand for the cure. Uncle Armand got shell-shocked in World War II. When Father D'Onofrio laid his hands on Uncle Armand's head, my uncle spit in his face and never did regain a healthy mind.

I wonder what it is that makes people in Worcester so hungry for preternatural religious experience or what makes the city so hospitable to the wondrous. The TV beeped twice and a weather alert scrolled across the bottom of the screen. Hurricane Fritzy was now a strong Category 3 storm and was located about 270 miles east of the Lesser Antilles. Fritzy was heading due west at 31 miles per hour. Less than two days away, looked like.

I heard Spot snore, wheeze, snuffle. I turned off the TV. His forelegs twitched. Probably dreaming about chasing a stretch limo up Sheridan Street. I stood. He opened an eye, looked my way. Don't even think about it, Johnny.

The Bathtub

Spot is so terrified by thunderstorms that I tell myself we ought to move to the desert, and maybe we will some day. (And then I think: dry and flaky skin; nose bleeds; flat, flyaway hair.) As soon as Spot hears the first grumble of thunder he starts panting, whining, pacing the house. I take a bottle of cognac, a plastic cup, and a pile of magazines to the bathroom. As the storm intensifies, Spot starts digging at the tile or the rug with his front paws, trying to furiously scoop out a protective bunker. I figured out that the safest place for us in a storm was the bathtub where Spot could dig all night without hurting himself or our house. I sit at the faucet end of the tub and drink and hug Spot when he tires and takes a fretful break on my lap. I pat him. I sing lullabies. I read him stories from *DoubleTake*. I tell him, It's okay; Daddy's here. So you see why I was worried about a hurricane. I wasn't sure I was up for thirty-six hours in the tub.

One Saturday morning last July I woke up, and Annick was staring at me. I said, What? She said, Are we too old to be spontaneous? I said we weren't. She said, Let's do something unexpected. Usually when we're together on Saturday, we sit on the couch and read our books until afternoon when we plan a menu, shop, cook, eat. I said, Like what? We drove to Key West. We left Spot in the garage with food, water, leather bones, and an open door to the backyard so he could do his business. Spot wasn't allowed in the house alone because he'd eaten most of a Mission end table I'd bought at Restoration Hardware. Annick and I planned to have a late lunch at Blue Heaven, listen to junkanoo music over a couple of drinks. On the drive home, we'd stop to see the key deer. Be back before dark. We hadn't counted on the weather. We ran into a line of violent thunderstorms at Mile Marker 56, and we took a motel room on Grassy Key.

In the morning I dropped Annick off at her house and went home to rescue Spot. You could tell from the downed branches and the flooded streets that the storm had hit hard. I opened the kitchen door, and Spot charged me. He was so deliriously happy to see me that he zoomed across the living room, ran over and across the couch, the comfy chair, the coffee table. He made that circle three times and then he was back licking my face. Spot had chewed and dug his way from the garage, through the drywall and the plywood, and had come out in the cabinet under the sink.

What My Sweetheart Annick and I Are Not Doing Tonight
We're not in her kitchen preparing spaghetti puttanesca, sipping martinis, making naughty jokes about noodles and sauce. And we're not sitting on the deck of the SS *Euphoria* sailing to the Bahamas, holding hands, staring up at Cassiopeia, chatting about our

aspirations. We're not at the movies, partly because I refuse to go anymore. I find them all dishonest, disheartening, and disappointing. Body parts and body counts. So Annick goes alone or she goes with her friend Ellen. She thinks I'm ridiculous about this, thinks if I love her I ought to be able to sit for ninety minutes by her side. But we'd only end up arguing. I'm insufferable, and I know it. It's all because I loved movies when they told stories about decent people in enormous trouble, when acting was a special effect.

When we first dated Annick told me she liked *Forrest Gump,* and I felt the life-force drain from my body. I thought, If she tells me she's a Republican I'll scream, and then I'll take my leave. When I'd mention Truffaut, she'd roll her eyes. I'd say Cassavetes or Spielberg: principle or spectacle; sentiment or sentimentality. She'd say, Cassavetes?

We're not at the movies and we're not in my bed, not in her bed, not in bed at the Riverside Hotel in Fort Lauderdale, which is what I had planned for this, our fifth anniversary as a dating couple. Dinner at the Himmarshee Grille, cruise up the New River on a water taxi, nightcap at Mark's on Las Olas. These days Annick considers herself my ex-sweetheart.

Screening

I left Spot with Barbie, went to the kitchen, and telephoned Annick. I got her machine. *Hello, you've reached Annick. Today's words are* cosset, oast, *and* judder. *Leave your name, your number, and your word for today, and I'll get back to you as soon as I can. Maybe.*

I said, Annick, it's me. Come on, pick up. I know you're there. Annick? One, two, three. Okay then. Call me. My word is *vaticination*. Bye. No sooner had I spoken my word than I wanted to take it back. And that's the terrible thing about speech—once it's articulated you can't revise. I hung up. A crumby Latinate word that will never enlarge anyone's world. A pretentious synonym for *prediction*. If I had thought a moment longer I could have said *rick* or *larrikin* or something interesting. With speech there's no time to see what you say until it's too late.

Ennis

Back in college, my friend Ennis Murphy fell in love with a girl from the Midwest. He married her in 1972 and divorced her in 1974. A year later he married again (both wives had the same first name and the same blonde hair) and had two kids, one of whom, the boy, got into some criminal trouble when he was fourteen. So Ennis and his wife search around for a proper boarding school for their son. Get him away from the crowd he's running with was their thinking. Ennis's wife's friend, a visual artist, suggested a school in Mitchell, South Dakota, that has a terrific reputation for turning wayward boys around. Saved her nephew Peter's life. Was into sniffing spray paint and now he's a clinical psychologist. This was in 1994, and Ennis could not have told you if his first wife was even alive.

So Ennis and his son flew to South Dakota, and Ennis spent a week at the Corn Palace Motel while his boy settled into his dorm and his routine. One morning over coffee at the Lueken Bakery, Ennis noticed an article in the paper about his ex-mother-in-law. He couldn't believe it at first, but there was her photograph, and Marlene didn't look much older than she had twenty or so years ago. She had won first prize at Dakotafest for her honey-spiced cornbread. And she lived in Epiphany. Ennis checked his road atlas, saw how close that was, smiled, called information and got Marlene's address.

When she answered the door, Ennis said, Marlene, you may not remember me, but I was your son-in-law. Marlene stepped back, opened the screen door, said Ennis Murphy, you're like some ghost, and she hugged him, and ushered him into her kitchen. He sat at the table while Marlene brewed coffee, warmed some cornbread. She told Ennis how her husband Tubba had died of emphysema six years ago. Never did quit smoking. That's when she sold the place up in Huron and moved out here, away from the hustle and bustle. She said her daughter lived in Mitchell now, taught literature at Dakota Wesleyan. Ennis had never known his ex-wife to be interested in literature. I'd call her right now, Marlene said, but she's in Rapid City at a conference. Ennis said, Well, you tell her hi for me. Marlene said, We know all about you, Ennis. We follow your career. We're so proud of you. (I should tell you I've changed Ennis's name. He's a moderately famous musician whom you might recognize.)

A year later, Ennis returned to Mitchell to perform at his son's school. He sent his ex two tickets to the show. She came alone. They got together later for drinks. She was a Willa Cather scholar, it turned out. Head of her department. Ennis told me, It didn't take us long to realize that our divorce wasn't working. After that weekend, he went home to his unsuspecting wife of twenty years, his devoted wife, and told her he was leaving her for his other wife. She said, This is some sick joke, right? It isn't funny, Ennis.

Ennis told me it was his great happiness over his resurrected love that gave him the strength to do what must have seemed so cruel to an observer. He told his wife he hadn't planned for this to happen. She said, Weren't we happy? He said, It was fate. She said, You can't do this to me. He said he was sorry, truly sorry that it had to happen, but it had happened, hadn't it? You'll be better off, he said. She hit him in the face so hard that she broke her elbow. Ennis drove her to the emergency ward. He was questioned by the triage nurse and then by two sheriff's deputies. His wife was hysterical. He waited for her in the lobby. His left cheek was bruised, his eye swollen shut. He called South Dakota with the news.

Ennis remarried his first wife on what would have been their 24th wedding anniversary. Their first marriage, I remember, took place in a field of wildflowers at an Audubon Sanctuary in Barre, Mass. We were all barefoot and garlanded, and high as kites. The second marriage was performed in a Lutheran Church in Mitchell, and Ennis's son, an A-student, was his Best Man. His daughter refused to attend the ceremony.

I made the mistake of telling Annick this story as we lounged on the couch the same night that Spot stole Barbie. So now she thought I wanted to reunite with my ex-wife. I said, That's crazy.

She said, You made that story up. I was hurt. I said, If I'd made it up, you'd have believed it. She was crying now. She put down her wine glass. She asked me how I could have told her such a desolate story. I said I thought it was a story of enduring love and grand passion. Annick shook her head. She said my past was the one place she could never be. And then she stood, told me she was leaving, and walked to the door. Spot followed her, wagging his garrulous tail. She patted his head, scratched behind his ears, under his chin, called him *Spot the Looney* in her baby voice, and let him lick her face. She told him to stay. After she shut the door, Spot sniffed at the threshold, whimpered. He woofed at me.

At first I was angry with Annick. I mean, you think you're building a cozy and resilient relationship with a person, and then she proves you wrong. It's not at all intimate like you had imagined, but merely amicable. It's not irrepressible, but rather fragile, unsubstantial. But then I considered my motivation. Why *had* I told her about Ennis and the two Violas? Had I meant it, unconsciously or not, as an unsettling cautionary tale? Was my story a smile and a shrug? A nasty little assertion of my independence? A gratuitous nod to the treachery and caprice of Time? And then I was angry at my vicious self. I realized that I had committed an unpremeditated, but intentional, nonetheless, act of cruelty. I've caught myself playing this game before, the game of undermining my emotional prosperity. Something irrational inside, something ungovernable and unknowable, some fear or impulse has convinced me that the road of happiness leads to the house of sorrow.

Canine Theater

I cleared my dishes, rinsed them, poured myself a drink, and went out to sit on the deck. I put my feet up on the rail, leaned back in my chair. Spot sat at attention and stared at me. He wanted to know where I'd hidden Barbie and, more importantly, why would I do such a thing. I said, Maybe she found out I was suing her for alienation of affection and decided to skip town. He put his paw on my leg. I said, I don't think obsession is healthy for a dog. He yipped. He rested his head on my arm, looked up at me with his Pagliacci eyes. He's good.

Barbie was in the exercise room, which is not where I work out, but where I store all the training equipment I've foolishly bought over the years, the free weights, the Solo-flex, the stationary bike, the Abdomenizer, the StairMaster, the treadmill, the NordicTrack. You might ask why have I kept these reminders of my failure and my unfitness around. Well, I paid for them, and I can't bear to give them away. The financial loss would only compound my distress. I've also got a closet full of shoes that I haven't worn in years. I've got red clogs, green espadrilles, white bucks, dirty bucks, oxblood brogans, black wingtips, blue huaraches, cordovan penny loafers, chestnut Earth shoes, purple creepers, saddle shoes, beaded moccasins, Beatle boots, cowboy boots, chukka boots, engineer boots, fringed suede knee boots. I've even got a pair of parti-colored bowling shoes that I wore home from Gasoline Alleys Candlepin Lanes when they gave my sneakers away to someone else. If I ever put in a garden, I'll wear the bowling shoes to till the soil because who cares if they get wrecked.

I wanted to take Spot's mind and heart off Barbie, so I figured we'd play Canine Theater. Spot's quite a fine performer. I like to think he brings clarity and dignity to every role he plays. Of course, he doesn't like the Scottish play. When Annick, as Lady Macbeth, rubs her hands and declaims, Spot runs for the door and whines to be let out.

I stood. I looked at Spot. I said, "Biff, what are you doing with your life, goddamit? You've got unlimited potential."

Spot cocked his head.

"Don't look at me like that, Biff. Your brother Hap, he's doing gangbusters. But you, Biff, you're the smart one. You've got the winning personality."

Spot woofed.

"Out west? There's nothing out west for a man with ambition." He growled.

"You're wrong, Biff. New York's the place for the Lomans. Willy and his sons."

Spot barked.

I picked up the Nerf football from the deck. I said, "Go long, Biff." I threw it as far as I could. Spot just sat there. I gave in. I got Barbie.

pannick@hailmail

I checked my e-mail: Speed Up Your Net Connection in Minutes GUARANTEED!!! Investor Alert! A Canadian Package That Matches Your Request. Archie MacPhee's On-Line Catalogue. And this from Annick:

> Johnny, I'm trying to give my future a shape. I don't want it being just more of the present. All my days are so alike now that they slip seamlessly into the past, and the past may be a fine place to visit, but I don't want to live there. Sometimes you make me so tired. It seems to me like I'm walking, you're standing still. You're stuck in your blue period. I'm going out to buy new paints. Time to get on with it. The opposite of change is death. Say hi to Spot. Have you heard about Fritzy?
> Annick

I went back to the deck.

Ways of Seeing

Some things you *look* at, and some things you *stare* at. You look at a photograph, but you stare at a flame. You look with intent and with intensity, but you stare without purpose or motive. When you look, you distinguish. When you stare, you witness. To look is to examine. To stare is to accept. Looking leads to comprehension, staring to reflection. *Look,* and you are fixed in time and space. *Stare,* and time dissolves, the world around you drops away. Me, I love the imposition of looking, but I prefer the susceptibility of staring. And that's why I love the night. Darkness obliterates distraction. I sit on my deck and stare at the stars. I see Perseus, Lacerta, and Cygnus adrift in the Milky Way. And I see beyond the stars to infinity, and in staring out I see within, see the faint shimmer of who I briefly am. Emerson said that if you want to feel alone, look at the stars. And I do. I feel alone, but also a part of something incomprehensibly vast and sublime. And I feel small, but not insignificant because I can wonder at it all, because I can think about the stars, and the stars cannot think about me, because I can tremble at the mystery.

The wind rattled through the queen palm. I smelled curry coming from the Pannu's house. I heard the squawk of a night heron. I saw the Northern Cross, and the Cross made me think of Ray. Rayleigh Baravykas, my girlfriend just before I met my wife. Ray and I were in our sleeping bag in the dunes in Provincetown, and Ray pointed out the Cross and Andromeda and the dim galaxy beyond it, and we stayed awake to watch the Perseid meteor shower—a night of shooting stars. And then a thunderstorm.

The next morning we sat together at the Laundromat, and a woman with a baby on her lap stared at us and smiled. She said, "You two look so beautiful together." But we're not together. Maybe we didn't believe in our beauty. I wondered how Ray was doing, and wondered how you could go from finishing each other's sentences to not talking for twenty years. There was a time I wouldn't let Ray out of my sight, and now I'm not even sure what she looks like.

I heard rustling in the heliconias. Probably a possum. Spot heard it and woofed. He's afraid of possums. I said, It's only Pogo. He growled unconvincingly. I guess my theme for the night was loss, or it was loneliness, because then I thought about two ex-friends who had the same first name (no motif intended). I've known the first Tony since second grade. He's my oldest pal. We used to sit in the schoolyard and talk about movies. Later we read Thoreau and Muir together, listened to obscure acoustic music. We planned trips out West, to Coeur d'Alene, to the Sawtooth, to Glacier. I'd buy maps, plan the routes, research the parks and campgrounds, and Tony would go with someone else. One morning he wouldn't be home and his mom would say he's off with Gary Smart (or Brian Houde or Henry Welch) to the mountains. I'd get to see the slides when they got back. Each time I was afraid to ask for an explanation.

One Friday night he called from his college dorm to tell me his girlfriend had left him, and how devastated he was, how suicidal. That Sunday morning I hitchhiked the fifty miles in sub-zero weather to see him, and when I arrived, his roommate told me that Tony was at a motel with the woman in question, and then he went back to sleep. *Miles* was the roommate's name. Miles to sleep. Miles to go before I sleep. Funny, I hadn't even known I knew his name. Miles, who later moved to Australia. Why do I remember that?

Tony was an only child. He had one aunt and no cousins. His aunt and parents died. Tony has known me longer than he has known anyone. I tell myself it's his childhood he's running from. But I think it's me. I call every six months, on Christmas and his birthday, and leave a message on his machine.

The second Tony and I did travel together—to Europe and across America. For years we were inseparable. And then he stopped talking to me. He told friends that I was stuck in the past, that I hadn't grown up. He may have been right, of course. He told them I had an indiscriminate sense of humor. Maybe it *is* better to put the past aside, but I never can. Tony moved back to his mother's house after she died. I wondered did he sleep in his old bedroom or move into Mom and Dad's. There's some cruelty in that thought, I know. I miss the Tonys. We could be having fun right now.

What if Ray and I had never split up? I tried to picture us now. (Yes, it's futile to think *what if?* about your life, but I've been doing it since I was a kid. What if Mom and Dad die in a car crash on the way home? How would I handle all that trouble? Could I go live with Aunt Bea in California? What if I had sprung my grandfather from the nursing home? [Would have needed a miracle here. In fact, I went to the nursing home, said, Pepere, you want to get out of here, never come back? He said, I know I'm supposed to know

you. Could you tell me who you are.]) I could only see Ray and
me in a cold place. Ray in a bulky wheat-colored sweater. We're on
a farm in coastal Maine. Goats. Wild raspberries. And then I remembered her grandfather's farm and what happened there. Ray's
uncle Edwin shot his father in the head and then shot himself,
but not before he doused the parlor with gasoline and dropped a
match.

I went back to the kitchen, made some coffee, sat at the table and
wrote a poem about Ray:

Still Life with Ray
Ray tells me what Sister Cecilia told her and the other girls back
in sixth grade, that St. Lucy plucked out her eyes and sent them
to her tiresome and lascivious suitor, the Consul Paschasius, to
save herself from shame. Yikes! It's 1969 and Ray and I are on
the beach in Provincetown waiting for the sun to set over the
bay. We have wine and chocolate and Portuguese bread. I wonder did Lucy have the eyes wrapped in silk and did she pay the
boy who delivered them. I make a joke about how Lucy was
from the school of aggressive chastity. I'm in love with Ray.
Ray's mother has just died. Ray says eyes don't see, the mind
does. I touch my forehead to her temple, and when she speaks
I feel her words in the bones of my head. She says we never see
only one thing at a time. Ray is a painter. She says if you look
at anything for a long time, it melts and shatters. I wonder if
she's talking about her memory of her mom or about the beach
grass, sea rocket, and bayberry in front of us. When the sun sets
Ray stands and looks behind us to the eastern sky. I look at the
fuchsia sun, the purple sea. I look at Ray, her blonde hair aflame.
She tells me to look at the purple band low in the sky. I put my
chin on her shoulder and look ahead to where she's pointing,
and finally I see it. We watch the band rise in the sky and then
dissolve into the darkness. Ray says we just watched the earth's
shadow cast on the sky. I hold her face in my hands. Ray averts
her eyes.

I typed it. By now it was the middle of the night, and I still couldn't sleep. My uncle Armand told me how the world was destroyed every night and put back together again by God before morning. I looked through photo albums and found what I knew I would—a black-and-white photo I had taken of Ray and her grandfather on one of our Sunday visits to the farm. Ray is sipping soup from a spoon and looking over at me with her turquoise eyes, and old Joe is holding his ball cap by its visor and scratching his head. The tip of his index finger is missing. He's wearing a torn corduroy coat over his coveralls over his sweatshirt. Beyond Joe on a shelf over a dry sink sits a tub of Jewel lard, a pitted enamel wash basin, a chalkware collie, a hurricane lamp, and a box of Ohio Blue Tip matches.

I took a drink with me out to the deck. Something else Uncle Armand told me: you can tell the real voices from the crazy voices because the crazy voices are just outside your ear. We look out to the end of the universe racing away from us. We can only look back, it seems. The future is invisible. How shall we know it?

Glow & O

When you tell people that you write fiction, they tend to respond in one of three ways. There are those who will stop talking to you because they assume you are going to write about them, you're going to appropriate their precious lives for your squalid little stories. My family's like this. Years ago I was made to promise that I would never again reveal the kind of familial impropriety that had gotten my uncle Didi blackballed at the Singletary Rod & Gun Club, that I would not embarrass my parents or aunts or in any way muddy the family name. Otherwise I could spend my holidays in solitude. And I have kept my word although I do have a dozen or so stories filed away awaiting the deaths of certain cousins and in-laws.

Then there are the folks who think that writers write only about themselves, and so they assume that writers lead adventurous, troubled, and reckless lives. These people are eager to listen to your madcap tales of turmoil and self-destruction. You tell them you don't smoke, don't drink (you lie) or carry on with the wives of friends. You explain that you no longer shoot heroin and you don't roam the predawn streets with packs of other writers. You tell them you sit in a room and work. These people are hurt that you don't trust them with your indiscretions. The hurt festers into anger and resentment.

The third response comes from those who think that fiction writers make everything up. These are sweet, kind, and naive people who want to make your job easier, and so they tell you stories from their own lives. Like my friend Ennis and his two Violas. Or like the seventy-five-year-old woman I met in Winter Haven who told me she'd carried on a forty-year love affair with a married physician, a radiologist, a man with a wife and four children. Moved here from Los Angeles to be near him. They went on a cruise to Paradise Island, and he died in their bed in his sleep. She had to call the wife from her cabin with the tragic news, arrange for the transport of the body back to Winter Haven. She could not attend the funeral. He was the love of her life.

Gloria and Omar fit into this last category. When Gloria first stopped by to welcome me to the neighborhood she was very pregnant and smelled like vanilla. As we sat in my kitchen and talked, she ate the empanadas she had brought me. She told me that her husband—she called him the Big O—was away on business, meeting with the Latin American Cosmetics King in Caracas. She told me how she knew that O loved her: since she told him how much she loved his lavender shirt, he'd worn it every day. She told me she took lessons: voice, dance, acting. It was O's ambition that she make it in show business, get her own program on Telemundo. I told her I wrote stories. She told me her voice teacher's cousin knew Gloria Estefan's housekeeper. I said, So, you have an in. She raised her brow, pointed at me like I was onto something. She asked me what my stories were about. I told her love and death. She wiped crumbs from her mouth, leaned back in her chair. She said, You can write my story.

When she was sixteen, Glow was madly in love with Billy Cassidy, with his dreamy blue eyes, his wavy black hair, his sweet disposition. They'd been going steady for a month when Billy's mom died quite unexpectedly (aneurysm). At the wake, Glow sat between Billy and his sobbing father and accepted the condolences of strangers. Billy chewed gum. His jaw cracked. He held Glow's hand for what must have been comfort, but felt to her like restraint, detention. Glow wished she could say a prayer at the casket, express her regrets, whisper to Billy that she'd be there for him, and leave with their other friends.

In the following weeks, Glow spent her afternoons and evenings at the Cassidy house, cooking, cleaning, watching television. Billy had become more affectionate, but less amorous, more tender, but less demonstrative, more reliant, grateful, needy, and therefore less deserving of her passion. She wanted love, not domesticity, wanted to be an obsession, not a substitute. She told Billy she was sorry about his terrible loss, and then she returned the silver crux ring he'd given her. She told me she missed him, always had. He teaches high school in Miramar. And then she told me the hidden meaning to her story: "Death is stronger than love, Johnny."

When I first met Omar he was wearing a silky red-and-gold soccer uniform, shin guards, and wrap-around sunglasses. He handed me a beer, and we leaned against his van. He told me his team, the Jaguars, had just defeated the Lions of Judah at Boggs Field. He scratched Spot's muzzle, spoke to him in Spanish. Spot sat, gave Omar his paw. I noticed the cases of lipstick in the van and asked Omar how he liked his job. He said a man's job was to love a woman. Whether the woman loved him back was unimportant. The woman's job was to be loved. He asked me did I have a woman. I said I did. He asked me to describe her complexion, eye and hair color. I said, Cream, coffee, copper. He put down his bottle, cut open a case of lipstick with a key, pulled out a gold tube and handed it to me. "Cinnamon Spice. For your woman."

"Thank you."

"My wife tells me you write stories."

"Yes."

"Why?"

"Every story uncovers a secret."

Omar smiled, looked toward his house, leaned into me, and told me his secret. He had another family in Venezuela. A wife, Graciela, and three sons, Pablo, four; Carlos, three; Celestino, one and a half.

"*Omar* is my American name."

"You wouldn't lie to me?"

"What would be the point?"

"How do you manage?"

"With difficulty."

"You have two identities? Two passports?"

He smiled.

"You seem happy."

"I love them all."

"What will happen? I mean you can't keep this up indefinitely."

"We shall see."

What Else Could It Be?

I squished my earplugs in as far as they'd go, adjusted my padded eyeshade, taped my Breathe Right nasal strip on my nose. I thought how this was a secret I kept from Annick. She'd never seen me armed for sleep. When we stay together, I sleep unfortified. I would be too embarrassed. Anyway, I like my dreams and want to enjoy them without interruption. But I'm a fretful and uneasy sleeper. Wind in the oleander wakes me, the refrigerator's hum, the dawn's light, passing cars, my own snoring. I puffed my pillow, smoothed the sheet, stretched my legs, relaxed them. For an insomniac, going to bed is like going to therapy. All the cargo you've weighted down with forgetfulness and disregard, and then dropped into the deep, comes popping back to the surface. Like my dad.

He had left a message on my machine, and I hadn't returned his call. He told me about the hurricane and about a woman named Fritzy that he knew during the war—before Mom. My dad was an inventor before he lost his sight. He didn't so much make new things as he found new uses for existing things. He made fishing lures out of bottle openers and teaspoons, made coat hooks out of plastic duck decoys. He once made a shaving mirror for the shower out of a harmonica holder and a woman's compact. And that's how he appeared to me as I tried to sleep—naked in the shower with the holder around his neck and the opened compact case snapped into the spring tension clamp. His face was lathered. He held a shaving brush in one hand and a razor in the other. He was far-sighted in those days, so he wore his reading glasses, which had fogged. He cracked me up sometimes. One day he ran out of shaving cream, so he shaved with Reddi-wip. He would point at an object and ask me what it was. I'd answer, and then he'd tell me what else it was. Like I'd say *ladder,* and he'd say *towel rack.* Or I'd say *ashtray,* and he'd say *soap dish. Wooden shoe—planter; flat iron—door handle.*

The reason I hadn't called my father back, the reason he was keeping me awake, had to do with the tape he wanted me to make. He wanted me to read my last book into a recorder so he could listen to it. I told Dad that Spot was in the book, that he belonged to the central character, a writer, not so unlike myself. I told him the writer's father had vision problems, so naturally he assumed the father is him. I did not tell him that the writer and his father have a problematic relationship. I did not want my father hurt by his misperception. Even if I told him now that he's not the character, he'll think I'm lying. Spot's Spot, after all. The writer's a pathetic little scribbler who left his loving wife, after all.

I took off my eyeshade. Maybe if I opened my eyes, I wouldn't see my wife. But there she was holding a peeled orange to her mouth, holding it with both hands, biting into it and crying. Just great! I pulled out the earplugs. Once again, thoughts had murdered sleep. I know that I made the novel up. I also know there are resemblances to my life. I know why the writer left his wife, but I don't know why I left mine. I like to pretend that writing is a plunge into reality, that it forces me to deal with what I'm ashamed of, with what I regret, with what I don't understand, with what I don't want to know about myself, but it can also be avoidance. Flight. It's easier to make someone up, after all, and give him the trouble and deal with his turmoil than it is to deal with your own. So much for courage and honesty. And I knew if I didn't do something soon, I'd be writing about the writer who lost his girlfriend.

I sat on the edge of the bed. I keep a memo pad and pen on the night table. I wrote this down: *a father is always a son; a son's not always a father.* I'd figure it out in the morning. If I hoped to get any sleep, I needed to get out of bed.

The Dead of Night

I've been despondent in my life. I've felt ponderous and numb, desperate and disabled, brittle and disposable, lost in a gloom so profound I wanted at once to hold onto anything and let go of everything. But I've come to understand that hope, our brief candle, is my only light in the darkness, and so I keep it with me.

I sat in the living room, feet up on the ottoman, staring toward the window. Spot snored on the couch. I realized you can't look at space, but only at objects in space. Without something to be seen, you are blind. I also realized I was avoiding what hurt. It was so quiet I could hear everything, the CFX freight rumbling alongside Dixie Highway, blasting its whistle at every intersection. And when that faded, I heard a semi whining along the Interstate. I pictured the driver wearing a T-shirt, smoking a cigarette. He knows he has seven hours to Savannah and then one more load to carry up to Augusta before he gets home to Myrna and the boys, gets a few days of rest and a chance to work on the dragster. He's thinking, because he always does, that he shouldn't have gotten into the long-haul business in the first place. Never at home. But how could he give it up now? That's what the car's about and why he needs to get it humming: the new life, the dreamed-of life, the real life he's not yet living, the life of a drag racer. He'll enter out at Silver Dollar this spring and then maybe Rockingham. He doesn't want to think about all this. He'll just get sad. He puts on the radio. Every station's in Spanish. Where the hell am I? He plugs in a Willie Nelson tape, and every song calls him home. His name's Keith. He's got a herniated disc in his lower back and a nasty scar that runs up the inside of his right arm.

While I thought about Keith, I felt okay, but I opened my eyes and the exhausted air was empty of light. How do we fill our emptiness? With jobs, with songs, with family, with friends. Even if we have to make them up. We connect how we can.

The night is both our blessing and our curse. It's a sanctuary from turmoil, a respite from the routine and clutter of our lives. Our days seduce us with activity. Our nights confront us with stillness. The night may seem false in its solitude, but it's the lie that speaks the truth. At night, we can't pretend that we're not dying. At night, we're reminded of this hurried interlude between oblivions. And that's why we choose to sleep, to dream. Dreams are the madness that keep us sane.

I saw Spot's legs twitch and realized my eyes had adjusted to the scant light that had been here all the while. I wasn't despondent. I was afraid. I thought about what I was missing, like my old friends, the old neighborhood, my old room, my old young and innocent self. Annick.

When I first met her—this was at a bookstore café—she told me her name was Annick, but she danced under the name *Blaze*. Blaze was the set-up. After our espressos, she shook my hand, said how nice it was to meet, to chat and all. She needed to find a book. I discreetly followed her, hoping she didn't head for *Self-Help* or *New Age*. She went to *Art & Architecture,* and this gave me the courage to approach and ask her if I might call her. She gave me her card. The card was the pay-off. I said, Very funny, Miss Pascal. You don't dance at all, do you? She told me she was a freelance scenic designer and worked mostly with local theaters. I said, Are you related? She said, He is my great-great-great-great-great-great grandfather. Later she told me her joke had been a test. If I hadn't recognized the name, she wouldn't have answered the phone.

I was, I knew, distracting myself with thoughts. I told myself not to think, but to feel, to wait quietly and the fears would present themselves. If I love Annick and she loves me, why don't I want what she wants? Why do I insist on separate lives? Do I love her in a different way than she loves me? Do I know what love is? Annick says, Love is simple. It's what you do, not what you think or feel. She also says that the only way to know the future is to imagine it. I'm not sure I want to know it, but I try. I see Annick and me in twenty years. We're living in Taos. It's a Saturday night in July, and we're driving down to Chimayo for dinner. And then I think, Twenty years—no Spot, so I just get up and go to the kitchen to make coffee. I turn on the TV. There's a live remote from Home Depot. It's half past four in the morning, and the place is packed. People are buying generators, sandbags, flashlights. The store's already out of plywood.

Walkies

I used to bring Spot to Bark Park up in Fort Lauderdale for his exercise, but he's been banned, *canis non grata*, labeled chronically aggressive, which is a lie, or, at best, a misunderstanding. What Spot did was he got a lot of otherwise docile and obedient dogs riled up, got them in touch with their inner puppies, so that in their exuberance, they ignored their owners' commands. Apparently, these dogs had never seen anything remotely like Spot's exhilaration and abandon. They watched Spot run like mad around the perimeter of the park, his ears waving, his tongue flapping, his body leaning into the turns like it does. He'd stop to pee on the statue of Dr. Dolittle or to chew some piece of canine agility equipment, and then he'd be off again, dogs following.

Spot gets a kick out of prissy little dogs, and every once in a while he'd see one across the park, and he'd charge at it and then leap right over it at the last second, leaving the little shih tzu trembling in its satin bows. I could see people calling to their recalcitrant dogs, whistling, gesturing, ordering them to stop chasing after Spot the dervish and get back here this instant! The owners would look at me with narrowed eyes and clenched jaws. I'd smile as if to say I'm just as nuts as the dog. Spot earned five demerits in his first week.

The final straw came when Spot, who'd been splashing through the drinking fountain, crashed a doggie birthday party at the puppy pavilion, a party to which he'd been explicitly disinvited. He stole a cardboard hat off a beagle and ran off with it. The beagle looked sad, confused. Then Spot bounded back and galloped through the cake. The party's human hostess, a sixty-something platinum blonde, told me I was just the kind of reprobate that gave dog owners a bad name. I told her Spot was just playing. She told me he doesn't play well with others. When I intimated that the party guests were maybe unduly prim, she said, no, they were gentle and dutiful. Bootlickers, I said. She said did I understand the first thing about the responsibilities of dog ownership. I said something about the fascist's need to control and dominate. I really wasn't making sense.

So now Spot and I walk around the neighborhood, and I carry a plastic Publix sack so I can collect his poop. We follow a route of Spot's choosing along the mangroves to the canal where he does his business, to the pond where he barks at the Muscovy ducks, and then past the strip mall where I deposit the sack in the bucket behind Asian Nails, and then up Coolidge. (Used to be there were monkeys in the mangroves—escaped from Chimp World in the '50s, but lately the state's been paying poachers to trap them. Haven't seen any in months, which is fine with Spot. They freaked him out. We also have walking catfish here and marine toads the size of catchers' mitts, and four-foot iguanas, and basilisk lizards that run along on their back legs. That's the kind of neighborhood it is.) Eventually we come to Annick's house. And normally we pay a visit. So this morning after my sleepless night Spot ran up Annick's porch steps and turned to me. I told him to come on. He sat, looked back over his shoulder to the door. There were treats and hugs inside. I, too, was hoping the door would open, and Annick would be standing there in her cowgirl pajamas, and she'd invite us in for breakfast and reconciliation, but it did not. I saw no lights on inside, no activity in the yard.

Back on our block, O was unloading sheets of plywood from a U-Haul truck. Spot sniffed through the hibiscus while I gave O a hand. O asked me did I want to buy some plywood to board up my windows. I told him I wouldn't know what to do with it. He shook his head, told me I ought to be more responsible than that. "Your house will blow away. What will you do then?"

"I'll come stay with you."

O didn't laugh. He opened his cooler, asked me if I wanted a beer.

"Seven-thirty's a bit early."

He opened two bottles of Polar and we sat on the lawn. Layla told Spot he looked adorable. She'd tied a sun bonnet on his head. The two of them sat on the porch steps. His tail wagged a mile a minute. And then I understood. Barbie was Spot's connection to Layla, that's why he kept her around. He had a crush on Layla. I felt relieved and guilty. I saw Glow at the screen door talking to someone on a cell phone. She waved to me.

O said that Channel 7 had called for a hurricane landfall somewhere between Haulover Cut and Hillsboro Inlet sometime before dawn tomorrow. I said I ought to paint a bull's-eye on my house. He said we were under a mandatory evacuation order. We've got till dusk, but by three the Turnpike and I-95 will be one-way north and grid-locked. He said he was boarding up, selling what he could of the plywood—Glow's on the phone to the neighbors now—and then taking off. He's got a room booked in Orlando, closest he could find. He told me I should get ready and get out. I said I might have to stay. He said did I have a gun. Did I want to buy one?

Tropical Anesthetic

At home I switched on the TV, and there it was out in the Atlantic, Fritzy's well-defined eye, bearing down on South Florida. I checked HurricaneCentral.com and saw the bright yellow cone of probable landfall centered on the Dania Cutoff Canal. The consensus in

the chat room was a powerful Category 4 event in our immediate
vicinity with a twenty-foot storm surge, which would put the
ocean seventeen feet above the sidewalk. This was not good news.
I looked out the window at Spot, studied him. I'd read that animals begin acting strangely before a cyclone hits. Spot was lying in
a puddle of sun on the deck. Maybe it was earthquakes I read
about. I told myself I wouldn't leave without Annick, and I immediately felt noble, valiant, and self-sacrificing, and I realized as
well that Annick would snicker at my idea of heroism, and then I
felt embarrassed even though I was alone. You wouldn't think that
could happen.

I called motels, and the few that had rooms didn't take pets, no,
not even in an emergency. So I just lied to the desk clerk at the
Osceola Motel in Valdosta, Georgia, told him I was dogless, even
though he hadn't asked. I reserved our room, but we'd have to
check in by 10 P.M. or they'd rent it out to someone else. I hung up
and then thought what if it's one of those motels where you have
to enter your room through the lobby. I hate getting caught in lies.
I hate sleeping in cars. I closed my eyes and pictured the Osceola.
I saw a red sign out by the street with white letters and a flaming
white arrow piercing the center of the O, and then a one-story,
U-shaped, white concrete building with jalousie windows and two
red tulip chairs outside each room. I was relieved and chose not to
look inside.

I needed to pack what I was going to take, needed to decide
what I would save. I walked around the house and thought first,
What do I want to take? Then: What do I *need* to take? Briefs,
T-shirts, socks. Then: What is irreplaceable? I realized I had a lot
of stuff in my life, most of it you would call junk, evidence of too
much time and money spent on ebay: old scrapbooks, movie
posters, match covers, baseball cards, advertising art, 78 rpm
records, vintage eyeglasses, Viewmaster reels, swizzle sticks. And
so on. I packed my computer and disks, my notebooks and photo
albums. I figured I could get a thousand books in the bed of the

truck. I'd just have to hope it didn't rain. Then I thought, Which thousand? All right, we start with the complete Chekhov. Shakespeare. The Bible. Christ this could take all day. Which Faulkner do I take? Which Tolstoy? Then I realized that Spot, Annick, and I wouldn't all fit in the cab of the truck. We'd have to take Annick's Tercel.

I put valuables in Tupperware containers in the fridge. I called Annick. Today's words were *pasquinade, herl, dornick*. I told her machine I'd be over in fifteen minutes. She should pack. I said, Our lives are at stake here, Annick. I paused. I said, I'm not leaving without you. Then I thought, I hope she hasn't left already. I told Spot we were going for a ride, and he ran to retrieve Barbie from under the deck. On the way to Annick's I saw that the truck was on *E*. I stopped at the Chevron on Federal and waited in line for twenty-five minutes. They had raised the price by a dime since yesterday. Capitalism is not our finest idea.

I drove to the liquor store. Spot waited in the truck. Prakash and Chandra were boarding up the windows. Don was clearing shelves. He said he kind of figured I'd be along, so he'd saved me a bottle of Hennessy behind the counter. Said they were closing up as soon as they stored the booze in the back. Don's about sixty-five, moved here a dozen years ago from Michigan, and lives in a residential motel off Dixie. He has double-vision, which can't be good, but he won't go to a doctor because he doesn't have health insurance. He bought an eye patch at Walgreen's, says he's fine. The headaches have stopped.

Annick still wasn't home. I peeked in her garage. Her car was gone. What if she really *had* evacuated? I enjoy irony as much as the next guy, but to drown while the woman you're trying to save lounges by a pool at the Tallahassee Holiday Inn was more than I could handle. But Annick is responsible. She would not have gone without storing the porch furniture. She's around. I drove home to check messages. Nothing from Annick, but an update from Dad. Seems they'd closed the Fort Lauderdale airport and were flying the planes to safety. I put on the TV. The evacuation of the

Keys was over. Whoever wasn't out, wasn't getting out. Card Sound Road and Route 1 south of Homestead were closed. Helicopter shots of 1-95 showed six lanes of solid traffic heading north. Meanwhile, in breaking news, two Miami mayoral candidates had each claimed the endorsement of little Elian Gonzales.

I sat on Annick's porch, sweating and fuming, thinking how inconsiderate her absence was. I watched the anoles do push-ups, spread their orange throat fans. The sky was cloudless, the air still and steamy. I looked at my watch. I didn't know why I couldn't leave Annick behind exactly, I just knew I couldn't, knew without thinking, not even to save myself or to save Spot. I looked at him sleeping on the lawn, collapsed like dirty laundry in the mottled shade of a mango. I've always had this knowledge—or maybe it's a belief (or maybe there's no difference)—that I would survive any emotional disaster in my life. Like if this really were the end of the affair with Annick, I might be sad, but I'd be okay. Was that what I wanted—to be okay? In order to think this way, I suppose I needed to believe that I was independent and unfettered. Does that mean there's a part of me that can never relax with anyone, never trust anyone, cannot commit and never will? That seemed pathetic. Not that I wanted to fall apart, either. What good would that do? I realized, too, that this reticence, call it, was often perceived by others as a strength and was admired. Ray told me one reason she liked me so much, one thing that attracted her to me in the first place, was that I seemed so aloof, so unapproachable, unknowable, self-contained. When she told me that, I was both flattered and disturbed. Evidently I had no idea who I was. Ray called me "The Island." She called me *"Jean le Fataliste."*

I got the house key from under the plaster lawn gnome (Chomsky, Annick called him). I knocked on the door. Waited. I opened the door, stood inside and yelled hello. No note for me on the kitchen table. No dishes in the sink. Nearly noon. We'd need to leave immediately if we hoped to reach Valdosta by ten in this traffic. I opened the garage, stowed the lawn and porch furniture inside. I took down the wind chimes, the bird feeders, the floral wreath, the chili pepper porch lights. I carried Chomsky inside. I changed my shirt. I saw Annick walking up the street. So did Spot. He ran to her. I waited by the truck.

I was deliriously happy and relieved to see her, but I was also apprehensive and angry though I had no right to be, and I knew that. I said, "Where have you been?" and I knew it sounded more hostile than concerned, which wasn't my conscious intention.

"At the beach."

Spot brought armless Barbie to Annick and dropped the doll at her feet. Annick tossed her, and Spot fetched.

I said, "Don't you know we're facing a catastrophe here?"

"Yes."

What did she mean by that? Had we just slipped into metaphor?

"The hurricane."

"Fritzy."

"And you're out strolling on the beach?"

"Thanks for putting everything in the garage."

"We live in a mandatory evacuation zone."

"So why are you still here?"

"I'm not leaving you."

"You don't owe me anything."

She was being disingenuous. "Come on, Annick, you know I love you." But why couldn't I have said it simply? The declaration without the agitation. I said, "Where's your car?"

"In the shop. Henk says I need a transmission."

"Shit. We'll squeeze in the truck."

"Are you trying to insinuate yourself back into my life?"

"I'd like to think I hadn't left it."

We went inside. We turned on the TV while Annick packed her things. Spot dropped Barbie de Milo on the floor and barked at her. He scrunched down, barked some more. He was angry, perhaps because her head was loose. Officials had already made all lanes northbound on the Turnpike and 95, and already the roads were clogged, traffic was stopped. Five million people trying to get out of Dodge. Cars were stalled—out of fuel and overheated. Fist fights had been reported in several locations, guns fired in Pompano Beach. A ten-car pile-up at Copans Road couldn't be cleared because authorities couldn't get at it. Annick said she'd rather be at home in a hurricane than parked in a truck on the highway.

At this point we had no choice. She told me I could stay. She reminded me that we hadn't made up, hadn't resolved a thing. I said, We'll get married. She said, Don't make fun of me.

"What?"

"You take it all so lightly." She cried. I held her. She said we'd have to talk about it later. Now we have to get ready. We need to fill up every container we can with water. Need to get out the candles, flashlights, batteries. We needed to get to an ATM and take out cash, move the truck away from the trees, check the rain gutters, move everything off the floor that we could, tie cabinet doors shut, and fill the tub with water. I looked at Spot. I said, We can't. Annick smiled. Oh, that's right.

Testimony

Annick and I walked to my place with Spot. We were oppressively cordial, warily chummy. I couldn't stand it. I confessed that I'd been behaving badly, and I apologized. I suppose I thought she would forgive me, would smile, wrap her arm around my waist, lean into my shoulder. She picked up a twig and tossed it ahead for Spot. The thing is I didn't really think I'd been bad, just honest. And now my graciousness was being rebuffed. How dare she?

Omar's house was boarded up, the rental truck was gone. The neighborhood was eerily quiet. Inside, we filled the tub and sinks with water. I filled a cloth book bag with items from my desk: binoculars, pens, eyeglasses, a portable tape player, headphones, a Howard Finster angel *(One day out of a whole lifetime you will die),* scissors, glue sticks, Eva Cassidy and Louvin Brothers tapes, a stopwatch, and a shortwave radio. We locked up and walked to the beach. The lifeguards had gone. We got lunch at Angelo's before it closed. We watched surfers ride the ten-foot swells as we ate. I said,

"Annick, I want to be with you no matter what. And if you want to be married, then I want to be married."

She said, "You just don't get it, do you?"

Strike two.

On the way back to Annick's we spoke to the bridge tender who told us he was locking the bridge down at three, per orders, and heading out to his girlfriend's house in Davie for a hurricane party. We bought Sterno at Publix, figuring even if the power went out, we'd have fondue. I showed Annick the photo of Bigfoot's boy. We bought Little Debbie snack cakes at the Dollar Store.

We watched TV reports of the devastation in the Leewards and in the Turks and Caicos. People stranded out on the parking lot that had been the Turnpike were setting up camps beside the highway. A couple of hundred stranded motorists on 95 had broken into Northeast High School and set up their own unauthorized shelter. Stores had been looted in Hallandale Beach and in Lighthouse Point, and nothing catastrophic had even happened yet. Dolph Diaz, the Channel 10 anchor, said he was going home to take care of his family and walked off the set. I asked Annick why we lived here. She said, The climate. At the Krome Detention Center in west Miami-Dade, the detainees, most of them Haitian refuges, fearing for their lives, had busted through the fence and fled into the Everglades. And then we heard the storm was slowing, strengthening. Estimated landfall in fourteen hours.

We turned off the TV and sat out on the deck. It seemed ridiculous that there was nothing we could do but wait. It started to rain. Radio reports indicated that these rain cells had nothing to do with the hurricane, but we didn't believe them. Annick kissed me. I was grateful, restored. I thanked her. We set up the bathroom which would be our fortification. Candles, the shortwave, a boom box with Puccini CDs, a Coleman lantern, batteries, plastic cups, cognac, Irish whiskey, blankets, water, alarm clock, books, magazines, dog dishes, dog food, dog biscuits, dog nest, dog chewies, what's-left-of-Barbie.

When we were first going out, Annick told me she had been an equestrian in the Big Apple Circus and had dated, had lived with, in fact, the lion tamer, Gunther Something, for three years. So for months I pictured the two of them in their trailer, her in a silky pink, sequined ballerina outfit with a feathery headdress and garish silver eye makeup and him in a one-piece gold-and-black tank-top deal with gold ballet slippers, the both of them, lithe and graceful, walking quickly on tiptoes around the place, stopping once in a while to pose for the other, to toss back their hair, to acknowledge a glance with upraised arms and a grand smile, to bow deeply, sincerely, with the sweep of an arm. This kept me awake at night. I determined to shape up at a gym. I thought it odd that she never wanted to go horseback riding. Then she told me she'd made it all up. Said really she was a meteorologist—not a weather girl—at KENW-TV in Portales, New Mexico. *Light rain showers will continue this morning across much of Southeast New Mexico into the Capitan and northern Sacramento mountains. A few areas of low clouds and fog may reduce visibility. Motorists should use caution.* And I believed that, too, for a while. I even suggested we vacation in her old stamping grounds, told her I had friends in Hobbs we could visit. She laughed, kissed me on the nose, asked me if I'd always been so gullible. I told her I just didn't expect people to lie is all. She said, You lie for a living. I even believed Annick when she told me she'd been abducted by aliens. I mean I believed that she believed she'd been abducted, not that she really had been. We were snuggling on her couch when she confessed. She said she went into the UFO because she was forced to under mind control. She said, "You don't have a choice. I was sleeping, and when I awoke I heard a buzz, and I was paralyzed, and they floated me up and through the ceiling."

I suggested that perhaps she had had a particularly vivid and frightening dream and was unable to separate it from reality just yet. She shook her head. She said, "They like bedrooms, cars, and swamps."

"Then we're safe."

"It's not funny."

Spot climbed onto the couch with us. Annick said that I'd also been abducted. "You have their scar on your wrist."

"I had a tumor removed."

"That's just the memory they implanted." She asked me if I'd ever dreamed of UFOs. I told her that as a kid I'd dreamed that communion wafers were UFOs. She nodded, smiled. She said, "Unexplainable things have happened in your life."

"I suppose . . ."

"You've got sinusitis."

"Yes."

"Have you ever noticed blood on your pillow when you wake up?"

"Yes."

"Have you ever woken up and not realized where you were?"

"Every morning."

"Ringing in your ears?"

"You know I have tinnitus."

"That's what Earth doctors call it. But they don't know what causes it, do they? Or how to cure it?"

Spot rested his head on Annick's lap and stared at me. Annick said, "And you don't remember anything about an abduction, do you?"

"Of course not."

"That seals it."

"You're kidding, right?"

"Do I look like I'm kidding?" She said these aliens were bluish with large heads and large lidless eyes and spindly legs with wide, flat feet. They look like that until you get to the ship. "It's just a disguise, as you can see from our friend here." She patted Spot the Plutonian. He moaned. She laughed.

I felt foolish and relieved. I said, "Were you probed?"

"Not very well."

So I can be excused, perhaps, for what happened next. After we set up the bathroom, we sat on the couch. Annick cried. She told me she'd been a mother once. I thought, Oh, she's good! I said,

"Bigfoot's boy?" She got up and walked into the kitchen. I waited a minute, pictured her in there waiting for me to take the bait. I heard her blowing her nose, sobbing. I went after her. When I said I was sorry, I half-expected her to crack up. Her shoulders trembled instead. I held her, and she told me the story.

She was twenty-seven, not married or engaged, having a difficult pregnancy. Took a leave from teaching. The boyfriend wasn't interested in a child, or in marriage, or in much of anything, really. An optometrist. This was in eastern Pennsylvania, where she grew up. She went into labor a month early. The baby weighed two pounds at birth and lived for two hours. She named him Jonas after her father, who had died when she was fourteen. She told me she still imagined her son alive, still spoke with him. He'd be sixteen.

We lay down on Annick's bed and slept. In my dream I saw a man biting a dog by the nape of the neck, shaking him. I saw men walking upside down on the surface of the water, trees full of perching cats, people with handles on their backs, people floating in air. And I knew if I kept walking I'd see Annick, and I did, and when I reached out to hold her she split into shards of glass and dropped to the ground. Sounded like bells. We woke up with the first crash of thunder and the sound of Spot scratching at the bedroom door.

Miracles

The thunderstorm passed, leaving Spot exhausted. He panted on my lap for a while. Annick sang, "Spot the Magic Setter," his favorite song. I took the mittens off his paws. He hopped out of the tub, drank all the water in his bowl, and collapsed in a heap. The radio report said this line of storms was only a hint of what was to come. Fritzy was nine hours away, wobbling a bit, but still on course for Broward County. Annick and I sat in the tub talking about miracles, which are what Annick figured it would take to get out of this jam. She took a drink of whiskey and passed the cup to me. I told her I didn't believe in miracles. She said walking on water was a miracle. I told her loons walk on water, and Jesus bugs. She said, How about rising from the dead. I said, An oxymoron is not a miracle. I knew I was treading on thin ice. Annick's a practicing Catholic, and she's got a shelf full of books about miracles in her bedroom, books she's had me read. She said what about those stories? "What about the man from Dallas who got a spooky feeling and decided at the last second not to get on that ValuJet flight that crashed into the Everglades?"

I said, "Changing your mind is a decision, not a miracle. Coincidence is not a miracle. Luck is not a miracle. Thinking your dead mother is in the room is not a miracle. A hallucination is not a miracle. An accident is not a miracle. A doctor's misdiagnosis is not a miracle. Finding something you lost ten years ago is good fortune, but not a miracle. Learning from your mistakes is not a miracle. The decision to quit drinking yourself to death is not a miracle. It's a courageous act. Realizing that you've been a ruthless prick all of your life is not a miracle, it's overdue, and you won't change the past or buy your way into heaven by giving your stolen money away because heaven isn't the White House and God doesn't sell pardons."

"You don't believe in God."

"Figure of speech."

"It's always politics with you, isn't it?"

Annick said she didn't care what I thought, but she believed that God put his hand on that fortunate Texan's shoulder and said, Son, don't get on the plane.

I said, "Then you must believe that that same God sent the other two hundred or whatever people to their fiery deaths without a second thought."

Spot raised his head when I raised my voice.

Annick said, "It's a miracle that I'm with you." And I couldn't argue with that. She kissed me, and I realized how wonderful this moment was and how I would be remembering it all my life, the kiss in the tub waiting for the storm, and in that life would be Annick and Spot the Wonder Dog. Lightning flashed through the house. Thunder exploded and the power failed. "Must have hit a substation," I said, not really knowing what I was talking about. Spot whined, woofed, clambered back into the tub, buried his head in my armpit. I lit the lantern and the candles. We settled in for a long night. I poured cups of whiskey. Annick and I played the rhyming game we call *Spot Shot* (a certain dog's photo). She said, "An Asian Attorney General."

"Filipino Janet Reno."

"Presidential Butt."

"Bush Tush."

The next storm lasted twenty minutes or so. I held Spot while he dug into the curve of the tub. We weren't going to get any sleep. We put on Puccini. Spot howled along to "Maid with the Flaxen Hair." We played *Two Truths and a Lie*. Annick went first. I had to guess which of her three stories was the lie.

"Number 1: I was a sophomore in high school, and I had a mad crush on Hilary Bronson, who was gorgeous and troubled. He'd already been to Juvenile Hall. I started smoking to impress him, started playing hooky to be with him. So one afternoon, Hilary and I were in his bedroom, and we had just finished doing it, and I lit up a True Blue, and I asked him, Does this mean that we're going steady?, and he laughed and said he was already going steady with Elaine Gosselin, and I stared at him and twisted the cigarette into my hand, crushed it out, and I didn't feel a thing.

"Number 2: I was a volunteer at the Nescopeck Manor Nursing Home. I ran the balloon volleyball games, organized Manicure Day and like that. One day I read how pets were supposed to be therapeutic for old folks, so I cleared it with the director and called up a dog track in Connecticut and adopted a greyhound. Mr. Bluster. The sweetest dog. Terrified of stairs. We'd get him running down the ward corridor for exercise and he'd slip and fall on his face or else he'd get going and not be able to stop or turn and he'd slide on into the wall. For some reason, the geriatrics didn't take to Mr. Bluster. He brought out the meanness in them. They treated him like the children that had abandoned them. Agnes Timoney chased him with her wheelchair. Archie Ledoux threw his radio at him. Mark Levine beat him over the head with his cane. The director had to go to court over cruelty to animals. I had to have poor Mr. Bluster put down.

"Number 3: I was driving alone to Scranton, and the car radio was busted, so I was singing all the songs I knew, and just when I was singing 'Ruby, don't take your love to town,' the radio starts up—dashboard lights come on and everything—and Kenny Rogers is singing right along with me. When we finished our duet, the radio went off."

I tried to imagine Hilary's bedroom. The broken lamp, the socks balled up under the bed, the pile of elbowed butts in the ashtray, the grit on the yellowed sheets, the busted alarm clock. And Hilary himself: India ink tattoos, acne, mossy teeth. I wanted Hilary to be the lie, but the answer had to be the nursing home. They wouldn't make old folks play balloon volleyball, would they? "Number 2."

Annick laughed. "Number 3. How could a busted-up radio just spontaneously begin to work?"

"Sun spots?"

"Your turn."

I told Annick how one time I came upon a car on fire in the middle of a two-lane road in the piney woods up near Smackover, Arkansas. Flames leaping thirty feet into the air. What was stranger than the fire was that nobody was around. I drove to town and called the Sheriff who thanked me for the heads-up. I asked him what he thought might have happened. He told me not to worry about it.

Then I told her about the night I was in Memphis and couldn't sleep—a loud party going on in the next room at the motel—and I went out for coffee and met Al Green. Sat beside him, said hi. Al introduced himself. He talked about himself in third person and laughed for no reason. He'd be like, "Al don't touch liquor no more," and he'd giggle. Or, "Al owes all that he has to Jesus Christ." When I told him he was my favorite singer, he began to hum, and pretty soon he was singing "Precious Lord" right there in the coffee shop. And then the customers started singing along, and the waitress, and me. Like in a movie.

"Number 3: My first girlfriend Patty was a diabetic, and she let me inject her thigh with insulin."

Annick said three, and she was right, and then she asked me why I would make up such a lame lie and if there really was a Patty at all. There was. She had a small diamond implanted in her front tooth. She was not diabetic. Her father was. Annick shook her head. She said, "'Take Me to the River' Al Green?"

Pressure Drop

During the night, Miss Fritzy inexplicably braked, wheeled around her eye, and drove south—miraculously, if embarrassingly so, according to the National Hurricane Center. Unfortunately, our miracle was Cuba's catastrophe. There had been no official damage reports from the island as yet, but Havana, apparently, had taken a direct hit. It was nearly nine o'clock. When the last storm ended an hour ago, Spot climbed out of our crowded tub, squeezed himself as far behind the toilet as he could, and fell into a fitful sleep. He was snoring now. According to News Radio 99, South Florida highways remained clogged with parked cars, most of them now in snake-infested water up to their chassis. We had missed the worst, but were not out of danger yet. The hurricane continued to spawn bands of severe storms, some of them potentially tornadic. The Governor had declared a State of Emergency, called out the National Guard. Public offices would be closed until further notice. All but essential medical and emergency personnel were to stay at home and off the roads.

I stretched my cramped legs, shifted my weight off my numb left side. Annick woke up, smiled, closed her eyes and nuzzled into the pillow on my chest. During a commercial for Griot King Take-Out, I changed stations to a call-in show. A man claiming to be on a cell phone from Havana described the ruins of the Presidential residence and said that no one inside could have escaped its collapse. The next caller, who identified himself as a representative of both the county government and the Cuban-American National Foundation, said that as soon as rumors of El Jefe's death were confirmed, there would be an official, government-sponsored gala celebration in the Orange Bowl to which citizens would be respectfully asked not to bring weapons or infants. Another gentleman— *first time caller from Hialeah; love your show, Rick*—suggested that even if Fidel were alive, this would be an opportune moment for an invasion. I turned off the radio. Annick said that maybe at long last Cuba would be free.

"To install another dictator," I said.

"Don't be cynical, Johnny."

"They loved Batista."

"They don't love Castro."

"The Miami Cubans don't. And that's because he's smarter than they are, and taller than they are, and more Cuban than they are."

"You wouldn't be talking like this on Calle Ocho."

"That's my point."

"So you're saying that some dictators are okay with you?"

"I'm saying I should hate the son of a bitch, but I don't."

Spot whined to go out. Annick sat up. I stood. My knees hurt. My back hurt. I looked at Spot. He woofed.

"All right already, we'll go out."

Spot sniffed the yard in all the usual places. He lifted his leg against the banana tree, turned his back to it and kicked up some turf with his back legs. I don't know why they even bother. The yard was littered with buttonwood branches, the hibiscus was stripped of its blue and purple flowers. Spot lapped up water from the birdbath. The eastern sky was black, not the serene dark of night, but the ominous green and purple, the bruised black your eye might be if you walked into baseball bat.

The power was out, would be for days it looked like. Annick and I sat at the kitchen counter eating the Little Debbies and drinking bottled water. Spot chewed on the last of Barbie's midriff. Annick told me about her cousin Destiny, how every six years she commits matrimony with some loser or other. Married at sixteen, twenty-two, twenty-eight, thirty-four, forty, forty-six, and fifty-two. Seven husbands, and in between them a series of even more miserable boyfriends. Dope fiends and drunks, batterers and cheaters. She can't seem to learn. I said, Maybe she's looking in the wrong places. Annick said, You think? I said, No need for sarcasm. She said, You're going to use this, I know you are. I said, Destiny Pascal?

"Destiny Pascal Rankin Kennedy Ayer Liechtenstein Chesterfield Smith."

"How do you remember her names?"

"Mnemonic. Despicable Partners Rankle Kin And Leave Cousin Stunned."

I tossed Spot a piece of a snack cake. "You could look at each marriage as a triumph of hope."

"Rankin cheated on her all over Tamaqua and slapped her around when she tried to leave. That's how smart he was. Kennedy defrauded retired people out of their life savings for a living. One night he moved to Bimini with his secretary. Ayer and Chesterfield were heroin addicts. Liechtenstein was a fundamentalist preacher who beat her when she cut her hair. Smith is a drunk."

"What's Destiny do for a living?"

"She's a psychotherapist."

"Is that a joke?"

"And a good psychotherapist. Destiny's the sweetest person I know."

"Where is she now?"

"Lives with Smith in Colorado."

"Denver?"

"Loveland."

"You're making this up."

"Just before each marriage ends, she goes in for surgery. She's had her tummy tucked, her ankles thinned, her varicose veins stripped, her eyes lasered, her nose reshaped, and her tear ducts removed."

"Tear ducts?"

"Said her eyes were always watering, and she was sick of it." Annick brushed crumbs from her lap. "What do you think all the surgery's about?"

I sipped some water. I didn't want to say *low self-esteem* or *self-mutilation* or anything else a psychotherapist might say. I shrugged. Tired of weeping! Where's my pen?

Spot heard the thunder before we did. He sat up and whined. He walked to the sliding glass door and barked at the sky. I said, "Okay, sweet pea, I'll take care of you." I wrapped Annick's cashmere tartan scarf around Spot's ears, tied it under his chin. He quieted. I slipped the Gore-Tex mittens over his front paws, tightened the pull cords. We all got back in the tub. Suddenly it felt like we had peaked on a roller coaster and had just begun free fall. The stomach in the throat business. My ears popped. The thunder was now a continuous rumble and Spot was digging like crazy and crying. I held him. The tub trembled. Our liquor bottles clanged against each other. The radio lifted off the floor and slammed into the wall.

Annick said, "Jesus Christ!"

I said, "Tornado."

Spot leaped out of the tub and ran for the closed door. The door sailed into the living room. The little window above us popped like a champagne cork, and the glass and screen vanished. I remembered reading about a man whose brain had been sucked out his ear by a tornado. Then I remembered we were supposed to drag a mattress in here with us to cover ourselves. The walls groaned and quaked. I remembered, too, that you're supposed to open all the windows in the house to prevent a vacuum from developing, and you're supposed to go to the northwest corner of the house. Or the northeast. Too late for us anyway. I grabbed Annick and lay on top of her. I shouldn't have, but I looked up, saw the walls flex, contract, and topple, and I saw Spot, still scarved and mittened, hovering above us, about where the roof had been, and I called to him as if he could have done anything about it, as if he even could have heard me above the earsplitting roar of the storm. Spot floated away from us like a helium balloon. The furniture in the house skated across the floor, tumbled to the lawn, and rolled down the street. The Goretkin's chiminaya flew over our tub and so did a bicycle, a propane tank, a floor lamp, and a television. And then it stopped. We didn't move. We listened to a silence so intense I was sure my ears were blocked. And then a gas grill dropped into what had been the living room and scared the hell out of us. Annick trembled. I held her, kissed her face a dozen times. We cried and then we smiled. I said, "We should find Spot."

Our radio and lantern were gone, but our bottles of liquor were undamaged. I smiled at Annick. I said, "There *is* a God." She picked up a flashlight, tested it. It worked. The kitchen counter was gone, meaning our batteries were, too. The only piece of Annick's furniture in sight was a single kitchen chair. I set it upright. We had an empty sink and a battered stove, minus an oven door. We discovered a providential case of bottled water where the garage used to be. The Lord giveth and the Lord taketh away. Three clown triggerfish flapped their bodies against the Mexican tile floor. I looked at Annick. She nodded. We plugged the sink, poured in two gallons of water, and released the stunned but grateful fish. We watched them float, bodies bowed, at the surface, saw them right themselves, ripple their lacy fins, and dart madly through the tepid water.

We sat on someone else's plaid sofa in the backyard and surveyed the incomprehensible devastation. Annick cried. The sofa wasn't very comfortable. I checked under the cushions and found several dollars worth of change, a pair of drug-store reading glasses, a TV remote, and a copy of *The Unabridged Journals of Sylvia Plath*. My truck was parked on its side in the next-door neighbor's living room. I hoped that my computer and disks were still in the cab, but I was too afraid to look just yet. I held Annick's hand, and all I could think of was that the worst part of this would be all the standing in all the lines at all the agencies that I'd be doing, all the forms I'd have to fill out, all the calls I'd have to make, all the paperwork and rigmarole involved in getting my life and Annick's life back to normal. And that's when I remembered that triggerfish live in salt water. I decided not to tell Annick. I called to Spot. I whistled. Annick said he'd be okay.

We spent the rest of the morning and the afternoon wandering the neighborhood calling to Spot. We seemed to be the only fools who hadn't evacuated. I found a replacement for my torn shirt in a pile of clothes on Harding Street— a Delta State University T-shirt: The fighting Okra. We stepped around power lines, fallen banyans, appliances, and household debris. What on earth were we all going to do without homes or possessions? Annick found a portable radio, and we sat on a houseless porch and listened. The tornado had leveled everything east of Federal Highway in Hollywood and Dania Beach. The highways were still parking lots and now the secondary roads in and out were blocked. We told ourselves it wouldn't be looting to take the radio. Annick tapped my leg. Look, she said. Two chimpanzees walked down the street holding hands. When they saw us they stopped and hugged each other. One of them bared its teeth. Then they fled across the golf course toward the water treatment plant.

When we rounded the corner to my street, I half-expected to see Spot waiting for us. When he left Annick's house he'd been flying in this direction. I still had a deck and a Solo-flex, a washer and dryer, an armoire with a TV in the cabinet, bookcases but no books. We found my tent underneath someone else's Barcalounger. The smart thing to do was to get out of there. Walk to the beach and follow it south until we found a hotel that would take us in. Annick said, We're not leaving Spot. I said, If we haven't found him by tomorrow, we'll have to go.

Annick set up the tent in the front of the house while I walked back to her house for water, liquor, and my computer. I made part of the trip back in an E-Z-Go golf cart I found by the Publix. I got back around dusk. Annick had a campfire going. She'd found sheets and pillows for the tent. At least we'd be safe from mosquitoes and sand fleas, from water snakes, roof rats, and God knows what all else. I told her we should just move. She said we couldn't.

We still had mortgages. We still owned the property. We'd have to rebuild and then sell and then move. I said if we both sold our houses we could buy a palace in some place more placid and less congested. She said, Montana. I said I didn't want to be cold. We drank cognac, listened to the radio. Castro had been seen on the devastated streets of Havana. In Bangladesh, 100,000 people had been killed in monsoon floods. In Boston, the Red Sox drove for the pennant. In France, union leaders had called for a general strike. We turned off the radio. We heard a helicopter somewhere nearby, and when that faded, the snore of tree frogs, and the exuberant call of a whippoorwill.

I thought about my pitiful collection of shoes and how years from now some kid kayaking through the mangroves will notice a curious, single, salt-stained, penny loafer wedged into the prop roots, and he'll stop rowing and stare at it, and he'll make up a story about how it came to be there, how one afternoon this junior at South Broward High found out that his girlfriend, his steady girlfriend, his steady, lavaliered girlfriend, was dumping him for a senior who was also the assistant night manager at Pollo Tropical, and how the spurned boy couldn't stand it anymore and started running like mad and eventually found himself sloshing through the swamp, wondering how he got there, and then he lost his shoe in the muck, and the shoe was lifted by the rising tide and floated down the inlet and dropped here, where it may have gone unnoticed forever, except that he, the innocent kayaker, happened along—he could have gone to the beach instead this morning—and happened to be just here when a mangrove crab flashed its white pincer from the cradle of the shoe.

I realized I had been unburdened of the stress and responsibility of proprietorship. I now owned nothing, and I felt reborn. I smiled at Annick. I understood that I was buoyant because I was with her. Privation is not something I could bear alone. In the end, all we have is who we love. My past had vanished, as it were, and now I could be anyone. Annick said, "Did you hear that?"

"What?"

"Listen."

I didn't hear anything.

"Jangling."

I shook my head.

"Like sleigh bells."

Coming from down the street. And then we saw a dim light about a foot or so off the ground, bobbing in time with the jingle.

I said, "Goddam."

"What the hell?"

It looked to be a faint halo, and iridescent, a scintillating glow. I got the flashlight, shined it at the apparition, and then I saw him, Spot the sundog bounding toward us with Los Alamos Barbie gripped in his jaw. He ran right past us, the plaid scarf now trailing rakishly behind him, one mitten on, one mitten off. He circled the tent, the campfire. He dropped luminescent Barbie and rolled on his back, squirmed like a fish, exploded to his feet, shook himself like he'd just stepped out of a swimming pool, and dashed into our arms. We petted him, accepted his messy kisses, told him how worried we had been, how happy we were. I threw another Mission end table on the fire. We all crammed into the tent. Spot lay between us, panting, drooling. Then he told us how he'd flown over West Lake and landed in a cushion of fallen Australian pines. Came by earlier, but we weren't here. He caught his breath, licked our faces, crawled out from between us, and curled into a ball like a roly-poly at our feet. I snuggled into Annick. She kissed my nose. Spot woofed. No more storms, he said. The three of us, we got to get out of here.

John Dufresne is a professor in the Masters
Creative Writing Program at Florida
International University. He has won the *Yankee*
magazine award for fiction, the *Transatlantic*
Review/Henfield Foundation Award, a PEN
Syndicated Fiction award. His novel *Louisiana*
Power and Light was a Barnes & Noble Discover
Great New Writers selection and a *New York*
Times Notable Book of the Year, 1994. He is also the author of a short-
story collection, *The Way That Water Enters Stone*, and the novels *Love*
Warps the Mind a Little (also a *New York Times* Notable Book of the Year,
1997) and *Deep in the Shade of Paradise*. His stories have appeared in
numerous literary journals, including *Mississippi Reivew*, *Missouri Review*,
and the *Greensboro Review*. He is one of the thirteen authors of the
mystery novel *Naked Came the Manatee*.

J. TOMAS LOPEZ

*I wanted to write about South Florida, a place I've lived for thirteen years,
so that I could begin to understand it. Fiction writers in South Florida
can't compete with daily life here. You already know that we can't figure out
how to vote. We've lost five hundred children in our welfare system. Right
now a hospital is accusing labor organizers of using voodoo to frighten the
workers into voting for union representation. A recent Miami police chief/city
manager was arrested for stealing money from the Do the Right Thing
Foundation so he could buy tickets to Marlin games and nights out with his
mistress. I can't make stuff like that up; you'd never believe it. Fiction has to
make sense. So I'd write a domestic story about a man and his dog. A man,
his dog, and his currently estranged girlfriend. Maybe the man's like me and
he wants to know what he's doing here. Spot's terrified of storms. Johnny
spends four months a year worried that we'll be clobbered by another
hurricane. He saw what happened when Andrew blew through here, and he
doesn't sleep well in storm season. He could lose everything.*

Lucy Corin

RICH PEOPLE

(from *Shenandoah*)

I went to the beach with Jennifer, with her parents and their house. They're rich. I said, "what's that" in the refrigerator, and she said, "paté" and took out a Coke I think it was, and closed the door. Which got me curious, so I waited through three days of meals and snacks for the paté to come out so I could eat some, and we ate *lots* of other things, a lot of fish, of course, and hamburgers with potato chips, and eggs, but then it was going to be my last day there and I'd hinted a couple times. We'd be eating something and I'd be sure to say, "would paté go with this?" But no paté. So I snuck down to the kitchen to look at it in the night. On the way I walked very carefully, so that by the time I got down the hall and to the stairs I could kind of tell where the stairs were, and I leaned a lot on the banister in case any of the steps creaked, but either I did a good job or there weren't any creaks. I got to the living room and edged myself along, touching one cushy chair and then the next, sliding one foot at a time ahead of me. In the kitchen, opening the refrigerator made the bottles in the door rattle. Light gushed onto the floor. I squatted and held the door open with my knee, and I took the paté out. It was wrapped in cellophane on a little plate with blue flowers. It was the shape of a fat slice of bread, and I tried to think of how to eat it.

I had to move to the counter and the refrigerator door shook closed. I turned on the light under the sink. I took out another small plate. I put the plate of paté next to the plate. I took a butter knife and trimmed around it, keeping the shape, depositing the slivers of meat onto the other plate, which was white with small blue flowers, like the one from the refrigerator. I ate the slivers, there over the sink, my hands bright, the gray meat faintly, faintly pink in places. When I looked back at the paté in the light that lit the clean sink I could not believe anyone could look at that piece of loaf and believe it. Jennifer, and her mom and dad, and her brother and his fiancée, and the fiancée's parents, and a couple guys the two of them knew from college who also lived near them in Manhattan now, all of them sleeping upstairs except for one of the guys who was asleep in the living room on the sofa, which I didn't know at the time but would know the next morning because he slept through breakfast, almost— all of them, they'd see a country mouse had nibbled at the paté with a butter knife, all around.

With a thumping heart I pulled the sliding glass door open to the ocean, and the wave sounds bounded into the house. I ran to the ocean in the romantic night and threw the paté as far as I could, using the plate to throw it into the dark. The moon was overhead, and the plate was over my head in my hand. Of course there was no splash, and I could have tossed the paté on bare sand for all I knew, but in my panic and shame it was all I'd thought to do.

It had been delicious. It had been more delicious than William Carlos Williams's plum. Because it was yours, but also because it was *complicated*.

I slipped the cellophane into the trash can, beneath other pieces of garbage. I went to bed in the room with Jennifer, with the twin beds and matching everything.

In the rush of people making breakfast I retrieved the two plates and the butter knife from my suitcase and slipped them into the sink with the dishes already accumulating. I put the butter knife at my place as I helped Jennifer set the table. "That's dirty. Get another," she said. The dishes slid around in the sink with their blue-flowered sisters and cousins. No one mentioned the paté, which it seems had already disappeared into the history of all the other things the family might or might not have eaten.

Lucy Corin's first novel, *Everyday Psychokillers: A History for Girls,* will be published in 2004. Her short stories have recently appeared in *Shenandoah, Ploughshares, The Southern Review,* and the Serpent's Tail anthology *Strictly Casual: Women on Love.* A story from *Mid-American Review* was included in the 1997 edition of *New Stories from the South.*

RIC O'CONNELL

I wrote this story for my best friend, Kristin Bergen. She called me a country mouse once. We went to the beach and spent one day walking around town with our dogs on leashes, looking at all the new and hideous mansions. One was marble. I was thinking about another time I'd been a guest at someone else's family beach house. I was fourteen and came downstairs in the night in my nightshirt to get a glass of water or something from the kitchen and my friend's father was in the living room. We said, "Hi," I think. In the morning his wife accused me of being sleazy. I was thinking, among other things, about the horror of finding you don't know the rules. Still, that's not something I knew until I wrote the little story. I wrote the story because indeed there was paté in Kristin's refrigerator, it's true that I wanted it, and that's when I thought of the plum.

Brad Vice

REPORT FROM JUNCTION

(from *The Atlantic Monthly*)

L ate in the afternoon Kurt Schaffer rides on his roan gelding up to his uncle Pleasant's feedstore, only to find that the old man has already left for the hospital in Johnson City, to visit his sick wife. Kurt doesn't much care for filling in at the feedstore. The public life of a merchant doesn't appeal to him. He prefers the solitary existence of working cattle on his father's ranch, or the excitement of playing football on the weekends. Working at the store means that he can become locked into pointless conversations; he's at the mercy of any son of a bitch with six bits for a bag of Ripsnorter sweetfeed.

The feedstore is only a mile or so away from the abandoned courthouse in Blanco. The county seat moved to Johnson City years ago. The year is 1954 and the Blanco River is dry. All of Texas is four years into a drought that has caused everything that was once green to turn brown, curl up, and blow away. The only vegetation that remains consists of a few mesquite trees, honey locust, and oceans of short cactus. Kurt will be a sophomore at Texas A&M before rain falls on his home again. That same year the Aggies will win their first Southwest Conference championship in fifteen years. But right now Kurt is beginning his last year of high school, and the Aggies are perennial losers. Even so, he has heard rumors that things are about to change for A&M. The newspaper reported last week that the new head coach, Paul "Bear" Bryant, is determined to institute an extreme brand of spartan military discipline.

Nine days ago Bryant drove his new team deep into the desert, to a place called Junction, where the team has been housed in abandoned military barracks. The players practice all day in a field of sand and clay drawn off in chalk lines, and they tackle one another atop jagged rocks and prickly pears. Denied water for hours at a time, the team continues to run and block and tackle no matter what. The boys carry on with sprained knees, dislocated shoulders, broken noses, broken ribs. According to the newspaper, hardly a man among them is still whole.

A syndicated columnist uses words like "bone-crushing" and "inhumane." He describes the players as "bloody" and "mangled" and compares them to soldiers on the Bataan Death March or to concentration-camp victims. Two days ago one of the players, Drake Goetze, a center from Paris, fell out with heatstroke and almost died of a heart attack. Pushed beyond their endurance, other members of the team have simply fled, sneaking out of the oven-like Quonset huts in the middle of the night in order to hitchhike away. Every day the reporter gives an update on the gruesome situation and publishes a list of names—the quitters. Originally a hundred and eleven players, the team has been reduced to around forty, and still the practice continues. Kurt vows to himself that next year, when his time comes to ride out into the desert, his name will not be printed in such a list. By the time he finishes next year's training camp under this new slave-driving coach, his daddy's ranch will have gone under, and maybe his uncle's feedstore, too. His aunt April will probably be dead, and his family may well have moved away from their home in Blanco County forever. At any rate Kurt will not quit, because he will have nothing to go back to.

T-Willy, Uncle Pleas's World War I buddy, walks out from the shadowy doorway onto the porch of the feedstore as Kurt ties his horse to one of the support beams. "Kurt, where in the heck have you been? Pleas was expecting you an hour ago."

Kurt isn't in the mood to be talked down to, especially by the likes of T-Willy. Kurt has spent the entire morning riding fence, and he's tired and disgusted. He goes about the business of unsaddling the roan without so much as a hello. Kurt needs help, but he won't ask for it. The horse stepped on his left hand a few days ago, and the last three fingers are broken and taped together, the nails black and split. Kurt has always been a little suspicious of T-Willy, partly because the old man's a half-breed: part German, part Mexican. But mostly Kurt dislikes T-Willy because he's never seen the old man do a hard day's work. He just sits here in the feedstore with the fans on him, drinking whiskey, smoking cigarettes, and playing checkers with Pleas, living off the skinny tit of a soldier's pension. Instead of asking for the old man's aid, Kurt grips the saddle horn tightly with his thumb and forefinger and manages to drag the saddle down off the horse's back without dropping it.

"You know I'm too down in my back to load up anybody's truck. I don't even know how to open up that cash register in there."

"Everybody pays with credit anyway," Kurt says. "Has anybody been in today?"

"Not since Pleas left."

"Well, then, it hasn't been a problem, now has it?"

"You worried Pleas. That's the damn problem. He doesn't need any more of that."

Kurt lays the saddle on the railing of the porch and then drapes a froth-soaked blanket matted with horsehair next to it. A saddle-shaped sweat outline on the gelding's back is already beginning to evaporate in the sun. Next Kurt takes his father's .45-caliber cavalry revolver out of his jeans and places it in the saddlebag in exchange for a pick, which he will use to clean the rocks and dung out of the horse's hooves. Every morning for the past two years Kurt has risen well before sunrise, put on his work clothes and a baseball cap, saddled up the roan, and ridden five or ten miles around the perimeter of his daddy's property. He carries the .45 in order to put water-starved cattle out of their misery. He has killed dozens since the beginning of the long, cruel summer—so many that he has begun to think of himself as the ranch's executioner, a kind of resident Angel of Death bringing peace to all the wretched animals the land will not support. And the job is getting to him.

Last week was the worst. Riding across the northeast corner of the ranch, Kurt spotted a pack of turkey buzzards wheeling in the cloudless morning light. He figured they were circling more dead cattle. But as he came closer, he could see that the head of one of his daddy's prostrate Herefords was still moving; the animal was beating itself senseless in the dust. Kurt kicked the gelding and charged up to a gruesome sight: unwilling to wait for death, the buzzards had just picked out the Hereford's eyes. Two or three of the birds bobbled with the strewn sticky nerves; the others tapped their beaks into the hollow sockets of the Hereford's skull. Kurt unloaded the pistol, killing one buzzard on the ground and two others in midair before the reports chased the rest out of range.

"Take off, you sons a bitches!" Kurt screamed, pointing the empty gun up in the air. Then he got off the horse and looked down at the savaged remains of the cow. It was all he could do to keep from vomiting. The cow stared blindly at him out of one of the upturned holes in her skull. The other side of her face she rubbed violently on the ground, her black tongue caking with dust. Kurt cursed himself for continuing to shoot after the buzzards were out of range. He had to reload in order to put the tortured Hereford out of her misery.

Nervous, the horse turned its hindquarters away from Kurt as he snatched up the reins. Kurt stuck the gun in his jeans so that he could fiddle around in the saddlebag while the horse's backside continued to drift away from him. Kurt jerked down hard on the reins to stop the horse from moving; the bit clenched against the roan's jaw, scaring him still. The horse laid his ears flat back on his head and shivered. It seemed to take forever for Kurt to find the box of shells. When he finally did, he let go of the reins, drew the gun, and fumbled with the pin that released the revolver's chamber. He dropped both the gun and the box of shells, and the bullets spilled out on the ground. Kurt fell to his knees and lurched for the revolver with his right hand. The ammunition rolled between the fetlocks of the roan. Without thinking, Kurt extended his hand, and the nervous roan stepped backward in retreat. The horse's front hoof landed squarely on Kurt's fingers. For a hellish moment the hand was simply stuck under the horse, and there was nothing Kurt could do to move it. The horse could have easily reared up and trampled him to death or turned and kicked Kurt in the head with one of his powerful back legs. All Kurt could do was stare at his crushed hand pinned to the ground, and think to himself, *Oh, my God. She is still alive. She is still alive.*

Kurt replays the bloody scene with the buzzards over and over in his brain as he lifts up one leg of the roan and scrapes debris out of the V-shaped groove in its hoof.

"Goddamn," T-Willy says, trying to start up the conversation again. "I do believe this drought is rougher than the one in the thirties. If it don't rain soon, every rancher from Austin to New Mexico will be broke."

"You reckon?" Kurt asks, rolling his eyes. Now that he is here to keep an eye on the store, he wishes the old man would go away. Kurt knows as well as anyone what's going to happen to the ranchers from Austin to New Mexico. It will only be a matter of months before his own daddy goes under, and when enough people like Kurt's daddy go broke, his uncle's feedstore will go broke, and the banks will take everything.

The day Kurt shot the Hereford, he returned home from his morning ride to eat breakfast. Instead of eating, he poured himself a cup of coffee and went outside on the front porch to drink it. His father rose from the kitchen table, where he had been picking at a mixture of eggs and hog brains, and followed. Kurt had already wrapped his fingers in a blue bandana.

"What happened to your hand, boy?"

Kurt hesitated only a moment before he told his father the story of the buzzards' monstrous attack. He almost cried when he came to the part about having to wait on the roan to release his hand. "It was stupid. Plain old stupid."

"I want you to know something, Kurt," his father said. "Something no one else knows yet. When you move off to College Station in the fall, I'm selling everything but the goats." Kurt's father seized his shoulder so hard that the boy almost dropped his coffee cup. "You're old enough to be on your own now, Kurt. Don't screw up your scholarship, son, because from here on out you're going to have to be responsible for yourself." His father lowered his gaze. "I'm sorry, I had to say that."

Kurt keeps his back to T-Willy as he grooms the gelding. He doesn't need a shiftless old man to tell him about hard times. "Why don't you try giving your mouth a rest for a little while," he says.

"Kurt, I'll swan," T-Willy says, scratching his curly gray head in wonder. "You are the aggravatinest thing I ever run across." He sits down in a rocking chair. "I hope somebody pops that fresh mouth of yours for you when you go off to school next year." The old man starts rolling a cigarette. It's not a pretty sight. First he takes his teeth out and sets them in his lap. After he has rolled up the tobacco, his wormy tongue peeks out of its toothless cave to seal the paper.

Kurt hates the idea of getting old. He runs his left hand up the buttons of his chambray work shirt and scratches his stomach, which is flat and hard, though a little black pit of fear rests under the muscles. His only physical imperfection is a scar under his left eye, a white star puncture wound, a memento from Kurt's childhood when he fell off a Shetland pony and landed facefirst onto a barbed wire fence. His coordination is better now; he has power and agility.

Kurt is tough and mean, but a bit of a runt. Because he works so hard on the ranch, he can't keep weight on. At 165 pounds, he is really too light to play college ball; A&M was one of the few major universities that offered him a scholarship. Jess Neely, at Rice, made him an offer, but the ties and jackets that Rice students have to wear to class are expensive. A military institute, Texas A&M provides uniforms. But if the news reports from Junction are true, Kurt will most likely get bounced around pretty good when his turn comes to practice in the desert, and he wonders if he has made the wrong decision. He will never have the luxury of backing down from a fight, or even the chance to rise casually from a pile-up. He must never allow himself to dog it, not even a little, when running the gassers or playing bull-in-the-ring. Kurt must positively shine with hustle and aggression if he hopes to win a position; otherwise, he will find himself riding the pine in the fall, and will maybe lose the chance to renew the scholarship.

"You have to act like a banty rooster." This is what his father, who is fond of cockfighting and boxing metaphors, tells him. "Half the size but twice as mean. That's you, Kurt." Sometimes before a tough game Kurt likes to hop himself up on white cross and bennies, cheap trucker speed that makes his brain itch and his teeth ache, but the pills keep him immune to fatigue or pain. Now he is so tired from working on the ranch that he wishes he had something with a little pep to keep him going. Then Kurt remembers that T-Willy usually carries more-soothing medicine.

"T-Willy, you got your bottle on you?"

T-Willy looks sideways, like he's thinking about holding a grudge, but then he grins, reaches into his overalls, and hands the kid the bottle. "Take it easy on that stuff."

Kurt takes a mighty swig from the bottle. It doesn't taste like whiskey—more like sweet wine—but it's still hot and strong like liquor. "Damn, what is this?" he says.

"They call it peach beer. It's brandy made with peach peels. My cousin sent it to me from Georgia. Ain't it smooth?"

Kurt grunts and takes another slug.

"Here, you best hand that back. Here comes your uncle. He'll have my hide if he knows I'm getting you drunk."

Kurt hands the bottle back as he spies a green Ford speeding toward the feedstore from Johnson City. But it's going much too fast to be Kurt's uncle, a cautious driver who rarely gets above 50 mph.

As the truck comes closer to the store, Kurt can see that it is similar to his uncle's but much newer; even through all the dust the chrome trim glimmers. T-Willy finishes his cigarette and replaces his teeth.

The truck pulls into the drive, runs right up next to the roan, and parks. Right off Kurt is sore with the driver, who doesn't think enough of his horse to park a few yards away. If the roan weren't gelded, it might have gotten nervous and reared up and possibly fallen over and hurt itself. More likely, it would have kicked the shit out of the shiny new truck and split a hoof. But the roan is tired too, so it simply pulls back on its halter and gives a shivering nicker. Kurt doesn't recognize the driver, which means he must be from pretty far off. When he steps out, Kurt sees that he's a big man, well over six feet tall and thick in the middle. He has a red moustache, and he's wearing an expensive Stetson, and a denim work shirt that is altogether too clean. A little blonde girl in pigtails, no more than seven and wearing brown overalls, jumps out of the passenger seat. The wind shifts, and even before the stranger has slammed the door of his truck, Kurt can smell that they have brought something with them, something that has been in the sun too long.

T-Willy, delighted to see the little girl, hunkers down in his chair and says, "Hey there, cowgirl, who you got there with you?"

"My daddy," she says, with an adult seriousness. Then she moves behind her father, so that she is difficult to see.

The man with the red moustache gives T-Willy an apologetic look and then turns to Kurt. "Pleas ain't here, is he?"

"Nope." Kurt shakes his head. "He's in Johnson City."

The stranger looks disappointed. "Would you mind coming over here and looking at something for me?"

Kurt and T-Willy exchange looks; then Kurt nods and walks to the back of the truck. The man lowers the tailgate, frowning. On top of a bed of canvas fertilizer sacks lies a newborn Red Angus bull, no more than a day or two old, and by the looks of it, the calf has spent a considerable amount of that time suffering out in the heat. It hasn't been licked clean. Dried afterbirth has crusted around its eyes and nostrils; its hide is matted with dried blood. Its nose is dull and pink. Already flies are gathering around the calf, lighting near its eyes and in the folds of its nostrils and on the umbilical cord. It is so tiny that it looks more like an orphaned fawn than a calf. The bull breathes slowly, dehydrated, too weak to even lift its head.

The little girl climbs on top of the back wheel and stands on tiptoes so that she can peer over into the bed and get a closer look. She smiles at Kurt. "His name is Chester."

The father turns to Kurt. "I can't figure why his momma don't want him. I guess it just happens that way sometimes."

"Lack of water," T-Willy offers. "It does things to their head. Makes cows plumb crazy. Or it might have been her first one and she didn't know what to do with it. That happens too."

"Look, my cousin's the cattleman, but he left town this morning. I just found this little fellow laying out near some brush not far from the house. I don't really know what to do with him. Somebody told me you can buy powdered milk here. Is that true?"

Kurt nods and walks up onto the porch and through the dark doorway of the store. He is almost bowled over by the rich smell of corn, oats, and molasses. He moves past stacks of crushed hay and cracked-corn feed, past the protein pellets and a pyramid of red salt blocks, all the way to the back of the store, where a few fifty-pound bags of powdered milk are stacked atop one another. Kurt selects one marked "Milk Starter"; it contains colostrum, the first milk a cow gives after birth, a thin, yellowish fluid full of minerals. Other bags are marked "Milk Replacer"—the hindmilk, the white milk.

Both the milk starter and the milk replacer are old. Since the drought most people don't bother trying to save an individual calf. Kurt shoulders the sack of colostrum and grabs a liter milk bottle off the shelf. The milk bottle is equipped with a long, vulgar-looking three-inch nipple that resembles a little boy's penis, pink and stiff. While Kurt is working in the back, he can barely make out the conversation T-Willy is having with the little girl's father. The man's name is something or other Dougan or Cougan, and he is an oilman, an executive, from Houston. But his relations live here in Blanco County. Walking back toward the doorway Kurt clearly hears the oilman say, "My cousin Bill wants me to buy in on his ranch, so I came to check the place out."

Kurt finds himself wishing that his father had some rich relatives, but his relatives are no different from himself, third- or fourth-generation Krauts, here from the time when Texas was still a part of Mexico.

Before Kurt can get back outside, T-Willy starts running his mouth about Aunt April, gossiping about her diabetic stroke, her blindness, how in all likelihood the doctors will have to amputate her legs, things he shouldn't speak about with strangers—with anyone. When Kurt gets out the door, he interrupts the conversation. "Here you go," he says, throwing the powdered milk onto the tailgate and setting the milk bottle on top of it.

"Mr. Cougan here is thinking about buying into Bill Worley's operation," T-Willy says. "They're cousins."

"Is that so?" Kurt says, not really asking. "You want me to show you how this works?"

"I'd appreciate that." Cougan tips his hat, cowboy style.

The little girl, still standing on the Ford's back tire, starts bouncing up and down, rocking the bed of the truck. She's so excited that Kurt can't help smirking. The poor girl must have lived all her life in the city.

Kurt pulls the drawstring on the powdered-milk sack and then steps up into the truck, seizes the tiny bull by the ears, and drags him to the tailgate. Cougan's daughter jumps off her tire and runs to the back of the truck so that she can watch what is about to take place. Kurt unscrews the nipple on the giant baby bottle and scoops about a cup of formula into the thick glass.

"What happened to your fingers?" Cougan's daughter is staring at the mess attached to his left hand.

"Damn, Katharine, that ain't polite."

For the first time all day Kurt laughs. "That's okay. She's just curious." But Kurt is unwilling to tell the real story behind his broken fingers, so he says, "Playing football."

"Football?" Cougan's eyes brighten. "You Kurt Schaffer?"

Kurt nods.

"You gonna be a redshirt Aggie next year?"

"Yep."

"Shoot, boy, I hope you're ready for one tough season. I hear that Bryant fellow works his players into the ground. He did it at Kentucky, too. That's why the Aggies got him. But from the way people talk, shit, he'll be lucky if he don't end up killing somebody. I read in the newspaper he's run off all but thirty-six men. You know, that boy from Paris is still in the hospital. If Bryant don't take those boys home soon, he won't have enough players left to field a team."

"Can we feed Chester now?" Katharine asks, impatient.

Kurt hands the milk bottle with the yellow powder in it to Katharine. "There's a bathroom inside the store. Go past the cash register, past the horse tack and harness, and turn right. Can you fill this up with hot water for me?"

Katharine says she can.

"Run the tap till it gets real hot, okay?" Kurt turns to Cougan. "Do you still have that newspaper on you?"

Cougan retrieves the local paper from the truck cab and hands it to Kurt. Kurt turns to the sports section and scans the headlines until he finds "REPORT FROM JUNCTION," by Allen Wier. The article recounts yet another hellish practice, a day full of blood and sand. At one point Wier describes a confrontation between Bryant and the father of Drake Goetze, the heatstroke victim from Paris. Goetze's parents had come to collect their son from the Junction infirmary. Because of his weak heart, they have demanded that Goetze never play another down of football. The article ends with a brief interview with the coach, in which Bryant's only comment on the matter is "If a boy is a quitter, I want to find out about it now, not in the fourth quarter." Then comes the list of four new names. Goetze's is among them, and this makes Kurt angry. If the boy had died on the practice field, would the papers have called him a quitter then, too? Kurt lowers the paper and looks at the bloody, flop-eared calf shivering in the sun, drawing flies.

He picks up the long pink nipple and pinches the tip. A tiny hole opens up through the thick rubber. "Those bastards at whatever factory makes these things should be shot. You leave it like this and the poor calf just winds up sucking air. Hey, T-Willy, you got your pocket knife on you?"

"Uh-huh."

"Toss it here."

Kurt catches the knife with his right hand and flicks open the blade. Cougan watches him curiously as Kurt slashes a little X into the top of the nipple and then inserts the tip of the blade into the tiny hole, coring it out. When Katharine returns, Kurt takes the bottle away from her, caps it, and shakes vigorously. Sitting down next to the calf, he grabs it by the neck and allows some of the colostrum to dribble onto the calf's tongue. Blackish placenta smears across the young man's shirt as he slips the nipple into the calf's mouth. The calf gags and regurgitates the milk into Kurt's lap. Soaked, Kurt smells like a mixture of chalk and eggs. He curses.

"You think he's too far gone?" Cougan asks.

"Nope. He just don't know how to suck yet. He'll get a taste for it in a second."

Kurt dribbles more of the milk into the calf's mouth. Instead of trying to make the calf nurse the bottle, he massages its throat, forcing it to swallow. He does this three times, and after the third attempt the calf gives a guttural cough as the milk slides down. Kurt puts the little bull in a headlock in order to keep its head elevated, and this time the calf offers a blind attack on the nipple, eventually sucking the milk.

When Kurt was a kid, before powdered milk and baby bottles were made for livestock, if a momma cow ever abandoned her calf, Kurt's grandfather would milk another cow, mix that milk with a raw egg, and use a kitchen funnel to pour the enriched liquid into a drenching bottle. A drenching bottle looked like a wine bottle but had a much longer neck. The old man would have Kurt tie a rope around the calf's neck and throw it over a rafter in order to elevate the calf's head. Then Kurt's grandfather would stick the long glass neck of the drenching bottle into the calf's mouth and down its throat, forcing it to swallow the thick milk.

It makes Kurt feel good to think about the days when his grandfather was still around, and everything was glistening and green as far as the eye could see. Kurt hugs the nursing calf in the headlock for quite a while. The little bull rubs its body up against the boy as he daydreams. Eventually the calf finds strength enough to bob its head a little, as if it were punching its mother's udder.

Kurt grins and pulls the bottle away. Katharine looks on in amazement. "Can I feed him?" she asks.

"Sure." Kurt nods, and asks her father to put her up on the tailgate. Kurt hands her the bottle. She stands on the tailgate, holding the bottle outward. Milk drips near her feet as Kurt picks up the calf and holds its face to the streaming nipple. Kurt starts to tell the little girl to tilt the bottle up high, so that the calf won't have any problem swallowing. Then he feels something move through the fingers on his good hand. He looks down to find several translucent worms, less than a quarter of an inch long, working their way through the caked-up corner of the calf's right eye. Kurt pulls the calf away from the nipple, flips it on its side, and brushes its eyes clean just in time to spot more maggots boiling up from the pink sores behind the eyelashes.

"Oh, hell."

"What's the matter?" Cougan asks.

"Man, your bull here's got the screwworms." Even when things were green, screwworms had been a problem for newborns. Screwworms are the larvae of blue-bellied blowflies, which lay their eggs in the wounded flesh of living animals. Kurt knows that some of the worms have probably already burrowed deep into the calf's body, and soon they will screw themselves into its vital organs and suck the life right out of it. In fact, with worms already on the calf's head, the maggots will most likely screw themselves into its brain and drive it completely mad before they exit back through its eyes. Kurt has never seen flies blow into the eyes before, although he has heard that they can blow inside the nose. Usually the flies lay their eggs in the navel of a newborn. This can be easily treated, by mixing kerosene and lard into a balm and applying it to the stomach. The kerosene kills the worms while the lard holds the chemical solution in place. But Kurt quickly realizes that putting kerosene on the sores around the calf's eyes will blind it.

"Look, uh, Mr. Cougan." Kurt weighs his words carefully, not wanting to upset the little girl. "You best leave Chester here with me. It'll probably be better if I take care of him myself."

"But, Daddy, you promised—you promised I could take care of him," the girl begs. "We need to take Chester back to Uncle Bill's with us. Please."

Cougan's eyes dart back and forth between Kurt and his daughter. "Actually, son, she's right. It ain't my calf to leave. It's my cousin's. He'll know what to do with him."

T-Willy attempts to intercede in Kurt's behalf. "I don't think you understand what the boy here is saying. That calf is in a lot of pain. It ain't going to get much better."

Cougan's eyes are fixed on Katharine, who is on the verge of tears.

Kurt lays the calf's head down on the tailgate to rest. "I'm telling you he's done for," he says. "There ain't no sense in dragging it out."

That does it. Katharine's face goes down into her hands, and she sobs.

Cougan puts his arm around her and cuts Kurt an evil look. "Well, son, why don't you let me be the judge of that." Then he whispers down to his daughter, "It's all right, honey. We'll take Chester home to Uncle Bill." Cougan cuddles the little girl, gently pressing her face into the swell of his broad stomach.

Kurt glances at the calf. The poor creature is shaking in pain, unable even to lick the yellow regurgitated milk off its nose. Kurt turns back to the rich oilman and his weeping daughter, her tears the only stain on his crisp, clean shirt. "Why, you silly son of a bitch."

Katharine stops crying. T-Willy winces. Cougan's expression of paternal sympathy shatters. "Katharine, get in the truck," he says. She knows better than to argue. She slowly climbs down off the tailgate and lets herself into the Ford. Cougan waits until she has closed the door. "Now, why don't you get off my truck, you little shit."

Kurt knows that as soon as he steps off the tailgate the oilman will swing at him. So he moves back and bounds in an athletic flash over the right side of the truck, hoping the roan won't decide to kick him as he flies through the air. The horse nickers and pulls back against its halter, as it did when Cougan drove up.

Already Cougan is stalking around the opposite side of the truck, fists balled for action, "Look, son, I'm going to show you not to cuss me in front of my girl." T-Willy puts a hand on Cougan's shoulders in an effort to calm him, but Cougan bats it down, knocking the thin old man to the ground. This gives Kurt just the time he needs to make it to the saddlebag and draw the .45. Cougan's eyes go flat with fear and hate as the boy turns the gun on him. For just a moment Kurt prays that the man will keep coming. He would love to shoot Cougan in his fat gut, watch all that good food and smugness spill onto the dirt. How much different could it be from easing the dumb suffering of a steer mad for water or a fevered calf with worms itching through its brain? He has done it dozens of times—the quick flick of the hammer, and then the mark of the dime-size hole, and then a little peace for everyone. All the past there ever was, all the future there is ever going to be, meet at this place and fold into a single moment—the pulling of the trigger. Kurt is exhilarated by the fact that he suddenly has the power to change his life, and he keeps the gun leveled as he tries to figure out if he should.

Jail, Kurt thinks, might even be a relief: no hellish football camps out in the desert, no land auctions to witness. No winners, no losers, just a small, dark cell with plenty of cool water to drink. But then Kurt's mind turns back to the ugly turkey buzzards blinding the Hereford, picking and picking their way through life. The murderous moment slips away from him.

Apparently Cougan has also surmised that Kurt isn't going to shoot him. He continues to advance. Cougan's face is puffy and red with hate, and Kurt wonders if he will still go to jail if he doesn't shoot but the oilman dies of a heart attack. Kurt decides to bluff. He cocks the hammer and yells something he heard in a roadhouse once, when one of his friends wanted to scare a big Yankee from Cleveland out of a fight. "Mr. Cougan, I'm just a little old country boy. But I'll clue you, I'm mean as hell." As soon as the words leave his mouth they seem stupid and frail, the threat of a hick, and Cougan is coming on as if he has heard nothing at all.

Kurt can think of only one thing to do. He swings the gun away from Cougan and points it toward the child in the truck.

"No!" Cougan cries. He stops long enough to look at his daughter. Katharine's face is pressed in horror against the window of the Ford. She doesn't have sense enough to duck under the dash. Instead she screams, "Daddy, Daddy!"

"No, please." The sight of his frightened daughter takes all the fight out of Cougan. He backs down, slides his body along the hood of the truck, and slowly makes a retreat to the other side. Kurt follows him halfway, keeping the gun pointed at the little girl until he backs up the porch steps. T-Willy has managed to get inside the feedstore and is peering out the dark window.

Cougan opens the door of the Ford. "This ain't over," he says. "I'll kill you for this." Kurt points the gun back toward the oilman and keeps it on him in case he has a pistol of his own under the seat of the truck or in the glove compartment. But Kurt is pretty sure that Cougan won't risk any shooting with his daughter next to him in the cab. Cougan pushes his little girl down in her seat and peels out in reverse, his ruddy face receding into a cloud of dust. But he floods the engine, and the truck stalls. Kurt raises the .45 again.

After two or three tries Cougan manages to turn the engine over. He shifts into first and floors the accelerator. The Ford lurches forward, violently flinging the little bull off the tailgate and onto the ground. The bottle shatters. The calf is too weak to cry out and lands in the dirt with a thud, as if it were already dead. When he sees this, rage wells up in Kurt all over again, and he is tempted to try to shoot out the truck's tires. But a little voice inside his head tells him to leave well enough alone. T-Willy comes back onto the porch, and they watch together as the green Ford disappears, a line of powdered milk running all the way to the highway.

"Kurt, I'm afraid you're out of your damn mind," T-Willy says, as he shrugs at Kurt and starts walking toward the calf. It lies lifeless, like a blown-out tire next to the road.

"You reckon?" Kurt asks, swinging the cocked gun in the direction of the old man. T-Willy puts up his hands. They stay that way for a second or two, and then Kurt unloads four rounds, not into the old man but into the calf—two in the belly, two in the skull. As be lowers the gun, Kurt feels a wave of regret wash over him. He is sorry that he pointed the gun at his uncle's friend, and thinking about pointing the gun at the little girl makes him feel sick at his cowardice. He even feels sorry he had to kill the calf with the screwworms twisting in its eyes, but mostly Kurt feels sorry for himself, because he knows that for all his trouble, his life hasn't changed a bit, and in the morning he will have to get up out of bed and put on his work clothes and saddle the roan, and the whole thing will start over again.

_____

Brad Vice has published stories in *The Georgia
Review, The Southern Review, Hayden's Ferry
Review, The Greensboro Review, The Carolina
Quarterly, The Atlantic Monthly, New Stories from
the South, 1997,* and *Best New American Voices,
2003.* His book reviews are frequently published
in the *San Francisco Chronicle.* Born and raised
in Tuscaloosa, Alabama, he spent his summers
working on his grandparents' cattle farm. He
teaches creative writing at Mississippi State
University.

EMILY STINSON

*I would like to dedicate "Report from Junction" to my dad, Leon Vice, who
died of leukemia shortly after I found out the story had been accepted by*
The Atlantic Monthly. *My dad was a freshman at the University of
Alabama in 1958, the year Bear Bryant became head coach. I had heard my
father mention Bryant's training camp in Junction, Texas, many times when
I was a kid, and the story of what took place there has become more or less
mythic in our imaginations. If you root for the Crimson Tide, Junction is
your Aeneid; we trace the foundation of the once-mighty Bama football
empire to the events that took place there. Veterans of the Junction camp such
as Gene Stallings and Bobbie Drake Keith would go on to be Bryant's first
assistant coaches and men-at-arms, and later, when I was a student at
Alabama in the early nineties, Stallings took us to a National Championship
himself.*

*Junction is one of those few times outside of books where the literal and the
metaphorical meet, and that is why I selected Bryant's hellish training camp
as the backdrop to my own story, which is not really about football but about a
tough kid trying to endure tough times. My dad was such a kid, though he
had a gentler disposition than my character Kurt.*

*Dad was invaluable in the writing of the story, the sort of guy who knew
all the secrets of raising motherless livestock as well as a great number of other
things that no one has bothered to write down in a book. Who else could have
told me about the existence of a drenching bottle or how to use it? Who else*

could have given me a recipe for treating screwworms? Since his passing, I frequently feel like the desperate Jewess in Isaac Babel's story "Crossing Poland," who, at the story's conclusion, demands of the narrator, "I should wish to know where in the whole world you could find another father like my father?"

THE BALLAD OF
RAPPY VALCOUR

(from *Image*)

The neighbors were watching the new couple moving in, some of them peering out from behind ancient shutters—some others boldfaced on their porches or standing right smack in the sidewalk, a few little barefoot wild children—two black, two white, one café au lait—circling in and out of the new couple's moving, like leaves in a muddy stream's eddy. The shotgun doubles that lined Saint Pé Street, a hundred years old if they were a day, seemed ready to crumble to powder and blow away not too long off in the future.

There was none of this gentrifying business that was happening other places in New Orleans: people with new money buying up houses they loved for their high ceilings, putting in central air, then silly elaborate ceiling fans—just pretty much for show—fresh Gothic gingerbread scroll-sawed out of pinewood by college-boy carpenters, skylights, stained glass, old brick patios out back, and all of it new. Saint Pé Street was still as it always had been, ever since decades and decades ago the families of okra and mirliton vendors, masons, and sheet-music salesmen had first moved into these houses, back when the air on Saint Pé Street was thick with guttural German, spicy Sicilian, and even occasional French flying this way and that.

But times had altered regardless, around that. The first and the second wars came and went, then that Korean mess; now the Vietnam War had been done for near a decade, and down on the Gulf, the Vietnamese fishermen who had survived had come over and done very well with their nets, making a whole lot of the Cajun shrimpers damn mad, if you got right down to it. This new couple carried that war with them: the husband had lost his legs, both of them, near about all the way up to the sockets, and the wife was hauling him up the stairs backwards in his silver wheelchair, him holding on tight to the chair-arms, and her huffing a little bit, trying not to jog him too much.

His name was Rapides Valcour, and his wife's name was Lilah. The neighbors knew this because already the mailman had told them. He had waved the first pieces of mail in the air like a herald two days before, then stuck them theatrically into the mailbox, with a flourish, as if to say *y'all take a look.*

They were nothing important or interesting: a bill for a sofa from Rosenberg's Furniture on Tulane Avenue—one of the neighbors had held it up to the light (they had not moved in yet, after all, so this was not like snooping on people you knew); a letter from some older relative who lived in Jeanerette, Louisiana—spidery, shivery handwriting—who they assumed was the wife's kin, since the surname in the upper left corner was not Valcour; then, finally, a notice about a rate change from the New Orleans Public Service, the power and light, addressed only to Occupant.

Nobody offered to come out and help Lilah Valcour, in her sweat-sticky rose-patterned dress, to hoist her husband up. She was not a big woman, just average height, with a generous bosom and lively dark hair that tended to escape from the rubber band gathering it. Such an offer, they adjudged, would have seemed impolite, suggesting that she was a weakling, or that they'd been watching nosily from behind shutters, and thus knew that her husband was legless and hopeless and pitied him.

Finally she got him up the last step and onto the porch. He cried out, "Wahoo! You done it, my Lilah Bean!" She opened the door, propped it carefully with the brick doorstop, and pulled him through, into the house's cool darkness.

Catercorner across Saint Pé Street, in a duplex whose paint had long ago disappeared, leaving the wood exposed and hence somehow invisible, a short but enormous black woman in a caftan scolded her six little grandchildren. "Y'all get down from that sofa," she said majestically, and, like little automatons, they jumped down. "Y'all don't be staring at that poor white man." The fabric of her caftan was from Ghana and had gold-ink highlights. She was thinking of jokes about quadruple amputees she had heard white boys make to each other in the grocery line. *What do you call a quadruple amputee who lies down in front of the door? Mat. What do you call a quadruple amputee who hangs on the wall? Art.*

"He got no legs, Gramma," said little DeQuan.

"I *said*," the woman reiterated.

"Yes, ma'am," said little DeQuan, like a perfect Marine. *What do you call a quadruple amputee who's dropped from a plane in the middle of the ocean? Bob.*

But then she thought: that man got arms, so he only a double.

"How come God give that man no legs, Gramma?" said De-Quan's little sister Sh'Vaunne.

"God done give 'em," said Mother "Peaches" Aloysius. "Man done take 'em away. I 'spect that man went to the Nam."

Under her breath she began humming a song that averred *she* wasn't going to study war no more.

"Y'all go eat y'all grill cheese," she said.

The children ran out to the kitchen, where the Reverend Gonzales Brown, one of Mother Peaches' assistant pastors at the Church of the Spirit's Delight, was laying grilled-cheese triangles on melamine plates on a pearly-topped table. The cheese oozed out joyous, lethargic. The children squealed. It was their third favorite lunch, next to alphabet soup or grits.

Reverend Gonzales Brown mopped the floors at Popeye's Fried Chicken most evenings, and got to practice his preaching sometimes if Mother Peaches had what she called "a little guitar" in her throat, an annoying catarrhal drip that made her have to stop and drink ice water, which then derailed her train of thought.

The last time the little guitar came up, she had mixed up in her sermon the names Obed and Obadiah. Any fool with half a grain of sense knew that Obed was Ruth's boy, the son of that wonderful selfless foreigner Ruth who took care of her mother-in-law, and that Obadiah was the minor prophet who waggled his finger incessantly at all those bad guys in Edom, the offspring of that spineless Esau. Easy distinction. Still, nobody in the congregation even noticed, and that piqued her a tad.

Lilah Valcour had been raised in Jeanerette by her father, "Red" Tramontana, whose flaming bright hair came from his maternal ancestors, the Irish side, and her mother, Alsace Jelineau. Red and Alsace Tramontana loved each other deeply. They had moved out to the country because the city was getting "too ruckus," as her mother put it, and they wanted to raise little Lilah in pastoral splendor.

Jeanerette did not turn out to be pastoral splendor, but Red was away from the Sicilian pinball-machine mobsters in Jefferson Parish who were rumored to have done in his two uncles who went to the Hibernia Bank one day but never came back.

In Jeanerette they were happy as clams. Lilah's mother called her husband "Red Bean," with seventeen spoonfuls of affection, even in front of the neighbors, and he in return called her "Jelly Bean." Alsace told her little girl bedtime stories each night when she got in her covers, stories from books, as well as stories out of her head.

One night little Lilah asked about Daddy's grandfather, who he was and did she know him and could we go see him sometime? Alsace knew that Daddy's grandfather had been a bootlegger, in tight with the Mafia, but she didn't want to say that, so she did the oblique thing.

"Honey, I think that the name Tramontana means 'across-the-mountains' and that must mean that way back Daddy's people were very brave travelers, don't you think?"

"Yes, ma'am," said little Lilah, and made beautiful pictures inside her head of those brave travelers.

Even though they were Catholics, no little brother or sister came for Lilah, after two years, after three, after four, and then ever. So the two lavished all of the love they had on this one little girl-child.

When Rapides Valcour met Lilah, when he was twenty-eight and she was twenty-four, after the Vietnam terribleness, Lilah was waiting tables in her little checked apron and nursery cap at the Porky Pig Diner, near the foot of Canal Street. Rapides Valcour was astonished that Lilah was not married. His friend Mac who had brought him there told him that, and it was true.

He noted the glow of love that radiated from her. He later attributed that to the surplus of love, a continuous infusion, pressed down, running over, that she'd gotten at home as a little girl: a whole lot of hugging, and reading, and rum cake at bedtime (he thought that exotic) with hot milk in a cut-glass cup whose handle looked like a clear-glass tree branch.

They still had the cup in the glass-fronted cabinet in the front room, along with some tiny blown-glass figurines, a couple of scenic plates with painted views of Luray Caverns and Mount Rushmore that Lilah's parents had brought home from trips, and a tiny wire replica of the Eiffel Tower that Rappy had given his wife on their first anniversary with a note that said, *Honey one day I will take you here.*

The third time Rappy Valcour ever set eyes on Lilah, which was the second time she waited on him, he proposed to her right there on his stool. This was before she had even served him his dry toast and his three eggs, sunny-side-up. She blinked in surprise at what he said. She did not even notice his wheelchair folded into the niche beside the jukebox, or the fact that he had no legs: she just noticed his lovely eyes, which were a gold Cajun brown and as warm as she'd ever seen.

She replied that, well, for right now he had just better eat his breakfast and they could talk about that some other time, because there were three people waiting for French toast and two people needing a refill on coffee, and the man from the linen supply would be there in a minute with dishtowels and probably new coffee filters, which she had to check because he sometimes brought a different size in a box that was labeled wrong. She sighed and turned her hands palm-up, as if to suggest that the world was a silly and difficult place. Would that be okay?

"Yes, ma'am," said Rapides Valcour, "That would be perfect." He shook his head, amazed.

"I hope your eggs are the way you enjoy them," she said. "If those yolks are too solid, you just wave me down." Because she was gripping the glass coffeepot handle in her right hand, she made a tiny quick movement of fingers-as-fluttering-flags-in-the-wind with her left. Then she moved off to replenish the coffee in a tubby truck driver's cup.

Rapides Valcour turned his head slowly, as if he had whiplash, to look at his friend Mac. His look said, *Hey, do you believe it?*

Mac raised his eyebrows and lifted his coffee and smiled in wide, pleased disbelief. Mac had two legs and could not get a girlfriend to save his life.

It was the second week of March now, and the Valcours had moved in the summer before. No one much in the neighborhood knew them, and so one day Mother Peaches decided that it was time to call on them. She rarely crossed the street. Usually she just came out to the curb and got into a car that pulled up and Gonzales Brown or one of her grown children drove her wherever she needed to go. She felt strange as she crossed the street.

She had had a prophetic dream that morning which woke her up just before dawn. Mother Peaches was God's woman, that was for sure, but she still found these dreams and these words from God—directions to do this or that thing that in her flesh she would never drum up—a little unsettling. She hated that resistance in herself, because she wanted to be in God's will, so she just grumbled, "Lord, let this cup *pass*," just like Jesus, then went on and did the damned thing, whatever it was, that God told her to do.

The dream was quite simple: she saw the Valcours' grayed-white housefront, with its two feet of shriveled petunias between the porch and the sidewalk, as if she were peering out from her own shutters, like those little grandchildren the very first afternoon. In the dream the house began to change, seeming to take on a pale yellow color, then brightening until it was like the yolk of a raw egg, bright gold, so gold that it seemed—like organza—to overlay rosy pink, and almost pulsing with life. She knew what it meant: something good was in the offing, and she, as the instrument of God's grace, was called to go check things out at the Valcours'.

She rapped on the door with the silver wolf-head of the cane that she used most of the time now, since she had grown stiff and then, slowing down, had gotten heavier. The sound of her knock was amazingly loud. She frightened herself, just a little. But no one would ever know she was frightened: the wide pale-brown freckled face of Mother Peaches glowed as impassive and calm as the harvest moon.

The door opened, and Lilah invited her in. She had seen Mother Peaches in her comings and goings, though they had never met. Mother Peaches brought a welcome present, a Mason jar of fig preserves she had put up the summer before, grown on the fig bush behind her house.

She brought also a little plastic-framed picture of Jesus with a carmine-red drape hanging over his tunic. He was knocking on the door of a house. Mother Peaches held the picture out to Lilah and waggled it from side to side. Jesus seemed to knock, then rear back, knock and rear.

Mother Peaches said solemnly, in a theatrical monotone, "Lo, I stand at the door and I knock. Revelations 3:20." Then she looked right into Lilah's eyes, which were clear and good. "Thass *weird*, that picture," she said as if half apologizing. She cocked her head and noted to herself that it looked a lot like the Three Bears' house in little DeQuan's big old book. She wondered how the bears would deal with Jesus, or he with them. "I likes it anyways." She set it down on the table with its little prop-leg poking out back as if it had always belonged there.

She went to the Rosenberg's sofa for which all the neighbors had heard the price, visible through the thin envelope, and sat her bulk down carefully, as if she might break something deep in herself. "Okay. Now, tell me all about y'all," she said, and she turned her full harvest-moon glow on her hostess, who sat entranced, holding upright in her lap the Mason jar filled with its globy squashed fruit hanging as if in amber.

When Mother Aloysius left, closing the door very slowly behind her, Lilah Valcour remained very still, listening to her new neighbor's cane-tip stumping down the stairs and then across the sidewalk to the street.

Lilah sat remembering all of the things she had told the old woman, things she hadn't quite even said to herself yet. That Rappy had moments of panic that frightened the bejeebers out of her: that at Mardi Gras, even in all that crowd, when a child nearby popped a balloon, Rappy almost pitched out of his chair, and then couldn't be calmed down until Lilah wheeled him back past the tamale stand where there were no people and said again and again, "Rappy. It's okay. Hon. Rappy. You're home. At the Mardi Gras. No grenades. Rappy. You hear me?" That once, before dawn, a police helicopter had flown over the house and Rappy threw himself off the bed, onto the floor, and spent almost an hour sobbing and shaking.

She hadn't told anyone these sorts of things, then the first time she met Mother Peaches she told her the whole thing. Well, not the whole thing, but a pretty good chunk. She had not told her the thing Rappy said the day after their wedding: "Honey, you going to have to raise me. Ain't nobody raised me. I do not know how to be regular."

Lilah sat thinking, remembering that. She remembered the way she had stared at him then, wondering what had changed. The day before, she had a bridegroom in a striped cravat, handsome if legless, and now here the next morning she had a person who claimed he was not even human, did not know how to be regular.

She remembered saying, "Rappy, what *do* you mean?" She wondered if everyone changed into someone else once they were married, if this was a secret of marriage that no one had told her. She remembered the very sad look in his eyes. She still had no idea. She loved Rappy even more.

Each day she went out to the Porky Pig Diner on the bus. Gonzales Brown and his brother Ricardo built a ramp for Rappy's wheelchair out the back door into the alleyway, and Rappy went to the Veterans' Hospital once a week, in his wheelchair, and somewhere else every day, to keep busy: the library, often, a movie, wherever. And then he came back to the house on Saint Pé Street and was there, lit up with joy, when she came home from work, and he loved her as much as a man could possibly love a woman.

Each Friday he brought home a rose, which he put in a vase on the end table next to the picture of Jesus knocking. Each night he held her close. Each morning he kissed her good-bye as if it were the last morning of the world. But the look in his eyes, those beautiful eyes, was of such devastation.

When Mother Peaches shut the door behind her, coming into her living room after having crossed the street from the Valcours', she said aloud to the empty room, "Lord, we got our work cut out for us."

From the kitchen, her daughter Tyeesha called in, "What, Mama?"

Mother Peaches said dismissively, "Not you, T. I was talking to the Lord."

Tyeesha, mother to Bree and Xavier, two of the other small ones who were everywhere here, was chopping up fat yellow onions for barbecue, wiping her cleaver on a damp dishtowel and moaning with onion pain. Her eyes ran with tears. "My land, Mama, when are you not talking to the Lord!" In the next room there was shrieking and bouncing.

"That Rappy man, we got to get the Lord working on him, T."

"Yes, ma'am," she said.

In the back door, through the shortcut from the avenue, came

her son Leander, the oldest, born before she was saved, from a father she didn't remember. He was dusty from work and he set his
hard hat in the sink and ran water on it. "Leander," she said, in her
most imperious tones, "that man across the street in that wheelchair?"

"Yes, Mama," Leander said.

"We going to pray him healed."

"Hah!" said Leander, who was in general fine with this church-
iness as long as it held its place but got salty when his mother
started this kind of stuff. "Grow back that man legs, right?"

Mother Peaches looked straight in his eyes. "And everything else,
and you look at me one more time that way, Leander, and you can
forget about barbecue. Not just tonight. Ever."

"Yes, ma'am," said Leander. He meant it.

The next week was the Feast of Saint Joseph. Out in California,
where no one on this block but Rappy had ever been (on the way
to Vietnam twelve years before), the swallows were flocking back
mystically, predictable as sunrise, to the old Spanish mission at San
Juan Capistrano. In other parts of New Orleans, the Italians and
the Sicilians were having their altars to Saint Joseph.

Mother Peaches, before she was saved, when she was just a teenaged girl, had ironed for some Catholics who did this. They had
a plaster statue of Saint Joseph, the foster father of Jesus, with
painted golden-brown hair and neat plaster feet poking out from
under his skirt, wearing golden-brown sandals. Mother Peaches,
who was still a girl then, had observed this with interest.

She had asked her employer, Mrs. DiLisio, what this was for.
Mrs. DiLisio seemed taken aback for a minute. "It's for Saint
Joseph," she answered, clearly hoping the girl would not want to
know more.

"I mean what do it do," the girl asked. "And why do you all do
this?"

Her hand swept the air, indicating the terraced, ad hoc altar built
out of tables and odd shelving, covered with linen and then cro-
cheted doilies, filling the room with plate after plate of food.

Candles stood flickering between the plates, casting strange shadows that danced like Balinese ladies. Holy pictures—of the Sacred Heart; of various pious and anemic-looking girl saints in white dresses and stockings and wreaths of pale flowers; pictures of Our Lady of Lourdes and Our Lady of Fatima and finally Saint Joseph himself, with his carpenter's tools—had been taken down from every other room in the house and brought into this one.

On the terraced tables at the DiLisios were frosted biscotti on cake plates, and buckets of meatballs in gravy, and deviled eggs fluted with creamy yolk filling and topped with pimentos. There were glass dishes of watermelon pickle. There were three beef roulades that Italians called *braciolone:* the rolled steak, the stuffing, and at the roll's center, a boiled egg, so that when the *braciolone* was sliced it presented a bull's-eye.

There were anise cakes and jars of peach butter and jellied-veal mold. There were bottles of homemade wine. There was a pea salad with peanuts in it, and something red-jewely nestled there too. There were at least a dozen varieties of pasta, in white sauce and red. There were musical instruments—saxophones, xylophones, drums—made of marzipan, yellow and pink and green. There were round little balls of white cookies with nuts in them that they called Mexican wedding cakes.

The teenaged maid waited to hear: did they think Saint Joseph ate this, like Santa Claus, or like the elves in the shoemaker story? Mrs. DiLisio said again, "Well, it's all for Saint Joseph, and this is, um, what we do." The girl shook her head and went back to her ironing. She did not come back until Tuesday and everything was back to normal, and all the stuff gone.

A dozen and more years later, she took over the Church of the Spirit's Delight the day after old Reverend Cornelius B. Jackson got taken home by the Lord right in the middle of a sermon about the Rapture, his hand laid flat across his heart, his eyes rolled to heaven, and he breathed out then never breathed in.

They just needed someone to hold things together awhile, but it went on and on and they started calling her Mother and paying her upkeep, and that was it. That next spring Mother Peaches remembered Saint Joseph's Day, and decided that the Church of the Spirit's Delight could use something like that. Kind of a party, for its own sake.

The Spirit's Delight altar to Saint Joseph had cabbage rolls, after-dinner mints, chocolate doughnuts, and chitlins; it had deep-fried shrimp, black-eyed peas, pots full of creamy and buttery white mashed potatoes. Because a Chinese man named Lee Ling Ho who lived next door to the church heard about the celebration and brought over a dish of thousand-year-old eggs, it had green un-shelled duck eggs, jade-slick and gorgeously veined, which really were not that old but looked mysterious, like eggs made of marble and dug from an emperor's tomb. Lee Ling Ho sometimes came to their services and clapped slightly off the beat, singing along in a kind of sincere nonsense language.

Because nobody knew what Italians did with the food afterward, Mother Peaches decided to give some of it to the orphanage, say, the doughnuts and mashed potatoes and black-eyed peas, because children would eat those things, and to bring some of the fancier stuff to a convent of cloistered Catholic nuns off Magazine Street, who could not come outside the gates and so had their extern take in the food on a revolving tray through the wall. Mother Peaches was put in mind of the modesty turntable in the ladies' room for passing urine to invisible lab folk the last time she'd gone to the hospital.

Her younger son, Leftenant, from the husband who died in a gas station robbery in Gulfport, had looked at the thousand-year-old eggs that morning and said, "Mama, don't you go bring them damn eggs to the nuns. They gone think you crazy."

She raised an eyebrow at him. She was about to tell him not to take the Lord's name in vain but then she realized he hadn't. "I believe they the best thing we got," she said. "That Mr. Ho say it took him since last summer to make them."

"Suit yourself, then," said Leftenant, after his wife Cheryl shushed him in mime from across the room. As she walked away he saluted his mother behind her back with his eyes wide in mock something-or-other, and Cheryl looked daggers.

So Mother Peaches, who had been thinking about the new neighbors a lot since she had had that dream the week previous, and then visited the next day with Mrs. Lilah Valcour, thought that she would bring the best thing they had over to the Valcours. And in case they didn't like thousand-year-old duck eggs, she brought a banana cream pie for good measure.

Lilah Valcour was surprised to see Mother Peaches at her door again. "Come in, come in!" she said. Mother Peaches had not told Lilah about her dream, in which the Valcours' house turned yellow, then seemed to be full of rosy life, like the sun rising. You couldn't tell people those things until you knew what you had there. "Set yourself down, Mother Peaches," she said. "What is all this?" She was looking at the pie and the platter of duck eggs. Mother Peaches had left her cane home and navigated across the street carrying all of it balanced precariously.

"This ain't nothing," said Mother Peaches. "This just an excuse," she said, and then was silent.

Lilah Valcour didn't know what to say, so she said nothing. The clock in the next room ticked loudly. The two women sat not speaking for several minutes. From the back of the house came the sound of a television. Crowds were cheering.

Mother Peaches pursed her lips. "Spo'ts," she conjectured. Lilah nodded. "You husband, he like to watch spo'ts?" Mother Peaches ventured.

Tears welled up in Lilah's eyes. "No," she said. "He doesn't. He just can't do anything else, much. And he isn't very happy, and I cannot make him happy, and, oh, Mother Peaches, I just want to die." Lilah Valcour fell onto her knees and put her head, plop, into Mother Peaches' capacious lap.

"Jesus say he have come that we may have *life*," said Mother Peaches, "and that more abundantly."

Lilah lifted her head and tossed back her hair. "Then why did he take Rappy's legs?" Her face was wet and messy.

Mother Peaches was taken aback for a moment. The image was startling: Jesus taking Rappy Valcour's legs? "No, no," she said. "That ain't the thing." She was trying to remember what the Bible said about this, or what Reverend Cornelius B. Jackson had said in some sermon, but none of it made much sense.

"And there's something else I haven't told you," said Lilah Valcour, with a kind of guilt, as if they had been talking their whole lives and she had withheld this. Mother Peaches sat at attention, her shoulders pulled up as if lifting her heart off her diaphragm to give it more room to beat. Her ears seemed to shift and change shape slightly, almost to take on elfin points.

"The day after our wedding my Rappy said . . ." She paused. "He said . . . I would have to raise him, that nobody had raised him." Mother Peaches' mouth was gathered like the mouth of a drawstring purse. Her ears shifted again. Something drew Lilah Valcour's eyes downward. Mother Peaches' toes in the open slippers she wore, made of fake mink, crossed and uncrossed, seemed to have a life of their own, like happy puppies deep in a fur basket.

Mother Peaches intoned it, an echo. "Ain't nobody raised him. What, he a orphan?" She was thinking about the orphans' home where Leftenant and Cheryl were taking the black-eyed peas, as they spoke. She thought, Lord, we all orphans.

"No," said Lilah. "His mama's just mean. She did terrible things to him when he was little. You don't want to know."

Mother Peaches groaned soundlessly deep down inside herself. The pulsing yellow house in the dream-vision, with all of its pink life inside it, came up in her mind's eye. She knew what it meant now. She hated these times, when she had to be channeling miracles. It just took everything out of her, but it was what she was called to do.

She remembered the pipe underneath her kitchen sink when Leftenant had replaced it, after the water stopped running except for a trickle. Leftenant was swearing and bumping his head, and Cheryl was raising her eyebrow and running out over and over to the TrueValue Hardware to pick up the stuff that Leftenant wrote down on the back of the last Sunday's church bulletin, and then to the drug store for something to fix his forehead.

Mother Peaches remembered the pipe when he'd finally gotten it free. "Feast you eyes," said Leftenant, accusingly, as if Mother Peaches had done something terrible. Inside the narrow pipe, thick as that, was crusty mineral buildup from years of hard water coursing through. Her last husband had died of the artery clog, from a life of fat building up inside him like that. She had never thought what that might took like. There was hardly enough room for a trickle to get through.

Mother Peaches made a sermon around that the following Sunday, the way that an oyster would build a pearl. She told the congregation that if we would have God use us, we must keep our pipes free of that buildup. She said God could send his grace through like a blowtorch, if that's what we wanted, in an instant. But we had to give him permission. She said it might hurt.

She knew she would have to do that after dinner, go into her prayer closet on the back porch that Leander had built her and hung with dark red velvet curtains and talk to the Lord about Rappy Valcour. And she knew the first step was that she herself had to repent of her sins, any sins she might have missed along the way, any new ones she'd committed today, so that God's grace could blowtorch through.

All this went through Mother Peaches' head in a split second. Lilah saw none of it. Mother Peaches said, "You man ever cry, honey? About he legs? About he mama?"

"No," Lilah said. "Not outside. But one time I heard him say out loud in the bathtub, as if he was talking to somebody, only nobody was there, 'This here is why people kill themself.'"

"You want me to say that again about Jesus?" asked Mother Peaches a little sternly. "I came that you might have life, and that more abundantly?"

"I heard you the first time," said Lilah, sounding slightly sullen, as if that were just a tease she would rather not hear at all. "But

Jesus can't bring Rappy's legs back. Or make all that terrible child-hood stuff go away."

"You telling me he *can't?*" said Mother Peaches. She seemed to be rising in her seat, inflating, as if like a dirigible she would lift off and bounce slow and soft off the light fixture overhead.

Lilah's face looked almost bruised with sadness. From the back of the house came the roar of a crowd at a game. A sport. Fun!

"No," she replied. She was thinking about all of those Bible stories, and whether she was supposed really to think that was possible. She decided to say she believed.

"Then you eat you damn pie," Mother Peaches said, actually rising now, and simultaneously asking God's forgiveness for talking like Leftenant under the sink. "And don't ever say nothing like that about Jesus again."

She inspected the pictures arranged on the wall. There was one of a baby, white-haired and dark-eyed. The picture was black and white, tinted a sepia brown. The baby sat on a blanket with fringe and reached with a chubby white hand toward something just out of sight. The soft bottoms of his feet made Mother Peaches want to touch them. They looked like a bear's. She said, "Thass you hus-band. Am I right?" Lilah nodded. There was another baby picture beside it, a little girl with brown curls, also sepia-tinted.

Mother Peaches walked slowly over to the glass-fronted cabinet and squinted to read the lettering on the Luray Caverns plate, and then the Mount Rushmore. "Y'all done been these places?" she said. Lilah shook her head no. "If you *was* to go somewhere, a trip, honey, where would y'all go?"

Lilah frowned slightly. "A trip?"

"You know," Mother Peaches said. "Like, on a Greyhound bus. Like you sends in a box top from . . ." She tried to pull a brand name out of the air and failed. "From something, and you wins a trip anyplace you wants to go."

Lilah rolled her eyes, thinking. "Wyoming?" she asked. She was picturing wide open spaces, and mountains, and velvet-grassed pastures, and cattle all russet and white, and perhaps—was that what that was? — tumbleweed, rolling and tumbling and rolling, and nice ponies watching it.

Mother Peaches said nothing, just walked to the door and went out. Lilah wondered about the cane, whether she only needed it some days. Apparently so.

That night in the kitchen Leftenant and Cheryl and Tyeesha and her boyfriend Raoul, whom Leftenant called Raoul the Fool, because he thought that Tyeesha had him wrapped around her little finger, played cards on the pearly-topped table. Mother Peaches believed that the Bible said nothing at all about card-playing, just as it said nothing about penicillin or dentists or television, so God let us figure things out for ourselves. "What y'all think he done give y'all y'all's brains for?" she said.

In the prayer closet on the other side of the thin wall, while the card game went on, Mother Peaches groaned loudly, and sang in her oddly weak tremolo, and thumped her head against the backboard of the prayer closet. Leftenant just shook his head and rolled his eyes.

Two of the children, LaJuana and Roosevelt, Raoul's children that his ex-girlfriend had left on his porch, came in from the TV room and begged for money to go buy some ice cream.

Leander came in then and they climbed on him. "Money, money, money," he chanted. "Y'all think I made out of money?" Yes, actually they did, because Leander never had married and so had a pretty big bank account.

On the other side of the wall, Mother Peaches called out to Jesus and banged her head on the backboard. The thick velvet curtains muffled the sound somewhat, but it was still quite impressive.

"What Gramma doing?" said little Sh'Vaunne.

Leftenant tossed his head. "Y'all done saw that movie, *King Kong*?" he said to Sh'Vaunne. She nodded yes. All of the little barrettes that held her braids — fuchsia, turquoise, and taxicab-yellow — danced merrily.

Leftenant said, "That ape done escape. Gramma fighting with him in the prayer closet." Cheryl slapped him on the back of his head with her long, brightly manicured fingertips, and Sh'Vaunne looked up at the door to the back porch in mixed horror and glee, expecting to see the great monkey.

Just then Mother Peaches lurched into the doorway. Her hair was awry and her prayer stole was askew. "Leander!" she said. "You go see if that Rappy Valcour okay."

Leander looked at her dumbly. He looked at the card players to see what they knew about this. They knew nothing either and gave him only wordless looks in reply.

Leander took his jacket, which he had just hung up, down from its hook. He put it on again. He left, and Mother Peaches stood in the doorway holding onto the doorjamb on both sides as she heard people did in an earthquake. The card players resumed their game.

In a few minutes Leander returned. "He fine, Mamma."

"What you see?" she demanded.

"He just sit in that wheelchair," Leander said. "Looking right flat out in front of him."

"What else?" she said.

"Nothing else," he said. "They done eat four of Mr. Ho eggs. She say they taste all right."

Mother Peaches went back to her prayer closet. The card game resumed. Leander was persuaded to leave his jacket on this time and go for the ice cream. The back wall of the kitchen seemed to bulge and retract with the old woman's groanings and intercedings.

Sh'Vaunne and DeQuan and Xavier and Bree and LaJuana and Roosevelt ran around in a loopy circle through the house until they all crashed in a pile in the front room and fell asleep.

Leander returned with the ice cream. "I knew it," he said, rolling his eyes at the sight of the piled children braided together and breathing damply in sleep like a giant dog.

Across the street, at the Valcours', Lilah was helping her husband into bed. His absent toes—on the ends of his absent feet, on the ends of his absent legs—were hurting him again tonight. "Ghost piggies," he called them. The doctors called this phantom pain, but he told Lilah, the toes might be phantom, the pain was not.

He had lost his legs throwing himself on a grenade, he told her. "Throwing yourself?" she echoed. He could not mean that. She'd misunderstood. Yes, he'd said, all the stuff from his childhood just made him want to die—he said the word with a quick exhalation of air—and at that instant he had seen a three-way chance to protect his buddy Hamlin Dennis, who was in front of him, to be remembered as a good person, and to die quickly and leave no remains to speak of. He did not want a funeral. He wanted obliteration.

The plan misfired, of course, and while Hamlin was saved from the grenade, he drowned swimming in a river in the Mekong Delta two months later, while Rappy lay in the Japanese hospital where the army had flown him.

Lilah Valcour, having tucked Rappy in, went to check the doors. When she looked out the front window, just at nothing in particular, she squinted. Something just seemed odd. There was a sort of a glow at the back of Mother Peaches' house: the only way she could describe it to herself was that it was as if someone were having a midsummer party and Japanese lanterns were strung around, loopy and jewel-like. There was also a hum in the air, like electrical wires on Saint Charles Avenue when a trolley was coming but you couldn't see it yet.

She turned out the living room lights and locked both of the latches, then went to bed. She climbed into the sheets beside Rappy and looked over at him. A tense whiteness came into his face when he hurt like this, like the look of a foot that has been far too long in its shoe, but of course that was a terrible way to put it, because Rappy had no feet at all. So she just thought, he looks very pale tonight. She said, "Rappy, did you like those thousand-year-old eggs?"

"They was okay," he said. "But you know what I like, Lilah Bean?"

She said, "What, Rappy?" She could tell something good was coming.

"You," he said simply, and fell asleep, tunneling his hand beneath hers, which was under her pillow, and holding on nicely.

The next morning was Lilah's day off at the Porky Pig, so she had not set the clock. She woke up with the sun lying like a hot towel across her face, and she turned away from the light. She reached over to put her hand on her husband's back but he was not in his usual spot. The covers were kicked askew. Her heart caught in her: she loved him so much she feared sometimes he would be stolen away. The one thing she wished in her life was that she could have saved him from all of the badness that came before.

She sat up with a start. The pillows were pushed around. Something was funny here. The smallest snuffling sound in the world rose from behind Rappy's pillow. She pulled the pillow aside.

A squeaky small gasp came forth from Lilah Valcour's throat. It was a baby there behind the pillow, a newborn, as silky and powdery-innocent as could be. She thought it, then said it out loud: "Rappy!"

She picked up the amazing creature. She held the child up in the light. Its hair was like corn silk, and white-blond. It was too new to smile, but it clearly had not had time to be hurt, and so was perfect and pure. Every finger and toe was there, chubby and pink and intact.

Lilah remembered her husband's words: "Lilah Bean, you'll have to raise me. Nobody raised me."

She said it out loud then: "No!" meaning not, *I won't,* but rather, *This cannot be.*

She wrapped the child up in a blanket and laid him down on the bed between two of the pillows for safety. She washed her face, gargled with Dr. Tichenor's, and dressed in a hurry. She looked in the mirror to see if she recognized herself. She did.

She picked up the baby and went across the street to Mother Peaches' house. It was quiet. She knocked and Tyeesha answered.

"Shh," Tyeesha said. "Mother Peaches not so well this morning. When she do intercession, it take everything she got out of her. Leftenant done took the children to visit they cousins live out in Chalmette." She motioned Lilah into the house.

Then she noticed the baby. "Hunh?" said Tyeesha, her eyes wide.

She folded aside the top flap of the blanket. The little pink in-nocent stared back at her like a star, like a flower, like the gorgeous little incongruous white-child doll that they used for the Baby Jesus in the Christmas pageant at Spirit's Delight.

Lilah just shook her head and smiled a bit off-centeredly. She had no way to explain this. "I want to see Mother Peaches," she said firmly to Tyeesha.

Mother Peaches was propped in her bed in a darkened room. She stirred up off her pillows when Lilah came in.

"Holy . . ." Mother Peaches began, and stopped short. "Did I do . . . ?"

"Yes," said Lilah Valcour. She handed the baby to the old woman. The room smelled like violets, and barbecue, and the lingering after-scent of Leander's hair pomade.

Intercession just did take it out of a person, Mother Peaches said, then she smiled a big smile which showed her gold front tooth that had a star cutout. She called it her "burying tooth" and she said the mortician could take it and sell it to pay his fees, because her mouth would finally be shut, in the coffin, but Cheryl and Tyeesha said would she please stop saying that, in Jesus's name, and they would take care of that stuff when the time came.

The next morning Lilah Valcour and the baby got on a Grey-hound bus. Leftenant and Cheryl had driven her to the bus sta-tion, with DeQuan and Sh'Vaunne and the others strapped into the seats of the church van behind them. The children alternated singing "Trust and Obey" with another song that they had learned from Kermit the Frog on *Sesame Street* called "It's Not Easy Being Green."

Leander staked her the ticket, and Tyeesha and Raoul the Fool promised to take care of all the loose ends. Mother Peaches was still in her bed, and might never get up, for all it looked like. Tyeesha was getting the sofa and some of the other stuff. Lilah had packed up some Huggies, a week's worth of clothes for herself, and the small Eiffel Tower, along with the cut-glass cup with the tree-branch handle, for when the baby got bigger.

The bus ticket was to Cheyenne, and she knew she could figure it out when she got there. There seemed to be nice places all around: Mountain View, Paradise Valley, and Medicine Bow were the three that first struck her when she looked at the map.

The little legend on the map said that the state flower was called the Indian paintbrush, and the state bird was the meadowlark. Surely there would be someplace nice out there, with all those wide-field expanses of Indian paintbrush and those scattered copses of trees filled with meadowlarks, to raise a baby right.

———————

Ingrid Hill has published stories in the *Southern Review, The Michigan Quarterly Review, Shenandoah, North American Review, Louisiana Literature,* and *Story;* and a collection of fiction, *Dixie Church Interstate Blues.* She has held fellowships from Yaddo and MacDowell and is a two-time National Endowment for the Arts recipient. She grew up in New Orleans, and is the mother of twelve children, including two sets of twins. She lives in Iowa City with her family.

A generally accepted rule suggests that no good fiction is published about any war until two decades later. That's false, of course, but there is a way in which one needs to let a war mellow to see what unique societal deformations it will produce. For years I have been thinking about writing a Vietnam-amputee story, but it was just too sad. So I left it alone. In the meantime, I've seen enough "miracle" healings that I began thinking: Now, what are the outer limits of possibility there? That question hovered for me. Still does. As a fan of Glenn Frey and the Eagles, I like to "take it to the limit" whenever possible, as in "Nothing succeeds like excess." Meanwhile, I was looking into another question that had intrigued me: The Saint Joseph's Day feasts I had half-known as a child in New Orleans. I never understood what all that was about. My research brought me no closer to truth. I decided that maybe I was being too left-brained and that the general looniness of celebration for its own sake ought to be enough. Suddenly Mother Peaches appeared full-blown, with her wolf's-head cane, her knocking-Jesus picture, and her entourage—Leftenant, Lee Ling Ho, the Reverend Gonzales Brown in his Popeye's Fried Chicken uniform, the six little grandchildren. From inside of Mother Peaches, I peered out through the shutters and saw . . . Rappy and Lilah Valcour, struggling up the stairs of that little old house on Saint Pe' (which exists only in my head, somewhere near Tchoupitoulas Street) and there came my story.

Steve Almond

THE SOUL MOLECULE

(from *Tin House*)

I was on my way to see Wilkes. We were going to have brunch. Wilkes was a minor friend from college. He played number one on the squash team. I'd challenged him once, during a round-robin, but he annihilated me with lobs. Afterward, in the showers, he told me his secret.

"Vision," he said. "You have to see what's going to happen."

Now it is five years on, and I still felt sort of indebted to him. This was idiotic, but I couldn't unpersuade myself. I kept remembering those lobs, one after another, as elegant as parasols.

Wilkes was in the back of the restaurant, in a booth. We said our hellos and he picked up his menu and set it down again.

"We've known each other a long time, haven't we, Jim?"

"Sure," I said.

"Eight years now, coming up on eight."

"That sounds about right."

"You wouldn't think less of me if I told you something, would you?"

"Heck no," I said. Mostly, I was wondering how much breakfast would cost, and whether I'd have to pay.

"I've got a cartridge in my head," Wilkes said.

He had that drowsy pinch around the eyes you see in certain leading men. He was wearing a blue blazer with discreet buttons.

He looked like the sort of guy from whom other guys would buy bonds. That was his business. He was in bonds.

"A cartridge has been placed in my head for surveillance purposes. This was done a number of years ago by a race of superior beings. I don't know if you know anything about abduction, Jim. Do you know anything about abduction?"

"Wait a second," I said.

"An abduction can take one of two forms. The first—you don't need to know the technical terms—the first is purely for research purposes. Cell harvesting, that kind of thing. The second involves implants, Jim, such as the one in my brain."

Wilkes was from Maryland, the Chesapeake Bay area. He spoke in these crisp, prepared sentences. I'd always thought he'd be a corporate lawyer, with an office in a glass tower and a secretary better looking than anyone I knew.

"You're telling me you've been abducted," I said.

Wilkes nodded. He picked up his fork and balanced it on his thumb. "The cartridges can be thought of as visual recorders, something like cameras. They allow the caretakers to monitor human activity without causing alarm."

"The caretakers," I said.

"They see whatever I see." Wilkes gazed at me for a long moment. It was eerie, like I was staring into the big black space where an audience might be. Finally, he looked up and half-rose out of his seat. "Mom," he said. "Dad. Hey, there they are. You remember Jim."

"Why, of course," said his mother. She was a Southern lady with one of those soft handshakes.

"Pleasure," Mr. Wilkes said. "Unexpected pleasure. No no. Don't make a fuss. We'll just settle in. What are you up to, Jim? How're you bringing in the pesos?"

"Research," I said.

His face brightened. "Research, eh? The research game. What's that, biotech?"

"Yeah, sort of."

I'd never done any research. But I liked the way the word sounded. It sounded broad and scientific and beyond reproach.

"Your folks?" Mr. Wilkes said.

"You'll remember us to them, I hope," Mrs. Wilkes said.

I had no recollection of my parents having met the Wilkeses.

"What are you two bird dogs up to?" Mr. Wilkes said. He was from Connecticut, but he sometimes enjoyed speaking like a Texan.

Wilkes was squeezed next to his dad and his voice was full of that miserable complicated family shit. "We were talking," he said. "I was telling Jim about the cartridge in my head."

Mr. Wilkes fixed him with a look, and I thought for a second of that Goya painting, Saturn wolfing down his kids like they were chicken fingers. Mrs. Wilkes began fiddling with the salt and pepper, as if she might want to knit with them eventually.

"How about that?" Mr. Wilkes said. "What do you think of that, Jim?"

"Interesting," I said.

"*Interesting?* That the best you can do? Come on now. This is the old cartridge in the head. The old implant-a-roony."

I started to think, right then, about this one class I'd taken sophomore year, the Biology of Religion. The professor was a young guy who was doing research at the medical school. He told us that the belief in a higher power was a function of biological desire, a glandular thing. The whole topic got him very worked up.

Mr. Wilkes said: "Do you know why they do it, Jim?"

"Sir?"

He turned to his son again. "Did you explain the integration phases to him? The hybrids? The grays? Anything?"

"He just got here," Wilkes said.

Mr. Wilkes was sitting across from me. He was one of these big Republicans you sometimes see. The gin blossoms, the blue blazer. His whole aura screamed *yacht*.

"They teach you any folklore in that fancy college of yours? Fairy, dybbuk, goblin, sprite. Ring a bell, Jim? These are the names the ancients used to describe our extraterrestrial caretakers. 'Their appearance was like burning coals of fire and like the appearance of lamps: It went up and down among the living creatures, and the fire was bright and out of the fire went forth lightning.' That's straight from the Book of Ezekiel. What's that sound like to you, Son? Does that sound like God on his throne of glory?"

"No," I said. "I guess not."

"There's a reason Uncle Sam launched Project Blue Book," Mr. Wilkes said. "He was forced to, Jim. Without some kind of coherent response, there'd be no way to stem the panic. Let me ask you something. Do you know how many sightings have been reported to the Department of Defense in the past ten years? Guess. Two point five million. Abductions? Seven hundred thousand plus. They are among us, Jim."

Our waitress had appeared.

"Do you serve Egg Beaters?" Mr. Wilkes said.

The waitress shook her head.

"Toast," Mrs. Wilkes said. "You can have some toast, dear."

"I don't want toast," Mr. Wilkes said.

Wilkes looked pretty much entirely miserable.

"What about egg whites," Mr. Wilkes said. "Can you whip me up an omelet with egg whites?"

The waitress shifted her weight from one haunch to the other. She was quite beautiful, though a bit dragged down by circumstance. "An omelet with what?" she said.

"The white part of the egg. The part that isn't the yolk." Mr. Wilkes picked up his fork and began to simulate the act of scrambling eggs.

"I'm asking what you want *in* the omelet, Sir."

"Oh. I see. Ok. How about mushroom, swiss, and bacon."

"*Bacon?*" said Mrs. Wilkes.

I didn't know what the hell to order.

The waitress left, and Mr. Wilkes turned right back to me. He'd done some fund-raising for the GOP and I could see now just how effective he might be in this capacity. "Mrs. Wilkes and I, we both have implants. It's no secret. Not uncommon for them to tag an entire family. Did Jonathon already explain this?"

"I didn't explain anything," Wilkes said. "You didn't give me a chance."

"Yes," Mrs. Wilkes said. "You mustn't dominate the conversation, Warren."

"Remember Briggs?" Wilkes said.

"Who?"

"Briggs. Ron Briggs. Played number four on the team. He's got an implant. He lives out in Sedona now."

"Do we know him?" Mrs. Wilkes said.

Mr. Wilkes waved his hand impatiently. "Now I'm not going to bore you with some long story about our abductions, Jim. How would that be? You show up for breakfast and you have to listen to *that*. What you need to understand is the role these beings play. If they wanted to destroy us, if that was their intent, hell, I wouldn't be talking to you right now. They're caretakers, Jim. An entire race of caretakers. I'm not trying to suggest that these implants are any bed of roses, mind you. You've got all the beta waves to contend with, the ringing. Val's got a hell of a scar."

Mrs. Wilkes blushed. She had an expensive hairstyle and skin that looked a bit irradiated. "He's going to think we're kooks," she said.

"Not at all," I said quietly.

"Hell, we *are* kooks," Mr. Wilkes said. "The whole damn species is kooks. Only a fool would deny it."

I waited for the silence to sort of subside and excused myself. I needed some cold water on my ears. I filled the sink and did a quick dunk and stared at the bathroom mirror—really *stared*—until my face got all big-eyed and desperate.

When I got back to the table, the food had arrived and the Wilkeses were eating in this extremely polite manner. I'd visited them once, on the way back from a squash match at Penn. All I could remember about their home was the carpets. They must have had about a thousand of them, beautiful and severe, the kind you didn't even want to step on. I couldn't imagine a kid growing up in that place.

My French toast was sitting there, with some strawberries, but I wasn't hungry.

Mrs. Wilkes frowned. "Is something wrong with your food, dear? We can order you something else."

"That was pretty funny," I said finally. "You guys really had me going. You must be quite the charades family."

The Wilkeses, all of them, looked at me. It was that look you get from any kind of true believer, this mountain of pity sort of wobbling on a pea of doubt.

I thought about my biology professor again. Toward the end of class, just before I dropped out in fact, he gave us a lecture about this one chemical that gets released by the pineal gland. He called it the soul molecule, because it triggered all kinds of mystical thoughts. Just a pinch was enough to have people talking to angels. It was the stuff that squirted out at death, when the spirit is said to rise from the body.

Mr. Wilkes was talking about the binary star system Zeta Reticuli and the Taos hum and the Oz effect. But you could tell he wasn't saying what he really wanted to. His face was red with the disappointed blood.

The waitress came and cleared the dishes.

Wilkes started to mention a few mutual friends, guys who made me think of loud cologne and urinals.

Mrs. Wilkes excused herself and returned a few minutes later with fresh makeup.

Mr. Wilkes laid down a fifty. It was one of his rituals and, like all our rituals, it gave him this little window of expansiveness.

"I don't know the exact game plan, Jim. Anyone tells you they do, head the other direction. But I do know that these beings, these grays, they are essentially good. Why else would they travel thirty-seven light-years just to bail our sorry asses out? It's the mission that affects me," he said. "Mrs. Wilkes and Jonathon and I, all of us, we feel a part of something larger." He gazed at his wife and son and smiled with a tremendous vulnerability. "I know how it looks from the outside. But we don't know everything. We all make mistakes." He tried to say something else, but his big schmoozy baritone faltered.

Mrs. Wilkes put her hand on his.

"What the hell do I know?" Mr. Wilkes said.

"We all make mistakes," his wife said.

"I'm not perfect."

"Nobody's perfect, love."

There was a lot passing between them. Wilkes started to blush. His father seemed to want to touch his cheek. "They're just trying to save us from ourselves, so we don't ruin everything."

The waitress had come and gone and left change on the table. All around us people were charging through their mornings, toward God knows what.

The Wilkeses were sitting there, in their nice clothing, but I was seeing something else now, these whitish blobs at the centers of their bodies. It was their spirits I was seeing. I wasn't scared or anything. Everyone's a saint when it comes to the naked spirit. The other stuff just sort of grows over us, like weeds.

I thought about that crazy professor again. He'd called me to his office after Thanksgiving to tell me I was flunking. He was all torn up, as if he'd somehow betrayed me. He asked if I'd learned anything at all in his class. I said of course I had, I'd learned plenty of things, but when he pressed me to name one or two, I drew a blank. Just before I left, he came over to my side of the desk and put his hand on my shoulder and said, *We all need someone to watch over us, James.*

"Do you believe that?" Mr. Wilkes said.

I was pretty sure I'd never see the three of them again and it made me a little sad, a little reluctant to leave.

Wilkes was smoothing down his lapels. Mrs. Wilkes smiled with her gentle teeth and Mr. Wilkes began softly, invisibly, to weep. His spirit was like a little kerchief tucked into that big blue suit.

"I think we're going to be all right," I said. "That's the feeling I get." This was true. I was, in fact, having some kind of clairvoyant moment. Everything that was about to happen I could see just before it did.

Outside, up in the sky, above even the murmuring satellites, an entire race of benevolent yayas was maybe peering down at me with glassy black eyes. I started waving. The waitress breezed by and blew me a kiss. Mr. Wilkes slid another fifty across the table and winked. The sun lanced through a bank of clouds and lit the passing traffic like tinsel. I waved like hell.

Steve Almond's first collection of stories, *My Life in Heavy Metal,* has just been published in paperback by Grove. His fiction has won the Pushcart Prize and been a finalist for the National Magazine Award. His stories have appeard in *Playboy, Tin House, Zoetrope, Ploughshares,* and elsewhere. He teaches creative writing at Boston College.

STEPHEN SETTE-DUCATI

*T*his sucker was the direct result of doing a reading with this great young poet named Peter Richard. Peter was reading from his first book, Oubliette (which rocks), and he told this story of going to see a friend of his who told him he had a cartridge in his head, implanted by aliens. Then he read a poem inspired by that incident. It was a beautiful poem, but it didn't really tell the story in a narrative way. So I did. I made up the parents and the squash and even that sad, beautiful waitress. The whole idea was to find a note of grace in the incontrovertibly strange. Not a bad aspiration, as these things go. Later on, both of us pretty wasted, I showed him the story. He wasn't mad at all. God, I love poets.

Paul Prather

THE FAITHFUL

(from *The Louisville Review*)

L ucille Johnson eases her Plymouth off the bypass onto Johnson Branch Road. In the passenger seat Betty holds a bowl
of pea salad in her lap with both hands. Betty's purse is on the
floorboard between her feet. She sits knock-kneed.

The turn takes them east. The sun strikes Lucille nearly blind,
even though she's wearing sunglasses. Laser surgery has left her
eyes generally improved but sensitive to light. She's humped over
the steering wheel squinting. Johnson Branch Road is more difficult to negotiate than the four-lane bypass. It rises, falls and winds.
No sooner have they started down it than a huge pickup comes
flying at them around a curve, riding the middle of the road.

"Oh, Lord!" Betty cries, hitting a phantom brake pedal with her
foot. She kicks over her purse.

Lucille wrenches the Plymouth to the right. The pickup's
driver swerves to his side of the road. Lucille glimpses just enough
of the truck's cab to see that the driver is wearing a white Sunday
shirt and has his wife in the cab with him. Lucille's car wobbles as
she wrestles the steering wheel. She keeps the Plymouth on the
blacktop.

"This road makes me a nervous wreck," Betty says.

Every Sunday when they go to church they're taking their lives
in their hands. Lucille dreads the trip, but believes it's worth the

danger. In any case she won't be making it anymore. Today's the day they're closing Johnson Branch Baptist Church.

Right behind the truck follows a whole line of traffic headed toward the bypass: a couple of minivans, another pickup, three or four SUVs. Lucille tries not to clip mailboxes or fence posts. The people who live on the road now all go to town to church, if they bother to go at all. They mainly are city folks who have built houses in new subdivisions with names like Shady Acres or Oaklawn. They don't farm. During the week they teach school in Ephesus or drive clear to Georgetown, an hour-and-a-half away, to the assembly line at Toyota.

Lucille has made the opposite migration. She had to sell her forty-eight-acre farm and move to a seniors' complex in town because she couldn't find anybody but Mexicans willing to work the land, and she couldn't communicate with them. When she sold the place five years ago she got $94,400 for it after the Realtor's fees, and she's had to spend most of that on living expenses and medicine. Betty, who faced identical problems, occupies the apartment next door to her. On pleasant evenings they sit on their adjoining concrete porches in plastic chairs and talk about their children.

"Lord, honey, will you watch what you're doing?" Betty says.

Lucille has let the tire dip off the pavement onto the gravel shoulder. "Hush, Betty," she says. "I do well to be on the road at all."

She successfully dodges another line of vehicles. If her eyes weren't so aggravating and the traffic weren't so heavy she would love to study the scenery going by. When she was a girl, she and her family traveled from Johnson Branch to town and back every Saturday, in a mule-drawn jolt wagon. This road was hardly more than a rutted dirt path, and the five miles could take hours. But you got to see and hear things: cardinals singing and darting among the maple trees that lined the road, or the glint of sunlight off Johnson Branch itself, or the lush grass of the green knobs behind the creek. Her family knew the names of the owners or tenants of each farm along the way and called to them as they passed. When they got to Ephesus, they would window shop at the dime store and go see a western at the Virginia Theater. Her daddy loved westerns. They would ride home exhausted and happy about dusk, in time to listen to the *Grand Ole Opry*. Her parents didn't buy a car or get electricity until after Lucille was married, but they did have that table-top, battery-powered radio.

They make it to the church in one piece. Lucille steers the Plymouth up the gravel path and parks by the door of the fellowship hall, so she and Betty won't have to carry their dishes far. Lucille's contributions are lined across the car's backseat: a sliced ham, dressed eggs, mashed potatoes, a butterscotch pie, her purse with the special gifts in it.

She leaves Betty in the car, unlocks the hall, and flips on the lights inside, then passes into the musty sanctuary, where she unlocks the church's front door. When she returns to her Plymouth, Betty is half in and half out, still fumbling with the purse she kicked over. Lucille has to go around to the driver's side and help her get it. She takes Betty's pea salad into the fellowship hall. Betty is only seventy-nine, younger than Lucille, but has every ailment from congestive heart failure to gout, and already was slow as Christmas when she was young and healthy. By the time Lucille makes several trips to get her own dishes, the rest of the congregation has arrived bearing food. Counting Lucille and Betty there are six of them now, all women, the youngest sixty-seven and the oldest ninety-two.

"It's a wonder somebody's not killed on that road," says Sister Lib Thomasson, the oldest, as she hobbles through the door on her walker.

"That Engels woman was killed on it last year," says Atha Holtzclaw, Mrs. Thomasson's niece and driver. She's the youngest. She carries Sister Thomasson's brown casserole dish atop her own Tupperware bowl and two baking pans covered in tin foil.

"That was three years ago," Lucille says. "Sister Thomasson, do you need help?"

"Honey, I need about every kind of help you can name. Just not any kind they can give me."

"Aunt Lib, why don't you go on into the sanctuary and sit down?" Atha says. All business, she's already arranging the cold dishes in the refrigerator.

Instead, Mrs. Thomasson stops and leans on her walker and looks around the low-ceilinged hall. Her husband, Brother Edwin Thomasson, was pastor of Johnson Branch Baptist for forty-three years. "My oh my. I hate to give this place up."

"Now Aunt Lib, don't get on a jag," Atha says. "You'll have us all bawling. Why don't you go on to the sanctuary?"

"Do you remember the time way up one winter when little Marvin Shawcross wanted to be baptized?" Sister Thomasson says.

"I think so," Lucille says. She hands Atha a macaroni salad.

"Well it was too cold to go to the creek. The water was froze so deep we couldn't break the ice. Edwin got this bright idea about baptizing Marvin here in the church, in a galvanized washtub."

"A washtub?" Betty says. She never remembers anything. She's sitting off to the side in a chair, one shoe off, rubbing her foot. "I never heard the like."

"Put your shoe on, Betty," Atha says. "You're in the Lord's house."

"I'm only in his dining room. The Lord knows this gout's killing me."

"Anyway," Sister Thomasson says, "this was before we got indoor plumbing here, much less a baptistery, you know. Me and Edwin hauled the tub up from our house on the back of the truck. Then we liked to never have got any water out of the pump outside, for the handle was froze, too. But somehow we did. We carried the water in one bucketful at a time. Edwin put that big old tub of cold water right in front of the pulpit."

"Are you sure?" her niece Atha says. "I don't recall that either, Betty."

"Why Atha, you were right *there*. How can you not remember

that? You were on the first row, for your mama was mad at you and she made you sit down front."

"She was always mad about something."

"Will you all let Sister Thomasson tell her story?" Lucille says.

"Well," Sister Thomasson says, "what Edwin didn't know was that Marvin was scared to death of water, even a little dab. So Marvin did sit down cross-legged in the tub, but when Edwin went to put him under—he said, you know, 'I baptize thee Marvin Shawcross, my brother, in the name of the Father and the Son and the Holy Ghost'—and just as he put his hand over Marvin's nose, well, Marvin starts thrashing like a scalded dog. Hit Edwin in the eye"—she raises upright from her walker and cackles—"and turned that tub over on the floor. Ruined the rug. And the water seeped down and buckled the floor. That spring we had to tear the boards out and re-lay the front of the sanctuary."

"I do kind of remember that," Atha says. "Whatever happened to Marvin Shawcross? He was an ugly boy. Had that wiry red hair."

"We never did get him baptized, love his heart," Sister Thomasson says.

"Didn't he get killed in Korea?" Betty says, working her shoe back on her foot.

"Missing in action," Lucille says. "They couldn't ever find him. His poor mother grieved herself to death."

"Now that I think of it, he asked me out one time before he went to the service," Atha says. "Mama wouldn't let me go. She always said, 'Never go out with a boy you wouldn't want to marry someday.' And when Marvin asked me out Mama said, 'I don't want no red-headed grandbabies.' She couldn't stand red hair."

The dining hall door swings open. "Praise the Lord!" the guest preacher announces in a voice way too loud and eager. "Here you are. I looked in the front door."

Lucille flinches. She's never met him. Generally she calls around the larger Baptist churches in Ephesus, or even way over at Georgetown College, and finds a retired pastor or a Bible professor who's willing to drive out to Johnson Branch for a few Sundays. For the past month they've had Brother Clifton Devine, who runs Living Word Bible College, a two-year school in Ephesus that holds classes in a former liquor warehouse. Lucille had hoped Brother Devine could conduct this last service. He's not Baptist, but he's a good preacher and a sensitive man. On Thursday he phoned to say his daughter was sick in Georgia, and he would have to send one of his pupils instead.

This boy is in his twenties. He weighs about two hundred and fifty pounds. His hair is slicked back. His navy suit looks cheap and shiny under the artificial lights. He's got a great big Bible tucked beneath his left arm.

"I'm Lucille Johnson."

The boy strides over and pumps her hand. He looks at her strangely and Lucille realizes she's still wearing her sunglasses. "Eye surgery," she says. His hand is soft as biscuit dough; Lucille's is hard from a lifetime of milking and hoeing.

"Brother Mitch Fowler, praise the Lord. I brought my wife, Linda." As the boy says this, a mousy little thing of about nineteen enters. She glances at the older women, forces a half smile, then ducks her head. Her flowered cotton skirt reaches to her ankles. Her brown hair hangs down her chest. She stays near the door, as if prepared to run.

Lucille takes off her glasses, blinks, then goes over to introduce herself. The girl's hand is as soft as the husband's, but thinner. She doesn't say hello.

By this time the preacher has made his way around the room and greeted the other women. "Where is everybody?" he announces.

"This *is* everybody," Betty tells him. She's got her other shoe off now.

The preacher's countenance falls.

Lucille leads the singing. Sally Barclay plays the old upright piano. Sally is as out of time as the piano is out of tune. She's the only one who still lives on Johnson Branch. She never married. Instead she took care of her parents until they passed away, then stayed on in their farmhouse. But she had to sell her land, and her house is surrounded now by the vinyl homes of a subdivision called Foggy Bottom.

They try three verses of "Standing on the Promises." On the front pew, facing Lucille, the young preacher booms out the song as if he's singing on national TV, on a Billy Graham crusade. His wife sits beside him but never looks up from her hymnal. Her lips scarcely move. Lucille recalls how Brother Edwin used to joke that while Christians ought to stand on God's promises, mostly they sit on His premises. The older women are scattered around the front half of the sanctuary, which was built to hold two hundred. Of the members, only Atha is dry-eyed.

They attempt two verses of "Bringing in the Sheaves" and two more of "Farther Along" before Lucille gives up. She asks Hazel Stamper, her second cousin on her mother's side, to take the offering. Hazel, a gangly woman gone stiff with age, used to be a secretary for the county extension office. As she totters up and down the aisles each of the members drops a few ones or a five into the plate. Hazel makes her way to the front again and extends the plate toward Brother Fowler and his wife but quickly withdraws it when they ignore her. All the while Sally pounds out what Lucille thinks is "Church in the Wildwood." During the war they had a piano player who got saved in a saloon in Ephesus. Brother Edwin walked in off the street and preached the gospel and led her out. Her name was Nancy. One Sunday during the offertory she forgot where she was and started playing "Brother, Can You Spare a Dime?" Nancy married a boy from Bethel and moved to Detroit in the late forties.

"You know," Lucille says to the flock when Sally has finished playing, "I wanted us to do something really nice today, it being the last Sunday. But there aren't enough of us left for much of a ceremony, and those of us who are here aren't able to celebrate."

The old women smile. Brother Fowler says, "Praise God." Betty frowns at the back of his head.

"I do have a little treat for us later. You'll have to wait for that. I've been going through the church records. I don't know if I remembered to tell everybody, but I moved them to my apartment so they don't get lost. This church started out in an old log house in 1831. A couple of years after it was founded a cholera epidemic swept through Kentucky. A third of the congregation died. Isn't that something? That must have been so awful. But the rest came back when the epidemic was over. They built this building in 1876. People have been worshiping here ever since. It's a sight to go over the rolls. Of course there's lots of Johnsons, who were Fred's people. And lots of my people, Cundiffs. There's Thomassons and Holtzclaws and all the rest, just generation after generation. All gone to be with the Lord. Or moved north. And our kids have all run off."

"Lord, Lucille," Atha says. "Just shoot us while you're at it." Atha's first husband left her for another woman. Her second husband, Den Holtzclaw, drank himself to death. She's been down on the world ever since.

"I'm sorry, Atha," Lucille says. "Sister Thomasson, I've been thinking an awful lot about Brother Edwin."

"Love his heart," Sister Thomasson says and dabs her eyes with an embroidered handkerchief.

"He was my pastor from the time I was just a teenaged girl until I was nearly sixty. He married Freddy and me. He buried Freddy. He baptized Freddy Junior and Horace. Brother Edwin used to say, 'Folks, I'm not the prettiest man in the county. I ain't the smartest. But if I can't do nothing else I can be faithful.'"

"That's what he said," Sister Thomasson agrees. "Edwin always said that."

"And so here we are, us old women. We've tried to be faithful like Brother Edwin, all these years. We've kept the doors open while the world went off and left us. But we can't keep them open anymore. The place needs too much work we can't do, and too much money we don't have. That Keath man bid five thousand dollars just to put on a roof. And there's cracks in the foundation to deal with. And—well, you know how much else there is. We can all hold our heads up before the Lord, though, I think, and say we did our best. I feel good about that."

"Amen," Sister Thomasson says. "That's a comfort, honey."

There's a lot more Lucille would like to say, but it's not a woman's place to preach and, besides, she doesn't want to lose her composure. So she nods at Brother Fowler and takes her seat on the end of the empty third row, where she has sat for sixty-five of her eighty-one years. Freddy's family, the Johnsons, always sat near the front. When she married she joined them. Her people sat halfway back on the left.

Brother Fowler stalks to the podium like he's about to whip somebody and spreads his Bible on the pulpit. Freddy's grand-father built the pulpit from an oak tree he'd cut on his farm, in the 1880s or '90s. It's worn and stained on the edges from a century of preachers gripping it. Lucille would love to keep the pulpit, but there's no place in her apartment for it and no one to move it there without hiring it done.

"This is an emotional day for all of us," Brother Fowler an-nounces. "An emotional day. Fortunately we have a rock we can cling to in difficult times amen?"

Only Sister Thomasson answers, "Amen."

"Turn in your Bibles to John, chapter 3, verse 16."

Obediently the women find the passage. They know it by heart, which is fortunate, Lucille thinks, because they can no longer read the fine print for themselves. Young Brother Fowler intones it loudly, though, and deliberately, as if they've never heard the verse before and they're all a little dense: "For God . . . so . . . loved . . . the world . . . that . . . He gave . . . His . . . only . . . begotten . . . Son . . ."

Afterward he lifts the Bible on his outspread palm. Its cover flops with each movement of his arm. He tears into a salvation message, shouting as if he's preaching on a noisy sidewalk in some heathen city like New Orleans. He strides back and forth across the narrow stage. He rakes loose the knot in his tie. His face reddens. He tells the ladies Jesus died on the cross in their place. They're sinners who have fallen short of God's grace. Unless they repent they're bound for eternal fires like so much kindling. Lucille thinks it's probably the only sermon he knows—and he probably heard *it* from somebody else. From where she's sitting she can see the profile of the preacher's wife. The girl stares straight ahead, looking bored stiff.

Atha arches an eyebrow at Lucille as if to say, "This is a fine fare-thee-well." Lucille shrugs. The pew makes her hips ache. The doctor wants to replace her left hip. At her age it's not worth the trouble, she thinks; she won't have to endure the pain all that much longer. Brother Fowler's agitated voice echoes around the room, intruding on her. He's getting more worked up, preaching himself happy, as Brother Edwin used to say.

Lucille remembers when Johnson Branch Baptist Church was the hub of the community, the site of pie suppers and gospel singings and cake walks and vacation Bible schools and two revivals a year, after spring planting and when the crops were laid by. In the fall of 1958 Brother Edwin invited in an evangelist from Knoxville, a Brother Sinclair, for a revival. Now that man could preach. They had seventy-some saved, and so many rededications the preachers lost count. The ushers had to put out folding chairs in the aisles. People sat on the floor and stood around the walls. Freddy Junior and Horace got saved in that revival.

Lucille tried to get Freddy Junior to fly back for today. He always loved church when he was young. He has retired early from the shipyard in California and he and Connie have moved to Arizona, where they play golf every day. He said he was too busy to come all the way to Kentucky for one service, but to tell everybody *hi*. He claims he belongs to a church in Flagstaff, but Lucille doubts he attends much; he never talks about the Lord on the phone. She didn't even ask Horace to come. He's in Boulder and hasn't been home since IBM transferred him out there in 1985. Horace sends her cards for Christmas, Mother's Day, and her birthday—or his new wife, Jeannie, does. The only other time Lucille hears from him is if she calls. He did fly her out there for the wedding. Colorado is pretty and Jeannie and her kids seemed sweeter than Horace's last wife and stepchildren. Still, Lucille was glad to get home.

When Brother Fowler has worn himself out, he calls Sally up to play an invitation. She gamely tries "Just as I Am," but the ladies don't walk down the aisle to grab Brother Fowler's arm and repent. They've been Christians since before his parents were born. Lucille kind of feels sorry for him. He's just a boy, really. He's got a lot yet to learn about the Lord and about himself. Most of it isn't going to be much fun for him.

In the fellowship hall they arrange the food on the counter and take the towels and plastic wrap off the dishes. In the old days there were so many people they had to eat their potluck dinners outside. They would place long boards across saw horses in rows and crowd the makeshift tables with bowls and pans. "Lord forgive us for the sin of gluttony we're about to commit," Brother Edwin would pray, grinning.

Still, even on this day there's too much food given the size of the group. None of the members is in the mood to eat, and anyway most of the ladies are on restricted diets. Lucille takes a dab of everything so as not to hurt anybody's feelings. The members congregate at one table. Brother Fowler and his wife sit at another. Lucille chooses a chair beside the Fowlers so the church won't appear unfriendly in their memories.

Brother Fowler's plate is heaped. "My, this is great," he says. "Praise God for good cooks." He empties his plate in nothing flat and returns to the counter to refill it.

"You're not eating much, honey," Lucille says to Mrs. Fowler.

"I don't like most of that stuff," the girl says.

Brother Fowler overhears. "She doesn't like anything but hamburgers and french fries."

"I do too."

"We had an evangelist who came through here," Lucille says. "One of the kids asked him how he realized God wanted him in the ministry. He said, 'Well, I woke up one morning craving fried chicken and feeling lazy—and I knew I had the call.' "

Brother Fowler and his wife don't even smile. "I don't get it," Brother Fowler says as he sits down and shoves a piece of ham into his mouth.

"Well, you know, people used to always take a preacher home with them for Sunday dinner. And nearly everybody fed him fried chicken. It got to be kind of a joke."

Brother Fowler tears a yeast roll in half. "But preachers aren't lazy. I would resent that, as a man of God, if somebody said I was lazy. The Lord's work is the most important work there is."

"I reckon you're right," Lucille says. She pushes around the food on her plate.

Before long Brother Fowler goes back to the counter for a third helping. His wife leans toward Lucille and whispers, "I never wanted to be married to a preacher."

The warm sun hangs overhead now instead of in Lucille's eyes. There's a breeze. Lucille walks among the tombstones that take up most of the churchyard. Walking helps her hips sometimes. Other times it makes them feel worse.

She drifts to a section where the stones are mossy and worn. There's one stone a bit newer than the others. It says, "Naomi Holtzclaw, Beloved Wife and Mother, 1858–1933." Old Mrs. Holtzclaw was Lucille's Sunday school teacher when Lucille was a girl. She sat in a wooden wheelchair that had a woven cane back. She used to tell Lucille and the other children stories about the Civil War, which Mrs. Holtzclaw had survived during her own childhood. One tale was about some Yankee soldiers who came through Johnson Branch scavenging for food. Mrs. Holtzclaw's mother hid the family's hams in an ash barrel. The soldiers found the hams but didn't want them because they were ash-covered and moldy. Being from the north, they didn't know Kentucky hams always looked moldy, and the ashes were easy to rinse off. So the Holtzclaws had ham meat all winter. Mrs. Holtzclaw looked as ancient to Lucille as a crone from a storybook. Lucille is older now than Mrs. Holtz-claw was when she died. There's nobody on earth besides Lucille and the old women in the fellowship hall who would have any idea who she was.

Lucille continues down the cemetery's rows. She finds Brother Edwin's stone. Beside his inscription, Sister Thomasson's date of birth already is carved in, her death date left blank temporarily. Beneath all that sod Brother Edwin must be spinning in his coffin to think the church's last service was preached by the likes of young Brother Fowler. Brother Edwin was convinced that only Baptists would make it into heaven. Lucille doesn't believe that herself, but she feels bad on his behalf.

After he died, Lucille kept praying the Lord would send another pastor like him, a man who would take the church into his heart and give his life to it, but that didn't happen. In Brother Edwin's declining years the attendance already had started to wane. The pastors who followed him didn't stay long. They planned bigger futures for themselves than they were likely to find at Johnson Branch Baptist.

The women haven't been able to decide what to do with the church property. The sanctuary is in too bad a shape and too far from town for another congregation to be interested in it. They might be able to sell the property to a developer, but Atha's the only one who wants to and, besides, what would a developer do with all these graves? For now they're just going to shut the utilities off, lock the building and leave it. Lucille knows it won't take vandals long to realize it's been abandoned. Teenagers from the subdivisions will knock out its windows and then eventually venture inside to spray-paint their names and ugly words on the walls. They'll build bonfires on the floors and drink beer and hold séances and claim the church is haunted. They'll tip over gravestones. She's seen it happen to other churches that were as dear to their people as this one is to her.

Two rows over from Brother Edwin she reaches the Cundiff plot, where her grandparents lie near her mama and daddy, her brother Chester and her sister Marie, who was three when she died of the whooping cough. Lucille decides she needs to come back next spring, if she lives and keeps her health, and plant new flowers on their graves even if the vandals just trample them down. To her it's the principle of the thing: You do what you can, and what you should, even if the results are out of your hands.

And then she makes it to Freddy's stone. It has a polished granite facing and rough-hewn sides. "Johnson" is engraved near the top on the front and, lower, in a small square it says: Frederick William, June 16, 1917–August 8, 1981. Next to that: Lucille Cundiff, March 22, 1920, with a hyphen.

The door to the fellowship hall opens. Brother Fowler emerges, followed by his wife. His suit jacket is folded across his arm. His wife is carrying his huge Bible. The preacher spots Lucille and bounds toward her. "Mighty fine meal! You all are wonderful cooks praise the Lord!" His wife hangs back.

He walks up beside Lucille. "If you ladies don't need us anymore, I guess Linda and I had better be getting on back to town bless God."

"Well, thanks for coming."

But Brother Fowler lingers. "Did you know a lot of these people?"

"Most of them. Knew *of* all of them."

"Praise the Lord. There must be some great saints out here."

Lucille doesn't answer. The preacher shifts from one foot to another. "We're to mourn at the day of birth and rejoice at the day of death, amen."

Finally, Lucille realizes what he's after. "Oh," she says. "I left the church's checkbook in the glove box." She leads him back across the graveyard.

The cars are loaded, the counter wiped. The women sit in the fellowship hall facing one another around a table. No one wants to be the first to go. Betty is in her stocking feet. Sister Thomasson has one baggy arm propped on her walker. Sally has gathered a sheaf of music as a keepsake.

"Did you all think this day would really come?" Hazel Stamper says. "After a hundred and seventy years?"

Atha says, "Everything in this world is born to die. Churches pass just like dogs and squirrels and people. That's a fact."

"It may be a fact, but that doesn't keep it from being a shame, too."

Sally shuffles her sheet music. Sister Thomasson starts to cry. "Lordy, lordy," she says. "Poor Edwin. Love his heart."

"Aunt Lib, it's time for us to head out," Atha says sternly.

"Wait." Lucille bends toward the floor. Opening her purse, she takes out several white envelopes and drops them on the table. "I've been asking the Lord for the right time to do this."

Each of their names is written on one of the envelopes.

"Now what's this?" Atha says.

"This is a little gift."

"A gift? From who?"

"I don't know, exactly," Lucille admits, feeling her cheeks blush. "From the church. Or me. Or the good Lord."

Lucille explains that, when she sat down to balance the books, the church still had over $900 in its account. "I left enough in to pay the preacher today and to keep the grass mowed 'til fall," Lucille says. "But then I got to thinking that if I left it all in there it would just end up going to the bank, or some lawyer, or the state, or whoever gets it when a church closes. I don't even know where it goes, really. I didn't ask. The men listed on the papers as trustees are dead and gone."

"Honey, what did you do?" Sister Thomasson says.

"Well, I drew out six hundred dollars. And I brought each one of us a hundred dollars apiece as a going away present."

"That's not right," Sister Thomasson says. "Is it? I mean, is it legal?"

"I don't know. But I'm eighty-one, and I've been treasurer since Kelvin Brashears died in nineteen seventy. I've never taken a dime. If the law wants to come after me for this, let 'em come."

"I am on a fixed income," Betty says. Her eyes have lit up. Last month she had to do without her blood thinner.

"We've endured," Lucille says. "I don't think the Lord will mind." She pauses. "Think of it as a reward. Or a little down payment on glory."

"To the victors belong the spoils," Atha agrees. "Isn't that in the Bible?"

"No, honey," Sister Thomasson says.

"Well, it ought to be."

They stare at the envelopes.

"Oh, I don't see why not," Sister Thomasson says at last, and that decides it.

They tear open the envelopes and eagerly pull out crisp hundred-dollar bills. Betty lifts hers by the ends and pops it. That makes Hazel Stamper pop her bill, too.

Then, to the astonishment of them all, Sister Thomasson rolls her hundred-dollar bill into a stick like a cigarette. Holding it between her liver-spotted fingers, she acts like she's smoking it. "I always did think I'd make a good tycoon," she says between puffs.

The others giggle like foolish schoolgirls.

Trying to outdo Sister Thomasson, Betty folds her money in half, raises a gouty foot and pretends to use the edge of the bill to clean her toenails through her stocking.

"That's nasty!" says Sally Barclay. But Sally's laughing so hard her upper plate slips loose from her gums. She catches it with her thumb.

All the women shriek. They laugh until they're wiping their eyes and patting each other's backs. They're so caught up that, as Lucille holds her stomach, shaking, she thinks she must be the only one aware of the treacherous drive back to town they still must survive, with the traffic coming the opposite direction, trying to run them off the narrow road.

Paul Prather is the pastor of a rural church near
Mount Sterling, Kentucky, and the son and
nephew of country ministers. He's also a former
writer for the *Lexington Herald-Leader.* Three
times the Kentucky Press Association named him
the state's best newspaper columnist. His books
include a biography of country singer John
Michael Montgomery and two works on spiritu-
ality. He has received awards for fiction writing
from the Kentucky Writers' Coalition and the
Kentucky Council for the Arts.

REX MARTIN

*I spend most days caring for my wife, who's battling advanced cancer.
Occasionally I decompress by driving alone along our country's backroads
with my camera, stopping here and there to snap pictures of old barns or
houses. During a couple of those drives I happened across two churches, one
abandoned and covered with graffiti and the other similar (from the outside)
to the one described in this tale. The photographs I took of those buildings
somehow made me think of my late grandmother and my great-aunts and
the potluck dinners their Baptist congregation used to have when I was a kid.
All these things—my daily intimacy with mortality, the time-worn church
buildings, and my memories of the women in my family—eventually joined
up in my head. Out came "The Faithful." I'm working on several stories
about the religious lives of various people in this same Kentucky town, but this
was the first of those I'd finished.*

Michael Knight

ELLEN'S BOOK

(from *Five Points*)

1. Every day, my wife and her mother drive down from the house in Ashland Place and eat lunch in Bienville Square. And, every day, I steal away from work and spy on them from the window of the drugstore across the street. My wife has been staying with her parents since she left me. Sunlight filters through the big oaks, drawing liquid shadows on her face and bare shoulders. Nearby, a quartet of old men is playing cards on a stone table. Ellen shakes her head, gives her mother a careful smile. I have no idea what they are saying. I only know they are not talking about me. Mrs. Allbright, in her yellow sundress and walking shoes and old lady bracelets, believes that bad things can be held at bay by leaving them unspoken. I watch Ellen finish eating and stuff a Tupperware bowl into her purse, watch her stand and smooth her shorts over her hips. I can see from here that the wrought-iron bench has left an intricate tattoo on the backs of her legs.

Ellen is barely five feet tall, but she moves like she's much taller, nothing but slink and skin and bones. Look there. The wind has snagged a paper napkin, and Ellen is dancing after it over the bricks.

I have decided to write a book about my wife.

2. Kosgrove Construction hires temps for on-site secretarial needs, and I've been called in to handle the filing and answer the phones. They're building a new middle school out by the airport. The land has been cleared, foundations poured, but this afternoon, the work has been delayed by bad weather. Through the window in the trailer, I can see the level, silvery expanses of concrete where the classrooms will one day stand, but so far it looks more like something destroyed than something in progress, torn-up ground, pools of rain water reddened with clay. Everything's quiet. Most of the construction crew has moved to a site where there is indoor work to do. I swipe a hard hat from the supply shed, tour the naked rebar and the rubbish heaps. The rain beats down on my shoulders. On the slab of what will be the cafeteria, I find the words *Henry Was Here* pressed into the concrete. Henry is the name Ellen would have chosen for our child.

3. My wife is a long-suffering insomniac. When she was a little girl, she lived in fear of missing something important while she slept, something cryptic and adult, the unedited solution to some antique mystery. After we married, she would glide out of bed when she couldn't sleep and rewrite my stories on the word processor in the spare room. Ellen found my fiction bland and deliberately remote. The men in my stories, she said, leaned too far toward emotional distance. She filled my bleak, ironic little numbers with romance. Brief glances became revelations of love. Missed opportunities, for better or for worse, were nearly always acted upon, and her characters could, at least, fade into the final paragraph without regret.

4. I call late enough that everyone should be asleep, but Ellen's father is manning the phones. He sounds groggy, maybe a little tight, and I can hear strains of classical music in the background. Wade Allbright is of the opinion music begins and ends with Beethoven.

"Keith?" he says. Then, "Jesus," when he understands that it's only his daughter's estranged husband on the line, and his family is safe, and this not one of those awful after-midnight wake-up calls.

"I didn't mean to bother you," I say. "I was hoping Ellen would answer."

Wade chuckles softly, like he has been in my shoes before, like I'm just in the doghouse and all of this will soon be a memory. That isn't true, I know, but I find his voice immensely reassuring. He had, I imagine, dozed off in his big leather club chair with a glass of scotch in one hand and the stereo remote in the other.

"She said you might be calling. The fact is, pal, she doesn't care to speak to you right this minute."

Ellen's father is one of those old Alabama smoothies who can talk friendly no matter what sort of bad news he is delivering.

"She'll call Wednesday," he says. "Just like last week."

My wife has not cut off communications entirely. She has agreed to one phone call a week, always, for some reason, on Wednesday, and always at the hour of her convenience. She believes that, in this way, she can achieve an honest separation, without ruling out the possibility of reconciliation. I'm not pleased with the arrangement, but I take what I can get.

"How's she doing, Wade?" I say. "Is everything all right over there?"

"It's been rough on her," he says. "She doesn't sleep much. You know this isn't what she wanted."

"I know," I say.

We are quiet for a moment, married men contemplating women in the waning hours of the night. Into our silence, string music swells. Wade is fiddling with his remote.

"You ever hear Beethoven's quartet in F major," he says.

"I wouldn't recognize it," I say.

"Deep," he says. "Goddamn." Ice clicks against his teeth. His chair creaks lavishly. When he says, "Nobody listens to Beethoven anymore," there is real sadness in his voice.

I will treat Wade Allbright kindly in the book.

"I'm sorry for all this," I say, but he's covering the phone with his hand. I can make out a muffled voice in the room with him, maybe my wife's, maybe her mother's.

"I have to hang up," he says. "I'm under orders."

"I understand," I say.

I'm lying in bed while we finish up. Old Dog is in Ellen's place. We rescued Old Dog from the pound. He's a medley of breeds, weighs about as much as Ellen. Sometimes, I wake in the middle of the night with Old Dog breathing on my mustache. I walk him outside, and both of us whiz into the boxwoods. The mustache is new. In the book, I will have copious facial hair as a way of revealing something important about my character.

5.   In part, Wade Allbright blames himself for getting his daughter mixed up in a failing marriage. He owns and operates a string of car dealerships out by the interstate, and his receptionist quit, without warning, to start a hemp farm in the foothills of North Alabama. Wade phoned for a temp to fill in while he interviewed for a full-time replacement.

That's where I come into the story.

Ellen was working for her father on the management end. She was just a few years out of college. Wade's employees treated her with the fondness and deference generally reserved for young children. I suspect her size played a part in their good will. She moved through the garage aswim in the elbows of large men. They spoke to her in soft voices. They tousled her hair with oily hands, and Ellen never seemed to mind. She remembered their names. She knew their histories. I'll need to come up with a more evocative phrase for the final draft, but, to my eyes, she was charmed.

She even took the time to introduce herself to temps.

"I only do this to pay the bills," I said, thumbing the telephone headpiece. "I'm a writer. I write fiction."

I nodded seriously, my armpits going clammy. We scanned the showroom as if the perfect subject for a novel were unfolding before our eyes.

"I always liked to write," she said. "I signed up for a class over at adult ed last year, but everybody was so depressed."

We did all the usual getting to know each other—marathon phone calls, kissing in public, you name it. Eventually, we wound up in my bed. My brain was a haze of endorphins and adrenaline and whatever else your glands are churning out when you're in the middle of falling in love.

"My sister was an accident," Ellen said. "Beth is sixteen years younger so I got to watch my parents raise a child. It was like home movies or something. They were terrific."

Ellen talked a lot about her parents, which was a surprise for me. I hardly remembered my mother. She died when I was five years old, and my father and I had settled on a cordially indifferent approach to our relationship.

"It would make a great story," Ellen said.

"You'd have to add some tension," I said, feeling the pulse in her wrist with my fingers. "The first time around the couple was happy and young. Things have soured over the years. They were planning a divorce until the second child. Maybe something like that."

"No tension," Ellen said. "This is a happy story." She pinched the hairs below my belly button, then swung out of bed and minced through the room in the dark looking for her clothes.

6. Mornings, I wake up early and stare at the computer, trying to imagine a beginning for Ellen's book. Dreary light slants in through the blinds, my shadow is pudgy at my back. The whole time I have the feeling that I'm being watched, but it's not Old Dog. He's snoozing in the kitchen. The hair on the back of my neck goes squirrelly. Goosebumps, etc. I take a break to check beneath our bed and paw through the closets. I peel back the mildewed shower curtain. I rattle the knobs to make sure I locked the doors.

7. My wife is watching TV through the display windows at Barney Electronics. Her mother has ducked inside to use the restroom.

They are on their way home from lunch in Bienville Square. Misting rain, but they stuck it out, polished off a pair of sandwiches beneath a red umbrella. Have I established the season? Late spring, pleasant despite the weather. I am hiding behind a bakery truck, gathering my nerve. If the truck pulls out before her mother returns, I will speak to her. If not, a meeting isn't in the cards. Ellen in a navy blue slicker, her toenails painted silver beneath the hem.

In the book, Ellen will be cagey and sad, always just beyond the reach of my understanding.

Then the truck pulls away, leaving me crouched on the damp pavement, my hair slicked over my skull. I wobble toward her on the sidewalk, behind and to her left, watch my reflection come even with hers in the plate glass, which is a nice detail. Ellen is intent on the TV and hasn't spotted me yet. At that moment, past our shapes in the window, I see her mother moving toward the door and I dodge behind a mailbox on the corner. I hear the bell announcing her exit, hear her mother say, "Were you talking to someone? I would have sworn I saw a man with an undergrown mustache."

8. I tell people that I'm still temping because it leaves me several days at a stretch for my real work. The truth is my real work amounts to a handful of short stories, only one of which has been published. It was picked up by a feminist literary journal called *Virginia's Room*, and that was an accident more or less. I posted one of Ellen's rewrites by mistake. I should have suspected something when I read the letter, which said, "The prose is uneven, but I started crying on the first page of "Satellite" and didn't stop for two days. How is it possible for one man to know so much about women?"

9. The Tuesday Night Prayer Group meets in a bar called Roget's Downtown. The name, a play on the actual Bible study meetings that convene all over Mobile, was Lamont Turner's idea. Lamont is a short-story writer who takes great pride in his agnosticism. There are four writers in the group—Lamont and Richard

Frost and Brenda Mayo and myself— and we have published exactly three stories between us, though Brenda is nearly finished
with her autobiography and, because she was raised by an abusive
father then went on to marry a drunken bully, we have high hopes
that she will find an agent. Tonight, we are hashing out the idea
of a book about my wife.

"Would you publish?" Lamont says.

"That's beside the point," I say. "She'll see it before then anyway.
The real question is will it win her back?"

"How long would it be?" Richard says.

Richard is the youngest in the group, maybe twenty-four or
twenty-five, a graduate student at the state university here in town.
He has a sinister goatee and his work is strictly hypertext.

"Does that matter?" I say.

"It could," Brenda says. "Your wife might be tempted to draw
a correlation between the number of pages and the scope of your
emotion."

"Is everyone so hung up on length?" Lamont says. He finishes
his drink and signals the waitress. "Why wouldn't a short story, perfectly drawn, serve your purpose just as well?"

I shrug, not wanting to get into this particular line of discourse.
Lamont has an inferiority complex regarding the short story. We
put the discussion on hold while the waitress takes orders for another round. When she's gone, Richard says, "You're talking about
fiction, right, a sort of parallel universe? Maybe you should use
footnotes, you know. To draw the analogy between your real life
and your book life."

"I don't want footnotes," I say. "I want my wife."

Brenda brushes her lips with a finger. She says, "Wait a minute,
now, Richard has a point. Why not just do the whole thing as a
piece of creative nonfiction?"

"That wasn't my point," Richard says. "What I was talking about
was layering the text."

"Layering the text?" Lamont says, his voice gluey with loathing.

He is looking at me when he says, "Does that even mean anything? Isn't anybody interested in craftsmanship anymore?"

We sit without speaking for a few seconds, all of us nodding solemnly, a moment of silence for the death of craftsmanship. The waitress arrives with new drinks, beer for Brenda and myself, bourbon for Lamont, red wine for Richard Frost, and waits for one of us to indicate that the time is right for an interruption. She is young, almost pretty, her legs descending from her shorts into white socks and running shoes.

"I couldn't help but overhear," she says. "I think it sounds great. The book about your wife. That's the most romantic thing I ever heard." She smiles at us, and we smile back. The moment keeps stringing itself out. "My name's Mandy," she says.

I say, "Well, hey, Mandy, thanks for the kind words."

"I really do think it's a good idea," she says. She gathers the empties, retreats to the bar. We peer grimly into our drinks. Finally, Richard excuses himself to go ask Mandy for her number.

10. Ellen and I had been together for seven weeks when she missed a period. We bought a drugstore test, and she was pregnant. I asked her to marry me because it was the right thing to do, and, to my surprise, she smiled and said she would, without giving it much thought. It was as if no one had explained to her that a bad thing can happen in this world.

"But do you love me?" I said.

We were sitting cross-legged on the grassy strip of median in the parking lot of my old apartment complex. Ellen was barefoot, her tiny toes unpainted. The sky was crazy with stars.

"Sometimes," she said.

"Like when?" I said, still dumbstruck.

She laughed and punched my chest, then realized I was serious and composed her face into a thoughtful frown. "Like last week," she said. "You were at the kitchen sink rinsing a mug."

• • •

11.   Ellen calls while I'm in the shower, and I barefoot down the hall in a hurry, toweling my head on the way.

"Hey," she says. "It's Wednesday."

Her voice sounds long distance. Old Dog picks through the mess on the bedroom floor and settles at my feet. He groans, like negotiating discarded clothes is the most difficult thing he's done in a long time. Old Dog's arthritis stiffens a little more each year, and rain makes him ache.

"The dog wants me to ask when you're coming back," I say.

A long quiet follows, and I imagine all the subjects we're avoiding backing up in the phone line like a gridlock. The clock beside the bed reveals that I'm running late for work.

Ellen says, "This is hard, Keith."

The simplest statement in the world and I don't know how to respond. I scratch my new mustache, rub my chin whiskers against the receiver. In the book, I'll have to smooth the edges of this scene, fill my head with thoughts too numerous, too painful for utterance, but for now, I lay back on the bed, hoping Ellen will mistake my silence for cogitation.

"Is this connection funny?" I say. "I can hardly hear you."

Ellen does an exacerbated sigh, so familiar I can see her face, the amused lips, the crow-footed corners of her eyes. "Mom?" she says, "Hang up the phone, Mom."

I hear a click, quiet as a whisper, and the line clears.

"She's just worried," I say.

Ellen doesn't answer, but I can picture her nodding a reply. Sometimes, my wife forgets she's on the phone and goes ahead with all sorts of nonverbal communication. She's in her old room, I think, her view pretty houses and big magnolias. She can hear traffic sounds drifting over from Dauphin Street. Maybe she is hiding in her closet like when she was a girl and she wanted to make a call in secret.

"I've been writing," I say, which sounds awful and self-important the moment the words are out of my mouth, but Ellen wants to know what it is I'm working on.

"A story?" she says.

"I don't know yet," I say. "I'm just taking notes."

Old Dog creaks upright and swipes halfheartedly at his neck. He is winded by the effort. His muzzle is all winter, his eyes rheumy and sentimental. Somebody should write a story about Old Dog.

"How about a sneak preview?" Ellen says.

Beyond the window, rain falls gently on the neighbor's hydrangeas. I close my eyes. I promise Ellen she'll be the first to read it when I'm done.

12. Ellen's version of "Satellite" is about a young woman married to a man incapable of tenderness. It's simple, poignant in a heavy-handed way. The wife is pregnant, worried, and unhappy, but she loves him and she wants to make a go of wedlock. She sends signals and makes loaded remarks. The husband, a top astrophysicist, finally gets the picture. Everybody's happy in the end. The principal metaphor features a moon in lonely orbit around a heedless planet.

The wife has a bit part in the original. My version is about mankind and his place in the mysterious universe.

13. My Taurus dies on the way to work, and I have to hoof the last couple of miles to the Kosgrove site. The grass is knee high beside the road, threaded with Queen Anne's lace and black-eyed Susans. Nobody notices that I'm late. I call a tow from the trailer and wait for it in the misting rain. The driver turns out to be a black guy, closing in on sixty. His name, according to his license, is Mohammed Ali. "Like the boxer," I say and Mohammed Ali goes, "Heh, heh." As we're leaving the site, headed back to my car, I see the word *Henry* spray painted yellow on a port-a-john.

14. Some nights, I call my father during the ten o'clock sports roundup. He never misses the TV 12 news. He lives up in Montgomery, and he has a crush on his local anchor lady, but he doesn't pay attention to sports so it's the perfect time for us to talk. I know

he's home, and he's awake, and I'm not bothering him. My old man does not like to be disturbed.

"Do you believe in ghosts?" I say.

"I heard whistling in the house for a month or so after your mother passed," he says. "Your mother was a gorgeous whistler."

She's been dead for years. There was nothing glamorous in her demise. My mother had cancer, like everybody else.

"I feel like I'm being watched all the time," I say.

"Weird," he says.

"I saw Henry painted on a port-a-john," I say. "Henry's what we would have named the baby."

"The whistling went away," he says.

"That's good," I say.

"I gotta run," my father says, his voice quickening. I imagine his anchor lady filling the TV screen. Her name is April West. Her lips are shiny, and she has bid farewell to her Southern drawl.

15. Ellen and I explained the situation to her parents on Good Friday. Mrs. Allbright wept for her daughter's innocence and for the baby, conceived in a union not sanctified by God. Wade took me aside and offered me a permanent position at Allbright Motors. I refused—graciously—on principle, and I think he respected me for that. Almost a year has passed. Those, I think now, were the happiest hours of my life.

16. Because the Taurus is in the shop and I haven't yet figured out the city bus schedule, I missed Ellen in Bienville Square today. I settle for a view of her bathroom window. The Allbright's house is only a couple of miles from mine, but even that's too much for Old Dog. He is napping, exhausted, at my feet. I watch Ellen scrub her face, her skin luminous and pale, her hair held back with a bandana. She smears lotion on her cheeks and gives her toothbrush a workout. I watch her bare her teeth at the mirror, checking her handiwork, the way she has done every night that I have known her, but tonight, my heart is a ricochet in my chest. There is some-

thing intimate about looking in on her like this, something thrilling, like I am on the verge of discovering my wife in a way I overlooked before.

Ellen kills the bathroom light, and I nudge Old Dog awake with my foot. He moans and looks at me like that's too much to ask. "All right," I say. I gather him in my arms and carry him to a magnolia with a view of Ellen's room. Her sister, Beth, follows Ellen in, wearing matching pajamas and slippers, and sits beside her on the bed. Ellen lets Beth brush her hair. Beth gabs excitedly, but Ellen's answers seem cursory from my vantage. Her mind is elsewhere. After a few minutes, her mother appears in a nightgown. When she speaks, her daughters laugh, and for an instant, Ellen looks happy.

Wade's women, the Allbright girls.

I notice, then, that Old Dog has realized why we're here. He is peering intently through the leaves at the scene beyond the window. He whines, beats his tall against my legs.

"Sorry, pal," I say. "I'm not welcome."

Old Dog couldn't be more disappointed. His muscles vibrate beneath his skin. Mrs. Allbright guides Beth out of Ellen's room, and Ellen heads over to the window. The dog looks at me with pained eyes. I don't think Ellen can see us, but I crab into the bush just in case. Ellen lets her brow drop against the glass. Her breath makes and erases ghostly ovals on the pane.

17. Ellen was three months pregnant on our wedding day. We said our vows on the elegant stairway in her parents' house. Despite the circumstances, Wade spared no expense. We could hear the orchestra tuning up during the ceremony, harried caterers putting the finishing touches on the menu. My father, insurance adjuster, widower, drove down from Montgomery. He wandered through the house marveling at banisters and mantels and the imported andirons in the fireplace. Late in the afternoon, I found him in Beth's room upstairs. He was standing at the window watching the reception on Wade's pristine lawn.

"This must have cost a fortune," he said.

"I didn't ask how much," I said.

He scratched the windowsill with his thumbnail.

"Your mother and I were married at the courthouse."

"I know," I said.

He said, "I had to be at work the next day."

Below us, natty guests strolled from one tent to the next. The grass looked impossibly green, and the whole day had a vaguely underwater feel. Ellen moved out from beneath a yellow awning, and we watched her lift her dress with both hands to keep the hem off the grass, watched her rise up on her toes to scan the crowd. At some point, she had kicked off her shoes. She was astonishing. She was my wife.

"She's looking for me," I said.

18.   Thursday night, Lamont calls an emergency meeting of the Prayer Group, which is to say he's drunk, and he wants company. Roget's Downtown is mostly quiet, and Lamont and I are alone at the bar. Brenda couldn't come. Her Battered Wives Team meets on Thursday to discuss their various tragedies. Richard Frost, however, has arrived and is making out with Mandy at the waitress station. He has somehow convinced her he's a genius.

"Admit it," Lamont says, "you think because I only write short stories my stuff is less important." Lamont is verging on bitter and morose. He is breathing open-mouthed, his lips moist, his eyes haggard. He grabs my wrist on the bartop. "Look at Carver, you bastard. Look at Raymond fucking Carver."

"You're a good writer," I say.

His features go soft all of a sudden. His eyes water up. He turns away before he starts to cry.

"I'm considering a subplot for the book," I say. "I don't know how it'll fit. It's about a dead baby haunting his father."

Lamont doesn't hear me. He can't take his eyes off of Richard and Mandy, Richard's hands up Mandy's shirt, Mandy's pretty mouth disappearing into Richard's beard.

"He's got the whole package," Lamont says, his voice weary with sadness. "The shaved head. The glasses. He's got the goatee. Women always think geniuses have goatees."

19. For several hours after I finished reading Ellen's version of "Satellite," I seriously considered proposing a joint literary venture. Together, I thought, we were capable of publishable work. I wanted her to know that half a talent was the worst thing in the world. That sort of ordinary can't help but break your heart.

20. Friday, I wake to the sound of Wade Allbright's voice, rise through layer upon layer of sleep to hear him barking orders on my lawn. It is as if I have slipped into a dream of yardwork.

"Right here, Pedro," he says. "The grass needs cutting, the hedge needs a haircut, and this azalea bed needs new mulch."

"Angel."

"What's that?" Wade says.

"My name is Angel. The old head groundskeeper, he retired last year, his name is Pedro."

"Mucho apologioso," Wade says. "Your name is An-hell. I want all this ragweed vamoosed by nine o'clock, An-hell. No telling how long the rain'll hold off for us today."

I open the window and hang my head outside, and there is Wade, in a short-sleeved shirt and striped tie, his hands on his hips, marshaling a trio of Hispanic yardmen.

"What time is it?" I say.

"Pushing seven," he shouts. "I brought my crew over from the dealership. Thought we'd give this yard a spruce." He storms over to the window and peers inside. The room is a masterpiece of disarray. Dirty clothes, dirty dishes, reams of wadded paper around the bed. "The house could use a once-over, too, looks like. Where's the car?"

"Alternator's busted," I say.

He gives me a hurt look. "You should've called me. When's it coming back?"

"Monday," I say.

"Monday my ass," he says. "How're you getting around?"

I say, "Bus." And Wade says, "Jesus on popsicle stick, Keith. What if Ellen was to come by here this morning? Where's your head, boy?" He jabs his index finger at me. "Listen up," he says. "I'll send Lavinia round for the house, and somebody from the dealership will handle the car. Now, get dressed. I'm driving you to work."

I pull myself together in a hurry, wet my hair in the sink, dump some food in a bowl for Old Dog, who is dozing in the kitchen. I'm ready for Wade in nine minutes flat, and he already has the Lincoln running. Wade is a big man, his frame softened by easy living. I like Ellen's father all over again, because he doesn't try to drum up conversation on the ride. Neither does he mention my new mustache, for which I am grateful, because it has arrived at something like a larval stage of growth. We cruise without speaking, past the strip malls and the hospital, Beethoven's *Fifth* murmuring from the tape deck.

"Take him," Wade says, tipping his head toward the dash. "There's a fella had some serious adversity between himself and beautiful music."

He is referring, I suspect, to Ludwig van Beethoven but I decide to keep my mouth shut until I'm sure.

"Ellen is a mess sometimes," Wade says. "I know that. And nobody could have helped what happened."

He shakes his head, raps his wedding band on the wheel. Sweat is beading on his upper lip. He's having a tough time. I tell him what I meant for him to hear the other night.

"I'm sorry for all this, Wade."

He exhales a yard of pent-up breath. "Lord in Heaven," he says. "This is my daughter we're talking about."

21. Ellen delivered a still-born male child near the end of the sixth month. I was temping for a locksmith when she went into labor. Because of a mix-up at headquarters, I didn't get the news for several hours. I barreled into the birthing room just in time to

witness Dr. Hershey emerging from between Ellen's knees, and I keeled over on the spot and woke in the hospital with Ellen in bed beside me. She was small enough that she fit on the strip of mattress between my body and the edge. The room was dark, except for a green light from a monitor by the window.

"Are you awake?" she said. "I thought I heard you wake up."

"I'm awake," I said.

"Do you remember fainting? Dr. Hershey said you looked like a vaudeville routine." Her voice sounded so matter of fact I wondered if I hadn't cooked up the scene in the delivery room from scratch. She propped herself on an elbow, ran her warm instep along my calf.

"I didn't mean to faint," I said.

"It doesn't matter," she said, and I knew, then, that what I remembered — the limp, slick, membranous creature — had nothing to do with my imagination. I could just make out her face, her features bunched and over-serious like a little girl. This will be a big scene in the book. The decayed flower smell and the sterile half light. The cross-hatched shadows. The fevery, anesthesia heat of Ellen's body at my side.

22. The good weather unleashes bedlam at work—everybody on the double to make up for lost time. I've got a phone at either ear most of the morning, one hand in the file cabinet, the other hacking out shipping manifests on the computer. While I'm polishing off the payroll, I come across the name Henry M. Hotchner, and it occurs to me to do a little sleuthing over lunch. There are three Henrys on the crew, it turns out—Hotchner, Shiflett, and Breedlove—and one by one I track them down. The day is all evaporation, the sun delirious with rediscovered strength. Each Henry looks at me like I'm crazy when I ask if he's the one who's been writing his name, and each in turn denies it. The last guy, Hank Shiflett, is a crane operator. He's got porkchop sideburns and a pompadour beneath his hard hat.

• • •

23. I wrote this sentence when I was eighteen: *After dinner, he knelt beside her chair without a word and rubbed her feet.* It was a story about old people. It's not much, I know, but it made me want to write another. I'll make myself a happy-go-lucky Ad man in the book. I'll have new suits and pressed shirts and polished shoes.

24. The door bell rings just as I'm selecting a Hungry Man from the freezer, and I pad down the hall, carrying my dinner like a school book. The peephole offers a blurred, compressed view of the yard, newly groomed, and the flagstone path which leads to my front steps. Prank, I think, neighborhood kids. I play along, crack the door, prepared to look angry and confused, and right then Ellen's hand flashes through the opening, and she catches me by the short hairs of my mustache.

"It *was* you," she says.

She spins me around by the lip and backs me against the wall, paralyzing me with pinprick pain.

"I mibbed you," I say. "I lub you, Ebben."

"Hell," she says.

Finally, Old Dog lumbers to my rescue. He wedges feebly in between us, slaps his tail against Ellen's thighs, shoulders his way through her legs. If he was a younger man, he would bear her to the ground with the weight of his affection. Ellen has to release my mustache to keep her balance. I press the frozen Hungry Man against my lip.

I say, "What tipped you off?"

"Daddy mentioned your new look," she says. "Momma saw a man with a mustache. I put two and two together."

"I'm sorry," I say.

Ellen keeps her eyes on Old Dog, runs her fingers through his fur until he collapses, spent, on the hardwood and offers her his belly. His eyes droop shut, his tail winds down. I crouch beside them and get to work on his ribcage. Ellen thumbs a wayward bra strap out of sight.

"You still writing?" she says.

"Yeah," I say. "It's a love story."

Ellen flicks her eyes across my face and back to Old Dog. "Does it have a happy ending?"

"I won't know until I get there."

Ellen pushes to her feet, then, her business concluded, and we stand in the hallway looking at each other for a long moment. Instead of working on the book, I should have been dreaming up a phrase or two for right now, here in the present tense. The air is full of birdsongs. My neighbors are bantering pleasantly across back fences. Mothers are calling their children home. Everyone knows their lines but me.

25. Most nights, Old Dog eats his dinner in front of the television. When he's finished, I take him for a walk. We drift around the block, past quiet porches and American flags and bird feeders in the trees, pausing now and then to peer up at the stupid stars. A neighbor's terrier greets us, without fail, as we make the last corner, and Old Dog runs her off with a rumble in his throat.

"You've still got it," I tell him.

That wretch, Old Dog, wags his tail.

26. Wade Allbright brings the Taurus round himself on Saturday. He must do his best work in the early morning because the sun is just pushing over the horizon when he barrels into the driveway, the horn, mysteriously, blaring Beethoven's "Ode To Joy." Old Dog groans and makes a face, scandalized by the hour of the visit.

Wade beats me to the door, lets himself in with his key. We meet in the front hallway, and he brushes by me, headed for the kitchen.

"Did I wake you?" he says.

"I was up," I lie, despite the sheet around my shoulders and the pillow-addled hair, despite the third day boxer shorts, and the bleary eyes. He is, after all, still my father-in-law, and I want to make a good impression. Wade is sporting tennis duds, a white sleeveless sweater over a blue shirt and white shorts, his grizzled old man's thighs still broad and muscular. I ease myself into a seat at the breakfast table, watch him pushing canned goods around the shelf above the range. It seems he has plans to make a pot of coffee.

"I had my wiring guy put the horn in last night," he says. "That's Beethoven."

"Thanks," I say.

"I'm only gonna say one thing. I am aware Ellen dropped by yesterday. We're not even gonna get into that. I didn't mean to blow your cover, but Ellen is under the impression that my sympathies lie with you. I want to be sure you know how wrong she is."

"All right," I say.

"I like you, Keith," he says, "but she's my girl. If she asked me to come over here twice a day and beat you silly with a whiffle ball bat, I'd start keeping one in my car, know what I mean."

Ellen's father understands the simple Algebra of manliness. I wonder if Wade has ever found himself so reduced by a pretty girl. In fiction, a tidy parallel might ordinarily come to light at this point. Wade would admit that he had stalked Mrs. Allbright for months before she finally gave in to his affections. But, on this day, with the pristine light against the window, with the insects chattering in the grass, all we have between us is the terrifying memory of bachelorhood.

"How did you and Mrs. Allbright meet?" I say.

He pauses, a coffee filter pinched daintily between two fingers.

"We were kids," he says. "It's not a very good story. I saw Annie at a public swimming pool."

Old Dog lurches into the kitchen, then, and flops onto the tile at my feet. Wade shakes his head.

"How old is that dog?" he says.

"We don't know for sure," I say. "He was old when we got him. The vet puts him somewhere around fifteen."

Wade returns his attention to making coffee. He fills the pot with water, measures out the grinds. There is an order to the way he works, deliberate, personal. He is, I suspect, in charge of handling the morning coffee at the Allbright residence. When his preparations are finished, he sits across from me and rubs his face with both hands. He says, "Did you know Beethoven was deaf as a tree stump when he wrote his ninth?" I nod, and he says, "That always made Ellen cry when she was little."

27. Marriage, as I had known it, ended on a Monday. Ellen was standing over me at the breakfast table in the kitchen. I was eating cereal and slipping Old Dog bacon slices which Ellen had undercooked. Neighborhood sounds. The way Ellen smelled in the morning, like newspapers, like a memory of soap. Newsprint on her fingers. Her fingers around a coffee cup. A coffee cup pressed into the V at the opening of her robe.

"This is sad," Ellen said.

I followed her gaze to the window, hoping she was referring to something in the backyard, the coiled garden hose or the mildewed picnic table, which did look somehow sad in their way. I avoided the obvious question. I knew what she meant. We had been biding time. This was three months since the hospital. I shoved off to work every morning, and at night, Ellen stayed up late so we wouldn't have to be alone together in the dark. In between, I could be found hiding in the spare room, tapping, like this, at the keyboard so Ellen would have something to work on when insomnia kept her from her dreams.

"Everything's fine," I said. "Nobody's happy all the time."

I set my spoon in the bowl. Ellen collected my dishes, scraped uneaten bacon into the trash, spilled leftover milk into the sink. She ran the faucet and rinsed her hands. I'll need to handle this moment carefully in the book. Had I only recognized the importance of the morning, had I only known that an hour later she would be packing, an hour after that she would be gone, I would have penciled myself in a better man.

28. Due to paranoia and grave loneliness, I have no luck at the computer. I punch up a sorry sentence, sweep it away with the

delete key, then hack the very same sentence out again. I write and erase, write and erase, etc. All the while, I can feel eyes on the back of my neck. I whirl in my chair, but the room is empty except for me and my nasty writer's block. I creep sock-footed to the door and leap into the hall ready for a confrontation, but there is only Old Dog napping on the rug. The eyes follow me everywhere and remain just over my shoulder no matter how fast or which direction I turn.

At noon, I pack it in and hike to the Dew Drop for an oyster loaf and fries. There, I find *Henry loves* scratched into the surface of my table like the writer was interrupted mid-defacement. My fingertips go electric. I ask the waitress how long the words have been there and she frowns and says, "Maybe an hour, maybe twenty years, who knows."

The sky is a confusion of yellow light. The eyes escort me home, past a black woman and a white man watering an overheated radiator, past an oak cracking the sidewalk with its roots. When I shut the door behind me, Old Dog peeks around the corner, sees it's only me and flops down, already snoring, in the hall. I climb into bed and draw the covers to my neck and dial the Allbright's number on the phone.

Ellen's mother answers on the first ring. In a spontaneous British accent, I ask if I might have a word with Ellen, but Mrs. Allbright says, "You aren't fooling anybody, Keith. You know Ellen doesn't want to hear your voice."

"Please, Mrs. Allbright, put her on for just a minute. I'm having a peculiar day."

"That doesn't surprise me," she says.

Yesterday, per Wade's instruction, Lavinia, the housekeeper, whipped my bedroom into shape. My sheets are clean and cool. The dirty clothes have been laundered and put away. I wriggle down beneath the blankets, but, even still, I have the prickly sense of being watched.

"Then ask her something for me," I say. "Please, Mrs. Allbright, it's more important than it sounds."

"What is it?" she says, her voice tired.

Annie Allbright is not a cruel or unfeeling woman. In the book, I will have to put myself in her shoes. From her point of view, I must look like nothing less than the agent of her daughter's ruin.

"I want to know if she believes in ghosts," I say.

"You must be out your mind," she says. "I will ask her no such thing."

"I love her," I say.

"That may be true, but it doesn't make a difference!"

Mrs. Allbright breaks the connection, leaving me in my marriage bed, miles and miles of silence on the line.

29. When I told Ellen about "Satellite" and *Virginia's Room,* she was weeding in the backyard. Her face was showing the faintest hint of chloasma, plum blotches on her cheeks like she was blushing all the time. Mask of pregnancy, her mother called it. Ellen was four months gone. She told me not to bother informing *Virginia's Room* of our collaboration. I could have the credit, she said, she'd only been messing around. She wiped her forehead with the back of her hand, smiled a harmless smile. For some reason, all of this made me angry—the smile, the modesty, the flawless generosity. I wanted her to understand that what the two of us had done, even if we never managed to do it again, was a rare and wonderful thing.

30. Saturday evening, the Allbrights hit the Carmike for a new release. From behind a huge, freestanding cardboard movie advertisement, I watch them load up on popcorn and Milk Duds and Diet Pepsi. Wade pulls out a wad of bills and complains good-naturedly about the expense. His daughters bump shoulders, pretend to be embarrassed, his wife wags her eyebrows. They have each heard his take on concession prices a hundred times. From my hiding place, I love them all. They have a rhythm, weaving across the crowded lobby, that my father and I can never quite get the hang of. Wade, popcorn in one hand, soft drink in the other, props the theater door open with his hip, and the women file past, Mrs.

Allbright and Ellen and Beth, always in that order, and Wade falls in behind them in perfect formation.

I know from experience that Ellen's bladder will drive her from her seat in a few minutes. If I'm lucky, she'll be by herself. The lobby empties gradually. The ticket taker abandons his window until the next seating. For a while, it's just me and the girls at the concession stand. Then, maybe a half hour into the movie, Ellen emerges alone and trots across the carpet toward the rest room, and I follow, wearing my most innocent face, the very face of a man who might wander into the ladies' room by mistake, but no one pays me any mind. Inside, I locate her sandals and take the adjacent stall.

"Please don't be mad," I say.

"Nope," Ellen says. "This is not happening."

From two stalls over comes a delicate, "Eeeck," then the sound of a handbag being gathered up and the click of heels on tile. The door wheezes on its hydraulic arm.

Ellen says, "If I were you, I'd be in a hurry to leave."

"Keep me company until security gets here," I say.

"I'll do what I came for," she says. "That's all." Her urine trickles into the bowl. "I thought being in the bathroom together gave you the creeps."

"It doesn't give me the creeps," I say. "I just don't like to think of you having worldly needs."

"That's a problem," she says.

She spins the toilet paper roll and flushes, and I watch her jeans rising up her legs. Her feet vanish one at a time, then her face appears above the stall, her fingers curled over the divider. She grimaces at the sight of me, hops down from the toilet and heads for the row of sinks. I listen while she washes her hands. From the lobby comes the murmur of impending commotion.

"Do you believe in ghosts?" I say.

"What?"

She shuts off the water. I can picture her at the bank of mirrors, dusting her eyebrow into place with her little finger. In narrative terms, I think, this is a pivotal moment. The bland, watery light. The pleasant echo of her voice. But before I can repeat my question, the door bursts open. This is not theater security. Somebody has called in the pros. I get to my feet, just as the stall is kicked in towards me, catching my forehead on the backswing. A female cop, built like a phone booth, fills my woozy frame of vision. She goes for my hair, and I flinch, which, apparently, makes her angry because her next move is a knee to the face, followed promptly by a headlock, and before I can get a word in edgewise, I'm pinned to the floor with my hands cuffed somewhere above my shoulder blades and her boot on the back of my neck.

31. Ellen left while I was still at work. I found Old Dog languishing in the kitchen. Taped to the refrigerator was a note: "I'll call Wednesday. You break my heart." That was the easily most terrifying piece of prose I'd ever read.

32. Prison is about what I would have expected, the holding cell all painted yellow bars and cinder block walls, iron benches on three sides, occupied by an assortment of second-tier criminals, most of whom are sleeping or swapping lies with the hookers in the women's cell across the way. The only thing that's missing is a freestanding toilet in the middle of the room, but in this jail, prisoners are escorted one at a time to a unisex number down the hall. This is good material, I think. It's my first time in the big house— as they say in crime novels— and I want to take it all in, the wet rag smell, the way guards and the regulars bullshit like old friends.

In the last two hours, I have stood in line for fingerprinting, had my possessions inventoried and confiscated, and been issued a pair of loose cotton pants, an over-small white T-shirt, and plastic flip-flops for my feet. I phoned my father in Montgomery, but right away, I could make out the sultry, nonregional tones of April West in the background. My father sounded impatient. I had interrupted his romantic evening. I didn't have the stomach to tell him the reason for my call.

Instead, I said, "How come you never remarried?"

"That's why you're bothering me?" he said. "I loved your mother. I guess I love your mother still."

It occurred to me, then, that not only did I have very little memory of my mother, but I had no recollection of my father before her death. In my imagination, he has always been a lonely old man.

"I could drive up next week," I said. "We could grab some dinner. We could watch the news."

"The news is on right now," he said.

The guard told me I could have another call in an hour, and meanwhile, I lurk in the corner, studying the band of pale skin where my wedding ring has resided for the last nine months.

Beside me on the bench is a black man, wiry and bald, vaguely familiar. He has been eyeing me since I sat down.

"Drugs?" he says.

"No thanks," I say.

He says, "Naw, man, like this: I'm aggravated assault on a not-paying-his-bill-busted-up-car-motherfucker, heh, heh. White guy look like you usually possession."

"I was arrested in a ladies' room," I say.

"Pervert," he says. "I gotcha."

I decide not to argue. His hand, knuckles big as class rings, is spread flat on the bench. At that moment, I notice HENRY WAS FRAMED scratched ragged in the paint beside his thumb. The hair on my neck bristles. My heart cranks up. I point and say, "Did you write that?"

"You been here longer than me tonight," he says.

That's when I recognize him—Mohammed Ali, my tow truck driver from the other day—and I'm instantly at ease. My blood slows down. My legs go weak with strange relief. The world is thick with coincidence, I think. These *Henry*s have been here all along. I'm primed to notice them is all.

From down the hall, somebody shouts, "O'Dell, Keith, you made bail."

I drift toward the bars, then down the long corridor and up the

stairs to find Wade Allbright seated in the lobby. He sees me coming, shakes a handful of leftover Milk Duds into his palm.

"You all right?" he says.

"I feel great," I say.

He double-takes, decides to ignore me. I sign some papers at the
desk. We walk outside together. Wade opens the passenger door,
and like a cop, he eases me in by the back of the neck.

"Ellen's at the house," he says. "She wanted to check on the dog."

I beam at him despite myself. I say, "Thanks for bailing me out,
Wade. I can hardly believe how well everything's coming together."

Wade shuts the door and walks around the front of the car, tossing his keys from hand to hand. He climbs in beside me and shakes
his head.

"You're a weird kid," he says.

33. I read somewhere that marital separations exceeding eight
weeks are nearly always permanent, which leaves me a month and
a half to whip all this into a book.

I have decided to write a book about my wife.

34. Here's what passes for an ending these days:

The first thing I notice when Wade drops me at the curb is that
the front door has been left open and all the lights are on. Right
off the bat, I think Ellen has swiped the dog and vanished from my
life forever. I watch Wade's taillights receding down the street. I
head up the front steps. There is no Old Dog to greet me at the
door. I think, this book is not turning out how I had hoped. I
think, this was supposed to be the scene in which I win her back
for good. Then, in a narrative turn too perfect to believe, I hear
what sounds like mumbling in the bedroom. I'm around the corner in a hurry, and, in the faint light from the whispering TV, I behold Old Dog and Ellen side by side in bed. She must have dozed
off waiting for me. Old Dog slaps his tail gently on the mattress.
Clearly, he wants to let her sleep.

"Shhh," I tell him.

I retrace my steps without making a sound. For a long time, I sit at the kitchen table doing exactly nothing. I'm with Old Dog. It's enough to have Ellen in the house for now. She might be gone again tomorrow. After a while, I dial Lamont Turner's number on the phone. He's always up late, always working. He does his best writing in the middle of the night. When he answers, I say, "How do you regard the epiphany in fiction?"

"It's bullshit," he says.

"That's what I thought," I say.

Lamont hangs up, and I make the rounds of the house. When the doors have been secured and all the lights are off, I sneak into the room, stretch out beside my dog and my wife. Half-asleep, Ellen murmurs, "I want to shave your mustache in the morning."

Michael Knight is the author of a novel, *Divining Rod,* and two collections of short fiction, *Dogfight & Other Stories* and *Goodnight, Nobody.* His fiction has appeared in *Paris Review, Esquire, The New Yorker,* and other places, including *New Stories from the South: The Year's Best, 1999.* He teaches writing at the University of Tennessee.

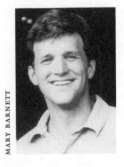

MARY BARNETT

T his story was a couple of years in the making. First, I was going to write an honest-to-God ghost story. Then, in order to avoid all the clichés of the honest-to-God ghost story, which had been bogging me down for what felt like a very long time, I decided to go superpostmodern with it. And failed. Finally, after about a year, on a day when I had nothing else to work on, I came back to it and discovered that lo and behold there was a simple story—boy meets girl, boy loses girl, boy wants girl back—underneath all the surface clutter, and I remembered that there is nothing wrong with that. That simple stories, as long as there's a hint of the ineffable in them, are usually my favorite kind.

ZZ Packer

EVERY TONGUE
SHALL CONFESS

(from *Ploughshares*)

A s Pastor Everett made the announcements that began the
service, Clareese Mitchell stood with her choir members,
knowing that once again she had to Persevere, put on the Strong
Armor of God, the Breastplate of Righteousness, but she was having her monthly womanly troubles, and all she wanted to do was
curse the Brothers' Church Council of Greater Christ Emanuel
Church of the Fire Baptized who'd decided that the Sisters had to
wear *white* every Missionary Sunday, which was, of course, the day
of the month when her womanly troubles were always at their absolute worst! And to think that the Brothers' Church Council of
Greater Christ Emanuel Church of the Fire Baptized had been the
first place she'd looked for guidance and companionship nearly ten
years ago when her aunt Alma had fallen ill. And why not? They
were God-fearing, churchgoing men; men like Deacon Julian Jeffers, now sitting in the first row of pews, closest to the altar, right
under the leafy top of the corn plant she'd brought in to make the
sanctuary more homey. Two months ago she'd been reading the
Book of Micah and posed the idea of a Book of Micah discussion
group to the Deacon Jeffers, and he'd said, "Oh, Sister Clareese!
We should make *you* a deacon!" Which of course they didn't. Deacons, like pastors, were men—not that she was complaining. But

it still rankled that Jeffers had said he'd get back to her about the Micah discussion group and he never had.

Clareese's cross-eyes roved to the back of the church, where Sister Drusella and Sister Maxwell sat, each resplendent in their identical, wide-brimmed, purple-flowered hats, their unsaved guests sitting next to them. The guests wore frightened smiles, and Clareese tried to shoot them reassuring looks. The gold-lettered banner behind them read: "We Are More Than Conquerors in Christ Our Lord," and she tried to use this as a focal point, but her cross-eyes couldn't help it, they settled, at last, on Deacon McCreedy, making his way down the aisle for the second time. Oh, how she hated him!

She would never forget—never, never, never—the day he came to the hospital where she worked; she was still wearing her white nurse's uniform, and he'd said he was concerned about her spiritual well-being—*Liar!*—then drove her to where she lived with her aunt Alma, whose room resounded with perpetual snores and hacking and wheezing—as if Clareese didn't have enough of this at the hospital—and while Alma slept, Clareese poured Deacon McCreedy some fruit punch, which he drank between forkfuls of chicken, plus half their pork roast. No sooner than he'd wiped his hands on the napkin—didn't bother using a fork—he stood and walked behind her, covering her cross-eyed eyes as though she were a child, as though he were about to give her a gift—a Bible with her very own name engraved on it, perhaps—but he didn't give her anything, he'd just covered her wandering eyes and said, "Sing 'On Christ the Solid Rock I Stand.' Make sure to do the Waterfall." And she was happy to do it, happy to please Deacon McCreedy, so she began singing in her best, cleanest voice until she felt his hand slide up the scratchy, white pantyhose of her nurse's uniform and slide up towards the control-top of her pantyhose. Before she could stop him, one finger wriggling around inside, and by then it was too late to tell him she was having her monthly womanly troubles. He drew back in disgust—no—*hatred,* then rinsed his hand in the kitchen sink and left without saying a word, not a thanks for the chicken nor the pork roast or her singing. Not a single word of apology for anything. But she could have forgiven him—if Sisters could even forgive Deacons—for she could have understood that an unmarried man might have needs, *needs,* but what really bothered her was how he ignored her. How a few weeks later she and Aunt Alma had been waiting for the bus after Wednesday night prayer meeting, and he *drove past.* That's right. No offer of a ride, no slowing down, no nothing. Aunt Alma was nearly blind and couldn't even see it was him, but Clareese recognized his car at once.

Yes, she wanted to curse the Brothers' Church Council of Greater Christ Emanuel Church of the Fire Baptized, but Sisters and Brothers could not curse, could not even swear or take an oath, for *neither shalt thou swear by thy head, because thou canst not make one hair white or black.* So no oath; no swearing, and of course no betting—an extension of swearing—which was why she'd told the other nurses at University Hospital that she would not join their betting pool to predict who would get married first, Patty or Edwina. She told them about the black-and-white hairs, and all Nurse Holloway did was clomp her pumps—as if she was too good for the standard orthopedically correct shoes—down the green tiles of the hall and shout behind her back, "Somebody sure needs to get laid." Oh, how the other RNs tittered in their gossipy way.

Now everyone applauded when Pastor Everett announced that Sister Nina would be getting married to Harold, one of the Brothers from Broadway Tongues of Spirit Church. Then Pastor Everett said, "Sister Nina will be holding a Council so we can get husbands for the rest of you hardworking Sisters." Like Sister Clareese, is what he meant. The congregation laughed at the joke. Ha, ha. And perhaps the joke *was* on her. If she'd been married, Deacon McCreedy wouldn't have dared do what he did; if she'd been married perhaps she'd also be working fewer shifts at the hospital, perhaps she would have never met that patient—the man who'd almost gotten her fired and at exactly that moment, it hit her, right below the gut, a sharp pain, and she imagined her uterus, that Texas-shaped organ, the Rio Grande of her monthly womanly troubles flushing out to the Gulf.

Pastor Everett had finished the announcements. Now it was time for testimony service. She tried to distract herself by thinking of suitable testimonies. Usually she testified about work. Last week, she'd testified about the poor man with a platelet count of seven, meaning he was as good as dead; Nurse Holloway had told him, "We're bringing you more platelets," and he'd said, "That's all right. God sent me more." No one at the Nurses' Station—to say nothing of those atheist doctors—believed him. But when Nurse Holloway checked, sure enough, Glory be to God, he had a count of sixteen. Clareese told the congregation how she knelt on the cold tiled floor of University Hospital's corridor, right then and there, arms outstretched to Glory. And what could the other nurses say to that? Nothing, that's what.

She remembered her testimony from a month ago, how she'd been working the hotline, and a mother had called to say that her son had eaten ants, and Sister Clareese had assured the woman that ants were God's creatures and wouldn't harm the boy. But the Lord told Clareese to stay on the line with the mother, not to rush the way other nurses often did, so Clareese stayed on the line. And Glory be to God that she did! Once the mother had calmed down she'd said, "Thank goodness. The insecticide I gave Kevin must have worked." Sister Clareese had stayed after her shift to make sure the woman brought her boy into Emergency. Afterwards she told the woman to hold hands with Kevin and give God the Praise He deserved.

But she had told these stories already. As she fidgeted in her choir mistress's chair, she tried to think of new ones. The congregation wouldn't care about how she had to stay on top of codes, or how she had to triple-check patients' charts. The only patients who stuck in her mind were Mrs. Geneva Bosma, whose toe was rotting off, and Mr. Toomey, who had prostate cancer. And, of course, Mr. Cleophus Sanders, the cause of all her current troubles. Cleophus was an amputee who liked to turn the volume of his television up so high that his channel-surfing sounded as if someone were being electrocuted, repeatedly. At the Nurses' Station she'd overheard that Cleophus Sanders was once a musician who in his heyday went by the nickname "Delta Sweetmeat." But he'd gone in and out of the music business, sometimes taking construction jobs. A crane had fallen on his leg, and he'd been amputated from below the knee. No, none of these cases were Edifying in God's sight. Her run-in with Cleophus had been downright un-Edifying.

When Mr. Sanders had been moved into Mr. Toomey's room last Monday, she'd told them both, "I hope everyone has a blessed day!" She'd made sure to say this only after she was safely inside with the door closed behind her. She had to make sure she didn't mention God until the door was closed *behind* her because Nurse Holloway was always clomping about, trying to say that this was a *university* hospital, as well as a *research* hospital, one at the very *forefront* of medicine, and didn't Registered Nurse Clareese Mitchell recognize and *respect* that not everyone shared her beliefs? That the hospital catered not only to Christians, but people of the Jewish faith? Muslims, Hindus, and agnostics? Atheists, even?

This Clareese knew only too well, which was why it was all the more important for her to Spread the Gospel. So she shut the door, and said to Mr. Toomey, louder this time, "I HOPE EVERYONE HAS A BLESSED DAY!"

Mr. Toomey grunted. Heavy and completely white, he reminded Sister Clareese of a walrus: everything about him drooped, his eyes like twin frowns, his nose, perhaps even his mouth, though it was hard to make out because of his frowning blond mustache. Well, Glory be to God, she expected something like a grunt from him, she couldn't say she was surprised: junkies who detox scream and writhe before turning clean; the man with a hangover does not like to wake to the sun. So it was with sinners exposed to the harsh, curing Light of the Lord.

"Hey, sanctified lady!" Cleophus Sanders called from across the room. "He got cancer! Let the man alone."

"*I know* what he *has*," Sister Clareese said. "I'm his *nurse*." This wasn't how she wanted the patient-RN relationship to begin, but Cleophus had gotten the better of her. Yes, that was the problem, wasn't it? *He'd* gotten the better of *her*. This was how Satan worked, throwing you off a little at a time. She would have to Persevere, put on the Strong Armor of God. She tried again.

"My name is Sister Clareese Mitchell, your assigned registered nurse. I can't exactly say that I'm pleased to meet you because that would be a lie and *lying lips are an abomination to the Lord.* I will say that I am pleased to do my duty and help you recover."

"Me oh my!" Cleophus Sanders said, and laughed big and long, the kind of laughter that could go on and on, rising and rising, restarting itself if need be, like yeast. He slapped the knee of his amputated leg, the knee that would probably come off if his infection didn't stop eating away at it. But Cleophus Sanders didn't care. He just slapped that infected knee, hooting all the while in an ornery, backwoods kind of way that made Clareese want to hit him.

She busied herself by changing Mr. Toomey's catheter, then remaking his bed, rolling the walrus of him this way and that, with little help on his part. As soon as she was done with Mr. Toomey, he turned on the Knicks. The whole time she'd changed Toomey's catheter, however, Cleophus had watched her, laughing under his breath, then outright, a waxing and waning of hilarity as if her every gesture were laughably prim and proper.

"Look, Mr. *Cleophus,*" she said, glad for the chance to bite on the ridiculous name, "I am a professional. You may laugh at what I do, but in doing so you laugh at the Almighty who has given me the breath to do it!"

She'd steeled herself for a vulgar reply. But no. Mr. Toomey did the talking.

"I tell *you* what!" Mr. Toomey said, pointing his remote at Sister Clareese. "I'm going to sue this hospital for lack of peace and quiet. All your 'Almighty this' and 'Oh Glory that' is keeping me from watching the game!"

While Sister Clareese murmured her apologies to Mr. Toomey,

Cleophus Sanders put on an act of restraining his amusement, body and bed quaking in seizurelike fits.

Now sunlight filtered through the yellow-tinted windows of Greater Christ Emmanuel Church of the Fire Baptized, lighting Brother Hopkins, the organist, with a halolike glow. The rest of the congregation had given their testimonies, and it was now time for the choir members to testify, starting with Clareese. Was there any way she could possibly turn her incident with Cleophus Sanders into an Edifying testimony experience? Just then, another hit, and she felt a cramping so hard she thought she might double over. It was her turn. Cleophus's laughter and her cramping womb seemed one and the same; he'd inhabited her body like a demon, preventing her from thinking up a proper testimony. As she rose, unsteadily, to her feet, all she managed to say was, "Pray for me."

All right. Get a hold of yourself. It was almost time for Pastor Everett to preach his sermon. To introduce it, Sister Clareese had the choir sing "Every Knee Shall Bow, Every Tongue Shall Confess." It was an old-fashioned hymn, unlike the hopped-up gospel songs churches were given to nowadays. And she liked the slow unfolding of its message: how without uttering a word, all the hearts of men and women would be made plain to the Lord; that He would know you not by what you said or did, but what you'd hoped and intended. The teens, however, mumbled over the verses, and older choir members sang without vigor. The hymn ended up sounding like the national anthem at a school assembly: a stouthearted song rendered in monotone.

"Thank you, thank you, thank you, Sister Clareese," Pastor Everett said, looking back at her, "for that wonderful tune."

Tune? She knew that Pastor Everett thought she was not the kind of person a choir mistress should be; she was quiet, nervous, skinny in all the wrong places, and completely cross-eyed. She knew he thought of her as something worse than a spinster, because she wasn't yet old.

Pastor Everett hunched close to the microphone, as though about to begin a forlorn love song. From the corners of her vision she saw him smile—only for a second—but with every single tooth in his mouth. He was yam-colored, and given to wearing epaulets on the shoulders of his robes and gold braiding all down the front. Sister Clareese felt no attraction to him, but she seemed to be the only one who didn't; even the Sisters going on eighty were charmed by Pastor Everett, who, though not entirely handsome, had handsome moments.

"Sister Clareese," he said, turning to where she stood with the choir. "Sister Clareese, I know y'all just sang for us, but I need some more help. Satan got these Brothers and Sisters putting m' Lord on hold!"

Sister Clareese knew that everyone expected her and her choir to begin singing again, but she had been alerted what he was up to; he had called her yesterday; he thought nothing of asking her to unplug her telephone—her *only* telephone, her *private* line— to bring to church so that he could use it in some sermon about Call Waiting. Hadn't even asked her how she was doing, hadn't bothered to pray over her aunt Alma's sickness, nevertheless she'd said, "Why, certainly, Pastor Everett. Anything I can do to help."

Now Sister Clareese produced her Princess telephone from under her seat and handed it to the Pastor. Pastor Everett held the telephone aloft, shaking it as if to rid it of demons. "How many of y'all—Brothers and Sisters—got telephones?" the Pastor asked.

One by one, members of the congregation timidly raised their hands.

"All right," Pastor Everett said, as though this grieved him, "almost all of y'all." He flipped through his huge pulpit Bible. "How many of y'all—Brothers and Sisters—got Call Waiting?" He turned pages quickly, then stopped, as though he didn't need to search for the scripture after all. "Let me tell ya," the Pastor said, nearly kissing the microphone, "there is *Someone!* Who won't *accept* your Call Waiting! There is *Someone!* Who won't *wait,* when you put Him on hold!" Sister Nancy Popwell and Sister Drusella Davies now had their eyes closed in concentration, their hands waving slowly in the air in front of them as though they were trying to make their way through a dark room.

The last phone call Sister Clareese had made was on Wednesday, to Mr. Toomey. She knew both he and Cleophus were likely to reject the Lord, but she had a policy of sorts, which was to call patients who'd been in her care for at least a week. She considered it her Christian duty to call—even on her day off—to let them know that Jesus cared, and that she cared. The other RNs resorted to callous catch phrases that they bandied about the Nurses' Station: "Just because I care *for* them doesn't mean I have to care *about* them," or "I'm a nurse, not a nursery . . ." Not Clareese. Perhaps she'd been curt with Cleophus Sanders, but she had been so in defense of God. Perhaps Toomey had been curt with her, but he was going into OR soon, and grouchiness was to be expected.

Nurse Patty had been switchboard operator that night, and Clareese had had to endure her sighs before the girl finally connected her to Toomey.

"Praise the Lord, Mr. Toomey!"

"Who's this?"

"This is your nurse, Sister Clareese, and I'm calling to say that Jesus will be with you through your surgery."

"Who?"

"Jesus," she said.

She thought she heard the phone disconnect, then, a voice. Of course. Cleophus Sanders.

"Why ain't you called *me*?" Cleophus said.

Sister Clareese tried to explain her policy, the thing about the week.

"So you care more about some white dude than you care about good ol' Cleophus?"

"It's not that, Mr. Sanders. God cares for white and black alike. Acts 10:34 says, 'God is no respecter of persons.' Black or white. Red, purple, or green—He doesn't care, as long as you accept His salvation and live right." When he was silent on the other end, she said, "It's that I've only known you for two days. I'll see you tomorrow."

She tried to hang up, but he said, "Let me play something for you. Something interesting, since all you probably listen to is monks chanting and such."

Before she could respond, there was a noise on the other end that sounded like juke music. Then he came back on the phone and said, "Like that, don't you?"

"I had the phone away from my ear."

"I thought you said, 'Lying is the abominable.' Do you *like* or do you *don't?*" When she said nothing, he said, "Truth, now."

She answered yes.

She didn't want to answer yes. But she also didn't want to lie. And what was one to do in that circumstance? If God looked into your heart right then, what would He think? Or would He have to approve because He made your heart that way? Or were you suppose to train it against its wishes? She didn't know what to think, but on the other end Cleophus said, "What you just heard there was the blues. What you just heard there was me."

". . . Let me tell ya!" Pastor Everett shouted, his voice hitting its highest octave, "*Jeeeee-zus*-did not *tell* his *Daddy*—'I'm sorry, Pops—but my girlfriend is on the other line'; *Jeeeee-zus*— never *told* the Omnipotent One, 'Can you wait a sec, I think I got a call from the electric company!' *Jeeeeeeee-zus*—never told Matthew, Mark, Luke, or John, 'I'm *sorry*, but I got to put you on hold; I'm sorry, Brother Luke, but I got some mac and cheese in the oven; I'm sorry, but I got to eat this fried chicken—'" and at this, Pastor Everett paused, grinning in anticipation of his own punch line, "'—'cause it's finger-licking good!'"

Drops of sweat plunked onto his microphone.

Sister Clareese watched as the congregation cheered, the women flagging their Bibles in the air as though the Bibles were as light and yielding as handkerchiefs; their bosoms jouncing as though they were harboring sacks of potatoes in their blouses. They shook tambourines, scores of them all going at once, the sound of something sizzling and frying.

That was it? That was The Message? Of course, she'd only heard part of it, but still. Of course she believed that one's daily life shouldn't outstrip one's spiritual one, but there seemed no place for true belief at Greater Christ Emanuel Church. Everyone wanted flash and props, no one wanted the Word itself, naked in its fiery glory.

Most of the Brothers and Sisters were up on their feet. "Tell it!" yelled some, while others called out, "Go 'head on!" The organist pounded out the chords to what could have been the theme song of a TV game show.

She looked to see what Sister Drusella and Sister Maxwell's unsaved guests were doing. Drusella's unsaved guest was her son, which made him easy to bring into the fold: he was living in her shed and had no car. He was busy turning over one of the cardboard fans donated by Hamblin and Sons Funeral Parlor, reading the words intently, then flipping it over again to stare at the picture of a gleaming casket and grieving family. Sister Donna Maxwell's guest was an ex-con she'd written to and tried to save while he was in prison. The ex-con seemed to watch the scene with approval, though one could never really know what was going on in the criminal mind. For all Sister Clareese knew, he could have been counting all the pockets he planned to pick.

And they called themselves missionaries. Family members and ex-cons were easy to convince of God's will. As soon as Drusella's son took note of the pretty young Sisters his age, he'd be back. And everyone knew you could convert an ex-con with a few well-timed pecan pies.

Wednesday was her only day off besides Sunday, and though a phone call or two was her policy on days off, she very seldom visited the hospital. And yet, last Wednesday, she had to. The more she considered Cleophus's situation—his loss of limb, his devil's music, his unsettling laughter—the more she grew convinced that he was her Missionary Challenge. That he was especially in need of Saving.

Minutes after she'd talked with him on the phone, she took the Number 42 bus and transferred to the crosstown H, then walked the rest of the way to the hospital.

Edwina had taken over for Patty as Nurse Station attendant, and she'd said, "We have an ETOH in—where's your uniform?"

"It's not my shift," she called behind her as she rushed past Edwina and into Room 204.

She opened the door to find Cleophus sitting on the bed, still plucking chords on his unplugged electric guitar that she'd heard him playing over the phone half an hour earlier. Mr. Toomey's bed was empty; one of the nurses must have already taken him to OR, so Cleophus had the room to himself. The right leg of Cleophus's hospital pants hung down limp and empty, and it was the first time she'd seen his guitar, curvy and shiny as a sports car. He did not acknowledge her as she entered, still picking away until he began to sing a song about a man whose woman had left him so high and dry, she'd taken the car, the dog, the furniture. Even the wallpaper. Only when he'd strummed the final chords did Cleophus look up, as if noticing her for the first time.

"Sister *Clare-reeeese!*" He'd said it as if he were introducing a showgirl.

"It's your soul," Clareese said. "God wants me to help save your soul." The urgency of God's message struck her so hard, she felt the wind knocked out of her. She sat on the bed next to him.

"Really?" he said, cocking his head a little.

"Really and truly," Clareese said. "I know I said I liked your music, but I said it because God gave you that gift for you to use. For Him."

"Uhnn-huh," Cleophus said. "How about this, little lady? How about if God lets me keep this knee, I'll come to church with you? We can go out and get some dinner afterwards. Like a proper couple."

She tried not to be flattered. "The Lord does *not make* deals, Mr.

Sanders. But I'm sure the Lord would love to see you in church regardless of what happens to your knee."

"Well, since you seem to be His receptionist, how about you ask the Lord if He can give you the day off. I can take you out on the town. See, if I go to church, I *know* the Lord won't show. But I'm positive you will."

"Believe you me, Mr. Sanders, the Lord is at every service. *Where two or three are gathered together in my name, there am I in the midst of them.*" She sighed, trying to remember what she came to say. "*He is the Way, the Truth, and the Life. No man—*"

"*—cometh to the Father,*" Cleophus said, "*but by me.*"

She looked at him. "You know your Bible."

"Naw. You were speaking, and I just heard it." He absently strummed his guitar. "You were talking, saying that verse, and the rest of it came to me. Not even a voice," he said, "more like . . . kind of like music."

She stared. Her hands clapped his, preventing him from playing further. For a moment, she was breathless. He looked at her, suddenly seeming to comprehend what he'd just said, that the Lord had actually spoken to him. For a minute, they sat there, both overjoyed at what the Lord had done, but then he had to go ruin it. He burst out laughing his biggest, most sinful laugh yet.

"Awww!" he cried, doubled over, and then flopped backwards onto his hospital bed. Then he closed his eyes, laughing without sound.

She stood up, chest heaving, wondering why she even bothered with him.

"Clareese," he said, trying to clear his voice of any leftover laughter, "don't go." He looked at her with pleading eyes, then patted the space beside him on the bed.

She looked around the room for some cue. Whenever she needed an answer, she relied on some sign from the Lord: a fresh beam of sunlight through the window, the hands of a clock folded in prayer, or the flush of a commode. These were signs that whatever she was thinking of doing was right. If there was a storm cloud, or something in her path, then that was a bad sign. But nothing in the room gave her any indication whether she should stay and witness to Mr. Sanders, or go.

"What, Mr. Sanders, do you want from me? It's my day off. I decided to come by and offer you an invitation to my church because God has given you a gift. A musical gift." She dug into her purse, then pulled out a pocket-sized Bible. "But I'll leave you with this. If you need to find us—our church—the name and number is printed inside."

He took the Bible with a little smile, turning it over, then flipping through it, as if some money might be tucked away inside. "Seriously, though," he said, "let me ask you a question that's gonna seem dumb. Childish. Now, I want you to think long and hard about it. Why the hell's there so much suffering in the world if God's doing his job? I mean, look at me. Take old Toomey, too. We done anything *that* bad to deserve all this put on us?"

She sighed. "Because of people, that's why. Not God. It's *people* who allow suffering, people who create it. Perpetrate it."

"Maybe that explains Hitler and all them others, but I'm talking about—" He gestured at the room, the hospital in general.

Clareese tried to see what he saw when he looked at the room. At one time, the white and pale-green walls of the hospital rooms had given her solace; the way everything was clean, clean, clean; the many patients that had been in each room, some nice, some dying, some willing to accept the Lord. But most, like Mr. Toomey, cast the Lord aside like wilted lettuce, and now the clean hospital room was just a reminder of the emptiness, the barrenness, of her patients' souls. Cleophus Sanders was just another one of those patients who disrespected the Lord.

"Why does He allow natural disasters to kill people?" Clareese said, knowing that her voice was raised beyond what she meant it to be. "Why are little children born to get some rare blood disease and die? Why," she yelled, waving her arms, "does a crane fall on your leg and smash it? I don't know, Mr. Sanders. And I don't like it. But I'll say this! No one has a *right* to live! The only right we have is to die. That's it! If you get plucked out of the universe and given a chance to become a life, that's more than not having become anything at all, and for that, Mr. Sanders, you should be grateful!"

She had not known where this last bit had come from, and, she could tell, neither had he, but she could hear the other nurses coming down the hall to see who was yelling, and though Cleophus Sanders looked to have more pity on his face than true belief, he had come after her when she turned to leave. She'd heard the clatter of him gathering his crutches, and even when she heard the meaty weight of him slam onto the floor, she did not turn back.

Then, there it was. Pastor Everett's silly motion of cupping his hand to his ear, like he was eavesdropping on the choir, his signal that he was waiting for Sister Clareese to sing her solo, waiting to hear the voice that would send the congregation shouting, "Thank you, Jesus, Blessed Savior!"

How could she do it? She thought of Cleophus on the floor and felt ashamed. She hadn't seen him since; her yelling had been brought to the attention of the hospital administrators, and although understaffed, the administration had suggested that she not return until next week. They handed her the card of the staff psychiatrist. She had not told anyone at church what had happened. Not even her aunt Alma.

She didn't want to sing. Didn't feel like it, but she thought, *I will freely sacrifice myself unto thee; I will praise thy name, O Lord, for it is good.* Usually thinking of a scripture would give her strength, but this time it just made her realize how much strength she was always needing.

She didn't want to, but she'd do it. She'd sing a stupid solo part — the Waterfall, they called it — not even something she'd *invented* or *planned* to do who knows how many years ago when she'd had to sneeze her brains out — but oh, no, she'd tried holding it in, and when she had to do her solo, those years ago, her near-sneeze made the words come out tumbling in a series of staccato notes that were almost fluid, and ever since then, she'd had to sing *all* solos that way, it was expected of her, everyone loved it, it was her trademark. She sang: *"All-hall other-her her grooouund—is sink-king sand!"*

The congregation applauded.

"Saints," the Pastor said, winding down, "you know this world will soon be *over!* Jesus will come back to this tired, sorry Earth in *a moment and a twinkling of an eye!* So you can't use Call Waiting on the Lord! *Jeeee-zus,* my friends, does not accept conference calls! You are Children of God! You need to PRAY! Put down your phone! Say good-bye to AT&T! You cannot go in God's *direction,* without a little—*genuflection!"*

The congregation went wild, clapping and banging tambourines, whirling in the aisles. But the choir remained standing in case Pastor Everett wanted another song. For the first time, Clareese found her monthly troubles had settled down. And now that she had the wherewithal to concentrate, she couldn't. Her cross-eyes wouldn't keep steady, she felt them roaming like the wheels of a defective shopping cart, and from one roving eye she saw her aunt Alma, waving her arms as though listening to leftover strains of Clareese's solo.

What would she do? She didn't know if she'd still have her job when she went back on Monday; didn't know what the staff psychiatrist would try to pry out of her. More importantly, she didn't know what her aunt Alma would do without the special referrals Clareese could get her. What was a Sister to do?

Clareese's gaze must have found him just a moment after everyone else had. A stranger at the far end of the aisle, standing directly opposite Pastor Everett as though about to engage him in a duel. There was Cleophus Sanders with his crutches, the right leg of his pinstriped pants hollow, wagging after him. Over his shoulder was a strap, attached to which was his guitar. Even Deacon McCreedy was looking.

What in Heaven's name was Cleophus doing here? To bring his soul to salvation? To ridicule her? For another argument? Perhaps the doctors had told him he did not need the operation after all, and Cleophus was keeping his end of the deal with God. But he didn't seem like the type to keep promises. Not unless they threatened to break him. She saw his eyes search the congregation, and when he saw her, they locked eyes as if he had come to claim her. He did not come to get Saved, didn't care about his soul in that way, all he cared about was—

Now she knew why he'd come. He'd come for her. He'd come *despite* what she'd told him, despite his disbelief. Anyhow, she disapproved. It was God he needed, not her. Nevertheless, she remained standing for a few moments, even after the rest of the choir had already seated themselves, waving their cardboard fans to cool their sweaty faces.

ZZ Packer was raised in Atlanta, Georgia, and Louisville, Kentucky. Her stories have appeared in *The New Yorker, Harper's Magazine, Story, Ploughshares, Zoetrope: All-Story,* and *Best American Short Stories, 2000.* Riverhead Books will publish her collection of short stories *Drinking Coffee Elsewhere* in March 2003.

MARION ETTLINGER

*E*very Tongue Shall Confess" *started as a need; I grew up in a Southern black Pentecostal church and I wanted— needed—to portray its vibrancy without judging it. My prior attempts at this story, however, ended up too cartoonish, too flip, too something.*

Previously, the story was Rashomon-like in structure, showing three different viewpoints during slightly overlapping moments of time. When I went to revise the story, I saw that I was asking the structure to do the work that only strength of character could accomplish (in short, it wasn't working). I began to reevaluate Clareese and decided that her viewpoint was the all-important one: she watches (mostly without observing), she does her duty, she sits back down in her choir mistress's seat, she goes to work.

I know so many women like Clareese—in and outside the world of the Pentecostal church—women who must keep moving and doing because reflection, for them, is tantamount to idleness. I am endeared to these lonely, soldierly women like Clareese, whose unwavering sense of rectitude is the fount of both comedy and tragedy in the story—or so I hope.

Bret Anthony Johnston

CORPUS

(from *Black Warrior Review*)

D riving to Bayview Behavioral Hospital took Charlie Banks half an hour. The sand-colored facility stood ten miles out-side Corpus Christi, Texas, among cornfields and grazing pastures. He drove a leased Lexus and liked shifting into fifth on Rodd Field Road, an abandoned straightaway where he could open up the en-gine. His top speed was 120 mph. He'd bragged about the num-ber at the office, though he didn't say where he was going. Edie had called the car pretentious, but Charlie viewed it as evidence that they were finally hitting their stride.

Bayview was nowhere near the bay. The surrounding area was staked with sun-bleached signs advertising acreage for sale; besides the hospital, there was only one gas station, a Kum and Go. ("Why not call it Kneel and Blow?" Edie had said the week before. "Why not Ejaculate and Evacuate?") Four shaggy-trunked palm trees an-chored the hospital's empty parking lot; the place resembled a de-serted country club. A man in fatigues stood outside the automatic doors, swigging from a leather flask. Military men always seemed to be at Bayview, loitering with wheelchair patients, littering the entrance, with cigarette butts. Nurses and orderlies smoked with them, too. Charlie made quick, kindly eye contact, then went in-side, registered, and took a seat across from a woman holding a motorcycle helmet. His stomach grumbled; he'd forgotten to eat lunch. Soon the soldier entered, trailing a cloud of viscous June heat into the air-conditioning. Charlie flipped through a magazine, the same as yesterday, and tried to quiet the fear that some calamity had befallen Edie since they'd spoken that afternoon. The anxiety was insidious and familiar, an acute disquieting that she'd cribbed some tranquilizers or carved her wrists with a piece of broken mirror. He opened his eyes wide and considered hustling out for a candy bar, maybe a tabloid and pack of cigarettes for Edie. But anything he brought in would have to be x-rayed and quarantined before she received it, so he stayed put.

The woman hugged the helmet, swinging her leg like a pendulum. The soldier sat beside her. He said, "Another five minutes."

"None of this makes sense to me," she said.

The soldier crossed his arms; his biceps bulged. He said, "Plenty of people in that boat."

"When we were young, a plane crashed behind our house," she said. "Donnie and I were outside and got covered in soot. Mother always worried it traumatized us. Maybe she was right."

"I doubt this has much to do with a plane."

The woman shrugged, as if there was still a chance whatever had happened could be explained away. Charlie thought someone close to her might have died. She was young, with fleshy arms and a faded dolphin tattoo on her calf. Keeping quiet seemed a chore for her. Edie had been that way for a while. The woman looked forlorn, which he also understood, though he had no idea what she was thinking.

She was thinking she needed to pull herself together. She'd been frazzled all day. First she'd gone to trade shifts at the Yellow Rose, but once there she realized this was her weekend off. Then she sped from Southport to the naval base, parked at the infirmary and rushed in, remembering too late her brother's message about being transferred to a civilian hospital. Outside, her keys hung in the ignition of her locked car. Her purse was there, too, with the cookies and comic books she'd brought for Donnie. *You stupid shit,* she'd said in the parking lot. *You stupid little shit.*

In the waiting room, she said, "I guess they'll make him quit the army."

"Discharge."

"Doesn't that sound too severe, like he's a spy?"

Just as he realized he was staring, Charlie found himself fixed in the soldier's gaze. He smiled apologetically, then glanced through the window. A chain of seagulls was flying back to the beach from the landfill. The Lexus sat alone in a row of parking spaces. The car still thrilled him. Before the Lexus, they'd owned a Ford that Edie called Fido because the old landlord had forbidden pets. This was in Dallas. She was thirty-four; Charlie was thirty-six. When the law firm in Corpus called to offer him their network support position (the salary so high he thought someone was joshing him), Edie flat refused to move. She liked her job doing nonprofit fund-raising and liked living close to the nursing home her mother's dementia had transformed into a grand hotel. He argued that they could buy a house and travel, perhaps find a hospital for her mother down south, but she stonewalled him and he began resenting her. Then, after two years of trying, Edie was pregnant, and he saw an opening and let reason shine through. He said, "Corpus would be a great place to raise children."

That was hardly a year earlier, but in Bayview the life seemed as far-off and turbid as the floor of the muddy, olive-tinted bay.

Dwana Miller wished she'd taken a cab from the naval base. But because unauthorized vehicles were prohibited past security, and because some documents (Donnie's, no doubt) needed to be delivered to Bayview, the infirmary attendant had suggested that Omar Delgado escort her to the hospital. She hadn't known he rode a motorcycle, nor that he'd feel compelled to wait while she saw Donnie. Nor had she figured how she'd return to her locked-up car, or for that matter, home. One disaster at a time, she thought.

They sat alone in the waiting room, twenty minutes before visitations. Whiskey on Omar's breath, a wet-smelling musk. Maybe she'd seen him at the Yellow Rose; army boys ferried over on week-ends, and after working there two years, she recognized them every-where. She wanted a change. She'd considered beauty college in San Antonio, but more recently she'd entertained notions of a clown school in Houston. An advertisement had promised work at parties, hospitals, schools, even rodeos. How easily she pictured herself painting on heart-shaped eyes, tying balloons into wiener-dog-style hats. She would run the idea past Donnie, amuse him. And she'd tell him she was sleeping with her boss's wife—"What else is new?" he'd say—a woman who two nights before had asked Dwana if she'd ever done a *taj mahal;* she'd meant *ménage à trois.*

"Me and my boys are shooting pool later," Omar Delgado said in the waiting room. "Always room for one more."

"You have children?"

He squinted, smirked as if being fooled. "Oh, no. Buddies, fel-lows from the base."

She forced a smile, feeling inane. She wanted to check the time, but resisted. "A lot of fun I'd be."

"Might feel good to relax." He'd been at her since they'd arrived, angling his thick neck so he could meet her eyes. He said, "And you don't have to worry about driving home."

"I guess I've already handed over my keys."

He laughed, then a silence settled. With the quiet came the memory that had resurfaced since hearing about Donnie. She is eight, he is six, playing in the field behind Memaw's house. He wears a plastic fireman's helmet, carries a kite that refuses to fly. He sees the plane first, a cropduster wobbling in the air, tendrils of smoke billowing from its tail. We should be on the ground, she thinks; our heads should be between our knees. But they stand, she behind him; she touches his shoulder. The plane flies low enough for her to see the pilot's goggles, his mouth moving. No. No gog-gles, a backward baseball cap, and he's wiping his eyes furiously. Then the ground buckles like a sheet snapped taut, and she runs into Donnie in a haze of smoke and pesticide.

"You don't look much alike," Omar said. "You and Don."

"I usually hear the opposite." Not true; no one ever compared them. She had dingy hair and blue eyes, her father's; Donnie's eyes and hair were black, shiny. For years she'd dreamed about the plane; he had, too. Their dreams were never nightmares, which seemed odd.

"Southport's a peach of a town," Omar said.

"It's where you're either drunk or fishing. They say that at the bar."

"Like I said."

She imagined serving longnecks in a rainbow wig and red squeak-ball nose.

He asked, "You got a sweetheart over there?""

"No," she lied, "just a husband."

Omar'd had enough of this flaky woman. He went into the parking lot for a smoke and a pull from his flask. The sky was hard, heat shimmering on the asphalt. A broken line of seagulls flew east from the dump; their shrieking sounded like an infant crying. Soon the line would fill in, hundreds of birds weaving their way back to the island. He picked a piece of tobacco from his tongue. A flash of a memory: Papa spitting tobacco juice into the sand. Maybe he *would* call the boys tonight. He'd drop the cook's sister at the base, shower and change clothes. Or maybe he'd swing by Sandra's first, let her wonder about this white woman behind him on the bike. A Lexus turned into the parking lot. A doctor's car, he thought, but the driver was too nervous looking, a frumpy man who had trouble activating the alarm. Probably a banker or a salesman, someone you met once and never saw again.

Donnie Miller disliked card games, but the monotony of poker in a psychiatric hospital was strangely relaxing. And the woman, Edie Banks, was enjoying herself, so he didn't mind spending the afternoon this way.

He'd arrived at Bayview after two weeks in the naval correctional facility—the army had no such facility on base—to undergo tests and counseling before the arraignment. He had arrived in handcuffs, escorted by MPs; he'd just turned twenty-four. Everything had started because of a comic book; rather, everything had *ended* because of it—Incredible Hulk #181, near-mint condition, worth two hundred dollars. A birthday gift from his sister. He'd shown the others and explained its value—the first cameo appearance of Wolverine, a haunted mutant who forever changed comics—but they'd hoped for a girly mag. Most were Donnie's age, lascivious, spring-loaded men who wore dress khakis to the Fox's Den on weekends. They called him queer and knocked over the water bucket whenever he mopped; on the soda machine someone had scrawled, *DM sucks sloppy cock.*

Watching Edie Banks put down two pair, he recognized a tenderness that made him want to please her. She reminded him of an old woman for whom he should open doors and speak loudly. She was in her thirties, sun-freckled, rusty-haired; she wore dental braces. She resembled Dwana's childhood friend Joanie Mahurin, a dewy-eyed girl who'd paraded around their house in panties. A tan-line on Edie's ring finger, perhaps that was the problem. Perhaps her husband had left, as Donnie's own father had. Maybe not. None of it mattered. Already he understood that none of it mattered.

He hadn't been looking for the comic book, but noticed it missing. He ferreted in places he'd never leave it, under his bed, in his duffel, behind the lockers. Of course they'd taken it, probably Buford, the wiry, fawn-skinned ring leader. Yet upon finding Buford in the rec room, the comic's cover folded as if he was enthralled by the story, Donnie felt briefly relieved. Two others played darts in the room, but they paused when he entered. Buford said, "Found your book."

Then they were behind him, holding his elbows, while Buford tore pages. The deliberate, excruciating noise of paper ripping and Donnie yelling. The screaming scorched his throat—he tasted the gritty texture of his own windpipe—and he was five years old again, grabbing a dogwood branch with a mud-dauber on it. Instantly pain shot from his palm through his body, like broken glass

in his veins, and he surrendered to it. He woke swaddled in cro-
cheted afghans; his mother and Dwana worried he was going into
shock. The memory came and dispersed in less than a beat, then
the rec room returned and he broke free as simply as slipping from
a shirt. He stomped one of the men's feet, felt the metatarsals snap;
he elbowed the other in his solar plexus, heard him heave and collapse. And now Buford was pinned against the paneled wall and
Donnie pushed a dart to his jugular. The soda machine droned beside them—*DM sucks sloppy cock*. The smell of menthol, Buford's
recent shave; under his jaw, a swatch of missed whiskers. Blood
dripped from his mouth, and although Donnie knew he must have
struck him, he didn't remember, so he did it again. Cracked his
forehead against the bridge of Buford's nose.

Then the not unfamiliar thought: maybe he was queer. Maybe
only queers would notice the curiously beautiful light in Buford's
eyes, the gray-flecked green, or the pleasing woodsy scent of his
hair. He felt every inch where their bodies touched, pressed his
weight harder against him, pushed his groin against Buford's thigh.
The contact neither aroused nor disgusted him. Buford was mumbling, whispering because his throat was blocked, but Donnie
made no sense of the words. He raised the dart to Buford's mouth,
parted his plump, tight lips; he heard them unstick. Blood-smeared
teeth, pink-white gums, bubbles of thick crimson saliva. He pressed
the dart's gold tip to the corner of one of those gorgeous eyes, ca-
ressed the skin, grazed the edge over his lashes. "You like that, don't
you," Donnie heard himself say. He slid the dart into one of
Buford's nostrils, pushed it against his septum. A needle into a
stubborn cushion. A stake into dry ground.

"I'm kicking your butt," Edie said in the hospital. "Full house."

"You're a card shark," he said. "I'm, like, a perch."

"My mother used to play on Sundays. Maybe I got it from her.
She lives in Dallas. She thinks she's a grandmother."

Confused, he arranged the cards.

"She has Alzheimer's. I've never told her I miscarried."

He shuffled the deck, wishing he could do it more quietly. A flyer on the wall advertised a seminar called *Preparing for the Unexpected;* another invited patients to join the bible study group.

"I send her framed pictures of babies from magazines. Does that sound calculating or cruel?"

"No," he said, though maybe it did.

"Those were my husband's words. He's a stickler for the literal truth, for facts."

He dealt the cards. By the patio door, a retarded man named Lester Riggs rested his forehead against the window. Probably he was watching the one-eyed cat that some people called Lucky. Others called him Jack.

"I decided to have a girl. I named her Esther, after my mother." Edie studied her cards. "Are jokers wild?"

"Yes, I think so."

"Charlie's a keeper, though. If we were stranded on an island, he would fashion a raft out of twigs. That's his character. I'd sit in the sand crying."

Edie drew three cards. Donnie held a pair of sevens, and a flare of excitement bloomed in his chest, his fingertips. He thought he might win.

"When I got pregnant, he was so excited he couldn't sleep for a week. I had to mix tranquilizers in milk. He never learned to swallow pills."

Donnie laid down his cards, hopeful until Edie fanned out three jacks. He averted his eyes to Lester who was marching in place.

"Charlie's mother left his family for an ostrich farmer," she said. Then she cackled, "Listen to what I'll tell a stranger. Maybe I *am* a nutso."

The MPs had put him in a padded cell on base—he hadn't known those really existed—and listed him on a suicide watch. He sat cross-legged in the middle of the room until morning, conjugating verbs in his head—Latin, Italian, Spanish, French. He never slept or spoke or moved, just to prove whoever was watching wrong.

• • •

Through the window that separated the ward from the common area, Charlie watched the nurse knock on a door. He felt suspended and vulnerable, as if life could unravel if she had to knock again or twist the knob herself. Then, release: Edie peered out and said, "Oh, it's Charlie." She shushed down the corridor in her terrycloth slippers, loosening her hair from a pony tail. He was surprised to recall how she thrived here. The daily arts and craft classes—she made stained glass (plastic) hearts—and the stray, one-eyed cat in the garden suited Edie as nothing had for a year. The same with the nightly bingo games, the book and cake-decorating clubs, the high school chorale that performed every Thursday. A juggling magician named Crazy Paul would visit over the weekend. Yesterday she had said, "We're thrilled. It's like he's one of our own."

Brightly colored tables crowded the cafeteria, the long, light-filled room where visitations took place. Twelve-step posters lined the walls; reinforced windows overlooked a dry, blond pasture. The starchy smell of dinner—meatloaf, pizza?—lingered, and he considered sneaking a roll to quell his hunger. The woman from the waiting room took a seat near the window; probably the soldier was outside again. Edie had staked herself at a yellow table near the far door, and approaching her, Charlie tried to gauge her spirits. Maybe sitting at a yellow table connoted a better mental state than sitting at a blue; he didn't know. His only thought was: she's here. When he reached her, she said, "Guess who's coming home Monday."

"Fantastic." The word tasted hollow. He'd expected her stay to be prolonged, more therapy scheduled, more tests ordered. He said, "Everything's waiting for you, right where you left it."

She smiled—her braces stoked his guilt, made him want to apologize—then she waved as a nurse ushered another patient into the cafeteria. Heavy, fortyish, wearing thick lenses that clouded his eyes, the man had the pale, doughy features of Down's syndrome. He stopped at the soda fountain and nudged the lever until an orange stream showered his hand.

"You need a cup, Lester," Edie said.

Lester laughed, affecting a chagrined surprise for forgetting his cup again. Edie watched him fondly, as she watched children. Charlie hadn't seen him before. Lester ambled to the window and pressed his fists to the glass, rocked to and fro. Edie whispered, "Lester the Molester. He points at women's crotches and says, *I know what that is.*"

"Points at you?"

"Oh, my knight. No, not me, but I've seen him."

Maybe she was lying, but he avoided pressing anything, especially here. He felt scrutinized by the nurses, cowed by what they understood of Edie that he didn't. He worried about sending her off to the races again.

"How's home? Is the nest still there?" Edie asked.

Earlier that year, a mother sparrow had nested inside the mailbox. Once, Charlie had thrown out the dense tangle of reeds and branches, and Edie called him a bastard and refused to eat for two days. When the nest reappeared, she slid bread crusts into it and made the mailman leave letters inside the screen door. How many times Charlie had caught her listening for hatchlings he didn't know. Now he realized he'd forgotten to feed the bird as Edie had instructed. He said, "We're all there, ready to roll out the red carpet."

A young, acne-pocked man entered the cafeteria and the woman from the waiting room ran to embrace him. Lester snapped his head toward them, then shifted back to the window. The woman started crying; the man rested his chin on her scalp.

"That's Donnie," Edie said. "He lets me win at cards."

"Why is he here?" Immediately, Charlie regretted asking this. The question assumed people had to do something, or not do something, to be hospitalized. So far he'd acted as though Edie's stay was routine, precautionary. "Like an oil change," he'd said that first night, trying to cheer her. He acted this way for both of their sakes.

"I think he beat someone up. Badly."

Donnie appeared incapable of causing damage, more like someone who'd been bullied all his life. He had a jittery manner that would invite cruelty. Charlie had pitied such boys in his youth, while he himself usually slipped under everyone's radar, avoiding altercations and attention of every kind; most days, he still felt invisible. What could people surmise from Edie's appearance—a thirty-four-year-old woman in wrinkled pajamas and braces? Maybe she seemed a person who'd lost her footing, but now rested, was fit to leave. And maybe she was, but Edie excelled at showing people what they wanted to see. How many times had they gone to parties where she interacted famously, then at home collapsed on the bed, too distressed to say good night? Not to mention the business with her mother. Esther called from Dallas at all hours and Edie plotted a sunny, alternate life in Corpus. Charlie had refused to indulge the fictions, and when he overheard their late-night talks, his stomach roiled.

Now, he tried to remember ever seeing another visitor get a soda. He thought anything in his stomach—a handful of cereal or a cold square of pizza—would sharpen his wavering concentration. Edie fingered the salt shaker, then rested her palms on the table. She said, "We talked about it today. In my session."

His muscles tensed, and he felt himself—not his arms or body, but everything inside—recoil. Edie wouldn't look at him. She ran her tongue over her braces. He said, "How did it go?"

"Sometimes I imagine the weight without trying to. It's like after swimming in the ocean, then a week later you still feel the waves."

This didn't sound like Edie, and he was trying to make sense of it when she said, "Let's leave Corpus for a while. The doctor suggested I reacquaint myself with the world."

"Sure," he said, automatically. Then, suddenly, unexpectedly, he was eager, awash with a grateful, weighted energy; his nerves tingled with the unmistakable electricity of hope. "We'll start planning on Monday. I'll talk to travel agents."

"Maybe to a desert. We can bathe in sand like Hindus. The new nurse told me about that."

"Anywhere at all." He liked the tone in his voice, the tone of an

actor in an important scene. Perhaps a week in Bayview *had* reju-
venated her, absolved her of that debilitating uncertainty. How
easy, he thought, to underestimate the wounded. Donnie and his
sister laughed behind her; this pleased Charlie. Lester moved from
the window and tapped the lever on the soda fountain again, but
pulled his hand away before getting splashed. He did it twice more,
then buzzed for the nurse. Edie waved again. Charlie did, too,
confidently now, flaunting his wife's renewed devotion.

Lester snickered, pointed at the woman: "I know what that is."

Leaving the hospital, Charlie felt jazzy. Hope and vigor always
returned after a visit, and accelerating past the split-rail fences
tonight, he vowed to harness his replenished optimism; X ray or
no X ray, tomorrow he'd bring her a tabloid, flowers. Stands of live
oaks were silhouetted along the road; the Kneel & Blow's sign
flickered in the distance. He cranked up a Tejano version of "Brown-
Eyed Girl" on the radio, and gathered speed through the humid,
heathered dusk. He imagined nights in the chilled desert and wondered how different they would feel, how much brighter the stars.
His stomach no longer ached; he'd cook at home. The speed-
ometer crested ninety. He floored the accelerator. He sang, though
he knew no Spanish.

Then time and event collapsed, imploded really, caved in on
themselves in a blur. He recognized the helmet and caught a clear
look at the woman's face; she stared south, unaware. Yet the soldier and motorcycle relieved him; steel and glass and a solid deaf-
ening thud, but nothing like this could be happening with two
people he'd just seen. He knew he could be killed but knew he
wouldn't. *I'm wearing my seatbelt. Hindus bathe in sand.* The hard-
hitting noise became everything, he tumbled and flailed inside it.
A peculiar softness to the collision, too, as of pressure released. The
bike's handlebars twisting like rubber; the passenger window
breaking so quickly, so completely that thinking no window had
ever existed made perfect sense. The Lexus slid. The seatbelt con-

stricted. The man said, *"Aggarrate! Aggarrate bien!"* The motorcycle flipped. Everything stopped.

Glass covered the seats, jewels in the moonlight; the showroom where he and Edie priced engagement rings. He didn't remember steering from the road, but he was parked on the narrow, crushed-shell shoulder. Lightning bugs flashed, the memory of returning to the jewelry store the same afternoon, afraid he'd forget which setting she'd preferred. Now, moving terrified him, but moving seemed tantamount to surviving, the first in a series of actions that would reveal themselves necessarily. He lifted one arm, then the other. Bent his knees, rotated his ankles, swiveled his wrists; slowly he twisted his neck. No airbag had inflated, why? Because the car had been broadsided? Smoke poured like liquid from the hood. The air reeked of scorched tread. Though the passenger side had suffered the impact, he expected his door to be jammed and was surprised when it opened easily; this seemed bolstering, promising. He'd slipped the ring on her finger while she slept, and when she woke the next morning, she said yes.

The night was hushed, darkening. Everything felt askew and surreal, as if he'd slipped through a gap in time's weave and all he'd known about himself was unrelated to where he was now. Walking in the glow of taillights and gauzy moon, his legs and mind were hollow. He expected his knees to give with each step. The oily air smelled of horses, cattle, manure. "You've had an accident," he said aloud. Insects whirred and clicked in the leaves; electricity sizzled in power lines. He expected voices, figures clamoring to ask if he was hurt. He paced fifty yards with only errant glints of broken reflectors on the asphalt, shards of plastic that might have been there for months. Perhaps he'd hit a deer or coyote, had suffered a head injury that spawned hallucinations of bending handlebars.

Then, near a tangle of mesquite trees, his breath left him. Had he not been watching the ground, he would have tripped. The soldier lay on his stomach, feet pointed inward, arms splayed. Charlie felt in a vacuum; the noise of the night rushed back in waves; he could no longer discern individual sounds. *There was a stop sign,* he thought. *They came from the west, they went somewhere after Bayview.* Over his shoulder, he glimpsed the Lexus—he'd not closed his door and light spilled out. No sign of the motorcycle or woman or anyone else at all.

"Hello," Charlie said. "Hello?"

He surveyed the area. Trees, sky, moon, ground, the lone gas station two miles ahead; each where it should be; each becoming another affirmation. Something rustled in the trees, then the sharp, resonant cracking of a single branch. His heart pounded. He waited for the woman to appear, but the rustling quieted. Whatever was there was gone. He placed two fingers on the man's neck and waited for a pulse. He'd never done this nor had ever imagined doing it. A quick thumping under his fingers; no, *in* his fingers, his own heart deceiving him, beating throughout his body. Edie knew CPR, had campaigned unsuccessfully for him to take the course with her. The flesh was grated and pulpy. He worried he pressed too hard or too soft, pressed the wrong place. Nothing. He found his own pulse pumping under his jaw, then tried the soldier's wrist. A raft of clouds moved across the moon, turned the skin a luminescent gray. The air became pungent, earthy. Closed eyes, open mouth and cracked-out teeth. Charlie had to shut a memory from his mind—Edie saying she wants braces, wants to laugh without covering her mouth. He choked back vomit. The pulse would not come. He waited another few minutes, afraid to stop waiting. Eventually, he stood and walked on.

Papa and Mama and the new collie, Obo, on Malachite Beach. Only in Corpus half a year and already Papa's located the best fishing spot—trout, sea bass, grouper, red fish. Aluminum lawn chairs; a Styrofoam cooler full of tamales and Fanta and Schlitz; Obo barking as Papa levers himself from his seat; the smell of Winstons and Hawaiian Tropics oil and the tonic in Papa's black, black hair.

"Give some slack, Omar."

He releases the line, though he wants to reel in. His arms tremble, his heels dig into the sand, granules between his clenched toes. In school he's learned that melted sand becomes glass, that mirrors are windows with one side painted black. Fourth grade, a bully has made him touch, with one outstretched, humiliated finger, his flaccid, brownish-purple penis.

"Now take him in, *un poquito*. Don't fight." Papa is excited, proud.

Omar reels. Two seagulls hover motionless overhead. Behind him the ear-splitting roar of a motorcycle, his mother calling Obo, the dog scavenging in the washed-up detritus—seaweed, a dead man-o'-war, mangrove pods. They bought Obo a month before. She was listed in the paper for $75, OBO; he'd believed it was the dog's name, which made his mother laugh through her nose, so Papa coughed up forty dollars. Obo sleeps beside the door, but Omar hopes she'll start jumping into his bed, giving him her warmth.

"Leave off, Junior."

"I am."

He will tell the whole school about the fish; Papa will tell his Thursday-night poker players; Mama will fry it; he will sneak Obo the skin; she will jump into his bed. The fish thrashes on the hook. Omar fears the line will snap and all will be lost, for suddenly existence itself depends on not bungling this. He offers more slack, this seems right, but Papa spits tobacco juice onto the sand and says, *"Aggarrate! Aggarrate bien!"*

Edie was four months along when the nurse called Charlie's office. He'd been waiting for the security desk to buzz when his wife arrived, though he'd thought nothing when an hour passed. Probably she was dallying in a fabric store. They only had the one car, Fido.

He took a cab to Spohn Hospital, acted stoic and amenable toward the driver, as if a purposeful composure could improve the circumstances. His breathing tightened. What his mind latched onto was the nursery—the antique bassinet bought at an auction,

Edie's ongoing search for the perfect hanging mobile, the picture books she'd started collecting. That she spent most of her days working in the room while he'd barely set foot in it turned his stomach so quickly he feared he'd throw up. Last week she'd had paint in her bangs; did she still? He imagined Edie exiting the freeway and being rear-ended and sent into oncoming traffic. He imagined the doctor waiting until he arrived to break the news about the pregnancy. Streaks of sweat tracked down his arms. The cab seemed stalled in traffic, even speeding toward the hospital.

She was leaning against a soda machine, talking to a nurse. No wheelchair, no bandages, no hovering, grim-eyed doctor. She seemed a visitor. "Fido got run over," she said, smiling. "I think we have to put him to sleep."

In bed that night, he picked up the joke again. "I'll miss the old boy."

"He's out of his misery."

"He'd want us to move on, to stay strong."

At first she seemed to be laughing, then he realized she'd started weeping into his shoulder. She said, "We've won the lottery, Charlie-boy."

Two weeks later, they woke on sheets soaked in blood. In his memory, Charlie always believed the thick, mealy stench roused them. An ambulance came, and within hours she'd bled so profusely she had to have a hysterectomy to save her life.

Dwana had the illusion of floating. The cropduster, the pilot's mouth moving; Donnie on his back, balancing her stomach on his raised feet, her arms extended like wings; the crystalline image of Omar Delgado's hands, though not really his, but her first lover's, a boy named Billy Mahurin; in a lifeguard stand, he had predicted she'd have perfect breasts; the moon coloring the beach cobalt, a pack of coyotes tussling in the water; she told Billy, "Donnie writes in four different languages. I never understand his letters."

Billy crouched beside her in the dark. They had just finished and lethargy overwhelmed him. She felt gravely embarrassed, disappointed and mystified, worried he was judging her against other girls. She couldn't stop blabbering. She said, "He waited a long time to say his first word. Then one day he just blurted, *I want a banana.*"

Billy said, "Are you okay there?"

"I'm wet." What a wonderful answer! The prospect of hearing how he'd volley back after being inside her was exquisitely terrifying, like swimming after dark or riding a motorcycle.

"There's been an accident," Billy said.

Not Billy at all; though the voice sounded familiar. From the hospital—Donnie is in Bayview, Billy is married or a father or dead, so much more than her first lover now, and she is beside a road, a pewtery night in Corpus—she *had* ridden a motorcycle!—the high pitch of mosquitoes, the moist scent of cow shit.

"I know," she told the man, but that was silly; she hardly knew anything. "Are people hurt?"

"I'm not sure," he said.

"I'm just a little cold."

Billy again, suddenly and completely; he removed his shirt and tucked it around her arms. She lay on her stomach, his touch shamefully comforting. She said, "Perfect."

"We'll sit tight. We'll catch our breath, then decide what to do."

"It might have been Omar's fault," she heard herself say. "He was speeding. And drinking. We'd seen my brother at Bayview."

"Did you go somewhere after—"

"They'll expel him, the army will. I never wanted him to enlist."

"My wife is there, too. He lets her win at cards."

In the lifeguard stand surrounded by coyotes—a pungent yet not unpleasant odor of wet fur all around—Billy and the man were both present. No ocean, though. The water had evaporated. She thought to scream this news, but the men seemed unalarmed, so no need to worry. She said, "He's just a baby. He used to be afraid of water. I don't know what he's afraid of now."

"That's okay," the man said. "He's safe there."

Billy and the coyotes vanished, as if spooked. She thought to say *Poof,* but asked, "Why is your wife in the hospital? Is that rude?"

"No," he said. "We lost our son."

"Oh, Lord," she said. "Lord, Lord." Her inclination was to prattle on, but she knew to hush. This man's wife had auburn hair and braces and a sad, dramatic jaw; she looked like Joanie Mahurin, Billy's sister, the first woman to break Dwana's heart. The man and his wife had sat near the soda fountain—who knew what they whispered? To know them, to understand who they essentially were, you only had to know what they'd lost. This was explicitly clear: everyone could be seen that way.

"How cold are you?" the man asked.

So, he stayed afloat by changing the subject. Good for him.

"We should find Omar," she said. "I'll help. I'll sit up."

"Wait—"

"I feel a little mixy. No. Woozy, that's the word. I guess that's normal. I don't feel broken anywhere."

"That's good news."

"I don't want to see Omar," she said. She'd thought they'd return straight to the base, but he'd detoured behind Bayview; he slowed in front of an A-frame, revved the engine until curtains parted in a kitchen window, then he popped the clutch and rocketed into the darkness. She said, "I wouldn't mind him being scared. Maybe his bike got crashed up."

The whine of sirens. Sirens coming to the field covered in glaucous green smoke, like fog; sirens coming to the lifeguard stand while she and Billy grope for clothes, she has his pants, he has her bra; sirens coming for Donnie as if he'd killed someone.

"The cavalry," she said. "Omar probably called them."

"Good," the man said, turning away. "At least we know he's alright."

The morning before the doctor committed Edie, the stink of cigarette smoke woke Charlie. As his eyes adjusted to the sunlight splashing into their bedroom, he fantasized that they had guests—a wife from the firm or neighbor. Edie had quit cigarettes for the baby, but he knew it was her, knew it as surely in bed as when he found her at the kitchen table in front of an overflowing ashtray. She said, "I'm smoking again."

She looked older than she was, a sullen, accelerated aging he'd noticed other mornings, but today it seemed permanent, not nascent wrinkles that would smooth with a shower and coffee. A moment before he saw them, he remembered the braces she'd gotten two months earlier.

She said, "I sneak out at night. I use mouthwash."

Their recent days flashed through his mind, a blur of filmy heat tinged with Listerine. She said, "Are you going to interrogate me, or can we just skip to my punishment?"

"What happened?"

"Interrogation it is."

"Honey, I just want to help."

She stayed quiet, a worrisome, irritating silence. He felt lured into dropping his guard when he should have seen this coming. He remembered that he only called her Honey when she bottomed out; he couldn't stop himself.

"I don't see how you do it, Charlie-boy."

"Edie . . ."

"You work, you socialize, you zip around in your hot little car."

"Honey, let's not—"

"When you were talking me into it, do you know what I kept waiting to hear?"

He did know; she'd said it before.

"*It's a great place to raise children.* I thought you'd say that about the car."

"I got a car, you got braces. We're not so different." As he said this, he wished he hadn't.

She nodded, once. Her expression suggested he'd incriminated himself, though he couldn't yet see that. Her cigarette had burned out. She had trouble lighting another one, as if aligning herself in a mirror where her movements were reversed. He reached to help, but she leaned back.

"I took some pills last night. Or this morning, I can't remember."

His heart went flat, his mind blanked. "How many?"

A disgusted little laugh sent smoke sputtering from her lips. "Apparently, not enough."

"I don't understand," he said, though he did. She had him cornered, and they both knew it. He noticed a bowl of pancake batter on the counter, cracked egg shells on a paper towel, the skillet on the unlit burner—a project that had proved too formidable. Those dishes, their air of defeated optimism, leveled him. There was nothing he could say now. He squeezed her hand, but it remained limp as raw steak. As cool, too. She lidded her eyes, then tears hung on her eyelashes, dropped to her cheeks, the table. Her mother, he thought. The phone had rung late last night, and even asleep, he'd understood Esther was asking about the baby. Maybe contriving details had sapped Edie. At once he understood his role. He knew to speak calmly, blithely, to call the doctor. He knew she was in no condition to stop him.

Hanging up, Charlie said, "He'll see us right away."

"What does he want to see?"

"Just a check-up. He'll run tests, then tell us where to go from there."

"*Us*? He'll tell *us* to go to Bayview, then he'll tell *you* to go home."

Years later, after Edie left because he reminded her of all she'd lost, Charlie would see the night as nothing more than coincidence, a series of circumstances that made sense in dim, regrettable lights. He'd remember a feeling of buoyancy, a survivor's euphoria, the subdued thrill of escape. Maybe such stability had been false at its core; that was not how life happened. Or maybe because it seemed so shatteringly absurd, it was exactly how life happened.

An ambulance had arrived at the accident, then a police cruiser. Paramedics fitted the woman with a neck brace and backboard, laid her on a gurney, and hoisted her into the ambulance. When one of the men asked her about Omar, Charlie mouthed, "She doesn't know," and the subject was dropped. The medics worked with fluid, satisfying efficiency, passing Charlie's shirt back to him while adjusting dials on monitors while discussing coyotes with the woman. Soon another medic—three now, though he'd first believed there were only two—directed him toward the police cruiser. His heart stuttered, his throat constricted; arrested, he thought. But he only needed to sign forms verifying he'd declined the medics' advice to go to the ER.

During all of this, he worried he'd not done everything he could for Omar, that he'd not waited long enough for breath, that the young soldier still lay suffering, praying a more competent soul would realize a sliver of life hadn't faded. Maybe all of this should have burned like hope, for if he were still breathing, maybe he could still be saved. Soon, though, a sheet covered the body like a mound of clumped snow. How strange to think: snow in Corpus. The sheet hovered in Charlie's peripheral vision, regardless of where he turned. The officer asked questions, and though Charlie couldn't admit to speeding, he answered as thoroughly as possible. He told about visiting Edie, about seeing the woman and Omar at Bayview. When he finally confided about Omar's drinking, he went under a wave of relief. Perhaps the officer went under, too; perhaps he'd already found the flask. A wrecker came for the bike, another for the Lexus. The sounds of the night amplified soughing wind, whispering fields, lines of far-off traffic. Another ambulance came for the sheet glowing in the moonlight, and the officer drove Charlie home, Patsy Cline in the speakers.

At home he drank bourbon; it seemed the thing to do. The whiskey relaxed him; was this how Omar felt, steering into the Lexus? Without realizing, Charlie had turned on every light in the house. His hunger returned and a lightheadedness set in, but he didn't eat. He sat at the table for another hour, doing exactly nothing, while the desire—the *need*—to talk with someone manifested. He felt pieces of the need gravitating together until they formed a complete thought: Call someone. Of course Edie came to mind, but with her came the improbability of negotiating answering services and nurses, convincing someone to wake her. Wait, then; let her rest. The same hesitation with the woman. He'd have to persuade the hospital staff, but that would be complicated by not knowing her name, nor even to which hospital she'd been admitted. His mother or father, a partner from the firm? He dismissed everyone. The night moved around him like mist.

The phone ringing. His mother-in-law, Esther, sneaked into the hall of the nursing home. When he told her Edie was in bed, she sounded affronted. A moment later, she asked, "How is Dallas this time of year?"

"Corpus. We moved. *You're* in Dallas."

"I can't wait to see you." Esther said, unfazed. She perpetually thought they were visiting the next weekend; Edie always told her they were. "I haven't spoken with the girl lately. I get worried, I worry something's happened."

"She'll call soon."

"The ragamuffin's wearing her out, I guess." She laughed. This was a grandmother's compliment.

Charlie walked to the window, feeling dizzy. He pictured Esther huddled in the hall, ready to bolt if an orderly rounded the corner. She wheezed. When he'd first met her, she'd been a member of a power-walking group, five widows who pumped around shopping malls before the stores opened. That she'd never spend a morning that way again felled him. She'd toiled for two decades in a dry-cleaning plant, then hawked Avon, then she started getting lost in parking lots, wandering off in her nightgowns; she had told him that Edie had learned to ride a bicycle behind a Catholic church. Suddenly the last thing Charlie wanted—it seemed the one abuse he couldn't endure—was for Esther to hang up. It was an opening in his body, the likes of which he'd not allowed himself to abide before, and the need aroused such alarm that it approximated relief, or on its sharpest edges, salvation.

The window was beaded and streaked with condensation. He said, "I'm looking at little Esther right now. She's sleeping. I have to whisper."

"Yes, don't disturb her." Esther had lowered her voice, too. Outside, June bugs bounced off a street lamp.

"Do you know what we've started calling her?" His voice sur-prised him. Then before she could answer, he said, "The little bug."

"Oh, she's a beautiful bug. I show her pictures to the nurses."

He knew her eyes were wide, her hands jittering with local tremors. When he'd signed the forms for the medic, he couldn't stop his fingers from shaking. His name came out spidery, illegible.

"Esther, I want you to hear something."

"Oh, Charles, would you?"

"Listen. Listen to her," he said and extended the phone into the air.

He'd always expected a rift to divide his life, a meridian by which he would measure before and after. Now he realized that no such divisions existed, just a steady letting go until you found yourself in a place you never thought you'd be. In an ambulance or nursing home, in a psychiatric ward, alone. More than ever he wanted to call Edie. He'd wanted to call since the morning they found blood on the sheets, for her to pull him to her breasts and console him. She had invited this, but he'd never been able to oblige, never would be able to. He thought to take one of her sleeping pills, but re-membered they were all gone.

He raised the phone. The line stayed quiet. He thought Esther had left the receiver dangling to hide from an orderly. Again it seemed he'd concocted the whole ordeal, that he only needed to dislodge this waking dream before it gained purchase in his mind. The veneer was thinning, though, like the night, and soon every-thing would be visible, undeniable.

"Esther?"

"Isn't that something," she said, "the little bug snores."

In less than a minute, the new nurse—Rahel Rama, two weeks on the job, left momentarily alone and more fearful of her patients than superiors—would knock urgently on Edith Banks's door and take an unprecedented, probably job-endangering chance to ask her to sit with Donald Miller; his sister was unconscious at Spohn and he'd asked for Edie. A strangely clarifying swirl of pride and despair would spread through her, a bracing call to arms that tingled in her cheeks and scalp. But the nurse hadn't yet knocked, and Edie lay in bed, Ambien-drowsy and about to remember the crabs.

She had loved the house, loved it. A two-story Victorian on Brawner Parkway, hardwood floors and a porch in a quiet neighborhood half a mile from the marina. Four bedrooms, theirs and a spare, one for Charlie's office and one to convert into a nursery. She visited Corpus's few museums—small, but lovely places to pass time, to bring children—and she drove over the causeway and watched men fish. She started writing a diary. A satin-covered notebook, filled with details of the pregnancy to eventually present to her daughter; though they had decided against an amneo, she always considered the child a girl. She wrote that eventually she wanted to volunteer at the library or a daycare, get involved with PTA. She wrote of driving around in Fido: *Fido is our car.* Or she wrote about staying home. How she opened the windows and let the balmy breeze ventilate the rooms; how she sat on the porch— *I'd always wanted a porch and now we have one!*—with headphones on her stomach, playing Mozart.

She had always known she'd be a mother, had known it more surely than she'd known she would ever marry. Fear had vanished. There was anxiety, but not doubt, not melancholy. She hoped the girl got her eyes, but not her rusty hair or bunched-up teeth. She wanted her to have Charlie's confidence, his bounding, resilient verve. He was like a boy, really, industrious and easily dazzled, deadly serious and shortsighted; how many nights had she reminded him to eat, to stop picking his nose while he read? Years before, she'd filled out a survey that asked how your partner would react if stranded on a deserted island; she'd said he would build sandcastles. But he'd become a stand-up father. In the mornings he slipped her feet into socks before they touched the floor; he handed her scissors handle-first; whenever she was going to the beach, he set out sunblock, shades, a floppy hat.

The beaches—Mustang Island, Padre Island, Malachite—were often deserted in the late mornings, her favorite time to go. An occasional surfer or fisherman, a boy riding a horse or an older couple combing the shore, but usually she was alone, listening to the waves roll and slosh. She hunted for sea glass and shells among the dried kelp, the barnacled driftwood. Once, she'd carted home a bag full of small conchs and soaked them in bleach overnight. When she woke the next morning—her body still craving its first cigarette but settling for water and a grapefruit—a dozen hermit crabs were scuttling around the table and floors, down the chair legs. Wake Charlie? No. She gathered the crabs in a shoebox and left him a note: *Gone to fabric store. Love, E.*

Why lie? Because he would worry.

The island was abandoned. The sky, like the water, was mother-of-pearl gray, the air unseasonably brisk, poised. She set the box halfway between the dunes and water, unsure which would be best. The crabs stayed so still she feared they'd suffocated. Whoops, she thought. Finally one stirred, then another and another; then they all came alive. Some were spindly and slow, some so swift and graceful they seemed to swim in the air. Maybe this gave her the idea, or maybe she remembered having always wanted to, or maybe no idea formed at all and she acted on perfect compulsion, instinct. She undressed. She waded out, holding her newly swelling belly. Her nipples tightened, the water cut into her calves, thighs. Sand slipped and shifted and collapsed beneath her heels. Her teeth chattered; she couldn't stop smiling. Then she ran, bound into the breakers and screamed and giggled in a widespread, beautiful lightness, a maternal ecstasy. She turned and surveyed the shore beyond the heaving waves. The sea oats feathering the slope of the sand, a rickety lifeguard stand in the distance, the mouth of a trail leading into the tawny dunes and the limitless mystery they promised lovers, children. Mystery? Yes, mystery. There was a secret life here —the sand dollars inching just under the surface; the kangaroo rat nibbling a tossed-out sandwich; the rattlesnake basking in the sun; the coyotes still damp-coated from slinking in the tide; the crabs claiming new shells; the Caspian terns hopping among the laughing gulls just about to take flight. Who knew where they'd land in an hour, next year? She only knew where they were now, with her, only knew her life was becoming more than it had been. Here we are, she thought. Here we are.

Bret Anthony Johnston was honored in *The O'Henry Prize Stories 2002* and was included in *Scribner's Best of the Fiction Workshops 1999.* His work has appeared in numerous magazines, including *Shenandoah, Greensboro Review,* and *Southwest Review.* A graduate of the Iowa Writers' Workshop, he teaches in the MFA program at Northern Michigan University and is working on a novel. "Corpus," is the title of his forthcoming collection. His novel, *Love in the Minor Keys,* is also under contract.

*I*n its first incarnations, "Corpus" was a linear narrative, seen exclusively through Charlie's eyes, and awfully, awfully boring. The events/ coincidences resolved rather than deepened the story's mysteries. Again and again I'd put the draft away, then return to it, each time getting closer to accepting that I'd probably be setting the story out to pasture, along with so many others.

But I liked Edie, found her implied situation intriguing, and one morning while working on another floundering story I heard her describing the city as she'd know it in the first months of her pregnancy. Through her, I learned that Charlie couldn't swallow pills, and after that, I learned she'd started a baby journal and that she'd woken to find the crabs on her chairs. These little details resuscitated the story and opened a door through which I heard the other voices. In fairly quick order, I saw Donnie sitting in his cell, Dwana locking the keys in her car, Omar struggling with his fish.

Finally, of course, Charlie remains, struggling to hold everyone and everything together, as he's always been wont to do. With as unruly a case as this one, it's no easy task, and rereading the story, I'm surprised—and grateful— for the fine job he's done.

Mark Winegardner

KEEGAN'S LOAD

(from *The Oxford American*)

The rumor was that Keegan had gotten married. As if that weren't improbable enough, the alleged wife was said to be years younger than Keegan and also pretty. We hadn't seen him, or each other, since May. Ours was the sort of forlorn Southern college where summer came and everyone scattered. Our composition director jumped on his motorcycle and zigzagged his way to California, looking up friends and lovers. Our theorist bought a hardscrabble hilltop vineyard. Our medievalist coached his kids' baseball teams. Our closeted, homosexual Romanticist hit Europe. Our fiction writer went to third-tier artists' colonies. Our poet took banjo lessons, divorced her husband, and finished her book of poems about taking banjo lessons and divorcing her husband. Our African-Americanist had a baby. Our Shakespearean went to Toronto. Those of us motivated enough by money or self-loathing to teach summer school skulked to and from the classroom with eyes as averted as a penitent's and dead as a pedophile's. Whatever we did that summer, we weren't thinking about Keegan.

When last we'd seen him—at commencement, trembling in white sunlight, reciting an occasional poem he'd written lauding the achievements of a Charlotte shopping mall developer to whom we were giving an honorary degree—Keegan wasn't so much as dating. He was sixty-six and looked eighty-six, tall and skeletal, with a long, white beard and stained polyester clothing he'd go days without changing. He also didn't change his voice: his every utterance was delivered in the Poetry Reading Voice—stilted, self-conscious, in awe of its own profundity. We disagreed among ourselves as to whether he had Alzheimer's or had always been like this. But, indisputably, Keegan had been unlucky in love. His first two wives had died. He'd politely asked out every unmarried woman at the college: every professor, every secretary, every librarian, all the young women in admissions, even our lesbian security cop. Some of us (out of pity? curiosity? guilt?) went out with him once or twice. But it had been years since he'd had a mildly significant other. Now he had a *wife?*

Yes, a wife. Her name was Bess. The first day of classes, we—at least those of us hip to the role face-time plays at a college like ours—went to hear the president's convocation speech. (When he said, "Our window of opportunity beckons," we briefly contemplated suicide.) At the reception, stationed in the middle of the atrium, sipping tepid white wine, nibbling cubes of marbled cheese, was Keegan and the new Mrs. Keegan. She was more than advertised: pretty in a neat, unaggressive way, in her late forties, and black. We tripped over ourselves in guilty liberal solicitousness, pleased as could be to make her acquaintance. Keegan had on a new gray suit. Bess wore a sequined black dress. He somberly introduced her. We tried not to form a reception line or to stare. Her head was tilted down, one shoulder dipped as a shield. She was the only spouse there who wasn't employed by the college, the only African-American who didn't teach black studies or coach a sport. She was a stranger to us all and overdressed. She called herself "just a housewife" and nodded serenely when we objected to the *just.* They'd met at church, she said. When occasioned, she took her napkin and dabbed dip from Keegan's beard so fast it embarrassed no one.

And so Keegan lost his homeless-man aura and showed up freshly scrubbed, Bess in tow, at lectures, readings, dinners, even the grim Friday happy hour in the faculty lounge that most of us thought had been abandoned years ago. They were sighted in trendy coffee shops, places Keegan had never been except to perform his poetry. Alone together, on the periphery of public events, her shy smile broadened to something like laughter, and Keegan, that lugubrious son of a bitch, looked content. We wondered, of course, what was in this for her. It was common knowledge that Keegan, though rumored to be the highest-paid member of our department, had no money. The idea of his naked, liver-spotted body quelled conjecture in that regard. The prevailing theory (we were big on theories) was that she had a caretaker complex. "She's a frustrated nurse," our comp director guessed.

"My take," said our African-Americanist, "is that, during a formative time in her life, she either saw her mother take care of an elderly loved one or did so herself."

None of us asked Bess about this directly. We were bigger fans of speculation than fact. Still, we liked her. Everyone said that.

Keegan's three children, from whom he'd been practically estranged, came to visit.

At work we saw a new Keegan. Ordinarily, when it was Keegan's turn to observe an untenured professor's class, he'd sit in front, remove his shoes, argue with us, then fall asleep. His letter in each of our files contained a brief fabrication of what had gone on in class and a rant about our misreadings of the assigned text. This semester it was our Romanticist's turn. Keegan sat in back, quiet, attentive, and fully clothed, then wrote a letter saying the class had made him want to go home and reread "Ozymandias." The Romanticist never seriously asserted that perhaps he was just a better teacher than we were.

Our students that term claimed that Dr. Keegan was doing more than going into class, reading the assigned poems, and gesticulating madly. There, he still took off his shoes, but his feet no longer stank. In class and out, he'd been given to Tourettic invocations of the Buddha and the Gospel of Luke. This abated. He also toned down the portentous pauses in his speaking voice.

Keegan's car, an old boat of a thing, was less frequently parked on the quad. Some of us began to feel happy for him. Knowing Bess would be there for him, knowing he would not be alone, helped us yearn for his retirement with clear consciences.

Years ago he'd posted a sign on his door advertising UNCONDI-TIONAL RAP W/ DR. KEEGAN. He was available, it said, every Monday in the department seminar room. Typically he was in there alone. Long ago someone (one of us?) had scrawled a C in front of RAP. This term, the old sign came down. Bess helped Keegan arrange to bring in guests: drug counselors, radical priests, weight-lifting motivational speakers, victims of apartheid. Flyers were posted. Attendance swelled to as many as twenty.

A few weeks into the term, Keegan published a new book of poems. His publisher, as had been the case for some time, was a former student who printed the books on a press in his parents' basement (before that he'd used a vanity press). Only the goodwill that Bess had engendered could explain why the fiction writer and the poet, after years of ignoring Keegan's books, organized both an on-campus reading and a book party for him, complete with a photo of the book's ugly cover screened onto a cake. The party was at the poet's retro-kitsch duplex. A reporter from our local daily, a friend of the fiction writer's, came to both the reading and the party. He got drunk and went home with one of our students. Another, a wholesome, large-foreheaded girl, seemed honestly to mistake Keegan's incoherence for depth. To be fair, we had many students in this camp. A week later the reporter did a story on Dr. Keegan that pretended he was not a fraud. It was such a fulsome valedictory that the joke around the college was that we were so sorry to hear that Dr. Keegan had died. Keegan lived.

In the '60s Keegan would have been the groovy professor, the one who'd already done everything the students thought belonged to their generation. He'd been against the war but was drafted and went (Korea, Vietnam, it was all the same to the sort of student we get). He'd come back and spent time in an ashram, a kibbutz, a seminary, and a *zendo*. He'd taught high school on an Indian reservation and in New Orleans. He owned a zither. You'd have to think that at some point drugs were involved. He'd gotten his doctorate on the GI Bill. He'd seen Muddy Waters and Miles Davis perform in nightclubs in bad neighborhoods. He'd brought Allen Ginsberg to our campus.

He'd married an art history professor. They fought passionately, the sort of couple everyone expects to get divorced and never does. They had two kids. After a particularly nasty public fight, she left him at a party and drove home into the teeth of a thunderstorm. She wrapped the family wagon around a tree. The kids were raised by her sister in Dallas.

The second wife had been his student, which was common in those days. She had a baby soon after they were married and went to art school at night. This was thought to be a good marriage. When a hair dryer fell into the tub with her, it was briefly investigated as a murder. The coroner ruled it an accident. We saw it as a suicide and didn't blame her. Keegan raised his third child himself. She spent her adult life in and out of rehab. We felt sorry for Keegan, for the girl (we didn't know her, but still). The better angels of our nature just wanted poor Keegan to be happy.

Was Keegan ever a legitimate figure in our profession? When he started out, anyone with a Ph.D. could get a college teaching job. At most schools, publishing was more a hobby of the obsessed than a condition of continued employment. His degree was from a solid university. We always meant to go to the library there and read his dissertation, to see if it was coherent. (Did we fail to do so because we were afraid it might be?) Right after he was hired (as an Americanist, not a poet), he published an article on William Dean Howells in a refereed journal that still exists. The article was workmanlike and so free of Keeganese (such as his incessant use of *resonance, organic, intrinsic, actualize, orchestration,* and *affirm*) that the department chair and the medievalist practically came to blows over the latter's drunken suggestion that it was plagiarized.

Not long ago, our Shakespearean found one of Keegan's exams on the copier glass of an old ditto master. Our department had stopped using ditto machines about when everyone else had. The exam contained twenty true-false questions and one essay. Sample true-false: "Faulkner, in *As I Lay Dying,* gives the fullest resonance of the human situation in opening the reader's heart to the spectrum of the souls of several sons who bear their mother, in their lives, to her grave." The essay question: "Name a writer you read this term who impressed you, and explain why." This from a four-time winner of our college's highest teaching award, who, not incidentally, gave grades that ran the gamut from A to A minus.

Scotch-taped to Keegan's office walls were yellowed letters from famous poets, sometimes next to snapshots of them with a younger, just as scraggly Keegan. This conveyed a certain gravitas. Until we read the letters. James Dickey thanks Keegan for sending him his book and says he plans to read it. Howard Nemerov points out that it's customary, when inviting a writer to campus, to offer a stipend plus expenses and corrects Keegan's grammar in the poem he'd sent. The postcard from Anne Sexton thanks Keegan for bringing her to our college and says she's never had a beer before a reading in a bar so dark. She's too busy, she says, to write on Keegan's behalf for a Guggenheim.

For years Keegan both advised our undergraduate literary magazine and published his own poems in it. (It was, in fact, the most well-known journal ever to accept a Keegan poem.) This continued when the Americanist, who had, in New Orleans, once been his student, took over as the campus magazine's adviser. When the college finally hired a real poet and the younger Americanist, by now the chair of the department, passed the advisership on to her, the poet instituted a policy excluding the work of the faculty. She'd presumed the students were publishing Keegan in an attempt to suck up to him. Rumor had it that Keegan was crushed. The poet received $650 as the magazine's adviser and was untenured. She reversed the policy. "What the hell," she told us. "If the kids want to publish him, who cares?"

When an ad hoc committee developed our department's Web site, the chair, to help us write the content, gave us a file folder of brochures that we had used over the years. In two of them—from the '60s and early '70s, judging by the wide ties and long-gone faculty—Keegan's bio calls him "our bard, who has been nominated for the Nobel Prize." We were stunned that this outrageous lie had been promulgated, believed, that the thought was even minted, but there it was. We were pleased to have proof that it wasn't Alzheimer's: Keegan had always been a fraud.

When it came time to be evaluated for tenure, we were required to compile a binder, which was to be, theoretically at least, the basis upon which everyone sitting in judgment—from the department tenure committee on up—would vote to grant us either lifetime employment or a pink slip. It was to include a curriculum vitae, copies of publications, course evaluations, teaching philosophies, grant applications, syllabi, lists of conferences attended, and letters from various authority figures within and outside the college. Our rules for compiling the binder explicitly prohibited letters solicited from other teachers at the college. That fall our poet inadvertently included letters from the medievalist and the fiction writer—letters she'd enlisted two years before when applying for jobs elsewhere, before she divorced her husband and realized she couldn't move (they had kids). She was a good poet but bad with paperwork and hadn't reread the letters. Both were glowing. Both noted that she was the first person our college had hired to teach poetry writing, after years of ceding such classes to an out-of-field colleague—a delicate situation that both said she handled deftly. Though she was more demanding than our students expected, they loved her. Her workshops filled. The fiction writer, who was scheduled to come up for tenure the next year and whose letter was the penultimate page of a binder as thick as a truck battery, was diplomatic about the Keegan situation. The medievalist's letter came last. It called Keegan "a hopelessly befuddled hobby poet, who gave everyone A's and was beloved thereby."

True as this was, it was a vestige of our sentiments toward Keegan before Bess was around. The director of composition was the first to sign the binder out. Around midnight he saw the letters and called the medievalist, who was his best friend. They ran marathons together. The medievalist was aghast. "Just pull it," he said.

"I already thought of that," said the comp director. "But there are two copies of the binder."

The chair, naturally, had the other one. By the time we got to campus the next day, the dean and the president already had copies of the letters. The chair told the medievalist that, because of the contents of the letter, he was sure to get fired. "I think not," the medievalist said. He was newly tenured and happily married to an expensive trial lawyer. "It's impolitic, but I stand by that letter. Look, I never even told her she could use it for that purpose. Plus, there's a rule against using letters like that."

"You'll get old someday, too," said the chair. "Don't you know that?"

"You think that's what this is about?" said the medievalist. "Pull the letter, which you have to do anyway, and this whole thing is done. I'll even apologize to Keegan."

"Even? First of all, under these circumstances," said the chair, "the letter stays. Second, you're suspended for the rest of the term."

"You can't do that."

The chair shook his head. "Please get out of my office."

The fiction writer, on the other hand, was sincerely mortified. She approached Keegan right before an Unconditional Rap session featuring an actual swami. Her plan was to pull him aside, apologize, then, in a goodwill gesture, stay for the swami lecture. She was also curious. She'd never met a swami. But at the door of the seminar room, Bess stood beside a beaming Keegan, who was quietly directing people to a classroom that was big enough to seat everyone. Shaking, the fiction writer asked Keegan if there would be a good time for them to talk, and he said right after the speaker finished.

There were many questions afterward. The fiction writer stuck it out. Bess saw her waiting and told Keegan she'd be happy to take the swami home. He nodded. She kissed him on the forehead.

On their way to Keegan's office, he and the writer didn't say a word. Once inside, she started talking, a river of words, and Keegan still didn't say anything. In her shame and contrition, she went on and on. Also, she'd had a few drinks.

"I affirm you," he finally said, and handed her a manuscript. No one knew Keegan had been writing a novel (naïve, we later realized; all of us were theoretically writing novels). He asked her if she'd read it and show it to her agent.

What could she do? She read it. It was the story of man who'd gone to Korea, become a sniper, and come home "with his body intact but his soul broken prismatically." He'd spent time in an ashram, a kibbutz, a seminary, and a *zendo,* and had wound up as a high school history teacher in a city resembling New Orleans. The last paragraph:

> His search for meaning brought him here, and it/He manifested itself/Himself in the classroom every day, the man was but a monkey of Jesus, some students would hear him, some would not be ready to hear, but intrinsically he was alive for this, to actualize the resonance of these kids.

The novel's title—not explained anywhere in the text—was *Samurai with Breasts.*

Meanwhile, Keegan was excused from the tenure committee's deliberations, though he could still vote. When the poet came to apologize, he told her that no one on this mortal coil could bestow true forgiveness. Nonetheless, he said, this matter would not affect his vote. He stood, put a hand on her shoulder, and said, "I affirm you."

The medievalist wasn't suspended, but the college seized his computer and reviewed every E-mail he'd sent and every Web site he'd ever visited. We even heard that a detective was hired to look for dirt on him. The committee met for a total of fifty-seven hours over eleven separate meetings. Its deliberations were confidential. The chair said anyone breaching same would be fired. The college attorney attended five of these meetings.

The poet had come up for tenure with more published work at that point than anyone in department history. ("Poems are short," the chair was rumored to have said. "Anyone can publish poems." The medievalist pointed out that Keegan never really had. The chair started to answer, and the college attorney clamped a hand over the man's mouth.) The medievalist's letter was destroyed more than once, by persons unknown, and replaced with copies. The committee used a secret ballot and denied the poet's request for tenure by one vote.

During all of this, the fiction writer bought Keegan lunch. Bess went, too. As they ate, the manuscript sat on a corner of the table. Bess and Keegan kept glancing at it, but no one said anything. They talked about Bess's sons—a cop, a jazz guitarist, and a city planner. They talked about Keegan's kids, too, about whom Bess had more to say than Keegan. She was compassionate and diplomatic about each child's difficulties, effusive about their triumphs, workaday and otherwise.

When the check came and the business part of lunch was inescapable, Bess offered to excuse herself. The writer said that wasn't necessary, hoping Bess would insist. Bess stayed. The writer wished she'd had a three-martini lunch. But she hadn't. She took a deep breath and began.

She said nothing dishonest. She praised the book's heart. She praised its authority. She said the book's theological overtones and digressions reminded her of late-period Tolstoy.

"Keegan sat there expressionless," she told us. "He reduced this piece of cake he'd ordered into a pile of crumbs and didn't eat any of it. Bess looked like some confused and eager student who just wanted to understand. Keegan, you could tell, was expecting the *but*."

But, she told him, she didn't really think the book was quite working, yet.

"All he said was"—and here she went into a note-perfect impression of Keegan's Poetry Reading Voice—" 'Could you. Just send it on to your agent. And see what he says?' "

She, she told him. Her agent was a woman.

He frowned and then asked if she knew any agents who were men.

"It pissed me off. Looking back," she said, "I guess he thought that was my point, that I was saying the book was wrong for a female audience. But at the time, damn. I just blurted out the truth: that he needed to revise the whole thing, with an eye toward what a stranger might find interesting."

Bess said that *she'd* found the book interesting. She put a hand on Keegan's thigh. She wasn't a stranger, obviously, or a professional in the writing field. But the book had moved her.

Keegan picked up his manuscript, stood, chastely hugged the writer, and left, Bess's hand on his shoulder all the way to his gigantic car.

That same semester, our theorist was up for tenure, too. In six years, he'd published only one refereed article and a feature story in an enology magazine. He'd garnered the dreadful student evaluations most theorists do. The committee discussed his case for four minutes. It recommended him unanimously.

We could get in a car, drive for two hundred miles in any direction, stop a random person on the street, mention where we worked, and be certain the person would say, "Hey, good school." Our campus looked like the set of a college movie from the 1950s, our weather was winningly temperate except in the summers, and our city was your basic Southern boomtown. People liked such places. We were expensive enough to be taken seriously by the rich, not so expensive that we couldn't compete with state schools for the rank and file. Like most colleges of this ilk, our faculty was committed to undergraduate teaching and was, to varying degrees, demoralized. That said, because the job market remained tight, and because ours had become the last profession in America that offered a hope of lifetime employment, whenever we went out to hire, we saw brilliant candidates. That spring, we brought three to campus competing for a Victorianist job. The prohibitive front-runner came first. He had a law degree from an Ivy League school and had been a true-blue Philadelphia lawyer for five years before chucking it to get a doctorate in Brit lit from a different Ivy League school. His dissertation was on literature and the law and seemed to be on the threshold of acceptance by the press of a third Ivy League school. In his letter, he made a point of mentioning that his wife's family lived near us. We thought we had a shot.

There were thirty students in his sample class. Halfway through, he knew all their names. He listened to them. He expertly balanced discussion and lecture. He was short, a little heavy, self-deprecating, and bald, which kept his intelligence and caged-animal pacing from seeming too much. At lunch, he always seemed to be talking about us and not himself, and yet we always came away having learned quite a lot about him.

By the time we sat down for the department interview, it was in the bag. He was making the intricate nature of his research lively and accessible, and we were already so won over that none of us asked one of those long questions that are really speeches about how we're smart and you're not.

When Keegan raised his hand, we were not initially alarmed. He typically asked one innocuous question at these things, late in the game, about the person's teaching philosophy. "I do not relish. The estimating of another's teaching," he said. He had the Voice going full-bore. "But don't you agree. That your approach to literature. Is too abstract for the students? I hear you talking about the law. But. What about the intrinsic themes. And the styles. Of the works?"

The candidate pursed his lips and nodded, as if this were a thorny, worthy question. To our horror we realized that the events of last semester had squelched the candor from us all. No one, not even the medievalist, had prepped the candidate for Keegan.

"I wouldn't call my approach abstract at all," the candidate said. "Legal issues of rights, ownership, and enfranchisement inform any work you can mention. They have a profound and even concrete effect on the lives of the characters and the life of the culture."

As the candidate cited several specific examples, Keegan started waving his hands slowly. He seemed to be pointing with his middle finger, the way old men sometimes do. We were afraid the candidate might think Keegan was flipping him off. Our African-Americanist reached over, put a hand on one of Keegan's arms. He ignored her.

"Stop," he said to the candidate. "What about the mother. Holding the child. In her arms?"

Apropos of absolutely nothing.

The candidate cocked his round head.

"The mother and the babe," Keegan said. He was still waving his arms. "The Madonna. And the Christ."

Here, several of us were about to say something, anything, but the candidate was too fast.

"Even motherhood," he said, "is a legal concept."

"My intrinsic response to that," Keegan said. He closed his eyes. He raised both hands before his face and extended his middle fingers. He had very long fingers. "Is stick it."

"Ha!" the candidate said, eyes wide, his expression a disconcerting blend of shock, fury, and amusement. He stood. "This interview is over."

He was out the door of the seminar room before Keegan reopened his eyes.

Not even the chair seemed to know what to say to Keegan.

"What's not befuddled about that?" the medievalist said to a few of us, though by now we weren't in the seminar room, either.

"What's not hopeless?" said the Romanticist.

"Word," said the medievalist.

Several of us piled into an SUV with the candidate and issued robust apologies all the way to the airport. On the way back, we stopped at a liquor store. Then we sat on the Romanticist's dock, on a brackish lake behind his house, and plotted ways we might get Keegan fired. Some of us thought this might be the thing that could bring about his retirement. We could go to the dean. We could go to the president. Maybe we could even enlist Bess's help.

Those who'd been here the longest said it was futile. Our poet, one of our best and brightest, would soon be out of a job, but Keegan would be here until he died. And he'd probably outlive us all. None of us believed he *would* be fired, of course. Not beloved Dr. Keegan. Still, somehow, he had to go. We were ready to relax our distaste for deus ex machina. Whatever it took, we were for it, even if Keegan needed to die.

Keegan lived. But days later, after we had lodged our quixotic complaints with the powers that be, Bess Keegan, forty-eight, died in her sleep. Brain aneurysm. Go figure.

The college had surrendered its church affiliation decades before, and our administration was unshy about its desire to tear down the chapel. It was a bastardized Federal-style building, old but not historic, a survivor of various shoddy renovations. The addition of air-conditioning was such a marvel of convoluted ductwork and later-boarded holes that crooked contractors brought their children here to sit on the tailgates of their pickups while they sipped whatever was in their travel mugs and savored the view of what was possible when enterprise collides with people who think they know everything. It was the only building on campus that was never locked. We bordered a bad neighborhood. Campus police often chased vagrants out of there. New officers, on their first days of work, were shown Keegan's picture in the faculty directory and told that he worked there, was not homeless, and should be left alone unless he asked for help. (*Help* involved jump starts, ball game scores, show times of movies, rolls of toilet paper, and requests to be let into his office to get his keys.) Keegan sat alone in that chapel all hours of the day—reading, writing, praying, sleeping. Our theorist said he saw Keegan grading papers there. Six months prior, Keegan and Bess had been quietly married in that chapel. Now it was the site of Bess's funeral.

At first glance, a stranger might have mistaken the funeral for a wedding. The flowers on the altar were red roses. The families and guests seated themselves as if there were ushers. On the bride's side sat about twenty black people. In front were three large and angry-looking young men we presumed to be Bess's sons. The groom's side was packed. Nearly all of us were very, very white. In the front row of our section sat Keegan, his three children, and their families. Only a handful of students, but more faculty than ever went to commencement (which was required, technically). Keegan had few real friends, and the excess of our turnout shamed us into conceding our weakness for pathos. Also, we felt guilty about our recent hateful feelings toward him. Bess's death seemed to have been engineered by someone's capricious, so-called God to make us take pity on Keegan. We studiously avoided the furious stares of Bess's sons.

At the appropriate time, the priest called upon Keegan to deliver the eulogy. He stood and shuffled to the pulpit. He mounted its stairs so slowly that the priest, seated on the opposite side of the altar, looked ready to leap up at any moment and steady the old guy. But Keegan made it alone. When he did, he closed his eyes, threw back his shaggy head, and stretched out his arms as if in invitation to be lashed to a cross.

This went on for an awfully long time. We exchanged glances. We wanted the priest to put a stop to this. We wondered if one of us would have to do it. We tried to keep from making eye contact with any of the people noisily clearing their throats on the other side of the aisle.

Finally, Keegan let down his weary arms. He pulled a stack of lengthwise folded paper from the inside breast pocket of the same gray suit he'd worn to last fall's convocation. It was the suit, he told us, that Bess had bought him for their wedding. We cringed.

He set the papers down on the Bible and smoothed them. "I have written a poem," he said, swallowing hard, "for Bess."

This gave us the courage to look across the aisle. People there seemed to relax, slightly.

The poem was more or less what we'd come to expect from Keegan's occasional poems, a blend of the earnestly literal with enough mystical babble to kill an adult horse. It included the names of

Bess's sons, which Keegan, eyes closed and head again tilted heavenward, shouted: *Derek! Alfonso! Tyrone!* We couldn't keep our eyes off those young men. They didn't move. Behind them, many of the black people wept, but the sons kept it together.

Keegan's pauses between stanzas were so long that we repeatedly thought the poem was over. When at last he finished, the priest rose.

"Yes, this, too, is for Bess." Keegan nodded, as if he were fulfilling a request. The priest sat.

This poem was included in Keegan's last book. Some of us had heard it the previous semester at his publication reading. Though we couldn't parse its gibberish, it had driven Bess into a fit of giggles. That, as Keegan read his poem, was what we thought of: poor Bess, happy. This got to us. We were not made of stone.

When at last he finished, the priest again rose. "I would like to honor Bess," Keegan said, "by reading another. Another poem. For Bess."

This time the priest didn't sit back down. He was also a professor in what was left of our religion department.

This poem was one Keegan had written years before he met Bess. We'd always understood the "she" in the poem to be the Virgin Mary.

Keegan finished and barreled right into another one. The priest looked to us for counsel and moved a couple more steps toward the pulpit.

When Keegan started another, a haiku this time, one of the sons stood. No matter our politics, we were, truth be told, the sort of people afraid of an angry young black man. The son walked toward Keegan. He arrived at the pulpit at about syllable fourteen.

"One final poem," Keegan said. The son and the priest flanked him, each with a foot on the pulpit steps and a hand on his shoulder. "I affirm you all," Keegan said, and soldiered on. When he finished, the priest and the son escorted him down. The young man put his arm around this old man, his stepfather. Keegan's children didn't move. Keegan took a place in the pew beside his stepsons. Our sense that they were angry had perhaps been culturally biased, and, anyway, an aneurysm was nobody's fault.

As the priest turned to cue the organist, Keegan stood and faced the congregation. "Copies," he said, "of the poems. I have read. In honor. Of Bess. And to grieve her."

Please, God, no! we thought.

"Are available. In the narthex."

He sat back down.

The stepsons patted him on the back. Keegan's own children crossed the aisle and did the same. They bravely took their places together in that front pew. Keegan began to sob silently. His shoulders shook. Hymns were sung, the priest executed a dull homily, and everyone pretended that nothing unusual had happened.

The poems were free, dittoed—somehow Keegan had found a ditto machine—and stapled together. There were maybe thirty sets of them stacked on a card table. They went briskly. No one we knew ended up with a copy.

It wasn't as if we didn't reach out to Keegan. We sent cards. We expressed genuine sympathy to his face. We made donations to the United Negro College Fund and to the church where Bess and Keegan had met. Naturally, some of us wondered if *this* might provoke him to retire. Then he could focus on the grieving process. But the chair told us that when he'd suggested a mere semester off, Keegan had been offended.

For the next few weeks, there was a frenzy of taking Keegan to lunch. He wore sweatpants to class but otherwise seemed to be bearing up well. His daughter, we heard, had landed an outpatient job at a food co-op and had taken an apartment not far away. He got a dog—a greyhound, from the rescue people. He renamed it Martha. Not only was he able in no time to get it to respond to that, but when he'd intone, "Martha, Martha, thou art careful and troubled about many things, but only one thing is needful," the dog would roll over, leap to its feet, look to the heavens, and bark.

It would have been sentimental, and perhaps unreasonable, to expect us to like Keegan more because a sad thing had happened to him. Bess's death had made the world a worse place for him, but Keegan had known her for less than a year. Soon our classes, our committees, our increasingly futile attempts to hire a Victorianist, our unhealthy obsessions, our families and their attendant crises conspired to push the care and feeding of Keegan from our agendas.

But over Easter weekend he was walking home from his daughter's apartment with the greyhound when a once-a-century ice storm hit. He was still four miles from home but did not turn back. He made it to within five blocks of his house when the dog bolted. Keegan fell, and the dog dragged him all the way to the mouth of his driveway. He was lucky, his doctor said, only to have broken his arm and ruptured his spleen. The ice must have made the enterprise go more smoothly. Keegan was expected to make a full, uneventful recovery.

Three of us—the teaching load here is three courses a semester— pitched in to cover his classes. The fiction writer took his modern American poetry class when the poet refused and the chair said he was spread too thinly already. When she got to the classroom, only five students were there. She asked if it was Dr. Keegan's class; it was. She asked if they'd heard about Dr. Keegan's accident (it had been in the school paper, along with several of his poems, as if he *had* died); they had. She asked where everyone was (there were thirty-one students enrolled, six over the cap); they said this was more than usual. She took out her book, and so did the two students who'd brought theirs. The other three hadn't even brought notebooks. When she began talking about Robert Frost, they looked at her as if she'd falsely accused them of date rape. We're not up to that, they said. We're doing Whitman.

She looked at the syllabus. It said Frost was on tap for today. Whitman was the first writer listed. The syllabus promised to spend two weeks on him. This was week twelve. "I'm the teacher of record from here on out," she said.

They considered her, blankly.

"Okay," she said. "Whitman."

The students seemed to find their shoes fascinating. Or were fascinated she was wearing hers.

Subbing for Keegan gave us access to his office. That was how our African-Americanist, while looking for something else, had come across the letter from the Swedish Academy, which curtly noted that Section Seven of the statutes of the Nobel Foundation forbids nominating yourself for a prize.

Did that make it better or worse? Worse, we thought.

Near the end of the semester, our poet won an award that many of us had heard of. Her picture appeared in the on-line version of the *New York Times*. Her tenure case, which had been denied right down the line, was on the desk of the president, who should have made a decision weeks earlier. For once, his pathological procrastination paid off. She received both a promotion and tenure.

To celebrate this, the department chair—undoubtedly one of those who'd voted against her—held a reception in the faculty lounge. Our theorist brought several magnums of his own surprisingly drinkable wine. Keegan arrived late, heavily bandaged and using a walker, despite which he'd brought his dog. We mooned over the dog. Our poet pulled out her banjo and played a hilarious medley of '80s hair-band songs, though she seemed disconcertingly unamused. "Speech!" someone shouted. Keegan rose. The poet didn't notice, or pretended not to. She thanked everyone for coming, and for their support, and announced that she'd been hired, with tenure and rank, by a large research university in one of America's rectangular states, a job she'd sought out of desperation and had accepted before her recent, unexpected reversals of fortune. We expected her to laugh, or to gloat, but she looked like she might cry.

Keegan sat.

The poet felt she needed to honor her commitment. She had no choice, she said, but to leave.

The chair rushed over to congratulate her. She was chagrined enough to flinch just slightly when he embraced her. Then he shouted down the buzz she'd kicked up and said he had an announcement of his own. After years of frustration, he'd finally found a donor—anonymous, as it happened—who was willing to endow a distinguished-chair position. It would be named for Keegan. Keegan would also be the first to occupy it. It came with a raise of some confidential amount and a one-one teaching load.

One-one. Same as that double-barreled bird he'd flipped.

Overcome, Keegan stood, whereupon the dog, stuffed with cheese that we'd fed it, crapped on the rug. Keegan was oblivious. The turd sat there. A few of us went over to shake his hand, because what else was there to do? As for the turd, we kept talking as if nothing had happened. No one did anything. Finally the dog ate it.

Summer came, and again we scattered.

After the year we'd had, many of us—particularly the poet, who spent the summer waging and losing a custody battle and then moved out West without her children—began to yearn for the day when we could urinate powerfully on Keegan's grave. That didn't make us bad people, did it? We'd never have the nerve to do it.

Mark Winegardner is the author of the novels *The Veracruz Blues* and *Crooked River Burning* and the story collection *That's True of Everybody*, of which "Keegan's Load" is a part. He is the Janet Burroway Professor of English and the director of the creative writing program at Florida State University. At present, he is at work on a novel that will continue the famed *Godfather* series.

MIRIAM BERKLEY

*W*hen I was nine, I fell in love with a series of what we'd now call *young adult novels by a* Sports Illustrated *writer named Tex Maule. His given name was Hamilton Prieleaux Bee Maule, which is also supremely cool, but not as good a name for someone writing books about pro football. The series started, if memory serves, with* The Quarterback. *It was followed by* The Running Back, The Linebacker, The Cornerback, *etc. Each took the reader through a season, each used the same fictitious team and league. This alternate reality is all I can blame for my decision, after publishing a story set in academia called "The Visiting Poet," to write a series of such stories, with titles such as, "The Untenured Lecturer" or "The Incoming Department Chair" or "The One-Legged Dean." I actually wrote "The Untenured Lecturer," which turned out all right, before I decided that the project was a stupid idea. "Keegan's Load" would have been called "The Endowed Chair," except that I was also sick of the title gimmick. It would have been published in the issue of the* Oxford American *that languished at the printer's while the magazine struggled to find the money to print it. Happily, that "Lost Issue" was published online; even more happily, that led to your finding the story here.*

Michael Parker

OFF ISLAND

(from *Five Points*)

for Lee Zacharias

A fter so many storms hit the island the people started to
move away. In the end it was only Henry Thornton on one
side of the creek, Miss Maggie and Miss Whaley on the other. Sisters: Miss Maggie with her dirty same old skirt and Henry's old
waders she used to slosh across the creek, Maggie hugging on him
nights when she got into her rum and came swishing down to his
place to hide out from her sister. Henry hid out from Miss Whaley
himself, stuck close to his house down the creek where his family
had stayed since anyone could remember. Three bodies left on the
island and a Colored Town right on until the end. Every day Henry
would cross the creek up to where his white women lived: sisters,
but Miss Maggie had got married and could go by her first name
instead of Whaley which her older sister by three years clung to like
the three of them clung firm to their six square miles of sea oat and
hummock afloat off the elbow of North Carolina.

Across the sound it got to be 1979. Henry's oldest boy, Crawl,
gave up fishing menhaden out of Morehead to run a club. He
wrote Henry that he'd purchased this disco ball. Miss Maggie read
the letter out to Henry on the steps of the church one warm night.
Henry told her, write Crawl tell him send one over, we'll run it off

the generator in the church, hang it up above the old organ, have this disco dance. Henry made a list in his head of everybody he'd invite back, all of them who'd left out of there after Bertha blew through and took the power and the light. Crawl wrote how that ball spinning under special bulbs would glitter diamonds all up and down your partner. Miss Maggie snickered, said, I ain't about to take a letter and tell him that. Imagine what Whaley would do come some Saturday night when we're dancing in a light bound to suffer her a hot flash. Up under his breath Henry said, We? Ain't no we. In his head he was twirling his Sarah around in a waterspout of diamonds. Tell everybody come back for the disco, Crawl, he wrote in his head. All of his eleven children and Miss Maggie's son Curt the prison guard up in Raleigh. Hell, Crawl, invite back those Coast Guard boys and some of the summer people even. He was sealing up his letter when he looked out across the marsh to where night came rolling blueblack and final over the sound. He ripped that letter open and crossed it all out and said instead, No thank you son to some disco ball, we got stars.

Every morning Henry poled his skiff out into the shallows to fish for dinner. He stayed out in good weather to meet the O'Neal boys, fishermen from Ocracoke who met the Cedar Island ferry every day for mail. Be sure you give me all them flyers, he'd say every time and the O'Neals would hand him a sack of grocery store circulars sent over from the mainland advertising everything. Miss Whaley liked to call out the prices at night. "They got turkey breast 29 cent a pound." All it took to make Henry wonder how come he stayed was to sit around long enough to hear Whaley say this three times a night about a two-week-old manager's special one hundred miles up in Norfolk. Crawl was always after him to move off island, had come after him six times since Bertha. You don't got to stay here looking after the sisters daddy till they die or you one. Come on, get in the boat. Crawl showed up wearing his hair springy long and those wide-legged pants made out of some rough something, looked like cardboard, to where your legs couldn't breathe. Boots don't ought to come with a zipper. Why would

Henry want to climb in any boat with duded-up Crawl? He would keep quiet watch his grandbabies poking around the beach and going in and out of the houses standing empty waiting on their owners to come back, sitting right up on brickbat haunches pouting like a dog will do you when you go off for a while. He would watch his grandsons jerk crabs out the sound on a chicken liver he give them and having themselves some big easy time until they hit that eyecutting age. Look at Granddaddy fussing after his white women, what for? Henry would look at them not looking at him and hear the words out of Crawl's mouth all across the Pamlico Sound and all the way back. Your granddaddy don't want to change none. That island gonna blow and him with it one of these days.

What would Henry Thornton be across the sound? Now, who? This he could not say but it wasn't what they all thought: scared to find out. Maybe fear was what kept the sisters from leaving, though they had their other reasons. Maggie would do right much what her big sister said do when it came down to it. Miss Whaley stayed on partly for the state boys who came down from Raleigh every spring before the mosquitoes rode the landbreeze over. Every April a boatload of them, always this fat bearded one with his bird glasses and often a young white girl who asked most of the questions. They'd get the answers up on a tape machine, so Henry called them the Tape Recorders. Miss Whaley'd put on her high-tider talk the Tape Recorders loved to call an Old English brogue. They said Henry spoke it too, though how he could have come out talking like an Old English, they didn't tell him that. He didn't ask. He didn't care to talk for them, but it didn't matter much because Miss Whaley loved a tape recorder. Every year she'd tell them about her father's daddy got arrested in Elizabeth City because he favored the man shot Abraham Lincoln who was loose at the time. She didn't mention he was over there on a drunk. Sometimes Maggie would though, and cackle right crazy loud. Miss Whaley every time would tell about Henry's younger brother Al Louie Thornton who cooked for the guests over at the first lodge before it washed away and who was known all over the island for wearing bras and panties and shaved his chest hairs and plucked around his nipples and painted his toenails. Sometimes he'd cook in his apron and shirt and that's all. Babe Ruth came over to hunt, they took him back in the kitchen to meet Al Louie. Babe Ruth took Al Louie's autograph, though Miss Whaley left that part out too.

One year the tiny white girl pulled Henry aside, said, That lady's digging dirt all the way around your family tree Mister Henry, serves her right if you want to return the favor. Wanting Henry to tell it on a tape machine, Miss Whaley almost getting married three times and then falling all over Miss Maggie's, her own sister's, husband, the no-fishingest man ever born on island and some said a thief. Henry could have taped that and more. He could have had Miss Whaley showing her white ass in some book right alongside Al Louie's black aproned ass. But he just gave that little girl a smile and said, I don't no more hear her than the wind after seventy-some years on this island and last six with just us three.

The Tape Recorders were all the time trying to get Henry to act like he hadn't ever been off island much at all. He played them like they wanted, even though he'd spent two years at the Coast Guard base up in Weeksville and six years in the Norfolk shipyards. There he took up welding and did decent at it. Now his children reached right up the east coast to Troy, New York, like stops on a train. Morehead, Elizabeth City, Norfolk, Baltimore, Philly, Newark, Brooklyn, up all the way to Kingston and Troy. He'd took that train many times when Sarah was alive. She loved it off island. All the time talking about moving, retiring she called it. But what was there to retire from? Wasn't any *after* to sit down from on this island. Henry came back to the island a damn good welder but what was it to weld? Can't weld conch shell, seaweed, fishbone. He bought some pigs and chickens off his brother and later on two milk cows from the O'Neals and got by selling crabs and flounder to O'Neal who turned right around sold to the wholesalers in Hatteras for what Henry knew was some serious profit.

Two storms before Bertha, the one that opened up a new inlet down on the southern tip of the island, Sarah bled to death on the kitchen floor. Henry had got caught over in Ocracoke on errands for the sisters and what it was was the wind. Henry'd tacked the kitchen on himself out of washed-up timber mostly and some he'd paid the ferryman to bring him from Belhaven, which wasn't much better grade than what the tide brung up. And Henry's hand-hammered kitchen falling, slashing a hole in his Sarah's forehead. Sarah lying on the floor in the rain, her blood running the brown boards black. Before he left he'd asked the sisters, y'all check up on Sarah while I'm gone. Sarah wasn't nearly as friendly with them as Henry. Maybe because they were women and it had got down to four of them, three women and one man to run man things. Sarah did not stomach Miss Whaley's attitude and as for Miss Maggie's mess when she took a drink and came right up close enough to Henry to blink crosseyed (maybe because at that particular nearness he wasn't even black, just blurry) well, Sarah knew it. She studied everything but didn't say one word to Henry about it even though he knew when she knew something, he could read her just like he could the wind and the sound and the sky. If Henry wasn't there to drag his wife across the creek nights she'd have stayed home singing those gospel songs Crawl's wife taped her off the radio. They had the lights then and Sarah favored this Al Green out of Memphis. Maybe she was singing her Al Green right up until Henry's kitchen came down on her and do you know the timber he cobbled that kitchen out of blew right off island? Ocean brung it to him, wind took it away. And left Sarah lying out on the floor holding a pair of scissors in her hand, what for? What was she fixing to cut? The sight of those scissors drove Henry crazy. He pried them out of her fist and flung them into the inlet and tried not to look at her head whichways upside the stove.

She wouldn't let me go after her, Miss Maggie told Henry talking about Whaley, which Whaley herself was big enough to admit. Why lose two to save one? she said. Sarah bled to death and it turned up big-skied sunny like it will do after a storm to make you feel worse and the sun dried the blood on the floorboards until it looked like paint. Toting the wood down-island is how he discovered the new inlet. And in his mind it was Sarah cut the island in two. Sheared right through the marshland with her sewing scissors. Low tide he'd walk over to the good-for-nothing-but-birdshit southside. He'd crouch and smoke him an El Reeso Sweet if he could get one off the O'Neals. Wasn't one thing over there worth seeing but he knew Sarah was wanting him where the sisters weren't.

But he couldn't be hiding all day down-island. They would be wanting their mail. Henry would pole out and the O'Neals would tie him up if they won't in a hurry and pass him a Miller's High Life. They liked to get him talking about the sisters. He knew they went right back to tell it all over Ocracoke and said how he was getting something off Miss Maggie and Miss Whaley liked to watch, he'd heard that, it got back to him. Brung back on the wind maybe. From his house down by the inlet you could see across to Ocracoke the winking lights of Silver Lake and the lighthouse tossing its milky beam around but neither Henry nor the sisters crossed over unless one got bad sick. The O'Neals brought groceries and supplies, which Henry mostly paid for with his catch, Whaley being too tight to part with what money was left the sisters from their daddy who even the Tape Recorders knew to have gotten filthy off a load of Irish whiskey washed ashore on Sheep Island in the twenties. Whaley when she paid him at all was so ill-mouthed about it Henry stopped asking. Sarah used to collect on it and because she knew Sarah was not scared of her, Whaley always paid her what she owed. Henry wasn't scared of neither of them but it seemed like with only three of them on the island and him keeping the two of them alive he could leave off acting the nigger and one way to do that was not go knocking on Whaley's door asking for anything he didn't leave over there the night before. Sometimes Maggie would pay him in dribbly change and yellow-smelling dollars she stole and hid God knows where on her person but it wasn't enough to make much of a difference.

Across the water Crawl wrote claiming it was 1980. He says

you're seventy-five this year, Henry, Maggie said to him one night on the steps of the church. Miss Whaley sitting in her lawn chair had her flyers to go through, she wasn't listening. When she had her newspapers spread out across her lap on the church steps where the three of them would sit just like people in town will linger after supper to watch traffic and call out to neighbor women strolling babies, she was just not there. Would a two-storied green bus come chugging across the creek, she wouldn't have lifted her head to grace the sight through her reading glasses. Henry thought at first she was loosening her grip, preparing to go off island by teaching herself what to expect to pay for a pound of butter across the water in 1980. But after four or five years he figured the flyers were part of what kept her here. She'd spit the prices out like fruit seed. She'd get ill at a bunch of innocent bananas for costing highway robbery, she would read her prices like Maggie would read the letters to the editor, taking sides and arguing with every one of them, My Land the way people live in this world she'd say every night when it got too dark to read and she folded up her newspaper like the Coast Guard taught Henry to fold a flag, that careful, that slow, like a color guard was standing at attention waiting on her to finish.

Crawl don't know nothing about how old I am, Henry said to the water.

Old enough to know better, said Maggie. She tugged at his shoelace while her sister studied the paper above them. Henry always sat on the second to bottom step and Miss Maggie'd start out on the top step and slide down even with him as the evening settled though her sister would rustle prices to try to halt her.

Too old to change, what it is, said Miss Whaley.

Henry swatted the back of his neck loud, but he didn't come away with any bloody mosquito because it was a sea breeze and there wasn't any bite. His head was getting ready to switch around and stare out Miss Whaley over her paper and he backslapped himself to keep still. The slap rang out like a hammering. Miss Whaley cleared her old throat. Miss Maggie to cover up got on with Crawl's letter but Henry didn't listen anymore. In his head he started his own letter to the sisters, one he knew he'd never ever send them even if he could write. Y'all ought not to have done me like y'all done me, he wrote in the first line, and that was as far as he got.

That night he lay talking to Sarah in the dark. He told her what Miss Whaley said and he discussed it. How come she talking about me not changing when it's her sitting up in her throne reading out her numbers on and on. Why you let that white woman hurt you so, Henry, he heard Sarah say. He heard her words like he heard the surf frothing on the banks, making its claim and then receding, taking it back, offering more words. A conversation. Sarah used to say to him, You the strongest man I ever met, you can work all day and all night if you care to and not make a noise about it to no-body. I seen you sit outside shucking corn in a nor'easter and you ain't scared of anybody who'd pull a knife on you. How come you let what people say get away with you so much? And Henry never answered though he knew how bad people could hurt him with what they said. He just hurt. He'd been knowing that. Maybe that was why he stayed by this island so long after everybody left and there wasn't anyone to hurt him anymore but Miss Maggie who was too sweetly dizzy in the head to hurt much and Miss Whaley who he thought he knew every which way she had of hurting him but she was good for coming up with a new one. Sometimes it didn't take anybody saying anything to him to his face, he'd remember what one of the men he used to fish with said to him sixty years before when they were boys swimming naked in the inlet and he'd be out in his skiff all by himself and he'd want to put his head down on his knees and let all the crabs and oysters and mackerel and blues and tuna go on about their business. He didn't care about reeling in a thing. Hurt nearly bad enough to let everybody starve.

Henry had been this way ever since he was born on this island that the wind was taking away as he lay there not sleeping. Wondering how old he really was, he thought of the island as it used to be when he was a boy, the two stores stocking shoelaces and bolts of colored cloth, the old hospital and the post office with over fifty boxes in the walls, little glass windows Henry would peek through and pretend he was looking right inside something mysterious— the innards of some complicated machine, some smart so-and-so's brain—like he was being offered a sneak at the way things worked in this life. And then the wind took that life away before he could put what he saw to any good use, and then the wind took Sarah and now what it was was him and the sisters holding out for the final storm to take them off island.

Because sleep would not come to Henry he got up and pulled on his waders and packed himself some bologna biscuits and a can of syrupy peaches like he liked and he boiled up last night's coffee and poured it in his thermos and took his flashlight out to search the weeds in front of the house for the stub of a Sweet he might have thought he'd finished one day when he was cigar flush. The beam sent sandcrabs sideways into their holes and Henry let the light play over the marsh wishing he could follow them down underneath the island where the wind could not get to them. Y'all be around way after I'm gone, he said to the crabs. Y'all wait, y'all still be here when this house is nothing but some rusty nails in the sand. He imagined his crabs crouched just below ground, ready to spring right back out once he switched his light off and give up on trying to find something to smoke himself awake good, imagined their big pop eyes staring right at him now, maybe their ears poked up listening to this sad old man out talking to the island like it cared to listen. He imagined the crabs calling to each other, hole to hole, old Henry Thornton won't never change.

What does it mean to change, Henry wondered as he cranked his outboard and throttled slow through the inlet towards the sound. What do I want over there across the water in nineteen hundred and eighty bad enough to give up whatever it is they're wanting me to give up? He'd spent the late 60s in Norfolk and all around him everybody was carrying on, army off fighting someplace he'd never heard of before or since, white boys growing their hair out and putting all kinds of mess down their throats, black people, his own children, trying to act all African, bushing their hair out and taking new names. Then crazies popping out the windows of tall buildings shooting presidents and preachers and the whole country catching afire. Henry brought Sarah home to stay. She tried to tell him wasn't anywhere safe left in this world, but Henry said he favored wind over flame, he'd rather be blown out to sea than die choking inside some highsky building with a brick lawn and blue lights streaking the night instead of the sleepy sweep of the lighthouse which he'd long ago learned to set his breath to.

Checking on the first of his crab pots, Henry told himself that Whaley said all that mess about him too old to change but was really talking about herself. Her sister too. What had the two of them done to change but choose to remain on this island where there weren't any bananas on sale, nor 19-cent-a-pound fryers, buy one get half off the other? He knew Sarah, had she lived, would have left him sooner or later, would have given up trying to talk him off island and gotten fed up with Whaley's ill mouth and Miss Maggie drunkstumbling across the creek to interrupt her Al Green tapes with a whole bunch of Where's Henry at, I need to ask Henry something, call Henry for me. Henry let the rope slide slowly through his hands, watched the empty pot disappear into the deep, and cut the engine. He knew he would have let Sarah go, would have stayed on just like he was doing, providing for the sisters, getting hurt over not much of nothing, spending half his days just waiting on that wind—the last one, the big one that would take the three of them out of this life where everybody was waiting on you to change.

Henry knew this too: if he went first, like they claimed men were likely to do, the sisters would have to leave. No way they could stay without him. Whaley could hurt him with her meanness, Miss Maggie could keep right on trying to get him to slip his hands somewhere they'd as soon not be, but neither of them could get on for more than a week without him. Without Henry there wasn't any island. Hell, I am that island, Henry said. Sarah when she passed cut me right in half. There's a side of me sits and smokes me a Sweet and just plain hurts, there's another part of me keeps the three of us and this island from blowing away.

Peering back on his island, Henry thought, This life ain't blowed away right yet. I can sit right here in the sound and let the wind take me wherever and still make a change. He could lie back and eat a bologna biscuit and talk to Sarah and let the change come on ahead, let the skiff drift right across the sound to Morehead where he'd call Crawl and tell him, Crawl, you ain't won, don't think you changed me, I'm just here because the wind brung me over here and I let it. He could sit outside Crawl's yard and mend nets for the boys who still pulled things out of the sea, and he could think while he mended about the sisters and about how he'd saved them. Made them change. He could sit outside on Crawl's porch and smoke on a Sweet and close his eyes and know he'd go before the sisters but that he would not leave them on that island because here he was taking the island with him, right across the water, him and the wind. He could close his eyes and see the sisters sitting right up front at his funeral, sea-salty tears raining down on the Sunday dresses they had not worn for years. Hoarse preacher shouting out some Bible and Sarah whispering right over him how she could surely forgive Henry for not taking her off island before it was time for him to change. All eleven of his children and their children and the babies of his grandbabies looking up at the casket where Henry had laid down one day halfway through his crabpots, let the wind take him off island. Inside that casket Henry was sipping peach syrup and wishing he had one last Sweet. The sun was high and it was a mean sun. The church was crowded and so hot the air conditioning was sweating and coughing like some sick somebody. Preacher called out a hymn. Let it be Sarah's singer sending me off sweetly. The sun and the water blended in brightness, the casket drifted, the wind picked up, the whole church rose up in song. Then came a lady in white passing out fans only to the ones who were moaning: sisters, hurting like Henry hurt, but thankful to be spared the wind.

Michael Parker's fourth work of fiction, *Daily Advance,* is forthcoming in Fall 2003. He teaches in the MFA Program at the University of North Carolina at Greensboro, where he lives with his daughter Emma.

BARBARA S. DOTY

*S*ometimes *I wish I knew where stories come from, but for the most part, I'm satisfied with the spontaneous combustion of image and language that ushers in the keepers. On the most literal level, this story grew out of a collaboration with the writer and photographer Lee Zacharias. In responding to Lee's photos of Portsmouth Island, I arrived finally at a syntax that seemed to capture the confluence of sun, water, sand, wind, and spirit that for me, a native Eastern North Carolinian, is our Outer Banks. There's a bit of fact here as well. The last three people to live on Portsmouth Island were two white women and the black man who cared for them. It was that relationship, enduring years after other natives had given up and moved inland, along with the vernacular poetry of the coastal plain, that drove me to get this story down on the page—and then, immediately,* right back up off *the page. For help with the latter, let me acknowledge my huge debt to the smooth-as-liver voice of Al Green.*

Dorothy Allison

COMPASSION

(from *Tin House*)

In the last days Mama's mouth cracked and bled. Pearly blisters spread down her chin to her throat. The nurses moved her to a room with a sink by the bed and a stern command to wash up every time you touched her.

"Herpes," Mavis, the floor nurse, told me. "Contagious at this stage."

I held Mama's free hand anyway, stepping away every time the doctor came in to wash with the soap the hospital provided. Mavis let me have a bottle of her own lotion when my fingers began to dry and the skin along my thumbs split.

"Aloe vera and olive oil," she told me. "Use it on your mama, too.

I took the bottle over to rub it into the paper-thin skin on the backs of Mama's hands. She barely seemed to notice, though a couple of her veins had leaked enough to make swollen, blue-black blotches. Mama's eyes tracked past me and even as I rubbed one hand, the fingers of the other reached for the morphine pump. That drip, that precious drip. Mama no longer hissed and gasped with every breath. Now she murmured and whispered, sang a little, even said recognizable names sometimes—my sisters, her sisters, and people long dead. Every once in a while, her voice would startle, the words suddenly clear and outraged. "Goddamn!" loud in the room. Then, "Get me a cigarette, get me a cigarette," as she came awake. Angry and begging at the same time, she cursed, "God-damn it, just one," before the morphine swept in and took her down again.

That was not our mama. Our mama never begged, never backed up, never whined, moaned, and thrashed in her sheets. My sister Jo and I stared at her. This mama was eating us alive. Every time she started it again, that litany of curses and pleas, I hunkered down further in my seat. Jo rocked in her chair, arms hugging her shoulders and head down. Arlene, the youngest of us, had wrung her hands and wiped her eyes, and finally, deciding she was no use, headed on home. Jo and I had stayed, unspeaking, miserable, and desperate.

On the third night after they gave her the pump, Mama hit some limit the nurses seemed determined to ignore. Her thumb beat time, but the pump lagged behind and the curses returned. The pleas became so heartbroken I expected the paint to start peeling off the walls. The curses became mewling growls. Finally, Jo gave me a sharp look and we stood up as one. She went over to try to force the window open, pounding the window frame till it came loose. I dug around in Jo's purse, found her Marlboros, lit one, and held it to mama's lips. Jo went and stood guard at the door.

Mama coughed, sucked, and smiled gratefully. "Baby," she whispered. "Baby," and fell asleep with ashes on her neck.

Jo walked over and took the cigarette I still held. "Stupid damn rules," she said bitterly.

Mavis came in then, sniffed loudly, and shook her head at us. "You know you can't do that."

"Do what?" Jo had disappeared the smoke as if it had never been.

Mavis crossed her arms. Jo shrugged and leaned over to pull the thin blanket further up Mama's bruised shoulders. In her sleep Mama said softly, "Please." Then in a murmur so soft it could have been a blessing, "Goddamn, goddamn."

I reached past Jo and took Mama's free hand in mine. "It's okay, it's okay," I said. Mama's face smoothed. Her mouth went soft, but her fingers in mine clutched tightly.

"That window isn't supposed to be open," Mavis said suddenly. "You get it shut."

Jo and I just looked at her.

Mama's first diagnosis came when I was seventeen. Back then, I couldn't even say the word, "cancer." Mama said it and so did Jo, but I did not. "This thing," I would say. "This damn thing." Twenty-five years later, I still called it that, though there was not much else I hesitated to say. That was my role. I did the talking and carried all the insurance records. Jack blinked. Jo argued. Arlene showed up late, got a sick headache, and left. In the early years it was Jack who argued and that just made things harder. Now he never said much at all. For that I was deeply grateful. It let us seem like all the other families in the hospital corridors—only occasionally louder and a little more careful of each other than anyone at MacArthur Hospital could understand.

"Who do they think we are?" Jo asked me once.

"They don't care who we are." What I did not say is that was right. Mama was the one the medical folk were supposed to watch. The rest of us were incidental, annoying, and, whenever possible, meant to be ignored.

"I like your mama," Mavis told me the first week Mama was on the ward. "But your daddy makes me nervous."

"It's a talent he has," I said.

"Uh-huh." Mavis looked a little confused, but I didn't want to explain.

The fact is he never hit her. In the thirty years since they married, Jack never once laid a hand on her. His trick was to threaten. He screamed and cursed and cried into his fists. He would come right up on Mama, close enough to spray spittle on her cheeks. Pounding his hands together, he would shout, "*Motherfuckers,* assholes, sonsabitches." All the while, Mama's face remained expressionless. Her eyes stared right back into his. Only her hands trembled, the yellow-stained fingertips vibrating incessantly.

Gently, I covered the bruises on Mama's arm with my fingers. Jo scowled and turned away.

"They should be here."

"Better they're not."

Jo shoved until the window was again closed. When she turned back to me, her face was the mask Mama wore most of our childhood. She gestured at Mama's bruises. "Look at that. You see what he did."

"He didn't mean to," I said.

"Didn't mean to? Didn't care. Didn't notice. Man's the same he always was."

"He never hit her."

"He never had to hit her. She beat herself up enough. And every time the son of a bitch hit us, he was hitting her. He beat us like we were dogs. He treated her like her ass was gold. And she always talked about leaving him, you know. She never did, did she?"

"What do you want?"

"I want somebody to do something." Jo slammed her fist into the window frame. "I want somebody to finally goddamn do something."

I shook my head, gently stroking Mama's cool, clammy skin. There was nothing I could say to Jo. We always wanted somebody to do something and no one ever did, but what had we ever asked anyone to do? I watched Jo rub her neck and thought about the pins that held her elbow and shoulder together. There was my shattered coccyx and broken collarbones, and Arlene's insomnia. At thirty, Arlene had a little girl's shadowed, frightened face and the omnipresent stink of whiskey on her skin. I had been eight when Mama married Jack, Jo five, but Arlene had been still a baby, less than a year old and fragile as a sparrow in the air.

"What is it you want to do? Talk? Huh?" Jo rolled her shoulders back and rubbed her upper arms. "Want to talk about what a tower of strength Mama was? Or why she had to be?"

My shrug was automatic, inconsequential.

A flush spread up from Jo's cleavage. It made the skin of her neck look rough and pebbly. Deep lines scored the corners of her eyes and curved back from her mouth. In the last few years, Jo had become scary thin. The skin that always pulled tight on her bones seemed to have grown loose. Now it wrinkled and hung. I looked away, surprised and angry. Neither of us had expected to live long enough to get old.

For all that we fight, Jo is the one I get along with, and I always try to stay with her when I visit. Arlene and I barely speak, though we talk to each other more easily than she and Jo. There have been years I don't think the two of them have spoken half a dozen words. In the ten weeks since Mama's collapse, their conversations have been hurt-filled bursts of whispered recrimination. At first, I stayed with Arlene and that seemed to help, but when Jo and I insisted that Mama had to check into MacArthur, Arlene blew up and told me to go ahead and move over to Jo's place.

"You and Jo—you think you know it all," Arlene said when she was dropping me off at Jo's. "But she's my mama too, and I know something. I know she's not ready to give up and die."

"We're not giving up. We're putting Mama where she can get the best care."

"Two miles from Jo's place and forty from mine." Arlene had shaken her head. "All the way across town from Jack and her stuff. I know what you are doing."

"Arlene . . ."

"Don't. Just don't." She popped the clutch on her VW bug and backed up before I could get the door closed. "Someday you're gonna be sorry. That's the one thing I am sure of, you're gonna be sorry for all you've done." She swung the car sharply to the side, making the door swing shut. If it would have helped, I would have told her I was sorry already.

Jo put me in the room where her daughter, Pammy, stashes all the gear she will not let Jo give away or destroy—shelves of books, racks of dusty music tapes, and mounted posters on the wall over the daybed. I fell asleep under posters of prepubescent boy bands and woke up dry-mouthed and headachy.

Jo laughed when I asked about the bands. "Don't ask me," she said. "Some maudlin shit no one could dance to—whey-faced girls and anorexic boys. All of it sounds alike, whiny voices all scratchy and droning. Girl has no ear, no ear at all."

Pammy had been picking out chords on the old piano Jo took in trade for her wrecked Chevy. She spoke without looking up. "You know what Mama does?" she asked in her peculiar Florida twang. "Mama sits up late smoking dope and listening to Black Sabbath on the headphones. Acts like she's seventeen and nothing's changed in the world at all."

Jo snorted, though I saw the quick grin she suppressed. She kicked her boot heels together, knocking dried mud on the Astro-turf carpet. That carpet was her prize. She'd had her boyfriend Jay-bird install it throughout the house. "She's eleven now," she said, nodding in Pammy's direction. "What you think? Should I shoot her or just cut my own throat?"

I shook my head, looking back and forth from one of them to the other. They were so alike it startled me, thick brown hair, black eyes, and the exact same way of sneering so that the right side of the mouth drew up and back.

"Hang on," I told Jo. "She gets to be thirty or so, you might like her."

"Ha!" Jo slapped her hands together. "If I live that long."

Pammy banged the piano closed and swept out of the room. My sister and I grinned at each other. Pammy we both believed would redeem us all. The child was fearless.

"We need to talk," I told Arlene when she came to the hospital the day after I moved in with Jo. Arlene was standing just inside the smoking lounge off the side of the cafeteria, waiting for Jack to arrive.

"She's looking better, don't you think?" Arlene popped a Tic Tac in her mouth.

"No, she an't. " I tried to catch Arlene's hand, but she hugged her elbows in tight and just looked at me. "Arlene, she's not going to get any better. She's going to get worse. If the tumor on her lung doesn't kill her, then the ones in her head will."

Arlene's pale face darkened. When she spoke her words all ran together. "They don't know what that stuff was. That could have been dust in the machine. I read about this case where that was what happened — dust and fingerprints on X rays." She tore at a pack of Salems, ripping one cigarette in half before she could get another out intact.

"God, Arlene."

"Don't start."

"Look, we have to make some decisions." I was thinking if I could speak quietly enough, Arlene would hear what I was saying.

"We have to take care of Mama, not talk about stuff that's going to get in the way of that." Arlene's voice was as loud as mine had been soft. "Mama needs our support, not you going on about death and doom."

Sympathetic magic, Jaybird called it. Arlene believed in the power of positive thinking the way some people believed in saints' medals or a Santeria's sacrificed chicken. Stopping us talking about dying was the thing she believed she was supposed to do.

I dropped into one of the plastic chairs. Arlene's head kept jerking restlessly, but she managed not to look into my face. This is how she always behaved. "Mama's gonna beat this thing," she'd announced when I had first come home, as if saying it firmly enough would make it so. She was the reason Mama had gone to MacArthur in the first place. Jo and I had wanted the hospice that Mama's oncologist had recommended. But Arlene had refused to discuss the hospice or to look at the results of the brain scan. Those little starbursts scattered over Mama's cranium were not something Arlene could acknowledge.

"We could keep Mama at home," she'd told the hospital chaplain. "We could all move back home and take care of her till she's better."

"Lord God!" I had imagined Jo's response to that. "Move back home? Has she gone completely damn crazy?"

The chaplain told Arlene that some people did indeed take care of family at home, and if that was what she wanted, he would help her. I had watched Arlene's face as he spoke, the struggle that moved across her flattened features. "It might not work," she had said. She had looked at me once, then dropped her head. "She might need more care than we could give, all of us working you know." She had dropped her face into her hands.

I signed off on the bills where the insurance didn't apply. For the rental on a wheelchair and a television, I used a credit card. Jo laughed at me when she saw them.

"You are a pure fool," she said. "Send back the wheelchair, but let's keep the TV. It'll give us something to watch when Arlene starts going on about how *good* Mama's doing."

Mama had had three years of pretty good health before this last illness. It was a remission that we almost convinced ourselves was a cure. The only thing she complained about was the ulcer that kept her from ever really putting back on any weight. Then, when she was in seeing the doctor about the ulcer, he had put his hand on her neck and palpated a lump the two of them could feel.

"This is it," Mama had told me on the phone that weekend last spring. "I'm not going back into chemo again."

She had been serious, but Jo and I steamrolled her back into treatment. There were a few bad weeks when we wondered if what we were doing was right, but Mama had come through strong. I convinced myself we had done the right thing. Still, when afterward Mama was so weak and slow to recover, guilt had pushed me to take a leave from my job and go stay at the old tract house near the Frito-Lay plant.

"We'll get some real time together," Mama said when I arrived.

"You need rest," I told her. "We'll rest." But that was not what Mama had in mind. The first morning she got me up to drink watery coffee and plan what we would do. There was one stop at the new doctor's office, but after that, she swore, we would have fun.

For three days, Mama dragged me around. We walked through the big malls in the acrid air-conditioning in the mornings and spent the afternoons over at the jai alai fronton watching the athletes with their long lobster-claw devices on their arms thrusting the tiny white balls high up into the air and catching them as easily as if those claws were catcher's mitts. I watched close but could not figure out how the game was meant to be played. Mama just bet on her favorites—boys with tight silk shirts and flashing white smiles.

"They all know who I am," Mama told me. I nodded as if I believed her, but then a beautiful young man came up and paused by Mama's seat to squeeze her wrist.

"Rafael," Mama said immediately. "This is my oldest daughter."

"Cannot be," Rafael said. He never lifted his eyes to me, just leaned in to whisper into Mama's ear. I was watching her neck as his lips hovered at her hairline. I almost missed the bill she pressed into his palm.

"You give him money?" I said after he had wandered back down the steeply pitched stairs.

"Nothing much." Mama looked briefly embarrassed. She wiped her neck and turned her head away from me. "I've known him since he started here. He's the whole support of his family."

I looked down at the young men. They were like racehorses tossing their heads about, their thick hair cut short or tied back in clubs at their napes. Once the game started they were suddenly running and leaping, bouncing off the net walls and barely avoiding the fast-moving balls. All around me gray-headed women with solid bodies shrieked and jumped in excitement. They called out vaguely Spanish-sounding names, and crowed when their champions made a score. Now and again one of the young men would wave a hand in acknowledgment.

I turned to watch Mama. Her eyes were on the boys. Her face was bright with pleasure. What did I know? Where else could she spend twenty dollars and look that happy?

When later, Rafael jumped and scored, I nudged Mama's side. "He's the best," I said. She blushed like a girl.

Mama was not supposed to drive, so I steered her old Lincoln Town Car around Orlando.

"You are terrible," Mama said to me every time we pulled into another parking space. It was an act. She played as if I were dragging her out, but every time I suggested we go back to the house, she pouted.

"I can nap anytime. When you've gone, I'll do nothing but rest. Let me do what I want while I can."

It was part of being sick. She wasn't sleeping, even though she was tired all the time. She'd lie on the couch awake at night with the television playing low. Every time I woke in the night I could hear it, and her, stirring restlessly out in the front room.

It was awkward sleeping in Jack's house. The last time I had lain in that bed, I had been twenty-two and back only for a week before taking a job in Louisville. Every day of that week burned in my memory. Mama had been sick then too, recovering from a hysterectomy her doctor swore would end all her troubles. Jo was in her own place over in Kissimmee, an apartment she got as soon as she graduated from high school. Only Arlene's stuff had remained in the stuffy bedroom; she herself was never there. At dawn, I would watch her stumble in to shower and change for school. She spent her nights baby-sitting for one of Mama's friends from the Winn-Dixie. A change-of-life baby had turned out to be triplets, and Arlene spent her nights rocking one or the other while the woman curled up in her bed and wept as if she were dying.

"They are in shock over there," Mama had told me. "Don't know whether to shit or go blind."

"Blind," Arlene said. The woman, Arlene told us, was drunk more often than sober. Still, her troubles were the making of Arlene, who not only got paid good money, she no longer had to spend her nights dodging Jack's curses or sudden drunken slaps.

"I'm getting out of here, and I'm never coming back," she told me the first morning of that week. By the end of the week, she had done it, though the apartment was half a mile up the highway, and even smaller than Jo's. I saw it only once, a place devoid of furniture or grace, but built like a fortress.

"Mine," Arlene had said, a world of rage compressed into the word.

Lying on the old narrow Hollywood bed again, I remembered the look on Arlene's face. It was identical to the expression I had seen on Jo when I was packing my boxes to drive to Louisville.

"We'll never see your ass again," Jo had said. Her mouth pulled down in a mock frown, then crooked up into a grin.

"Not in this lifetime."

All these years later I could look back and it was exactly as if I were watching a movie of it, a scene that closed in on Jo's black eyes and the bitter pleasure she took in saying "your ass." I know my mouth had twisted to match hers. We had thought ourselves free, finally away and gone. But none of it had come out the way we had thought it would. I hadn't lasted two years in Louisville, and Arlene had never gotten more than three miles from the Frito-Lay plant. Twenty years after we had left so fierce and proud, we were all right back where we had started, yoked to each other and the same old drama.

"Take me shopping," Mama begged me every afternoon, as if no time at all had passed. I had looked at her neck and seen how gray and sweaty the skin had gone and known in that moment that the chemo had not worked out as we had hoped.

"Tomorrow," I had promised Mama, and talked her into lying down early. Then gone back to curl up in bed and pretend to read so that I could be left alone. Every night for the two weeks I stayed there I would listen to Jack's hacking through the bedroom wall. Every time he coughed, my back pulled tight. I tried to shut him out, listening past him for Mama lying on the couch in the living room. She talked to herself once she thought we were asleep. It sounded as if she were retelling stories. Little snatches would drift down the hall. "Oh James, God that James . . ." Her voice went soft. I listened to unintelligible whispers till she said, "When Arlene was born . . ." Then she faded out again. In the background, Jack's snoring grated low and steady. I curled my fists under the sheets until I fell asleep.

When she took me shopping, Mama bought me things she said I needed. She made me go to Jordan Marsh to buy Estée Lauder skin potions. "It's time," she said. Her tone implied it was the last possible day I could put off buying moisturizer. I submitted. It was easier to let her tell me what to buy than to argue, and kind of fun to let her boss around the salesladies. I even found myself telling an insistent young woman that, no, we would not try the Clinique, we were there for Estée Lauder. Afterward, we went upstairs to do what we both enjoyed the most—rummage through the sale bins.

"I need new underwear," Mama said. "Briefs. Let's find me some briefs. No bikinis, can't wear those anymore. They irritate my scar." She gestured to her belly, not specifying if she meant the old zipper from her navel to pubis, or the more recent horizontal patches to either side. I sorted the more garish patterns out of the way, turning up a few baby-blue briefs in size seven.

"Five now," Mama muttered. "Find me some fives, and none of those all-cotton ones. I want the nylon. Nylon hugs me right, and I hate the way cotton looks after a while. Dirty, you know?"

Sevens and eights and sixes. I kept digging.

"Excuse me." The two women at Mama's sleeve looked familiar.

"Mam," the first one said, pushing into the bin. "Excuse me." She reached around Mama's elbow to snag a pair of blue-green briefs. "Excuse me," she said again.

The accent was even more familiar than her flat grayish features and tight blond cap of hair. Her drawl was more pronounced than Mama's, more honeyed than the usual Orlando matrons. It was a Carolina accent, and a Carolina polite hesitation, too. The other woman reached for a pair of yellow cotton panties, size seven. Mama moved aside.

"So I told him what he was going to have to do," the first woman said to her friend, continuing what was obviously an ongoing conversation. "No standing between me and the Lord, I told him. We've all got a role in God's plan. You know?"

Her friend nodded. Mama looked to the side, her eyes drifting over the woman's figure, the pale white hands sorting underwear, the dull gold jewelry and the loose shirtwaist dress. That old glint appeared in Mama's eyes and a little electrical shock went up my neck. I moved around the corner of the bin to get between them, but Mama had already turned to the woman.

"I know what you mean." Mama's tone was pleasant, her face open and friendly. The woman turned to her, a momentary look of confusion on her face.

"You do?"

"Oh yes, there is no fighting what is meant. When God puts his hand on you, well . . ." Mama shrugged as if there were no need to say more.

The woman hesitated, and then nodded. "Yes. God has a plan for us all."

"Yes." Mama nodded. "Yes." She reached over and put both hands on the woman's clasped palms. "Bless you." Mama beamed. This time the woman did frown. She didn't know whether Mama was making fun of her, but she knew something was wrong. Her friend looked nervous.

"Just let me ask you something." Mama pulled the woman's hands toward her own midriff, drawing the woman slightly off balance and making her reach across the pile of underpants.

"Have you had cancer yet?" The words were spoken in the softest matron's drawl but they cut the air like a razor.

"Oh!" the woman said.

Mama smiled. Her smile relaxed, full of enjoyment. "It an't good news. But it is definite. You know something after, how everything can change in an instant."

The woman's eyes were fixed and dilated. "Oh! God is a rock," she whispered.

"Yes." Mama's smile was too wide. "And Demerol." She paused while the woman's mouth worked as if she were going to protest, but could not. "And sleep," Mama added that as it had just occurred to her. She nodded again. "Yes. God is Demerol and sleep and not vomiting when that's all you've done for days. Oh, yes. God is more than I think you have yet imagined. It's not like we get to choose what comes, after all."

"Mama," I said. "Please, Mama."

Mama leaned over so that her face was close to the woman's chin and spoke in a tightly parsed whisper. "God is your daughter holding your hand when you can't stand the smell of your own body. God is your husband not yelling, your insurance check coming when they said it would." She leaned so close to the woman's face, it looked as if she were about to kiss her, still holding on to both the woman's hands. "God is any minute pain is not eating you up alive, any breath that doesn't come out in a wheeze."

The woman's eyes were wide, still unblinking; the determined mouth clamped shut.

"I know God." Mama assumed her old soft drawl. "I know God and the devil and everything in between. Oh yes. Yes." The last word was fierce, not angry but final.

When she let go, I watched the woman fall back against her friend. The two of them turned to walk fast and straight away from us, leaving their selections on the table. I felt almost sorry for them. Then Mama sighed and settled back. With an easy motion, she snatched up a set of blue nylon briefs, size five. She turned her face to me with a wide happy smile.

"God! I do *love* shopping."

"Wasn't she from Louisville, that woman had the sports car? The one with those boots I liked so much?" Jo and I were folding sheets. We had cleared about a month of laundry off the bed, shifting sheets and towels up onto shelves, and stacking the T-shirts, socks, and underwear in baskets. Jo's rules for housekeeping were simple; she did the least she could. All underpants, T-shirts, and socks in her house were white. Nothing was sorted by anything but size—when it was sorted at all. If I wanted to sleep, I had to get it all off the bed.

"No," I said. "Met her after I moved to Brooklyn."

"Sure had a lot of attitude. And Lord God! Those boots. What happened to her, anyway?"

"Got a job in Chicago working for a news show."

"Oh, so not the one, huh?" Jo made a rude gesture with her right hand. "You talked like she had your heart in her hands."

"For a while." I shook out a sheet and began to refold it more neatly. "But when I moved in with her, things changed. Turned out she had Jack's temper and Arlene's talent for seeing what she wanted to see."

"That's a shock." There was a sardonic drawl in Jo's tone. "Didn't think there was another like Arlene in the world."

"There's a world of Arlenes," I said. "World of Jacks, too, and a lifetime of scary women just waiting for me to drag them here so you can talk them out of their boots."

"Well, those were damn fine boots."

Jaybird came in then, dragging his feet across the doorsill to knock loose the sand. Jo waved him over. "You remember the red boots I bought in Atlanta that time?"

"They hurt your feet." Jay took a quick nibble on Jo's earlobe and gave me a welcome grin.

"Just about crippled me. But you sure liked the way they looked when I crossed my legs at the bar that weekend."

"You look good any way, woman," Jay said. "You come in covered in dog shit and grass seed, I'll still want to suck on your neck. You sit back in shiny red high-heeled boots and I'll do just about anything you want."

"You will, huh?" She snagged one of his belt loops and tugged it possessively.

"You know I will."

"Uh-huh."

They kissed like I was not in the room, so I pretended I was not, folding sheets while the kiss turned to giggles and then pinches and another kiss. Jo and Jaybird have been together almost nine years. I liked Jay more than any other guy Jo ever brought around. He was older than the type she used to chase. Jo wouldn't say, but Mama swore Pammy's daddy was a kid barely out of junior high. "Your sister likes them young," she complained. "Too young."

Jay was a vet. He had an ugly scar under his chin and a gruff voice. Mostly, he didn't talk. He worked at the garage, making do with hand gestures and a stern open face. Only with Jo did he let himself relax. He didn't drink except for twice a year—each time he asked Jo to marry him, and every time she said no. Then Jay went and got seriously drunk. Jo didn't let anyone say a word against him, but she also refused to admit he was little Beth's daddy, though they were as alike as two puppies from the same litter.

"To hell with boots," Jo joked at me over Jay's shoulder. "Old Jaybird's all I really need." She gave him another kiss and a fast tug on his dark blond hair. He wiggled against her happily. I hugged the worn cotton sheet in my arms. I'd hate it if Jo ran Jay off, but maybe she wouldn't. Sometimes Jo was as tender with Jay as if she intended to keep him around forever.

Arlene lived at Castle Estates, an apartment complex off High-way 50 on the way out to the airport. It looked to me like Kentucky Ridge where she was two years ago, and Dunbarton Gardens five years before that. Squat identical two-story structures, dotted with upstairs decks and imitation wood beams set in fields of parking spaces and low unrecognizable blue-green hedges. Castle Estates was known for its big corner turrets and ersatz iron gate decorated with mock silver horseheads. It gleamed like malachite in the Florida sunshine.

When I visited last spring, I went over for a day and joked that if I wanted to take a walk, I'd have to leave a trail of bread crumbs to find my way back. Arlene didn't think it was funny.

"What are you talking about? No one walks anywhere in central Florida. You want to drown in your own sweat?"

In Arlene's apartments, the air conditioner was always set on high and all the windows sealed. The few times I stayed with her, I'd huddle in her spare room, tucked under her old *Bewitched* sleeping bag, my fingers clutching the fabric under Elizabeth Montgomery's pink-and-cream chin. Out in the front room the television droned nondenominational rock and roll on the VH-1 music channel. Beneath the backbeat, I heard the steady thunk of the mechanical ratchets on the stair stepper. Since she turned thirty, Arlene spends her insomniac nights climbing endlessly to music she hated when it was first released.

The night before we moved Mama into MacArthur, the thunking refrain went on too long. I made myself lie still as long as I could, but eventually I sneaked out to check on Arlene. The lights were dimmed way down and the television set provided most of the illumination. The stair stepper was set up close to the TV, and my mouth went dry when I saw my little sister. She was braced between the side rails, arms extended rigidly and head hanging down between her arms. I watched her legs as they trembled and lifted steadily, up and up and up. A shiver went through me. I tried to think of something to say, some way to get her off those steps.

Arlene's head lifted, and I saw her face. Cheeks flushed red; eyes squeezed shut. Her open mouth gasped at the cold filtered air. She was crying, but inaudibly, her features rigid with strain and tightened to a grotesque mask. She looked like some animal in a trap, tearing herself and going on—up and up and up. I watched her mouth working, curses visible on the dry cracked lips. With a low grunt, she picked up her speed and dropped her head again. I stepped back into the darkened doorway. I did not want to have to speak, did not want to have to excuse seeing her like that. It was bad enough to have seen. But I have never understood my little sister more than I did in that moment—never before realized how much alike we really were.

Jack has been sober for more than a decade, something Jo and I found increasingly hard to believe. Mama boasted of how proud she was of him. Her Jack didn't go to AA or do any of those programs people talk about. Her Jack did it on his own.

"Those AA people—they ask forgiveness," Jo said once. "They make amends." She cackled at the idea, and I smiled. Jack asking forgiveness was about as hard to imagine as him staying sober. For years we teased each other. "You think it will last?" Then in unison, we would go, "Naaa!"

Neither of us can figure out how it has lasted, but Jack has stayed sober, never drinking. Of course, he also never made amends.

"For what?" he said. For what?

"I did the best I could with all those girls," Jack told the doctor, the night Arlene was carried into the emergency room raving and kicking. It was the third and last time she mixed vodka and sleeping pills, and only a year or so after Jack first got sober, the same year I was working up in Atlanta and could fly down on short notice. Jo called me from the emergency room and said, "Get here fast, looks like she ain't gonna make it this time."

Jo was wrong about that, though as it turned out we were both grateful she got me to come. Arlene came close to putting out the eye of the orderly who tried to help the nurses strap her down. She did break his nose, and chipped two teeth that belonged to the rent-a-cop who came over to play hero. The nurses fared better, getting away with only a few scratches and one moderately unpleasant bite mark.

"I'll kill you," Arlene kept screaming. "I'll fucking kill you all!" Then after a while, "You're killing me. You're killing me."

It was Jo who had found Arlene. Baby sister had barely been breathing, her face and hair sour with vomit. Jo called the ambulance, and then poured cold water all over Arlene's head and shoulders until she became conscious enough to scream. For a day and a half, Jo told me, Arlene was finally who she should have been from the beginning. She cursed with outrage and flailed with wild conviction. "You should have seen it," Jo told me.

By the time I got there, Arlene was going in and out—one minute sobbing and weak and the next minute rearing up to shout.

The conviction was just about gone. When she was quiet for a little while, I looked in at her, but I couldn't bring myself to speak. Every breath Arlene drew seemed to suck oxygen out of the room. Then Jack came in the door and it was as if she caught fire at the sight of him. For the first and only time in her life she called him a son of a bitch to his face.

"You, you," she screamed. "You are killing me! Get out. Get out. I'll rip your dick off if you don't get the hell out of here."

"She's gone completely crazy," Jack told everyone, but it sounded like sanity to me.

The psychiatric nurse kept pushing for sedation, but Jo and I fought them on that. Let her scream it out, we insisted. By some miracle they listened to us, and left her alone. We stayed in the hall outside the room, listening to Arlene as she slowly wound herself down.

"I did the best I could," Jack kept saying to the doctor. "You can see what it was like. I just never knew what to do."

Jo and I kept our distance. Neither of us said a word.

By the third morning, Arlene was gray-faced and repentant. When we went in to check on her, her eyes would not rise to meet ours.

"I'm all right," she said in a thick hoarse whisper. "And I won't ever let that happen again."

"Damn pity," Jo told me later. "That was just about the only time I've ever really liked her. Crazy out of her mind, she made sense. Sane, I don't understand her at all."

"What do you think happens after death?" Mama asked me.

She and I were sitting alone waiting for the doctor to come back. They were giving her IV fluids and oral medicines to help her with the nausea, but she was sick to her stomach all the time and trying hard not to show it. "Come on, tell me," she said.

I looked at Mama's temples where the skin had begun to sink in. A fine gray shadow was slowly widening and deepening. Her closed eyes were like marbles under a sheet. I rubbed my neck. I was too tired to lie to her.

"You close your eyes," I said. "Then you open them, start over."
"God!" Mama shuddered. "I hope not."

Jo was a breeder, ridgebacks and rottweilers. A third of every litter had to be put down. Jo always had it done at the vet's office,
while she held them in her arms and sobbed. She kept their birth
dates and names in lists under the glass top of her coffee table, chris-
tening them all for rock-and-rollers, even the ones she had to kill.

"Axl is getting kind of old," she told me on the phone before I
came last spring. "But you should see Bon Jovi the Third. We're
gonna get a dynasty out of her."

After her daughter Beth was born, Jo had her own tubes tied.
Still she hated to fix her bitches, and found homes for every dog
born on her place. "Only humans should be stopped from breeding," she told me once. "Dogs know when to eat their runts. Humans don't know shit."

Four years ago Jo was arrested for breaking into a greyhound
puppy farm up near Apopka. Mama was healthy back then, but
didn't have a dime to spare. Jaybird called me to help them find a
lawyer and get Jo out on bail. It was expensive. Jo had blown up
the incinerator at the farm. The police insisted she had used stolen
dynamite, but Jo refused to talk about that. What she wanted to
talk about was what she had heard, that hundreds of dogs had been
burned in that cinderblock firepit.

"Alive. Alive," she told the judge. "Three different people told
me. Those monsters get drunk, stoke up the fire, and throw in all
the puppies they can't sell. Alive, the sonsabitches! Don't even care
if anyone hears them scream." From the back of the courtroom, I
could hear the hysteria in her voice.

"Imagine it. Little puppies, starved in cages and then caught up
and tossed in the fire." Jo shook her head. Gray streaks shone
against the black. The judge grimaced. I wondered if she was getting to him.

"And then"—she glared across the courtroom—"they sell the ash
and bone for fertilizer." Beside me Jaybird wiggled uncomfortably.

Jo got a suspended sentence, but only after her lawyer proved the puppy farmers had a history of citations from Animal Protection. Jo had to pay the cost of the incinerator, which was made easier when people started writing her and sending checks. The newspaper had made her a Joan of Arc of dogs. It got so bad the farm closed up the dog business and shifted over to pigs.

"I don't give a rat's ass about pigs," Jo promised the man when she wrote him his check.

"Well, I can appreciate that." He grinned at us. "Almost nobody does.

"How'd you get that dynamite?" I asked Jo when we were driving away in Jay's truck. It was the one thing she had dodged throughout the trial.

"Didn't use no dynamite." She nudged Jaybird's shoulder. "Old Bird here gave me a grenade he'd brought back from the army. Didn't think it would work. I just promised I'd get rid of it for him. But it was a fuck-up." She frowned. "It just blew the back wall out of that incinerator. They got all that money off me under false pretenses."

Every time Jack came to the hospital, he brought food, greasy bags of hamburgers and fries from the Checker Inn, melted milk shakes from the diner on the highway, and half-eaten boxes of chocolate. Mama ate nothing, just watched him. The bones of her face stood out like the girders of a bridge.

Jo and I went down to the coffee shop. Arlene, who had come in with Jack, stayed up with them. "He wants her to get up and come home," she reported to us when she came down an hour later.

Jo laughed and blew smoke over Arlene's head in a long, thin stream. "Right," she barked, and offered Arlene one of her Marlboros.

"I can't smoke that shit," Arlene said. She pulled out her alligator case and lit a Salem with a little silver lighter. When Jo said nothing, Arlene relaxed a little and opened the bag of potato chips we had saved for her. "He's lost the checkbook again," she said in my direction. "Says he wants to know where we put her box of Barr Dollars so he can buy gas for the Buick."

"He's gonna lose everything as soon as she's gone." Jo pushed her short boots off with her toes and put her feet up on another seat. "He's sending the bills back marked 'deceased.' The mortgage payment, for God's sake." She shook her head and took a potato chip from Arlene's bag.

"He'll be living on the street in no time." Her voice was awful with anticipation.

Arlene turned to me. "Where are the Barr Dollars?"

I shook my head. Last I knew, Mama had stashed in her wallet exactly five one-dollar bills signed by Joseph W. Barr—crisp dollar bills she was sure would be worth money someday, though I had no idea why she thought so.

"Girls."

Jack stood in the doorway. He looked uncomfortable with the three of us sitting together. "She's looking better," he said diffidently.

Arlene nodded. Jo let blue smoke trail slowly out of her nose. I said nothing. I could feel my cheeks go stiff. I looked at the way Jack's hairline was receding, the gray bush of his military haircut thinning out and slowly exposing the bony structure of his head.

"Well." Jack's left hand gripped the door frame. He let go and flexed his fingers in the air. When the hand came down again, it gripped so hard the fingertips went white. My eyes were drawn there, unable to look away from the knuckles standing out knobby and hard. Beside me Jo tore her empty potato chip bag in half, spilling crumbs on the linoleum tabletop. Arlene shifted in her chair. I heard the elevator gears grind out in the hall.

I was gonna go home," Jack said. He let go of the doorjamb.

"Good night, Daddy," Arlene called after him. He waved a hand and walked away.

Jo twisted around in her chair. "You are such a suck-ass," she said.

Arlene's cheeks flushed. "You don't have to be mean."

I can't even say his name. You call him Daddy." Jo shook her head. "Daddy."

"He's the only father I've ever known." Arlene's face was becoming a brighter and brighter pink. She fumbled with her cigarette case, then shoved it into her bag. "And I don't see any reason to make this thing any worse."

"Worse?" Jo twisted further in her chair. She leaned over and put her hand on Arlene's forearm. "Tell me the truth," she said. "Didn't you ever just want to kill the son of a bitch?"

Arlene jerked her arm free, but Jo caught the belt of her dress. "He an't got shit. He an't gonna give you no money, and he can't hurt you no more. You don't have to suck up to him. You could tell him to go to hell."

Arlene slapped Jo's hand away and grabbed her bag. "Don't you tell me what to do." She looked over at me as if daring me to say something. "Don't you tell me nothing."

Jo dropped back in her seat and lifted her hands in mock surrender. "Me, you can say no to. Him, you run after like some little brokenhearted puppy."

"Don't, don't . . ." For a moment it was as if Arlene were going to say something. The look on her face reminded me of the night she had screamed and kicked. Do it, I wanted to say. Do it. But whatever Arlene wanted to say, she swallowed.

"Just don't!" She was out the door in a rush.

I took a drink of cold coffee and watched Jo. Her eyes were red-veined and her hair hung limp. She shook her head. "I hate her, I swear I do," she said.

I looked away. "None of us have ever much liked each other," I said.

Jo lit another cigarette and rubbed under her eyes. "You an't that bad." She pulled out a Kleenex, dampened it with a little of my black coffee, and wiped carefully under each eye. "Not now anyway. You were mean as a snake when you were little."

"That was you."

Jo's hand stopped. An angry glare came into her eyes, but instead of shouting, she laughed. I hesitated and she pushed her hair back and laughed some more.

"Well," she said, "I suppose it was. Yeah." She nodded, the laughter softening to a smile. "You just stayed gone all the time."

"Saved my life." I laced my fingers together on the table, remembering all those interminable black nights, Jo pinching me awake and the two of us hauling Arlene into the backyard to hide behind the garage. Bleak days, shame omnipresent as fear, and by the time I was twelve, I stayed gone every minute I could.

"You were the smart one." Jo looked toward the door. I watched how her eyes focused on the jamb where his hand had rested.

"You were smart, I was fast, and Arlene learned to suck ass so hard she swallowed her own soul."

I kept quiet. There was nothing to say to that.

"I dreamed you killed him." Mama's voice was rough, shaped around the tube in her nose.

"How?" I kept my voice impartial, relaxed. This was not what I wanted to talk about, but it was easier when Mama talked. I hated the hours when she just lay there staring up at the ceiling with awful anticipation on her face.

"All kinds of ways." Mama waved the hand that wasn't strapped down for the IV. She looked over at me slyly.

"You know I used to dream about it all the time. Dreamed it for years. Mostly it was you, but sometimes Jo would do it. Every once in a while it would be Arlene."

She paused, closed her eyes, and breathed for a while.

"I'd wake up just terrified, but sometimes almost glad. Relieved to have it over and done, I think. Bad times I would get up and walk around awhile, remind myself what was real, what wasn't. Listen to him snore awhile, then go make sure you girls were all right."

She looked at me with dulled eyes. I couldn't think what to say.

"Don't do it," she whispered.

I wanted to laugh, but didn't. I watched Mama's shadowy face. Her expression stunned me. Her mouth was drawn up in a big painful smile, not at all sincere.

• • •

"Did you want to kill him?"

I turned away from the black window, expecting Jo. But it was Arlene, her eyes huge with smeared mascara.

"Sure," I told her. "Still do."

She nodded and wiped her nose with the back of her hand.

"But you won't."

"Probably not."

We stood still. I waited.

"I didn't think like that." She spoke slowly. "Like you and Jo. You two were always fighting. I felt like I had to be the peacemaker. And I . . ." She paused, bringing her hands up in the air as if she were lifting something.

"I just didn't want to be a hateful person. I wanted it to be all right. I wanted us all to love each other." She dropped her hands. "Now you just hate me. You and Jo, you hate me worse than him."

"No." I spoke in a whisper. "Never. It's hard sometimes to believe, I know. But I love you. Always have. Even when you made me so mad."

She looked at me. When she spoke, her voice was tiny. "I used to dream about it," she whispered. "Not killing him, but him dying. Him being dead."

I smiled at her. "Easier that way," I said.

Arlene nodded. "Yeah," she said. "Yeah."

That evening Mavis stopped me in the hall. She had a stack of papers in one hand and an expression that bordered on outrage. "This an't been signed," she said. Her hand shook the papers. I looked at them as she stepped in close to me. She pulled one off the bottom.

"This is from Mrs. Crawford, that woman was in the room next to your mama. Look at this. Look at it close."

The printing was dark and bold. "Do not resuscitate." "No extraordinary measures to be taken."

I looked up at Mavis, and she shook her head at me. "Don't tell me you don't know what I mean. You been on this road a long time. You know what's coming, and your mother needs you to take care of it."

She pressed a sheaf of forms into my hand. "You go in there and take another good long look at your mother, and then you get these papers done right."

Later that evening I was holding a damp washrag to my eyes over the little sink in the entry to Mama's room. I could hear Mama whispering to Jo on the other side of the curtain around the bed.

"What do you think happens after death?" Mama asked. Her voice was hoarse.

I brought the rag down to cover my mouth.

"Oh hell, Mama," Jo said. "I don't know."

"No, tell me."

There was a long pause. Then Jo gave a harsh sigh and said it again. "Oh hell." Her chair slid forward on the linoleum floor. "You know what I really think?" Her voice was a careful whisper. "I'll tell you the truth, Mama. But don't you laugh. I think you come back as a dog."

I heard Mama's indrawn breath.

"I said don't laugh. I'm telling you what I really believe."

I lifted my head. Jo sounded so sincere. I could almost feel Mama leaning toward her.

"What I think is, if you were good to the people in your life, well then, you come back as a big dog. And . . ." Jo paused and tapped a finger on the bed-frame. "If you were some evil son of a bitch, then you gonna come back some nasty little Pekingese."

Jo laughed then, a quick bark of a laugh. Mama joined in weakly. Then they were giggling together. "A Pekingese," Mama said. "Oh yes."

I put my forehead against the mirror over the sink and listened. It was good to hear. When they settled down, I started to step past the curtain. But then Mama spoke and I paused. Her voice was soft, but firm.

"I just want to go to sleep," she said. "Just sleep. I never want to wake up again."

The next morning, Mama could not move her legs. She could barely breathe. There was a pain in her side, she said. Sweat shone on her forehead when she tried to talk. The blisters on her mouth had spread to her chin.

"I'm afraid." She gripped my hand so tightly I could feel the bones of my fingers rubbing together.

"I know," I told her. "But I'm here. I won't go anywhere. I'll stay right here."

Jo came in the afternoon. The doctor had already come and gone, leaving Mama's left arm bound to a plastic frame and that tiny machine pumping more morphine. Mama seemed to be floating, only coming to the surface now and then. Every time her eyes opened, she jerked as if she had just realized she was still alive.

"What did he say?" Jo demanded. I could barely look at her.

"It was a stroke." I cleared my throat. I spoke carefully, softly. "A little one in the night. He thinks there will be more, lots more. One of them might kill her, but it might not. She might go on a long time. They don't know."

I watched Jo's right hand search her jacket pockets until she found the pack of cigarettes. She put one in her mouth, but didn't light it. She just looked at me while I looked back at her.

"We have to make some decisions," I said. Jo nodded.

"I don't want them to . . ." She lifted her hands and shook them. Her eyes were glittering in the fluorescent lighting. "To hurt her."

"Yeah." I nodded gratefully. I could never have fought Jo if she had disagreed with me. "I told them we didn't want them to do anything."

"Anything?" Jo's eyes beamed into mine like searchlights. I nodded again. I pulled out the forms Mavis had given me.

"We'll have to get Jack to sign these."

Jo took the papers and looked through them. "Isn't that the way it always is?" Her voice was sour and strained. The cigarette was still clenched between her teeth. "Isn't that just the way it always is?"

"Mama's pissed herself," Arlene told me when I came back from dinner. I was surprised to see her. Her hair was pushed behind her ears and her face scrubbed clean. She was sponging Mama's hips and thighs. Mama's face was red. Her eyes were closed. Arlene's expression was unreadable. I picked up the towel by Mama's feet and wiped behind Arlene's sponge. Jo came in, dragging an extra chair. Arlene did not look up, she just shifted Mama's left leg and carefully sponged the furry mat of Mama's mound.

"Jo talked to me." Arlene's voice was low. Without mascara she seemed young again, her cheeks pearly in the frosty light that outlined the bed. Behind me, Jo positioned the chair and sat down heavily. There was a pause while the two of them looked at each other. Then Mama opened her eyes, and we all turned to her. The white of her left eye was bloody and the pupil an enormous black hole.

"Baby?" Mama whispered. I reached for her free hand. "Baby?" she kept whispering. "Baby?" Her voice was thin and raspy. Her thumb was working the pump, but it seemed to have lost its ability to help. Her good eye was wide and terrified. Arlene made a sound in her throat. Jo stood up. None of us said a thing. The door opened behind me. Jack's face was pale and too close. His left hand clutched a big greasy bag.

"Honey?" Jack said. "Honey?"

I looked away, my throat closing up. Jo's hands clamped down on the foot of the bed. Arlene's hands curled into fists at her waist. I looked at her. She looked at me and then over to Jo.

"Honey?" Jack said again. His voice sounded high and cracked, like a young boy too scared to believe what he was seeing. Arlene's pupils were almost as big as Mama's. I saw her tongue pressing her teeth, her lips pulled thin with strain. She saw me looking at her, shook her head, and stepped back from the bed.

"Daddy," she said softly. "Daddy, we have to talk."

Arlene took Jack's arm and led him to the door. He let her take him out of the room.

I looked over at Jo. Her hands were wringing the bar at the foot of the bed like a wet towel. She continued to do it as the door swung closed behind Arlene and Jack. She continued even as Mama's mouth opened and closed and opened again.

Mama was whimpering. "Ba . . . ba . . . ba . . . ba . . . ba . . . ba."

I took Mama's hand and held it tight, then stood there watching Jo doing the only thing she could do, blistering the skin off her palms.

When Arlene came back, her face was gray, but her mouth had smoothed out.

"He signed it," she said.

She stepped around me and took her place on the other side of the bed. Jo dropped her head forward. I let my breath out slowly. Mama's hand in mine was loose. Her mouth had gone slack, though it seemed to quiver now and then, and when it did I felt the movement in her fingers.

Across from me Arlene put her right hand on Mama's shoulder. She didn't flinch when Mama's bloody left eye rolled to the side. The good eye stared straight up, wide with profound terror. Arlene began a soft humming then, as if she were starting some lullaby. Mama's terrified eye blinked and then blinked again. In the depths of that pupil I seemed to see little starbursts, tiny desperate explosions of light.

Arlene's hum never paused. She ran her hand down and took Mama's fingers into her own. Slowly, some of the terror in Mama's face eased. The straining muscles of her neck softened. Arlene's hum dropped to a lower register. It resounded off the top of her hollow throat like an oboe or a French horn shaped entirely of flesh. No, I thought. Arlene is what she has always wanted to be, the one we dare not hate. I wanted Arlene's song to go on forever. I wanted to be part of it. I leaned forward and opened my mouth, but the sound that came out of me was ugly and fell back into my throat. Arlene never even looked over at me. She kept her eyes on Mama's bloody pupil.

I knew then. Arlene would go on as long as it took, making that sound in her throat like some bird creature, the one that comes to sing hope when there is no hope left. Strength was in Arlene's song, peace its meter, love the bass note. Mama's eye swung in lazy accompaniment to that song—from me to Jo, and around again to Arlene. Her hands gripped ours, while her mouth hung open. From the base of the bed, Jo reached up and laid her hands on Mama's legs. Mama looked down once, then the good eye turned back to our bird and clung there. My eyes followed hers. I watched the thrush that beat in Arlene's breast. I heard its stubborn tuneless song.

Mama's whole attention remained fixed on that song until the pupil of the right eye finally filled up with blood and blacked out. Even then, we held on. We held Mama's stilled shape between us. We held her until she set us free.

Dorothy Allison was born in Greenville, South Carolina, and still dreams of that landscape, though these days she lives with her partner, Alix Layman, and ten-year-old son, Wolf Michael, just outside Guerneville, California. Her novels include *Bastard Out of Carolina* (1992) and *Cavedweller* (1997). In addition she has published a book of essays, *Skin: Talking about Sex, Class and Literature,* and a book of poetry, *The Women Who Hate Me.* Her collection of short stories, *Trash,* was recently republished in a new edition by Plume, and includes the new story, "Compassion." She is working on a novel.

LEON BORENSZTEIN

I started trying to write "Compassion" after my mother died, in the fall of 1991, but it took me years to get a version down on the page. I wanted to find a way to talk about how it is that embattled families occasionally act with unexpected grace—as my own sisters and I had managed in the long months of my mother's last illness. How is it that people can manage to both love and hate each other at the same time? I got a rough version of the story going and read from it at a number of small colleges and benefits. But somehow I could never quite finish it. I set the short story aside—shoved the draft in a file and forgot about it.

Then an odd thing happened. Every now and then people would come up to me at readings or events and ask me about that story—the one about the sisters. Had it been published? Where could they read it? Sometimes they would repeat to me the mother's question "What do you think happens after you die?" And then they wanted to know if my sister actually raised dogs. No, I had to say. I've never quite gotten that story right. And no, I am the one who has dogs.

I went back to the draft in the filing cabinet. There were half a dozen different drafts of the ending—one so sentimental it made my teeth hurt. That wasn't right. These were not sentimental women. I started doodling with the characters. What if Arlene was not as pitiful as I had first imagined her? What if Jo were not nearly so strong? What if I didn't try to tie it up all neat at the end? Ten years after I had started, I finally got a version I could stand.

Peter Meinke

UNHEARD MUSIC

(from *The Gettysburg Review*)

James Vilag liked the idea of driving through unheard music, so
at night he would leave the radio off as he made his rounds, his
car nosing into endless waves of possibility, his shiny left shoe tapping like a metronome. He was most moved by the more emotional
music he couldn't hear, pieces by Chopin and Tchaikovsky, Dvořák's
Slavic Dances or Debussy's *En Blanc et Noir.* When he rolled down
the window, he could feel them flow over him like tides in a harbor,
filling the car with as much intensity as he could handle. Largo,
maestoso . . . the idea that they were all "out there" at the same time
made him breathe so heavily that the seat belt hurt his chest.

"That's just your imagination," Janice said. "And keep that seat
belt on even if you think the whole goddamn London Symphony
Orchestra is in the backseat."

"Seat belts lead to careless driving," he told her. "You wear your
seat belt for twenty years and never have an accident, it's been a
complete waste of time. To make it worthwhile you've got to have
an accident or two."

"You're a looney tune," she said, "and I won't let you drive on
your rounds unless your seat belt's on." So he would start each
night safely buckled and later undo it as the music flooded in.

He was an insomniac and had volunteered to drive the late-night
crime watch in his neighborhood on a more or less regular basis.

He didn't need much sleep anyway, and his job as editor of the in-house bulletin of St. Anthony's Hospital wasn't demanding. During the two months of his watch, there had been no burglaries, and everyone was giving him full credit, though he had never seen or even heard anything suspicious. He didn't tell them he did it partly for the unheard music and partly to avoid his dreams. He didn't care about burglaries; they seemed like petty crimes at most. People became too attached to *things*. James couldn't think of any *thing* he'd really mind losing.

His dreams had always been bad: for many years he dreamed he had killed someone, a stranger, at random, and would lie awake night after night grinding his teeth in agitation. There was a time in his life, before he met Janice, when what he did and what he dreamed became confused. When he was awake he thought he was dreaming. When he was asleep he'd dream of going to sleep and dreaming other dreams, often about dreaming, so the effect was like a hall of mirrors where the real self gets lost in a maze of distorted images.

One time during this period, he or his dream self was walking home from dinner in a strange part of town. The dinner itself had been upsetting: the waiter, insinuating and ambivalently sexed, had a pink face and a throaty feminine voice.

"Where have you been?" the waiter said. "You've never been here before."

"No, it's a little out of the way for me. I went to a concert and it got to be later than I thought." Why was he talking to this waiter? The concert had been a piano duet and the last piece, *Le Bal Martiniquais,* was still thrumming in his head. "I'd like the schnitzel, I think, and a glass of the white zinfandel."

"Oh my god, not the schnitzel!" The waiter arched perfectly clipped and rounded eyebrows. "Anything but the schnitzel. Our cook is Polish and hates anything German."

"Well, what do you recommend?"

"The duck with baked apple is pretty good tonight, or the chicken cacciatore."

"OK, the duck." He closed the menu and began tapping out a cigarette, but the waiter remained by the table. James asked, "Are you waiting for something?"

"The captain has asked that all cigarettes be distinguished," the waiter said and smiled. James wasn't sure he had heard him right and continued tapping, saying nothing.

"Not the zinfandel," said the waiter, still smiling. "Not with duck."

"Jesus, bring me anything."

"Yes, sir." When he bowed, the waiter's bald spot showed, seven long hairs pasted over it. "*Egri Bikaver,* Bull's Blood." He padded away, with a slight penguin waddle.

The dinner was further marred by an Englishman, perhaps an Australian, at a nearby table who sat quietly with a bottle of Foster's Ale in front of him, reading a letter with foreign stamps on it. He would smile as he read and suddenly begin crying, then start all over again, reading and rereading the letter. At the time, James lived alone in a single room cluttered with books and records; watching the Englishman, he felt drowned in loneliness. Who would write *him* such a letter?

He ate as fast as he could, to get out of there. The duck, he had realized too late, was so expensive he could hardly taste it anyway, and the tip he left—all the money he had—was insufficient. This made him both embarrassed and angry with the waiter: the schnitzel was five dollars cheaper. Each table had its own loaf of bread, bread knife, and cutting board, and as if this were a way to get even, he slipped the serrated, wood-handled knife into his pocket. He thought of taking the breadboard, too, sliding it under his shirt, holding in his stomach, but it seemed like too much trouble, and he settled for the knife and the book of matches that—oddly, he thought—was white and blank. Had the Englishman noticed? James didn't care. He waited until the waiter went into the kitchen, then he tucked his last bills under the wine glass and hurried into the night.

It was raining lightly, and on his walk he slipped and stumbled over the uneven sidewalks. It never snowed in Florida, but the rain looked like snow under the street lamps and like colored confetti in front of the bars and restaurants with their blinking neon signs. In places, his own reflection rose toward him like the cardboard mannequins on a bayonet field. He was tingling with an unfocused fear—stealing the knife had been an atypical and stupid thing to do—and he walked randomly in a westerly direction, heading toward the river rather than his own apartment. Mendelssohn's *Andante and Variations,* from the evening's concert, surged in his ears as if someone had turned on a switch.

At some point he realized that he had begun following a well-dressed man in a pale overcoat whose black shoes reflected the light and made sharp tapping sounds as he walked. James felt the man was drawing him like a whirlpool, against his will, down into the darkest part of the city, where redbrick buildings crowded the sidewalk and swallowed what little light there was. The footsteps began to echo at his sides and behind him, and in his fear and accompanied by music, he walked faster and faster, and when he at last caught up with the man, he found the bread knife in his hand and stabbed him with all his might high in his back, and the man groaned and dropped like a side of beef at James's feet.

He felt nauseated, terrified. His first instinct was to run, but as he looked around he knew this was only a dream . . . he was almost certain it was a dream. *Just the same,* he thought, *dreams are real, too, they don't come from nothing, this is a part of what I am.* And suppose he *wasn't* dreaming: here he stood, with blood on his shoes, a knife in his trembling hand and a dead man at his feet. It seemed best to do something, to act it out.

No one was around. The neighborhood looked dead, too, except for a few dingy, lighted windows down the street. James bent over and grasped the man under his arms, dragging him to an open iron gate that led down to a darkened apartment below street level. As he pulled the body down the few steps, he backed into a garbage can, making such a clang that his heart nearly stopped. He froze there for a minute, standing on the bottom level, the man's feet still three steps up. For the first time James looked at his victim's face. He was a middle-aged man with thick, graying hair, a healthy face frozen in a grotesque semblance of a smile like the mask of comedy. He looked familiar: the Englishman from the restaurant? James didn't think this was possible; he thought he, James, had left the restaurant first, but thinking back on it, he wasn't sure. Holding his breath, he tugged the man's wallet out of the tight back pocket.

There was a small amount of money, and he put that in his pocket without counting it and then looked at the driver's license: Jack Phillip Middleton, 77 Franklin Street. James wiped the wallet clean and forced it back into the man's pocket, an act that seemed as violent as the actual stabbing. He pulled the body behind the garbage cans and went up into the street. A young couple scurried through the shadows on the opposite sidewalk. James kept his face averted and headed for the river. He felt exhausted now, as if he had been walking underwater for hours; he had to kick the air aside with every step. When he reached the river, he threw the knife as far as he could—*This is my message to the world,* he thought—and turned for home.

The next morning, after he woke up, that was the tricky time. First he checked his shoes: no blood. But he could have cleaned them last night; he was a careful man. He found two incriminating items: money in his wallet and the matches in his pocket. These could be explained, too—he often resupplied his wallet at night for the next day, keeping a small supply of cash in his desk drawer for that purpose, and a pack of matches was hardly evidence that he had killed someone.

No, the real question was whether he had dreamed it or not and which side of the dream he was on. He often had dreams that encompassed several days in a row, dreams in which he went to bed and woke up, that were indistinguishable from real life. He thought about this all the time as he drove his rounds at night. It was diabolical. It made it impossible to check on himself. So what if he read the newspaper from front to back and there was no mention of a body found near the river? He could be dreaming right now. He found it hard to take action. Editing someone else's words and—a few years later—driving in circles on his crime watch was about all he was capable of performing. And there was Janice now, helping him keep his balance: without her it was difficult to breathe.

"You're my ozone," he told her. "You're my safety margin."

"Ozone, shmozone," she said. "Buckle up." She had always been solid and quick—that's what he liked about her. He was so slow himself, everything seemed slippery to him. Earlier, when he had called her on the telephone to ask her to a movie, she had wanted to talk.

"Phones make me nervous," he said. "I don't think I've ever said anything intelligent over the phone."

"Why don't you read me a few pages of Henry James and break your record?" she'd asked. He wanted to be like her.

Sometimes he thought, *What if I actually saw a burglar?* Would he chase him and corner him? He could tell him, *I killed a man at random and I'll kill you, too, if you don't give yourself up.* These scenarios were ludicrous, but as James enacted them in his mind, his hands turned cold on the steering wheel and he put his fingers on the even colder tire iron Janice insisted he keep on the seat beside him.

A while ago he had gone to a prominent psychiatrist, Dr. Walton Pharr, for help, but he proved impenetrably stupid. James often thought there was nothing wrong with the world that a little more intelligence couldn't solve. He felt surrounded by people strolling around with three pounds of suet in their skulls. He believed he would have been brilliant at college if his father had chosen to send him—he had won every spelling bee he had ever been in. If he had been born ten years later, when they began having national spelling bees, he might have been famous—picture in the papers, the works.

The psychiatrist had asked about his father. And his mother, and his childhood, and the army. What he couldn't seem to understand was that James already *knew* about these things. He knew he was marred from childhood—who wasn't? Dr. Pharr, who was fat and chain-smoked, obviously had problems with self-esteem himself; any idiot could see that. What James wanted to know was, simply, how to tell real life from dream life.

"Try pinching yourself," the psychiatrist suggested. He was really a dip.

"You can dream you're pinching yourself," James replied.

"Tell me about your dreams."

James described some of his dreams but was reluctant to tell him about the night at the weird café; that would be too much like a confession, and perhaps dangerous. He didn't trust Fatso farther than he could throw him. "I've been dreaming of an animal," he said. "I'm standing by a tree in a large backyard, maybe behind the house I grew up in, and this dark animal crawls up over a stone wall on the other side of the tree. At first I think it's relatively harmless, like a fat beaver or a porcupine, but as it gets nearer it elongates and gets bigger and turns into a wild boar. I've never seen a wild boar, but I know that's what it is. Its eyes are red, and it has ugly fangs or tusks.

"Anyway, nothing much happens, but I'm terribly frightened. We stare at each other. I pick up a heavy stone. Then, usually, he turns away and goes back over the wall. Sometimes he just disappears, and I have the feeling he may pop up on any side."

"Very interesting," said Dr. Pharr. "What do you think it means?"

"Maybe I'm eating too much pork." The psychiatrist brought out the worst in him. He knew Dr. Pharr wanted him to link the boar with his father, the apple tree—now he saw it was an apple tree—with his mother. But he could do that himself; he didn't have to pay seventy-five dollars an hour to find that out.

One time, during James's sophomore year in high school, his father burst into a house at 2 A.M. and struck him across the face in front of three of his friends. They had been playing chess and lost track of the time—James in particular would fall into the world of bishops and knights and all else would disappear. He was supposed to have been home at eleven.

"What the hell's wrong with you?" his father shouted, while the other boys froze in their chairs. "Your mother's worried sick!" And then he slapped him, the sound cracking like a gunshot in the silent room. *You would think,* James thought later, *a father would be proud of a son staying up all night to play chess.* He, James, would be proud if *his* son had done that, if he had a son. But he didn't say anything at the time. He was as tall as his father already, and he just stared at him for a minute, and they both knew this was the last time the older man would hit him. Then he followed his father out into the car.

He thought about all this, peering into the darkness for burglars, nosing the car slowly around corners, music rising and falling through the limp leaves of magnolias, jacarandas, and twisted live oaks. He had asked Dr. Pharr, "Tell me, how do I know I'm not dreaming *you?*"

"You know I'm real when you get my bill." That was the extent of the psychiatrist's sophistication.

Early on, James tried to solve the problem himself. For several days he carried around in his mind the vivid imprint of the Englishman's name and address: Jack Phillip Middleton, 77 Franklin Street. Finally, one evening after work, he gathered up the nerve to look it up then impulsively called a cab and gave that address. Franklin Street was a middle-class city block with a few trees and attached houses, each with a front stoop and a little patch of grass behind an iron railing. Number 77 was in the middle of the block, and rain started pouring down as he stood, bareheaded, heart bouncing like a headless fish, staring at its unlighted windows that stared blankly back.

From the street he could barely make out a nameplate underneath the number, and he forced his leaden limbs to open the gate and go up the brick steps to the door; but even as he was reading the name and feeling the rain running down his face, he knew with anguish that he couldn't tell if he were wide awake or dreaming.

Peter Meinke's collection of stories, *The Piano Tuner*, received the 1986 Flannery O'Connor Award. He has published six books of poetry, the most recent being *Zinc Fingers* (2000) and *Scars* (1996). His poems and stories have appeared in *Poetry, The New Yorker, The Atlantic Monthly, The Georgia Review,* and *The Gettysburg Review,* among many other magazines. He directed the Writing Workshop at Eckerd College for many years, and he has been writer-in-residence at over a dozen colleges and universities, including Hamilton College, Davidson College, the University of Hawaii, the University of North Carolina at Greensboro, and most recently, Converse College in Spartanburg, S.C. He and his wife, the artist Jeanne Clark, have four children, and have lived in the same house in St. Petersburg, Florida, for over three decades.

JEANNE MEINKE

U*nheard Music" got its start when I was taking my turn on Crime Watch in our somewhat spooky neighborhood. Parked on a dark corner with my lights out, I turned off the car radio and began making notes, eventually coming upon the idea that the music was still out there, surrounding me, waiting to come in. The experience of being on "Crime Watch," now common for huge numbers of Americans, is a dreamlike one, far from our sunny "real" lives—and it leads to thoughts and dreams with violent content (suppose one actually confronted a criminal?). More, it brings up questions like "Am I really doing this, or am I dreaming it?" and "How am I different from the criminal?" At least it did for me. Like the protagonist, I'm a mild insomniac, and once I got the story started I stayed with it for many nights, to the great detraction of the neighborhood's safety. After I finished it, I returned to writing in the morning, my usual habit.*

APPENDIX

A list of the magazines currently consulted for *New Stories from the South: The Year's Best, 2003,* with addresses, subscription rates, and editors.

Alabama Literary Review
272 Smith Hall
Troy State University
Troy, AL 36082
Semiannually, $10
William E. Hicks

American Literary Review
P.O. Box 311307
University of North Texas
Denton, TX 76203-1307
Semiannually, $10
Barbara Rodman

The Antioch Review
P.O. Box 148
Yellow Springs, OH 45387-0148
Quarterly, $35
Robert S. Fogarty

Apalachee Review
P.O. Box 10469
Tallahassee, FL 32302
Semiannually, $15
Laura Newton

Appalachian Heritage
CPO 2166
Berea, KY 40404
Quarterly, $18
George Brosi

Arts & Letters
Campus Box 89
Georgia College & State University
Milledgeville, GA 31061-0490
Semiannually, $15
Martin Lammon

The Atlantic Monthly
77 N. Washington St.
Boston, MA 02114
Monthly, $39.95
C. Michael Curtis

Black Warrior Review
University of Alabama
P.O. Box 862936
Tuscaloosa, AL 35486-0027
Semiannually, $14
Tommy Zurhellen

Boulevard
6614 Clayton Road, PMB 325
Richmond Heights, MO 63117
Triannually, $15
Richard Burgin

The Carolina Quarterly
Greenlaw Hall CB# 3520
University of North Carolina
Chapel Hill, NC 27599-3520
Triannually, $12
Fiction Editor

The Chariton Review
Truman State University
Kirksville, MO 63501
Semiannually, $9
Jim Barnes

The Chattahoochee Review
Georgia Perimeter College
2101 Womack Road
Dunwoody, GA 30338-4497
Quarterly, $16
Lawrence Hetrick

Cimarron Review
205 Morrill Hall
Oklahoma State University
Stillwater, OK 74078-0135
Quarterly, $24
E. P. Walkiewicz

Columbia
415 Dodge Hall
2960 Broadway
Columbia University
New York, NY 10027-6902
Semiannually, $18
J. Manuel Gonzales

Confrontation
English Department
C.W. Post of L.I.U.
Brookville, NY 11548
Semiannually, $10
Martin Tucker

Conjunctions
21 East 10th Street
New York, NY 10003
Semiannually, $18
Bradford Morrow

Crucible
Barton College
P.O. Box 5000

Wilson, NC 27893-7000
Annually, $7
Terrence L. Grimes

Denver Quarterly
University of Denver
Denver, CO 80208
Quarterly, $20
Bin Ramke

Epoch
251 Goldwin Smith Hall
Cornell University
Ithaca, NY 14853-3201
Triannually, $11
Michael Koch

Esquire
250 West 55th Street
New York, NY 10019
Monthly, $15.94
Adrienne Miller

Fiction
c/o English Department
City College of New York
New York, NY 10031
Quarterly, $38
Mark J. Mirsky

Five Points
GSU
University Plaza
Department of English
Atlanta, GA 30303-3083
Triannually, $20
Megan Sexton

The Florida Review
Department of English
University of Central Florida
Orlando, FL 32816
Semiannually, $10
Pat Rushin

Gargoyle
P.O. Box 6216
Arlington, VA 22206-0216
Semiannually, $20
Richard Peabody

The Georgia Review
University of Georgia
Athens, GA 30602-9009
Quarterly, $24
T. R. Hummer

The Gettysburg Review
Gettysburg College
Gettysburg, PA 17325-1491
Quarterly, $24
Peter Stitt

Glimmer Train Stories
710 SW Madison St., #504
Portland, OR 97205
Quarterly, $32
Susan Burmeister-Brown
    and Linda B. Swanson-Davies

Granta
1755 Broadway
5th Floor
New York, NY 10019-3780
Quarterly, $37
Ian Jack

The Greensboro Review
English Department
134 McIver Bldg.
University of North Carolina
P.O. Box 26170
Greensboro, NC 27412
Semiannually, $10
Jim Clark

Harper's Magazine
666 Broadway
New York, NY 10012

Monthly, $18
Ben Metcalf

High Plains Literary Review
180 Adams Street, Suite 250
Denver, CO 80206
Triannually, $25
Robert O. Greer, Jr.

Image
3307 Third Ave., W.
Center for Religious Humanism
Seattle, WA 98119
Quarterly, $36
Gregory Wolfe

Indiana Review
465 Ballantine Ave.
Indiana University
Bloomington, IN 47405
Semiannually, $12
Laura McCoid

The Iowa Review
308 EPB
University of Iowa
Iowa City, IA 52242-1492
Triannually, $18
David Hamilton

The Journal
Ohio State University
Department of English
164 W. 17th Avenue
Columbus, OH 43210
Semiannually, $12
Kathy Fagan and Michelle Herman

Kalliope
Florida Community College
3939 Roosevelt Blvd.
Jacksonville, FL 32205
Triannually, $16
Mary Sue Koeppel

The Kenyon Review
Kenyon College
Gambier, OH 43022
Triannually, $25
David H. Lynn

The Literary Review
Fairleigh Dickinson University
285 Madison Avenue
Madison, NJ 07940
Quarterly, $18
Walter Cummins

The Long Story
18 Eaton Street
Lawrence, MA 01843
Annually, $6
R. P. Burnham

Louisiana Literature
SLU-10792
Southeastern Louisiana
    University
Hammond, LA 70402
Semiannually, $12
Jack Bedell

The Louisville Review
Spalding University
851 South 4th Street
Louisville, KY 40203
Semiannually, $8
Sena Jeter Naslund

Lynx Eye
c/o ScribbleFest Literary Group
P.O. Box 6609
Los Osos, CA 93412-6609
Quarterly, $25
Pam McCully, Kathryn Morrison

Meridian
University of Virginia
P.O. Box 400145

Charlottesville, VA 22904-4145
Semiannually, $10
Jett McAlister

Mid-American Review
Department of English
Bowling Green State University
Bowling Green, OH 43403
Semiannually, $12
Michael Czyzniejewski

Mississippi Review
Center for Writers
University of Southern
    Mississippi
Box 5144
Hattiesburg, MS 39406-5144
Semiannually, $15
Frederick Barthelme

The Missouri Review
1507 Hillcrest Hall
University of Missouri
Columbia, MO 65211
Triannually, $22
Speer Morgan

The Nebraska Review
Writers Workshop
Fine Arts Building 212
University of Nebraska at Omaha
Omaha, NE 68182-0324
Semiannually, $11
James Reed

New Delta Review
English Department
Louisiana State University
Baton Rouge, LA 70802-5001
Semiannually, $8.50
Andrew Spear

New England Review
Middlebury College

Middlebury, VT 05753
Quarterly, $23
Stephen Donadio

New Millennium Writings
P.O. Box 2463
Knoxville, TN 37901
Annually, $12.95
Don Williams

New Orleans Review
Box 195
Loyola University
New Orleans, LA 70118
Semiannually, $12
Christopher Chambers, Editor

The New Yorker
4 Times Square
New York, NY 10036
Weekly, $44.95
Deborah Treisman, Fiction Editor

Nimrod International Journal
The University of Tulsa
600 South College
Tulsa, OK 74104-3189
Semiannually, $17.50
Francine Ringold

The North American Review
University of Northern Iowa
1222 W. 27th Street
Cedar Falls, IA 50614-0516
Six times a year, $22
Grant Tracey

North Atlantic Review
15 Arbutus Lane
Stony Brook, NY 11790-1408
2 years, $18
John Gill

North Carolina Literary Review
English Department

2201 Bate Building
East Carolina University
Greenville, NC 27858-4353
2 years, $20
Margaret Bauer

Northwest Review
369 PLC
University of Oregon
Eugene, OR 97403
Triannually, $22
John Witte

The Ohio Review
344 Scott Quad
Ohio University
Athens, OH 45701-2979
Semiannually, $16
Wayne Dodd

Ontario Review
9 Honey Brook Drive
Princeton, NJ 08540
Semiannually, $14
Raymond J. Smith

Other Voices
University of Illinois at Chicago
Department of English (M/C 162)
601 S. Morgan Street
Chicago, IL 60607-7120
2 years, $24
Lois Hauselman

The Oxford American
303 President Clinton Ave.
Little Rock, AR 72201
8 issues, $29.95
Marc Smirnoff

The Paris Review
541 E. 72nd Street
New York, NY 10021
Quarterly, $40
George Plimpton

Parting Gifts
March Street Press
3413 Wilshire Drive
Greensboro, NC 27408
Semiannually, $12
Robert Bixby

Pembroke Magazine
UNC-P, Box 1510
Pembroke, NC 28372-1510
Annually, $8
Shelby Stephenson

Ploughshares
Emerson College
120 Boylston St.
Boston, MA 02116-4624
Triannually, $22
Don Lee

PMS
Univ. of Alabama at Birmingham
Department of English
HB 217, 900 S. 13th Street
1530 3rd Ave., S.
Birmingham, AL 35294-1260
Annually, $7
Linda Frost

Post Road
853 Broadway, Ste. 1516
Box 85
New York, NY 10003
Semiannually, $16
Rebecca Boyd

Prairie Schooner
201 Andrews Hall
University of Nebraska
Lincoln, NE 68588-0334
Quarterly, $26
Hilda Raz

Puerto del Sol
Box 30001, Department 3E
New Mexico State University

Las Cruces, NM 88003-9984
Semiannually, $10
Kevin McIlvoy

Quarterly West
200 S. Central Campus Drive
Room 317
University of Utah
Salt Lake City, UT 84112-9109
Semiannually, $14
Stephen Tuttle

Rainbow Curve
P.O. Box 93206
Las Vegas, NV 89193-3206
Daphne Young

River City
Department of English
The University of Memphis
Memphis, TN 38152-6176
Semiannually, $12
Mary Leader

River Styx
634 North Grand Blvd.
12th Floor
St. Louis, MO 63103
Triannually, $20
Richard Newman

Santa Monica Review
Santa Monica College
1900 Pico Boulevard
Santa Monica, CA 90405
Semiannually, $12
Andrew Tonkovich

Shenandoah
Washington and Lee University
Troubadour Theater
2nd Floor
Lexington, VA 24450-0303
Quarterly, $22
R. T. Smith

The South Carolina Review
Department of English
Clemson University
Strode Tower, Box 340523
Clemson, SC 29634-0523
Semiannually, $20
Wayne Chapman

South Dakota Review
Box III
University Exchange
University of South Dakota
Vermillion, SD 57069
Quarterly, $22
John R. Milton

The Southeast Review
Department of English
Florida State University
Tallahassee, FL 32306
Semiannually, $10
Ed Tarkington

Southern Exposure
P.O. Box 531
Durham, NC 27702
Quarterly, $24
Chris Kromm

Southern Humanities Review
9088 Haley Center
Auburn University
Auburn, AL 36849
Quarterly, $15
Dan R. Latimer and Virginia M.
    Kouidis

The Southern Review
43 Allen Hall
Louisiana State University
Baton Rouge, LA 70803-5005
Quarterly, $25
James Olney

Southwest Review
307 Fondren Library West

Box 750374
Southern Methodist University
Dallas, TX 75275
Quarterly, $24
Willard Spiegelman

Sou'wester
Department of English
Southern Illinois University at
    Edwardsville
Edwardsville, IL 62026-1438
Semiannually, $12
Allison Funk and Geoff Schmidt

StoryQuarterly
431 Sheridan Road
Kenilworth, IL 60043-1220
Annually, $10
M.M.M. Hayes

Sulphur River
P.O. Box 19228
Austin, TX 78760-9228
Semiannually, $12
James Michael Robbins

Tampa Review
The University of Tampa
401 W. Kennedy Boulevard
Tampa, FL 33606-1490
Semiannually, $15
Richard Mathews

Texas Review
English Department Box 2146
Sam Houston State University
Huntsville, TX 77341-2146
Semiannually, $20
Paul Ruffin

The Threepenny Review
P.O. Box 9131
Berkeley, CA 94709
Quarterly, $25
Wendy Lesser

Tin House
P.O. Box 10500
Portland, OR 97296-0500
Quarterly, $29.90
Rob Spillman

TriQuarterly
Northwestern University
2020 Ridge Avenue
Evanston, IL 60208-4302
Triannually, $24
Susan Firestone Hahn

The Virginia Quarterly Review
One West Range
P.O. Box 400223
Charlottesville, VA 22904-4223
Quarterly, $18
Staige D. Blackford

West Branch
Bucknell Hall
Bucknell University
Lewisburg, PA 17837
Semiannually, $7
Robert Love Taylor

Wind Magazine
P.O. Box 24548
Lexington, KY 40524
Triannually, $15
Chris Green

The Yalobusha Review
Department of English
P.O. Box 1848
University, MS 38677
Annually, $10
Joy Wilson

Yemassee
Department of English
University of South Carolina
Columbia, SC 29208
Semiannually, $15
Lisa Kerr

Zoetrope: All-Story
The Sentinel Building
916 Kearny Street
San Francisco, CA 94133
Quarterly, $19.95
Tamara Straus

ZYZZYVA
P.O. Box 590069
San Francisco, CA 94159-0069
Triannually, $36
Howard Junker